Sea Sick

By

John Avanzato

KCM PUBLISHING
A DIVISION OF KCM DIGITAL MEDIA, LLC

CREDITS

Published by KCM Publishing
A Division of KCM Digital Media, LLC

Sea Sick by John Avanzato

ISBN-13: 978-1-939961-81-5
ISBN-10: 1-939961-81-5

First Edition

Publisher: Michael Fabiano
KCM Publishing
www.kcmpublishing.com

Icon made by Freepik from www.flaticon.com

KCM Publishing
a division of KCM Digital Media, LLC

Books in the John Cesari series by
John Avanzato

Hostile Hospital

Prescription for Disaster

Temperature Rising

Claim Denied

The Gas Man Cometh

Jailhouse Doc

Dedicated to those who cruise the high seas in search of adventure.

Acknowledgements

I would like to thank all those who helped me put this story together especially my wife, Cheryl, for her unwavering support, Terry McNulty, for her incredible editing prowess, Kim Worley Buczkowski, Heather Lynne Thibodeaux, Michele B. Kaufman, Pharm.D., BCGP, Peter Lutz, Vivien Warren, Patti Nogle, and Tracy Ambrose. A warm shout out to the crew of the Queen Victoria who patiently answered all my questions concerning the functioning and maintenance of their boat.

Most importantly, I owe my deepest gratitude to my brother, Anthony, who not only gave me the idea for this novel one summer evening but its title as well. I learned that night never to underestimate the power of cocktails and a good steak to stimulate the imagination. I owe him much more than that, but that tale is for another day…

Contents

Sea Sick

Chapter 1

The plane touched down at Marco Polo International Airport at exactly 10:00 a.m., a couple of hours behind schedule due to a delay in our departure from JFK in New York. A couple of sleeping pills and a half bottle of Chianti had done little to help me sleep during the overnight flight, and packed like a sardine in a can for eight hours with hundreds of other travelers, left me stiff, grumpy, and exhausted. I needed an espresso in a hurry and looked forward to finding a café with a seasoned barista. Peeking out the window, I could see it was a beautiful morning. The sun shone brightly over the snow-capped Dolomites in the distance, and there wasn't a cloud in the sky. Autumn in Venice. I could feel my luck changing already.

The airbus taxied to a stop and almost on cue, the passengers spilled out of their seats in unison to urgently retrieve their luggage from the overhead compartments. Waiting patiently, I watched them jostle for position in the aisles to leave the jet as if there was some prize for getting out as quickly as possible. Once the plane had mostly emptied, I retrieved my carry-on and said good-bye to the crew lined up politely in a long row by the exit.

A dark-haired, dark-skinned Italian beauty greeted me warmly as I reached the door. We had several typical interactions during the flight. You know, *can I have another glass of wine* type of stuff, but nothing more serious than that. I had noticed her smiling and glancing in my direction several times, but had chalked it up to international hospitality. Her name was Vincenza. She stood there now, last on the receiving line with a big smile on her face.

Beaming brightly, she said, "Ciao carino. Io ricordero sempre il mio bell'Americano in fila quindici posto corridoio." (Goodbye sweetheart. I will always remember my beautiful American in row fifteen, aisle seat.)

The flight attendant next to her giggled and I could see that they didn't think I spoke any Italian. But I did. I wasn't fluent by any means and intended on sharpening up my conversational skills during this trip. This was as good an opportunity as any. It wasn't my intention to flirt, but as long as they wanted to play…

I stopped and looked at her, choosing my words carefully. "Grazie, Vincenza, ma tu sei troppo gentile. So quanto sono brutto." (Thank you, Vincenza, but you are too kind. I am well aware of how ugly I am.)

She blushed, realizing I understood her. Chuckling she shook her head and said with a heavy accent, "Is no true. You are very handsome."

"Thank you again. I don't speak Italian very well. May I practice with you for a moment?"

She looked down the receiving line. The captain was ten feet away chatting with a passenger and the others were waiting for several stragglers to deplane.

She said, "Sure."

I said, "Vincenza, dolce Vincenza. Penso che tu sia la donna più bella del mondo. Ti amo con tutto il cuore e non posso vivere senza di te." (Vincenza, sweet Vincenza. I think that you are the most beautiful woman in the world, and I love you with all my heart. I can't possibly live without you.)

Suddenly dropping to one knee and with desperation in my voice said loudly, "Mi sposerai ... oggi ... ora ... questo minuto?" (Will you marry me…today…now…this very minute?)

I said it loudly enough that the entire flight crew, including the captain at the other end of the line, heard and started laughing. Someone clapped and shouted, "Bravo!"

The flight attendant next to her said, "Sposalo, Vincenza. Faremo una festa." (Marry him, Vincenza. We will have a party.)

Vincenza's face turned eight shades of scarlet as she grinned, appreciating my sense of humor. She complimented me as I stood back up, "I am a very flattered. Your Italian. She is very good."

I winked and said, "So's my fettucine Bolognese."

She held my gaze and lowered her voice, becoming serious. "Maybe…you could make a some for me? I no leave Venezia for two days."

There it was. She was ripe for the picking, and stared at me in anticipation of what should have been an invitation to dinner, but I was going to have to throw this fish back into the sea. This was a healing journey for me, and I wasn't looking for easy conquests. I said gently with a smile, "Maybe on my next trip, Vincenza. I must go now. Thank you for a wonderful flight and for being so nice."

As I moved to step past her, she reached out and grabbed my arm, a clear violation of protocol. Her friend said in alarm, "Vincenza, what a you do?"

I wanted to know the same thing. She moved a little closer and sniffed me. I raised my eyebrows in surprise. "Can I help you?"

"You smell so nice. What is it you wear?"

I couldn't imagine anyone wanting to get close to me after an eight-hour flight. I shrugged, "Just an inexpensive after-shave."

She furrowed her brow in concentration. "No, is no after-shave I smell. Is a something sweet...something...delicious." She sniffed again. "I know now. Is a cannella, how you say, cinnamon, like in biscotti or gelato. Gabriella, smell him."

The other flight attendant was horrified. "I will do no such a thing. Let go of him or I tell a the capitano."

I gently tugged my arm free, and reluctantly she drew back, smiling. The exchange ended when the captain clapped his hands and announced it was time for everyone to get back to work. He did call out to me though, "Arrivederci signore. I am a sorry, but you must find another pretty girl to marry. You will have a no trouble finding one in Venezia. They are like rays of sunshine on a clear day. You can no miss. Just open up you eyes."

As I made my way out of the terminal, I sniffed myself and was quite certain I didn't smell anything even remotely as pleasant as an Italian dessert. I walked to the pier to find transportation and hired a vaporetto, a water taxi commonly used to navigate around Venice's intricate maze of canals. As we splashed our way through the narrow waterways, I chided myself for flirting with Vincenza. I couldn't help myself sometimes; although, nothing I did could explain her behavior. But that was the way it was with women. Once you rolled the dice, you never knew what was going to happen.

Part of my agenda on this trip was to learn self-control when it came to the fairer sex. Just because someone offered you candy, didn't mean you had to accept it. I had a habit of falling for the bait every time, and I promised myself that was going to change. *I will resist, I will resist, I will resist.*

The vaporetto dropped me off at the front of the albergo Campiello, a reasonably priced three star hotel in close proximity to the Piazza San Marco. The concierge was young and friendly and check-in was painless. Most people in Italy spoke English to some degree and Venice being one of the most highly touristed cities in the world was no different. He was surprised to see I only had one piece of luggage, but I always travelled light. I'd rather buy what I needed than lug stuff around I didn't.

The room was small but typical for European lodging. It had tall ceilings, ornate wood, trim, and moldings, a queen bed, and a non-functioning air conditioner. It was only for one night and would serve its purpose. I fell face down on the bed and passed out, waking up several hours later with my cell phone buzzing next to my ear.

I yawned into the phone. "Vito, what's up? Checking to see if my phone works?" Vito was a childhood friend. The kind that never grew up and never would. We all have one like him. When we were kids running around the Bronx, one of our favorite games was 'guns'. With toy rifles and pistols, we'd chase each other making shooting sounds and pretending we were soldiers. Harmless enough at the time, but now he does that for real. I put my toys away and became a doctor, and he became a mobster.

"No, I'm calling to give you some good news," he said.

Scratching the back of my head as I sat up, I asked, "And what's that?"

"I decided to join you on the cruise."

I was silent for a minute as my recently wakened brain digested that, prompting him to add, "Don't you have anything to say?"

"Sure I do. Since when do mafia guys go on cruises?"

That stung him a bit. Mostly because the truth hurts. "There's no such thing as the mafia, moron."

I smiled. He knew that I knew better than that, but he was always on the alert in case some federal agent was listening in on his calls. "How could I forget?"

"You don't sound very happy."

"I'm not. I'm irritated that you don't know how to listen. I don't want you to join me on the cruise. I thought I made that clear to you when I booked the trip. Do me a favor and stay in New York. Who's going to beat people up if you leave the country?"

"Thanks for the sarcasm. Do you have any idea what kind of strings I had to pull to get on board at such a late hour? I practically had to promise to name my firstborn child after the travel agent."

That was funny. A committed bachelor who couldn't stand kids made that possibility unlikely. "Vito, I decided to go on this cruise to get away from it all and retool my soul, and you are part of the *it all* that I need to get away from."

"Cesari, three weeks is a long time on a cruise ship by yourself." He hesitated somewhat reluctant to continue but he did anyway, "Pam didn't think you should be alone for that long. She's worried that you might do something stupid."

"I'm not by myself. I have three thousand and eighty fellow passengers and nine hundred crew members for companionship and since when does an ex-girlfriend get to dictate how I spend my free time? Is she worried that I might get over her?" I took a deep breath and let it out. I was on a roll. "And why is my girlfriend talking to you about me anyway?"

"Ex-girlfriend, remember? And she has every right to talk to me about anything she wants to. It's called the first amendment. Well, now you'll have three thousand and eighty-one passengers to keep you company. What's done is done. I'll see you in Dubrovnik when the ship docks there for its first port of call. Besides, I'm kind of looking forward to it. I've never been on a cruise ship, and don't be mad at Pam. You just seemed so depressed and she was concerned about you. She would have come herself but she felt she should give you space after the way you dumped her."

Rolling my eyes, I declined to let him provoke me so I sidestepped the landmine of my breakup with Pam. I didn't dump her, not exactly. I just stopped returning her calls. Pam was a well-respected psychologist in Manhattan and held a faculty position at NYU. We had dated for about six months and were becoming quite close. Close enough that she gave me a key to her apartment, and close enough that she felt comfortable telling me about her fantasies of sexual domination.

Telling me about her dreams soon escalated to requesting that I do things I didn't feel comfortable with. Long story short, I couldn't satisfy her in the way she needed. One day, I stopped by her apartment to prepare her dinner while she was supposed to be working late and found her in the bedroom, tied up, getting paddled by two guys wearing phantom of the opera masks. It didn't help that she later told me the two guys were assistant professors in the English department. Unbelievable! Two guys who read poetry for a living could make her feel fulfilled as a woman, and I couldn't.

Rather than make a fuss, I decided to go on a long vacation. Vito was an old friend, but was on a need to know basis when it came to my personal life, and he didn't need to know the details of my humiliation. Needless to say, Pam was playing it low key as well. She didn't want word to get out about what had happened any more than I did.

I said, "Vito, I'm not mad at anybody and neither am I suicidal. I just need to find my center of gravity. Well, look, I can't stop you, but I don't want you bothering me either. I plan on doing a lot of yoga and meditation, and I don't want to be harassed."

He sounded astonished. "Do you even hear yourself? This is why Pam is worried? One minute everything is fine and the next you're leaving town like a hurricane is moving in to find your center of what and do what? This isn't like you."

He was right. I made the decision abruptly and was very lucky there were still a few occupancies left on board the luxury liner. We were scheduled to tour the Mediterranean in opulent style. "Well, I guess I'm full of surprises."

"You mean full of bull. You know, sooner or later you're going to have to tell me what really happened with Pam."

"When did you become a couples' counselor?" I looked at my watch. He was starting to bug me and I was hungry. "Hey, you're starting to breakup."

"Don't pull that on me."

"Can't hear you anymore. Got to go, bud. Talk soon."

I hung up on him.

Chapter 2

Feeling refreshed from my nap, I showered, shaved, and threw on fresh clothes. Passing through bustling Saint Mark's Square and over a small bridge, I entered Harry's Bar on Calle Vallaresso at 7:00 p.m. A short stroll from my hotel, it was just what I needed to kick off my Mediterranean odyssey. I was one of the few men wearing jeans, which in Europe was the same as wearing the American flag.

Harry's Bar was a legendary Venetian watering hole and magnet for tourists. It was opened in 1931 by bartender Giuseppe Cipriani and named after Harry Pickering, an American adventurer, who folklore says gave Cipriani the money to buy the bar. Amongst other things, Harry's is known for its most famous cocktail, the Bellini, a combination of pureed white peach juice and prosecco, a sparkling white wine.

The bar was crowded, long, and dark with lots of wood trim. A waitress pointed to a small table for two along the wall and I took a seat. I was tempted to try the Bellini but it seemed a little too girlie for me, and since this trip was about restoring my manhood, I ordered a Montgomery instead which I learned was a very dry martini; fifteen parts gin to one part vermouth. The Montgomery was named after British Field Marshal Bernard Montgomery, who kicked Hitler's ass in North

Africa and Europe in World War II. He liked to have a 15-to-1 ratio of his own troops against enemy troops on the battle field. Ernest Hemingway is said to be the first person to have ordered a Montgomery at Harry's Bar. That was enough testosterone right there to jump start my mojo. Besides, at only twenty-three euros, it had to be good.

I requested Hendrick's gin, which in addition to the traditional juniper infusion, used Bulgarian rose and cucumber to add flavor. It was a subtle yet discernible enhancement which my palate approved. Listen to me. I wasn't in Europe twelve hours and was already starting to sound like a coddled nobleman.

The cocktail was served in a classic stemless martini glass with two tiny olives, and I savored my first sip perusing the dinner menu. Deciding to go with the cuttlefish and risotto, I signaled my waitress, placed the order, and settled down to study my surroundings.

Most people there were well-dressed, good-looking, and on average, a solid ten years younger than I was. As always and everywhere, there were way more women than men. I wondered why that was. I had read somewhere that global child birth statistics showed that slightly more boys than girls are born every year, but due to a much higher death rate from all causes, especially homicide, accidents and heart disease, male populations declined with age. Eventually the higher ratio of males to females equalizes and then reverses. Looking around me now, I would have to agree. Well, it certainly made for a pleasant sight-seeing environment for a wounded heart such as mine.

I downed the martini quickly, ate the olives, and finally started to feel like I was on vacation as a wave of relaxation swept down to my toes. I heard a fair amount of English mixed in with Italian and wasn't at all surprised. Tourists generally outnumbered the local population in Venice on any given day by two-to-one, and Harry's Bar was a hot tourist destination. Everyone seemed to be enjoying themselves and that was all that mattered. I needed to be around happy people.

Smiling at the waitress as my dinner arrived, I ordered a second Montgomery and told her to hold the vermouth this time and not be so shy with the gin. Who was kidding who? It was my intention to begin my seafaring adventure with a bang. She nodded in understanding. The cuttlefish was delicious, and I thought about my itinerary. I didn't have one, other than to get plastered every night and wallow in self-pity.

The Queen Boudica, flagship of the Cunard line, boarded tomorrow morning at 8:00 a.m. and set sail at noon, reaching its first port of call two days later at the coastal city of Dubrovnik in Croatia. From there, the boat meandered its way slowly down the Adriatic and made a sharp turn by Greece, sweeping up and around Malta and Sicily eventually finishing its journey in Rome. I had three days of peace before Vito boarded the ship in Dubrovnik, and I intended to make the most of it.

The Boudica was named after the famed Celtic warrior queen, who in 60 A.D. led a ferocious uprising against the Roman Empire resulting in the destruction of multiple Roman cities and settlements in Britain. Close to a hundred thousand Romans lay dead before the rebellion was eventually and ruthlessly squashed. According to Roman historians, the seminal event triggering the carnage was when the Romans, in a singularly foolish act of authoritarianism, flogged Boudica and had her young daughters raped in front of her; a bad idea in retrospect.

A girl at the bar sipping a Bellini caught my attention. She was young, attractive, and alone sitting with her very long legs crossed. I caught a glimpse of her face in the mirror behind the bar and liked what I saw. She must have seen me looking because she suddenly swiveled around to face me, catching my eye. She had interesting features, large, almond-shaped blue eyes, reddish shoulder length hair, full pouty lips, and delicate freckles. Her skin was milky white.

Turning away quickly, I felt myself blushing. She was much too young for me and I hated when I got busted like that. I was on the wrong side of thirty-five and could already feel middle-age stalking me. I was in good shape, worked out regularly, and still had all my hair, but I was acutely aware that I was no match for some of the girls in this place. Besides, I was out of here in the morning and didn't want any trouble with anyone for any reason.

Staring down at my risotto, I ate in silence for the next few minutes until I sensed a presence nearby. I looked up. She was standing next to me with one hand on her hip and her cocktail in the other. Man, she was tall, easily over six feet and she wasn't even wearing heels. I wondered if she was a model. She was thin but not skinny or gaunt. She seemed very healthy and I guessed she spent quite a bit of time in the gym too. The hemline of her short skirt was almost at eye level and quite distracting.

She said in a thick eastern European accent, "American, no?"

Surprised by that opening, I raised my eye-brows. "American, yes. What gave me away? The jeans?"

"No, not jeans. Only Americans look at girl and then run away when girl look back."

I didn't know how to respond to that, so she continued. "I sit?"

She pointed at the chair on the other side of my table and I nodded. "If you want." Up close, I could see she was a little older than I had first guessed but not by much, maybe early twenties. She was kindling, and I had no intention of lighting her fire.

She put her glass down and reached into her bag, retrieving a metal cigarette case. She took one out, sat down, and lit it, blowing a puff out of the side of her mouth.

I looked around waiting for someone to go ballistic. When it didn't happen I said, "Are you sure it's okay to smoke in here?"

She smiled, "No one give sheet. This Eataly. My name Katarina, and you name is?"

"John, John Cesari." I offered her my hand and she took it.

"Nice to meet you John Cesari."

She unabashedly held my gaze and I just sat there not sure of whether I should continue eating or just get out of there while I still had the chance. Feeling very self-conscious, I said, "Would you like something to eat?"

She shook her head, "No, thank you. You eat, I drink Bellini."

I took another bite of the cuttlefish and washed it down with gin. I felt obligated to say something. "So, is this your first visit to Venice?"

"Venezia? No, I here many times."

"And what brings you to Harry's Bar?"

She thought about that. "Bar is where men are. I need man."

Jesus Christ! It just hit me. She's a hooker. I let out a deep breath and smiled to myself. Now I understood. An American sitting all by himself in a bar. You didn't have to be a genius to figure this one out. For some reason, knowing what her game was made me feel less tense.

I nodded my head. "I see, but I think there's been a misunderstanding. I'm not really looking for a date tonight."

She looked puzzled. "What mean?"

"I mean I don't have enough money on me to pay for you."

Realization came to her and she laughed. "I no prostitute. I captain of Croatian women's volleyball team. I am big star."

Blushing again and truly embarrassed, I stammered, "I apologize. I meant no disrespect. I didn't understand. That's wonderful. You're a professional athlete. That's truly amazing."

"Why you think I am whore?" she asked with a twinkle in her eye. I was uncomfortable, and she knew it.

I sat back. "I don't think that. I don't know why I said that and I'm very sorry. Please, let's just put it behind us."

With a quizzical look she persisted, "Women in America no get horny? Go to bar? Look for man?"

It was an interesting question when put so bluntly like that. This wasn't exactly the kind of conversation I thought I'd be having over cuttlefish in a bar my first night in Europe. I said, "They do, but they don't usually say it like that."

She blew a smoke ring in my direction. "No? How they say?"

Thinking about it for a moment, I was starting to find her amusing. Slowly, I said, "Well, they'll say things like 'Hey, buy me a drink,' or 'It's noisy in here. Let's go someplace quiet so we can talk.'"

She considered that for a second or two before saying, "Hey, it's noisy in here. Let's go someplace more quiet so we can talk."

I laughed. "That's perfect."

She wasn't laughing. "I serious. Finish eat. Then we go someplace quiet. You have hotel room?"

Okay, it was to time to lay the cards on the table. I shook my head. "No, Katarina. We're not going to my hotel room or yours. I came here to have a quiet dinner and a few drinks and that is all." I thought I was a little harsh and should have let her down just a little more gently, so I added in a softer tone, "You're very attractive and I'm very flattered but I have to get up early in the morning."

She pouted, sipped her Bellini and I said, "Look around you. There are plenty of other men in here. Most are closer to your age anyway."

She looked at me as if I was crazy. "If I want boy, I sit with boy. I want man, so I sit with man."

Fair enough. That was her right. "How old are you, Katarina?"

"Twenty-five. You want see passport?"

I shook my head. "That won't be necessary."

She smiled. "Is old enough?"

Not for me. I said, "For what?"

She liked this type of back and forth and giggled. "For you wash my back and I wash yours."

I had to admit, she was fun but it was time to end this before it got out of control. I signaled the waitress for the bill. As I did so, a big, sharp-featured guy, wearing a stylish blue suit and tie entered the room. Looking angry, he spotted her and shouted, "Katarina!"

She glanced in his direction and let out a deep frustrated breath. Ignoring him, she said, "Sheet."

I immediately computed the significance of what was happening and said sarcastically, "Great."

It had to be her boyfriend. She was mad at him about something and sought out a stranger in a bar to irritate him or make him jealous. I was glad I didn't fall for it. He quickly pushed his way through the crowd and stood tableside between us. Close up he resembled a bull without the horns and only half as nice. Disregarding me, he snorted at her, "Is time to go, beetch."

She blew a smoke ring directly at him and with utter disgust in her voice said, "Piss off or my boyfriend, John, will kick you ass."

My eyes went wide. He was two inches taller than me and at least fifty pounds heavier, and from the way he filled out his suit it didn't look like fat. I was six feet tall and 220 pounds. I could handle myself, but like Montgomery, preferred an overwhelming advantage on the battlefield. I also had a two-martini handicap going against me. A quick assessment of the situation told me that this was not going to have a fairy-tale ending if I didn't defuse the situation in a hurry.

I said calmly, "Hey friend, how about we all relax? I'm sure we can we work it out."

He looked at me and said, "American?" Before I could answer, he turned back to Katarina and said something in Croatian. I don't know what, but she held up her middle finger to his face. He grabbed her wrist roughly and started to lift her out of her chair saying, "We go now."

I stood abruptly. Damsels in distress were my fatal weakness and I just couldn't help myself. "Hey, let go of her."

With his other ham hock-sized hand, he grabbed the front of my shirt and said, "Hey, George Bush cowboy, we don't need your help." With a mighty shove, he pushed me backwards. I stumbled into the table next to ours knocking plates and glasses to the floor. The couple sitting there jumped to their feet and the rest of the room suddenly went quiet as the commotion grew in intensity.

Now I was pissed. No one calls me George Bush and gets away with it. As I recovered my balance, he turned to leave the room dragging Katarina, punching and kicking at him futilely. A waiter stood frozen nearby watching the spectacle. He held an ice bucket with a bottle of prosecco chilling inside. I grabbed the bottle by the neck and racing to catch up to them, I smashed it on the back of his head. He crumpled to the floor unconscious as shards of glass and sparkling wine showered the room. The crowd recovered from its inertia, and cellphones started coming out fast and furious, to record the event and call the police.

Damn! That was the last thing I needed. I looked at Katarina and she smiled. "He's going to be really pissed off when wake up."

"I have to get out of here. You can stay and deal with him if you want."

"No, I go with you."

I grabbed a cloth napkin and covered my face from the would-be photographers. We ran from the bar and headed to Piazza di San Marco where we were soon lost in the throngs of revelers.

Chapter 3

The next morning, I boarded the Queen Boudica uneventfully and was shown to my stateroom on deck 6. Smack in the middle of the twelve-story vessel, my room was an extravagant suite with a king bed, sofa, private balcony, and a commanding starboard view. The Queen Boudica was the top of the line cruise ship and spared no expense when it came to pampering its guests. All the suites boasted small kitchenettes with tiny tables and countertops. There was a microwave, coffee maker, and small refrigerator which made me feel right at home, not that I planned on eating in a lot. A royal blue, feather-soft terry cloth robe with matching slippers waited for me in the bathroom. On the desk in the sitting area was personalized stationery, a bottle of champagne, fresh strawberries dipped in chocolate, and a handwritten reminder that I could call the pillow concierge any time if I wasn't thrilled with the one they gave me. A pillow concierge? I tried to picture in my mind going to school for something like that.

I unpacked and lay on the bed to test it out. It was very nice. Staring at the ceiling fan, I thought about last night. Katarina and I had parted company in St. Mark's Square shortly after fleeing Harry's. At first, she tried to follow me back to my room but I firmly nixed that idea and sent her off from whence she came. I'd had enough excitement for one night. I didn't ask her who the goon was. I didn't care. It was my experience that when a girl can cause that much chaos, that quickly, it was best not to get overly involved and to put as much space between the two of you as possible. She did, however, reassure me that the guy wasn't going to be a problem, and I believed her. Why I believed I didn't know. She exuded confidence. Part of me was intrigued by her but mostly I was glad I was never going to see her again. She was trouble with a capital T for sure. The last thing she did before walking away was to throw her arms around my neck and plant a long one on my lips just to make sure I didn't forget her, and it was working.

I liked women, I really did, but I didn't like the power they had over me. It was too primitive, too compelling, and once they knew they had you in their crosshairs there was no stopping them. Men didn't have the same power over women. Women were too evolved. They needed men from time to time when the urge struck them, sure, but they could control their passions when necessary. A man's need for women was very close to his need for food. A guy could miss a meal from time to time but he couldn't go hungry for very long. I tried explaining that to a woman once and she threw a glass of water in my face.

The ship left port on schedule to much fanfare, horn-blowing, and cheering, and I spent the afternoon watching the coastline slowly drift by from my balcony lounge chair sipping champagne and reading an Italian newspaper. I was determined to improve my Italian comprehension and speaking skills on this trip and had picked up a dictionary and phrase book at the airport bookstore. Growing up, my parents spoke half-English, half-Italian and most of that was Sicilian dialect. In college, I had studied proper Italian, the dialect of Florence and specifically of Dante Alighieri, the most important poet of the Renaissance. *La lingua Toscana*, my Italian professor would say over and over, was the most beautiful of all the romance languages. His name was Mr. Cipollino, which meant little onion. He was short, wore a suit and tie every day, and smoked cigarettes right in class while he wrote on the blackboard. He had style and I liked him.

Being a diligent student, I had become fairly proficient, but had little opportunity to practice speaking, and linguistic skills were like any other skill; if you don't use it, you lose it. I had said that once to a girl I was trying to talk into doing something naughty and received another glass of water in the face. By the time I was twenty-five, I guessed that I had the cleanest face in the Bronx.

I was proud of the way I had spoken with the flight attendant, Vincenza, but unfortunately, all that remained of my four years of college-level Italian was my ability to flirt. If I was stranded in a Naples ghetto, homeless and starving, my only option for survival would be to propose to some girl I didn't know in exchange for food and shelter. In Italy that would be considered a fair deal.

The gentle breeze, rolling motion of the ship, and the champagne eventually took its toll on me and I fell asleep. At 6:00 p.m., the cool evening air woke me and I realized that I had just wasted my first day of a very expensive vacation. Evening was approaching fast, and I caught a glimpse of orange as the sun started to set in the west. Dinner was at 7:00 p.m. and was supposed to be a black tie affair. I had packed a sport coat only with intentions of renting or buying a tuxedo at the on-board men's haberdashery. I looked at my watch. It was too late for that so I cleaned up, put on dress slacks and shirt, and donned my navy blazer, hoping not to look too out of place. After adjusting my tie in the bathroom mirror, I splashed some after-shave on and headed to the main dining room.

Entering the grand ballroom on deck 2, I immediately realized I looked like a dairy farmer at a debutante ball. The room was ornately decorated with crystal chandeliers, brass wall sconces, marble colonnades and oil paintings. The wait-staff all wore black tuxes with white bowties as did the ten-piece jazz band. The singer was a beautiful brunette in a sequined, flowing, white gown. People milled about in formal attire and massive amounts of bling, sipping martinis and swirling high-end scotch in crystal tumblers enjoying the music. I guessed I had arrived in the middle of happy hour, and undeterred by my fashion faux pas, snaked my way to the bar.

Squeezing onto the last remaining stool, I sandwiched myself between two older women in elaborate evening gowns. The one on my right wore teal while the one on my left wore traditional black. The bartender noticed me and nodded.

I said, "Scotch, please. Oban if you have."

He was a polite fellow with only a trace of a German accent. "I'm sorry, sir, but it's black tie only. I'm afraid I won't be able to serve you."

Taken aback, I replied, "You can't be serious?" I almost said, 'Do you have any idea who I am?', but held back.

"My apologies, sir."

The old lady in teal on my right caught wind of the interaction and said, "First cruise, I gather?" She sounded American.

I chuckled. "Yes, and apparently, I have a lot to learn."

"They sent you an email and a brochure explaining the ship's rules and expectations?"

"Probably. I'll check when I get back to New York."

She smiled affably and sipped her martini. I guessed she was in her mid-to-late-sixties, and as she turned to face me better, her plunging neckline revealed a healthy dose of cleavage covered by a jewel encrusted necklace from which dangled at the apex, the largest diamond I had ever seen. The emeralds, rubies, and other gems twinkled in the light, but paled in comparison to the radiance of the diamond, and I estimated the necklace was easily more valuable than my entire net worth and possibly the collective net worth of ten or twelve doctors just like me.

She saw me staring and seemed pleased. "What are you having?"

"I was hoping for a scotch."

"Neat?"

"Does the Pope wear a dress?"

She smiled and raised her hand. The bartender approached, and she said, "Frederick, please get me a scotch, neat. I'm almost done with my martini." Her martini glass was three-quarters filled.

He smiled. "Yes, Lady Beth. Will Macallan 40 be adequate?"

"Yes, and make it a solid pour. I'm parched."

He came back with a crystal tumbler filled half-way with forty-year-old Macallan and placed it in front of me. "Enjoy your scotch, sir."

I chuckled. I couldn't even begin to imagine what a bottle of forty-year-old Macallan cost. "Thanks."

She raised her martini glass in toast. "Cheers. That's one way to skirt the rules."

"Lady Beth?"

"Elizabeth, but my friends call me Betsy. It's an honorary title, I assure you. My husband, Roger and I, donated a couple of million pounds to the restoration of London Tower a few years back and voila, we are now Lord and Lady Harrington of Boston."

She nodded at an older gentleman sitting next to her who was facing away, thoroughly engrossed in conversation with another couple. She continued, "And you? You're obviously American."

Extending my hand, I said, "Dr. John Cesari—of the Bronx, and it's a pleasure to meet you. Thanks for the drink, but I wonder what's going to happen with dinner?"

She took my hand and grinned. "A doctor? How marvelous. You can never have enough of those on a cruise filled with old people. I wouldn't worry about dinner, dear. It'll work out. I'm sure."

After the reaction I got from the bartender, I wasn't quite as confident as she was. She continued, "So, what kind of doctor are you?"

"I'm a gastroenterologist."

"One of those doctors with the tubes and cameras? Well, I've met your type before, several times in fact—professionally, of course."

"Of course."

"Hmm."

"So, is it safe to assume this isn't your first cruise, Lady Beth?"

"Betsy, please, and heavens no. We practically live on the ocean. So, is there a Mrs. Cesari or a lady friend who will be joining you later?"

"No, I'm unattached, cruising the high seas for adventure."

She liked that. "Hmm." That was twice she did the hmm thing. What was that all about? "You'd better take care," she said, "the high seas are filled with all kinds of predators, but I'll give you a hint how you can recognize them." She leaned close and whispered, "Most of them are wearing high heels."

Almost unconsciously, I glanced downward and noticed she was wearing black high heels. I chuckled, "I'll take that under advisement."

Watching me watch her, she crossed her legs to give me a better view of her shapely calf. I couldn't help but notice how attractive she was. Time had been very kind to her, and I could barely find a wrinkle on her face. She had high cheek bones and large seductive brown eyes. I was close enough to smell her perfume.

"Dr. Cesari, as a gastroenterologist, you must be thoroughly familiar with all the ins and outs of female anatomy."

I hesitated and looked past her at her husband to see if he was paying attention. He wasn't. This was a new game for me; flirting with a woman whose husband was inches away. She smiled and said, "He couldn't hear a word even if you screamed into his good ear."

I said, "The female anatomy is quite complicated as you can imagine which only makes sense if you consider the complex nature of women themselves." I was proud of myself and felt like King Solomon with that response.

"So you believe women are by their very nature, complicated."

"Very."

"Hmm."

There it was again. "You don't agree?" I asked.

She held my gaze for a moment, studying me, probing me, trying to figure me out. In less than five minutes, I already felt like I was being reeled in. I knew I had to be imagining it, but this was the problem with guys. A woman pays them a little attention and before you know it, we're all jumping to the wrong conclusions.

She said, "I think women are quite simple to understand, but then again I'm a woman, so for me they are easy."

I nodded. "That makes sense."

"I'd like to discuss this more with you, Dr. Cesari, if you don't mind? Which table are you seated at?"

I pulled the invitation out of my coat pocket and read it. "The mate's table, wherever that is, and please call me John."

She took the card from me and signaled the bartender. “Frederick, let the maître d know that Dr. Cesari will be joining my party at the admiral’s table. I’m sure they’ll be able to squeeze in an extra place setting, and make sure they know not to bother him about his attire.”

He nodded and took my invitation from her. “Of course, Lady Beth. I’ll take care of it immediately.”

I said, “You don’t have to do that, Betsy.”

“Nonsense, I insist. Besides, if you’re cruising the high seas looking for adventure then…” she paused to wink at me, “you’re off to a good start.”

A bell rang signaling the end of cocktail hour. We stood and Betsy put her arm through mine. “Would you mind escorting an old woman to her chair, John?”

What could I say? “Sure.” I looked over my shoulder and saw that her husband was still in animated conversation with the other guests. He appeared not have noticed that we left the bar.

Betsy saw me looking in his direction. “Don’t give him another thought, John. Roger hasn’t concerned himself with whom I invite to my bedroom since the great crash of 2008.”

This vacation wasn’t quite getting off to the start I had in mind.

I said, “Hmm.”

Chapter 4

We were the first to arrive at the round table for eight and I assisted Betsy into her chair, taking the seat on her right as the band played *Sentimental Journey.* A woman wailed melancholy riffs on the clarinet as her turn came to interpret the music.

"You like jazz?" Betsy asked, noticing me tapping my fingers on the table.

"Yes, in general, but there is something very haunting about this particular melody and this arrangement is pure genius."

"You may not know this, John, but this was one of the most popular songs ever recorded. It was released in 1945 and coincided with the end of World War II. It became the homecoming anthem for a generation of soldiers, their families and a war-weary nation. My father cried every time he heard it right up until the day he died."

"Was he a veteran?"

She smiled, "Was he ever; sergeant, U.S. marine corps, '41 to '45, two purple hearts and a bronze star. He was at Saipan, Okinawa, and Iwo Jima, and limped his whole life because of shrapnel from a landmine that took the legs off one of his men. His brother was beheaded in a Japanese prison camp because he was too weak to stand for morning roll call, so don't bother asking him about the morality of the atomic bomb."

I nodded. "I won't."

She grinned. "It won't come up. We played *Sentimental Journey* at his funeral."

We were soon joined by the Captain, Betsy's husband, Roger, followed by a large, boisterous man named Brad and his wife, Joyce, a platinum blonde in her late thirties with breasts way too large to be real. She wrinkled her nose at me in a flirtatious manner and I immediately sensed trouble. The two seats to my immediate right were unoccupied. Somebody was late. The wait staff filled crystal champagne flutes with Dom Perignon.

The ship's captain, Bjorn Hagen, was a stiff, bearded, Norwegian man in his fifties who spoke impeccable English. He wore dress whites and acted very deferential toward the Harrington's. They seemed to know each other very well. Roger wasn't a bad guy. Gray, thinning hair made him appear older than Betsy but by how much I couldn't say. His skin was bronzed and leathery as if he spent a lot of time in the sun. I suspected he had been athletic at one point in his life. He had a solid, well-developed frame. He laughed too much and too loudly and didn't seem to care at what. Some guys were like that. I noticed he paid little or no attention to Betsy and I could see why she went her own way. I guessed Roger, for whatever reason, wasn't tending the home-hearth anymore and she was still too young to pretend it didn't matter.

That was an interesting question. When did our libidos give up the ghost so to speak? Most men would tell you that a woman's sex drive died right after they finished saying their wedding vows. That always seemed funny to me, but I had never been married.

Brad was big, brash, and already smashed from one too many old-fashioneds during happy hour. He was born and raised in Hoosick Falls, New York, a small city in upstate, and according to him, that was a big deal. After receiving his MBA from a prestigious online university, he was named CEO of Hoosick General, the only hospital in the town. This was in no small part due to the fact that his father-in-law, who was president of the local chamber of commerce, had passed away suddenly, leaving several million dollars to the hospital contingent upon the hiring of his son-in-law as CEO. In Brad's view of things, this made him important. The most amazing thing was that he didn't mind telling everyone his life story. Ruddy faced and six feet-four, 280 pounds, he was literally the proverbial big fish in the small pond.

Joyce was hot and trashy with bottle-dyed hair, spiked heels, and long dangerous fingernails. Her breasts must have cost a fortune and if I were asked to offer one piece of advice it would have been to back off a bit on the collagen injections. Her puffy lips made her look a little like Mick Jagger, and I wondered if there was a karaoke contest on board because she'd win hands down on points. I didn't like the way she looked at me, but then again, I didn't like the way any woman looked at me these days. I was getting paranoid.

At the designated moment, the captain rose from his chair and the room went silent in anticipation. He introduced himself and greeted the guests wishing them a wonderful time during their voyage. He then clasped his hands and said a small prayer to begin the meal. Raising his glass of champagne, he toasted the room; good health, good friends, and good times. As he finished, the room erupted with clapping and cheering.

As the soup course arrived so did the tardy guests to my right. The captain and Roger stood to greet the newcomers. Hesitantly, Brad joined them and I figured I'd better stand as well. My jaw dropped when I turned and saw Katarina decked out in a long, black, form-hugging dress, pearl necklace, and white elbow-length dress gloves. She was beautiful and did not try to hide her surprise at seeing me there. Wearing heels tonight she towered over me by several inches.

Before I could react, she flung her arms around me and hugged me tightly. Everyone watched with great curiosity. She turned to the older, well-culled gentleman by her side and spoke rapidly in Croatian pointing at me repetitively.

She introduced him as her father. His name was Berislav and he was a powerfully built, stocky man, slightly taller than his daughter. Maybe in his early seventies, he was still in great shape and gripped my hand firmly, shaking it hard enough that I felt a vibration in my shoulder for the next five minutes.

He said, "Katarina say she meet you last night. Is true?"

Was she out of her mind? Total ignorance was the correct way to play this game. I hesitated, not sure what to say. To admit that we met last night would almost certainly lead to an acknowledgement that I assaulted someone in a bar in her defense and then fled the scene. The captain might be obligated to detain me as well as notify the Italian authorities. Almost anything that even vaguely resembled the truth could end disastrously for me. Why would she say anything at all? Why would she hug me? Just play it cool. My brain raced for a response but found none.

Katarina stepped in for me, explaining, "He is very shy man, Papa. He is hero for me." She turned to the rest of the table and with tears welling up in her eyes, said, "This man save my life last night. Three men attack me outside bar. They want sex with virgin and he rescue me. He is cowboy."

Oh brother!

Betsy covered her mouth in shock. My eyes went wide as did everyone else's at the table. Her father threw his arms around me in a bear hug. "You are hero, save daughter's honor from animals. Sadly, man I send to protect Katarina is in hospital in Venezia. He was attack from behind by cowards but you save little girl and I, Berislav Juric, forever in your debt. Anything you need…anything, and it is yours."

Katarina added with a big smile, "Yes, anything…anything at all."

I looked around. Everyone expected me to say something so I did. "It was no big deal."

Katarina objected. "Is modest." She turned to the table. "They were four of the ugliest brutes born of woman, and hands all over me. I wash and wash to get rid of stench."

Four now? She was incorrigible.

Everyone at the table congratulated me for my heroic behavior and we sat, Katarina literally pushing Berislav aside to take the chair next to me. Captain Bjorn raised his champagne a second time. "Words cannot express the gratitude of every man and woman on this ship for your valor, doctor. If only every man were to act with such selfless gallantry. May you live long and prosper."

The commotion died down and we got to know each other over lobster bisque. Roger and Betsy, it turned out, made their money in shipping and were the majority owners of the Queen Boudica as well as god parents to Captain Bjorn's oldest son, Andreas. Although they had homes in Boston and London, they spent most of their time sailing around the world on the Queen Boudica in pursuit of philanthropic missions. Berislav was an entrepreneur and self-made billionaire who owned multiple sports teams throughout Europe as well several soccer stadiums. Katarina's mother had passed away several years ago. Brad blustered incessantly about his accomplishments desperately trying to impress the table and I wondered if Joyce was a retired porn-star…maybe not retired.

As multiple bottles of expensive French burgundy were uncorked, chateaubriand was served, with sautéed baby carrots, grilled asparagus, and potatoes dauphinoise. Berislav stood with his glass raised and said, "I make announcement. Is special occasion. Is daughter's twenty-first birthday tomorrow."

Everyone clapped and Katarina took a sitting bow. I glanced at her and she smiled again knowing I had caught her in another lie. She had told me she was twenty-five. She was something else.

Berislav continued, "Am no shame to admit how proud am I of daughter. Captain of national volley ball team, Croatia, and most valuable player two year in row. Graduate university of Zagreb with highest honors."

Another round of applause and another bow. He continued. "This special cruise. For in Croatian culture, twenty-first birthday is time to be marry and make the grandchildren."

I snorted under my breath.

"But my Katarina, is so devoted to fellow man and God that she has decline hand in marriage from most eligible bachelor in all Dubrovnik, and instead, plans to devote life to service of church. When ship land in Rome, we go straight to Vatican where she join Sisters of Piety missionaries to help poor throughout world. Is so proud am I."

That was the last thing I expected to hear and nearly gagged on my wine. I started coughing and both Betsy and Katarina patted me on the back. I raised my hand and said, "Thank you. I'm okay."

Turning to Katarina I leaned close and whispered, "A convent?"

"Yes, I do God's work."

My jaw dropped and I stared at her. She gave me a feigned indignant look. "Don't look so surprise. I am very holy."

"Oh, for God's sake."

She grinned at my consternation and I rolled my eyes. Dinner went more or less smoothly after that as I divided my time between Katarina on my right and Betsy on my left. Conversation was polite if not slightly stilted and flirting was kept to a minimum on both sides. Except for the occasional foot rub and thigh squeeze under the table, I barely knew Katarina was there. I didn't ever want to be alone with her again, but I was dying to ask her what the hell was going on. I just didn't see her as nun material.

Brad who was nearly blind drunk toward the end of the main course, bellowed across the table with a mouthful of medium-rare beef, "Would someone care to tell me why the hero over there is the only one in the room not wearing a tuxedo?"

Joyce tried to rein him in, and in a high-pitched, nasal New Jersey accent said, "Oh Brad, leave him alone. You're just jealous. I think he's cute."

Nearly apoplectic at the rebuke, his ruddy cheeks got even ruddier. "I'm serious. It said in all the communications we received that this was a black tie affair and that there would be no, I repeat, no exceptions. It didn't say anything about saving virgins being an exception."

I replied calmly, "This voyage was a last minute decision for me. I barely made my flight out here, and I didn't have time to pick up a tux. An exception was made out of kindness, not because I'm worthy of special treatment."

Barely mollified, he shoved another gargantuan piece of meat into his mouth. "Well, it's disrespectful to the rest of us who followed the rules. You know, doctor, I would never tolerate behavior like this from anyone on my medical staff at Hoosick General. I run a tight ship, see. Any doctor steps out of line and I let him know who the boss is right away." He swallowed the beef and washed it down with a slug of wine. "That's exactly what I do."

I was getting red in the face but before I could respond Katarina jumped in. "Papa, let us get tuxedo for John. Least we can do, no? After all, he is hero for me. Save life and virginity." I looked at her and was perplexed by her sudden concern for my wardrobe.

Berislav countered with, "Is good idea, daughter. Maybe two tuxedos?"

I said, "Thank you, but that's really not necessary."

Berislav insisted, "Nonsense, I send tailor to room tomorrow."

"Is good idea, Papa. Send tailor to room. What is room number, John?"

Now, I saw what she was up to. There was no way I was going to tell her my room number. I said, "Your generosity overwhelms me, Berislav, and I only accept it with great reluctance, but I insist that I go the tailor myself. I'm sure he's a very busy man and has more important things to do than come to my room."

He said, "Seem fair. I call tailor first thing in morning."

Katarina made a sly face. "Yes, fair, but I would like to show thanks too. I send basket of fruit to room, yes? So tell number."

I said sternly. "I don't eat fruit."

She smiled. "Then special wine. I will have blessed by priest."

I didn't answer right away and Betsy said, "John, for heaven's sake. You saved the girl's life. She's just trying to do something nice for you. Tell her your room number."

After a moment's hesitation, I said, "6092."

Berislav added, "I am so proud of you, daughter. Is nice thing you do."

"Thank you, Papa."

After dinner, as coffee and dessert were served, the lights went dim and the band started to play a mix of waltzes, fox-trots and rumbas. Couples gradually drifted toward the center of the room to hold each other and sway rhythmically to the music. Several couples had obviously taken dance lessons and showed off their rehearsed moves for the crowd. Betsy and Roger were experienced dancers and gracefully twirled around the room to a Viennese waltz. I had turned my chair around to watch as I sipped what was arguably the best espresso I had ever had.

Katarina had gradually inched her chair close behind me. In a whisper, she said, "You want dance with me?"

I whispered back, "I don't dance, and I don't trust you as far as I can throw you." I knew exactly what she would do to me if she ever got me alone in the middle of a dark dance floor. I've been mauled like that before.

Not discouraged in the slightest, she giggled, "6092. We dance later—in the dark, lights out, clothes off. I thank you for saving virginity."

I turned to her and saw her father talking to Brad and Joyce. I reached for a napkin I didn't need and covering my lips, said under my breath, "You're such a liar. I can't believe what I heard tonight."

Without moving her head or acknowledging what I said, she blew me a kiss. In the low level lighting no one noticed, but I was rapidly becoming alarmed at her growing temerity. I was trapped on a ship with a twenty-one-year-old loose cannon who didn't seem to believe that rules applied to her. Somehow, I didn't think this boded well for me.

The music had stopped momentarily, and Betsy and Roger returned to the table. Betsy placed a hand lightly on my shoulder and I turned toward her. Roger sat down. He had worked up quite a sweat and was chugging down a glass of water while he flamboyantly conducted music with his outstretched arm waving wildly to a tune only he could hear. A strange sight for sure. "How about a dance, handsome?" Betsy asked.

I almost declined but I thought this would be a good opportunity to let Katarina know I was in control of my own life so I said, "Sure."

We walked to the center of the dance floor just as the band launched into a beautiful rendition of *I'm in the Mood for Love*. "Is Roger all right?" I asked, still watching him.

She glanced in his direction and smiled. "I'll keep an eye on him. I'm used to it."

I didn't pry any further and she said, "Do you have any moves?"

I shook my head. "Not even one."

"Then just put your arms around my waist and we'll take baby steps back and forth. That's what most people do anyway."

She put her arms on my shoulders and I put mine around her waist. We rocked and swayed gently, small steps leading us in one direction and then the other, gently arcing around the room. With each step she moved in just a little closer until she was pressing against me. She looked up at me smiling.

"So how is it that a handsome, young doctor like yourself is on a cruise all by himself?"

I decided to come clean. "I'm just coming off a complicated relationship. It didn't end well, and I thought a little vacation would clear my head."

She nodded knowingly. "A woman can raise a man to dizzying heights of pleasure and success or she can utterly destroy him."

"Boy, you hit that one on the head."

"What do you think of Katarina?" she asked.

"Seems like a nice girl."

"Hmm."

There it was again. "Why do you ask?"

"What really happened last night?"

"You don't believe her story?"

She chuckled, "Oh please."

Grinning I said, "You don't believe I can handle four guys?"

She squeezed my bicep. "That's the only part I did believe."

I studied her face. She was beautiful and I thought that she must have been absolutely stunning when she was younger. She didn't try to hide behind cosmetic surgery or too much make-up. She colored her hair but only enough to shave off five or ten years. She didn't try to turn back the clock all the way. Accepting the onslaught of time with grace, gave her an air of dignity which I found very appealing. I was starting to feel something stir inside.

We were silent for a moment, and then she rested her face against my chest, saying, "God, you smell nice."

I sighed, "What am I going to do with you?"

She looked up and smiled. "Do you want instructions?"

Shaking my head, I laughed, "No, I'll figure it out."

"The real question is what are you going to do with Katarina?"

"Not my problem. She's entering a convent."

"That's what she said."

"But you're not buying it?"

"She'll spread for you like butter on toast."

I grinned. "Womanly intuition?"

"Like I said, I can read any woman and she's easier than most. Be careful."

"I'll keep my eyes open."

The song ended, and she stood there holding me for an extra moment. Very slowly, she stepped back, and looked into my eyes. As we returned to the table, I felt her discreetly slip something into my pocket.

It was her room key.

Chapter 5

By 11:00 p.m. the party was shifting gears as blood alcohol levels rose. The mood had decidedly changed and most of the older patrons, including Betsy and Roger, beat a hasty retreat to their quarters yielding the playing field to a younger, more exuberant crowd. The music had taken an uptick as electric guitars, replacing trombones and horns, started hammering out rock tunes. As the saying goes, the joint was jumpin'. I'd had enough fun and felt it would be prudent to leave before Katarina, emboldened by too much wine, tried to get a hold of some of my DNA.

Not being very tired, I decided to explore the ship. The casino was on deck 3 and I went there first. Entering through the massive portico, I was amazed at how closely it resembled even the best ones in Las Vegas, both in size and grandeur. It felt like all three thousand passengers and nine hundred crew members were here at once. I sat down at a five dollar black jack table with two other guys and said hello to the dealer, a short, business-like brunette named Francine. I gave her a hundred bucks and she gave me some chips.

A cocktail waitress spotted me and I ordered Glenmorangie neat. Placing my first bet, I pulled out Betsy's room key to study it as the hand was dealt. She had adjoining staterooms with Roger on deck 8. She told me they'd had separate living arrangements for years. They didn't hate each other. In fact, they got along very well, but more like good friends than anything else. Although she pursued companionship like mine from time to time, she didn't like to flaunt her activities in his face for fear of hurting him. She said almost any night was good for her but advised me to wait at least until after midnight to be sure he was tucked away in his own room before coming to visit. I thought about what Vito would say about me sleeping with a woman thirty years my senior.

I chuckled quietly because I didn't care what he or anybody would think. When I was in the mood, I was in the mood, and right now, I was in the mood. I had promised myself I would practice self-discipline on this trip, but she had solicited me, so I didn't feel that this counted. I studied my cards; jack of diamonds, six of clubs, and signaled to Francine to hold. The guy next to me scored twenty-one, and the one next to him drew one too many times. Francine flipped her card revealing an eight of spades underneath an ace of hearts. I lost.

Big bad Brad and Joyce walked by without noticing me. They were arguing about something. She was angry and hissed at him, "You said you were getting a divorce. What's this bullshit?"

He whined back, "I know what I said, honey, but it's complicated. I need more time."

"You've had enough time. If you don't tell her about me, I will."

"Aww, c'mon, Joycie. Be reasonable. Everything's in her name. I got nothing without her. I have to be careful."

And then they were out of earshot. I laughed. Too funny. He had introduced her as his wife. Obviously, she wasn't. Another hospital CEO with too much time on his hands. They were all jerks. No exception to that rule. In fact, I was so sure of that, I made a promise to myself that if I ever found a CEO who wasn't a jerk, I'd buy him dinner at the best steakhouse in whatever city I was in. I laid another five dollar chip down and watched the clock tick away to fifteen minutes after midnight. When it did, I waved goodbye to Francine. I had lost thirty and won thirty-five in the course of an hour. I left her a ten dollar chip as I left the table.

The elevator let me off on deck 8 and I found Betsy's room. I took out the key, but hesitated. Was this really what I wanted to do? Sleep with another man's wife? Why was I doing this anyway? Just to stroke my ego? What the hell was wrong with me? My whole life had revolved around sex. One girl to the next to the next. No end in sight. I let out a deep breath, but I wanted her. I didn't know why. I just did. A man's sex drive was a curse. It controlled us from puberty until the day we died. There was no turning it off. If we were lucky, certain diseases slowed us down, but I've worked in nursing homes where demented old men were constantly stroking their magic lantern hoping to see the genie one last time. They didn't even know what they were doing. God, was that going to be me? I hoped not.

There was no point in fighting it so I slid the key into the lock and opened the door. The lights were on but no one was there. It was a very large suite, at least twice the size of mine. The door joining her room to Roger's was closed. The bathroom door was also closed and I went over to it knocking politely. There was no answer and I turned the knob to look in. She must have been there because the necklace she wore at dinner lay neatly on the counter sparkling in the light waiting to be tucked away someplace safe. I studied it more carefully. The gems were large and irregularly shaped; green, red, blue, yellow, purple and the large spectacular diamond. They were amazing to behold, and I was tempted to pick up the necklace for a closer inspection but decided against it. I learned a long time ago not to touch things that didn't belong to me.

Suddenly, I thought about Betsy not belonging to me. I went back to the living room trying to decide what to do. This wasn't part of the scenario I had envisioned playing out. I waited patiently for a few minutes but then the thought crossed my mind that she might suddenly appear with Roger in tow having forgotten her invitation to me. I thought about the necklace. I thought about Betsy. I thought about how pretty things always seemed to carry some risk with them. Ultimately, I took Betsy's absence as a sign and left.

I thought about returning to the casino, but it was now a quarter to one. My instincts told me that even on a cruise ship nothing good ever happened at this hour so electing to save my energy for tomorrow, I returned to my room. I'd get a good night's sleep and start over in the morning, beginning with the all you can eat breakfast buffet, a trip to the tailor, the pool, and an hour-long massage after lunch. I stripped, brushed my teeth, and opened the balcony doors. Standing there in the raw taking in the moon over the peaceful Adriatic Sea, I wondered if Betsy would be upset or annoyed that I wasn't there when she returned to her room. I doubted it. She was too mature for that kind of childish behavior. I hit the hay and was asleep within minutes.

A gentle rapping on my door woke me at 2:15 a.m. I threw on my terry cloth robe and went to answer it. Looking through the peep hole, I saw Katarina standing there with a hoodie partially hiding her face as she glanced nervously back and forth. She had a small bag with her. Now I was angry. I opened the door a crack and hissed, "What do you want?"

Through the peep hole I couldn't get a good look and could now see that she had been crying. She pushed the door open and threw her arms around me. "I'm so scared. Never seen father so angry at Katarina. I don't know where else go."

Confused, I stepped back into the room with her clinging to me. The door closed behind her and relaxing my tone I asked, "What are you talking about?"

Sniffling she said, "Very complicated. I not completely truthful."

"No kidding."

"Father no believe I go join convent like say."

I gently pulled her arms from around me. "He's not the only one. Let's sit down and talk." She was sniffling and choked up and I started to feel bad. "Can I get you some water?"

She shook her head no and we walked over to the sofa to sit. I pulled my robe tight and she shook the hoodie off her head. I saw she was wearing pajama bottoms and slippers.

I turned to her. "I'm listening."

She took a deep breath. "Is no easy for to say. Berislav is no real father. Is stepfather. Mostly nice but greedy. Always money, money, money. Croatia not America. Things is different."

I yawned. "And you felt you had to tell me this at two in the morning?"

Sighing deeply, she continued, "In Croatia, rich man want marry girl he pay father."

That caught my attention. She paused as I tried to soak that in. I said, "And…?"

"Old man want marry Katarina. Rich old man. Offer stepfather lots money. Lots. Stepfather say yes. He say, '*Katarina, Marry old man. He die soon. We get all money.*'"

"I thought Berislav was already very rich?"

"Is lie. Try to impress everyone at table. He owe money everybody but especially to, how you say…gangsters."

"Let me get this straight, Berislav wants to sell you to some old rich guy to be his wife but what he's really hoping is that the old man will die quickly so you inherit the money and naturally share it with him."

"Is right."

I was curious. "How old is this guy? I mean people can live a long time in this day and age."

"Is eighty plus eight years old, but if no die right away Berislav help."

I raised my eyebrows in surprise at her forthrightness. "I see." I was starting to think there was a whole lot more to Berislav than met the eye. "Just to be clear. When you say *help* you mean like push him off cliff?"

"More like smother him with pillow."

"Okay, I get it."

"No, you don't. If Berislav don't pay back gangsters by last day of cruise, they kill him and probably me too. They already on ship. Old man also on ship waiting for answer. If yes, he pay off gangsters for Berislav as soon as marry Katarina and, you know, go someplace quiet to talk."

I was almost too stunned to respond. This was unbelievable. "He wants to marry you right here on the ship and then go someplace quiet to talk. Then he'll pay off the gangsters?"

She nodded. "Yes."

I was starting to feel sorry for her. Talk about a situation. "So, you told Berislav you're too devoted to God and that you'd rather join a convent than marry the old man?"

"Yes, he very angry and lock me in room. He no believe. Say if no change mind by morning he beat me. I sneak out through balcony."

"You climbed over the balcony?"

"Many balcony until find open door. Come here. Berislav come here too when find out I gone."

"How will he know where you are?"

"He no like you. Say so after dinner. Think you want to take Katarina someplace quiet to talk."

Jesus!

I rubbed my now throbbing temple. "Katarina, I know this is difficult for you but what are you and Berislav going to do about the gangsters if you don't marry the old man?"

"It don't matter I marry old man or not."

"Why not?"

"Deal only good if old man marry virgin."

I looked at her and said slowly. "I see and you're not…?"

She gave me a little smile. "You want find out?"

I shook my head no to the proposition. "I'll take your word on that. I gather Berislav doesn't know this?"

"No, he doesn't. He be twice as angry. That why have bodyguard follow me to bar in Venice. Keep men away."

"So, you don't want to marry the old man because you know that there's no point because you're not a virgin. But here's a question, if you were still a virgin, would you go through with it?"

She thought it over and shrugged her shoulders. "Maybe." Suddenly appearing very lonely and vulnerable she asked, "May I stay? I have no place go. Don't even have clothes."

I thought it over and sighed. "Sure, but you get the couch."

She glanced over to my sofa and shook her head. "Couch is too small. I no fit."

She was right. It was only five feet long. "There are extra blankets and sheets in the linen closet. You can sleep on the floor."

"The floor? Why not bed? Is gigantic. I no bother you."

"You already bother me. You get the floor."

"Fine. I go bathroom to pee."

"Thanks for the update."

As we stood, there was a knock on the door. We looked at each other. She whispered, "Berislav!"

I looked around quickly for a place for her to hide. The room was a nice size but not big enough to hide a six foot tall volley ball player. The balcony was risky and I didn't want her doing anymore climbing tonight. I said, "Quick, under the bed."

"But I have to pee."

"Get under the bed and shut up."

She wiggled underneath the king bed and I walked to the door as the knocking continued. I took a deep breath to calm myself and looked through the peep hole.

It was Betsy, and she was wearing a lightweight raincoat with the hood pulled up to mask her appearance. I opened the door and said, "Betsy, it's almost three in the morning."

"I know. I couldn't help it. I was lying in bed thinking about you and well…Aren't you going to invite me in?"

"Of course." I opened the door more fully. She walked past me and turned around. The rain coat dropped to the floor revealing black lingerie and high heels. Man, she was in great shape, but this was very bad timing. She wrapped her arms around my neck and pulled me down for a very long and passionate kiss. Her closeness made my heart race.

She whispered in a throaty voice. "I couldn't wait another minute."

Frozen in space and time, I was at a loss for words for the first time in a long time. She grabbed my hand and pulled me to the bed. Standing in front of me she pulled my robe apart and studied me.

She caught her breath and said, "Oh my God! You're beautiful."

"Betsy?"

She pushed me gently back onto the bed and climbed on top of me. Staring into my eyes, I could tell there was no turning back. With her breathing coming in short rapid bursts, she whispered hoarsely,

"We'll talk later, okay?"

Chapter 6

Katarina fumed, "Is disgusting. I will never be the same."

She was beginning to irritate me. "Will you stop already? You're giving me a headache."

Betsy left just before dawn and I had ordered room service for Katarina and myself. It was 9:00 a.m. and she was venting her spleen at me over croissants and freshly brewed coffee served in a silver urn. She had showered and was now wearing my robe with her hair wrapped up in a white bath towel.

"I give you headache? I can't even eat. I may never eat again so disgusting. Sex with old lady. Never in whole life have ever thought such thing happen in front of my eyes. I may need psychiatrist to get over this."

She shuddered at the memory of having spent two hours under the bed listening to me and Betsy go at it. "Stop it. You're the one who's supposed to marry an old man."

"Is different. Old man and girl different…normal. What you do is no normal. And why not just do once and send home. No, once, twice, three times. Disgusting. And why she make so much noise? What you do to her?"

I took a sip of coffee. "Are you done?"

"No, why not want me instead of old woman?"

I strummed my fingers on the table. "Because I don't want any trouble."

She became indignant at that. "I no trouble."

"I beg to differ. You are the definition of trouble. I shouldn't even have let you in my room last night. I should have thrown you overboard."

"Fine, I go back stepfather. He beat me. I no care."

"Oh please, stop it."

"Well, you say mean thing."

Oh brother.

"Fine, I'm sorry." We looked at each other for an icy minute before I changed the subject. "Look, I don't know why, but I'd like to help you and Berislav. I just don't know where to begin."

"Neither do I. Why I go convent."

"That's only if you get off the ship alive."

She nodded.

I continued, "Do you know who these gangsters are?"

She shook her head. "Not name, but I know by sight. They come to room to threaten Berislav about money. Why?"

"I don't know yet. What about the old man? You've met him, right?"

She rolled her eyes. "Yes, is disgusting. Makes noises whenever see me."

"Just how much money does Berislav owe these gangsters?"

"Not sure. I think I hear say ten million American dollars. Something like that."

I rolled my eyes and took a deep breath. That was a lot of money. "Can he pay any of it? You know, liquidate assets. Stuff like that."

She shook her head. "No, he broke. Owns nothing. Make up story at table about wealth. He has apartment Dubrovnik and car, but business all fail. He compulsive gambler. Always borrow money. Borrow money for this trip."

"What was the point of this trip anyway?"

"Berislav want keep close eye on me so no run away. Also, I think hope make business deal with rich person he meet. He do like this before."

"Business deal? What kind of deal?"

She thought about how to better explain what she meant. "No real deal, phony deal. How you say?"

"A scam?"

"Yes, a scam."

"He plans on finding some rich passenger on board and scamming them?"

"Is what I say."

I looked at her carefully. Her freckles were adorable. "Are you really a star volleyball player?"

"That part true."

I finished my croissant mulling it over. She asked, "What you thinking?"

"I think I like you much better this way."

Smiling she said, "What way?"

"With a towel on your head."

She laughed, "You are hole in butt."

"You mean asshole."

"That too."

"So, who was that guy in Harry's Bar I hit on the head with the prosecco? If Berislav is broke how can he pay for bodyguards?"

"Only one man. He hire before coming on ship. Man don't know Berislav broke. Berislav hope things work out and I marry old man quick and get money to pay."

Compulsive gamblers were the same everywhere. Always scheming, plotting, and scamming their way in and out of debt. "Okay, tell me why I shouldn't just bring you back to Berislav myself and we can all try to work it out together?"

Her eyes grew wide. "Insanity! He would kill you himself and beat me for telling you family secret. Croatian men very proud. Kill for much less over honor."

I could see that she was genuinely frightened over that idea. "All right. All right. It was just a thought. You Croatians have a funny sense of honor. Okay, first things first. You need some clothes. Can you go back to your room?"

She thought it over. "He probably calm down by now. Will probably be worry. He not really bad man, but will kill you if find me here. So, I guess I go back."

I snapped my fingers. "Why don't you tell him that you've changed your mind and agree to the marriage. Then he won't be angry anymore."

"But I can't marry old man. He will know I not virgin."

"You're not going to marry him. This is just to calm everyone down while we think it through. You tell him you've agreed to the marriage after all but that you insist on the wedding taking place on the last day of the trip. That will give us three weeks to think of a way out of this mess."

"Us?"

Hesitantly, I took the plunge. "Yes, us."

This made her very happy and she jumped up causing her robe to fly open. Throwing her arms around my neck and pressing her naked body into me, she locked her lips with mine. I kissed her once, stiffened up and gently pushed her back, closing her robe for her.

I said, "Thanks, but nothing's changed here."

She said sarcastically, "Oh yes. How could forget. You like old wrinkled women. Remind you of Mama?"

Getting serious, I put my face right next to hers. "Use my mother as the butt of a joke again and I really will throw you overboard. Understand?"

She nodded and seemed contrite. "Fine."

"Now finish your breakfast."

Pouting, she sat down. I said, "I'm going to spend some time today trying to come up with a plan. I'll meet you in the Golden Lion Pub on deck 5 for a drink before dinner, let's say at six, to talk things over." I looked at my watch. "But right now I have to go get fitted for the free tuxedo Berislav promised me. That is, if he really meant it. So you get dressed and try to sneak out of here without being seen."

"He mean it. He like show off in front of people what big man he is even if not his money."

"I know a lot of guys like that. Okay I'll see you later."

I downed the remains of the coffee and left her in my stateroom to go find the tailor. He was a little Italian guy from Genoa named Pasquale. Balding, with thick glasses, and a no-nonsense attitude, he took his work very seriously. Berislav had kept his word and called ahead with the billing arrangement, so I ordered two tuxedoes, one with a traditional black jacket and the other with a white jacket. They had several in stock roughly my size but needing some minor alterations. Pasquale wasn't in a great mood. I made several jokes while he fitted me, but I couldn't even get him to crack a smile. And then, when I told him I wanted at least one of them ready in time for dinner, I thought he was going to wrap his tape measure around my neck.

"You think a I have nothing better to do but wait a here for you to come in and give me the extra work? I have a million and a one thing to do. Thank a you very much. You tux a be ready three o'clock. Don't forget a you come or I burn it."

"I won't forget, Pasquale, and thank you very much."

I made a mental note to bring him a Xanax when I returned.

Chapter 7

After a light lunch, I went to the pool to soak up some sun, read some more Italian, and study the inside of my eyelids. Betsy had worn me out pretty good and I was going to need a nap before dinner. I had an hour to kill before my massage and stretched out on a lounge chair near the deep end deciding whether to order a mojito or not. It was a hot, sunny, lazy day and I vetoed that thought in favor of sparkling water with a twist of lemon. There would be plenty of time for booze later.

Looking around, I made a mental note to pick up a speedo as soon as possible. Apparently, that was the preferred swimwear for European men regardless of the shape they were in. My brightly colored, floral patterned, knee-length suit was yet another telltale sign of my lack of breeding while my Roy Orbison style dark sunglasses added to my uniquely American appearance.

I read for a while but was too distracted with recent events to focus well. My brain was torn between Katarina's problem and the anticipation of sleeping with Betsy again. She was incredible in the sack. Experienced and confident, she showed me a couple of new tricks as she brought me to the brink over and over again. Time hadn't slowed her down at all. Thinking about her in that way caused a stirring down south and I hurriedly threw the Italian newspaper over my lap.

Jesus!

A sixty plus-year-old woman was getting me crazy just thinking about her. I needed to calm down. I sat up as the situation worsened. Think baseball. Think baseball. It wasn't helping.

"Hey, you're going to get burned like that."

I looked over my shoulder. Joyce was setting up in the lounge chair next to me wearing a black, thong-style bikini. Great, just what I didn't need. "Hi Joyce. What do you mean?"

"You don't have any sun tan lotion on. You want some?"

I looked down and then back again over my shoulder at her. "I'll be fine. I tan pretty well. It's that Sicilian skin."

"That's got nothing to do with it. It's the U.V. light that causes cancer. Something to do with the ozone layer. Dark skin doesn't protect you from that. I thought you were a doctor? Here, want to borrow mine. I have plenty."

She offered me her suntan lotion, but I wasn't ready to turn around, and probably wouldn't be for a while. Not good. "Thanks, Joyce, I appreciate your concern. Do you think you could give me a minute?"

"What are you sick or something? It's really hot out here. Maybe you've been in the sun too long?"

"I'm fine, Joyce. Just one minute, please."

"Oh I get it. You want me to put the lotion on you. No problem."

"That's not what I meant."

"Don't be shy."

She squirted suntan lotion on my back and I flinched from the unexpected feel of the cool liquid. This was followed by deep massaging hand strokes up and down and side to side. "Joyce…"

"You don't have to thank me," she said softly, running her hands down from my neck to my shoulders and then squeezing them. "You're pretty muscular. Do you work out?"

"A little."

She put some more lotion in her hands and rubbed my biceps and forearms. Getting in close she whispered in my ear, "I saw the way you looked at me last night, and I totally approve."

Her face was inches from mine and she was practically drooling on me. I said, "I'm not sure what you mean."

She smiled. "You don't have to play hard to get with me. I like horny guys."

"What makes you think I'm one of those?"

"Sitting hunched over with a newspaper on your lap?" She paused to giggle. "Sweetheart, I've danced in enough gentlemen's clubs to know what that means. Go ahead. Get rid of the newspaper and let's see what's going on."

I didn't move or respond to that and she continued, "That's what I thought. I don't know who you were daydreaming about but I hope it was me. You know, there's only one real way to fix a problem like this."

Before she could finish that thought, I stood, tossed my sunglasses on the lounge and ran quickly to the pool, jumping in with a big splash. I let myself sink to the bottom and stood there looking around for a while before kicking upward. My head broke through the surface of the water, and I drew in a deep breath as I shook water from my face. A couple of strokes brought me to the side of the pool and I rested there. Joyce came over and sat down next to me dangling her legs in the water, grinning from ear to ear.

"Did it help?" she asked, thoroughly amused by my antics.

"Yup."

She chuckled. "You're something else, Dr. Cesari. Did you know that?"

"Where's Brad?" It was time to change the subject.

"Nursing a hangover in the room. Man, did he tie one on last night."

"I'm surprised. He looked like he could handle his liquor."

She rolled her eyes. "Oh, please. He can't handle anything; not his liquor, not his temper, not his…"

"Wife?"

She hesitated for a moment. "No, he can't handle me, either."

"I didn't mean you."

She smiled coyly, and I said, "I have good instincts."

She nodded. "He's supposed to be at a conference, and she's visiting her sick mother on the west coast."

"Nice."

She shrugged. "It's a living."

I chuckled at that. She said, "He says he loves me and I believe him…sometimes. Look at me telling you all my secrets and I don't even know you. How'd you do that?"

"I'm a good listener."

"Maybe, or maybe it's your too cute for words face."

She was cracking me up. "Me?"

"What's that scar on your chest?" she asked.

"I was in a knife fight when I was a kid."

"Who won?"

"Guess."

"I would guess that you don't lose at much of anything."

"Good guess."

"So what do you think, Dr. Cesari? They cost a small fortune."

I looked up at her and she jutted her breasts out for me. She was spilling out of the suit. "I thought you were in love with Brad?"

"What's that got to do with anything?"

"They're very nice."

"Thanks. Will you be at dinner tonight?"

"Yes, I wouldn't miss it."

"And afterward…?"

"Aren't you with Brad?"

"He'll get drunk again tonight for sure. It's his routine. He'll be in a coma by midnight. If you want, I can come to your room. 6092. Isn't that what I heard you tell that brat last night?"

"Joyce, don't take this the wrong way, but…"

A loud voice boomed, "Joyce! I've been looking for you."

We both turned at once to see Brad approaching quickly wearing an orange speedo with his big, hairy belly hanging over the top. Definitely looked like a CEO. He was holding a scotch in one hand and a cigar in the other. Sitting down next to Joyce, he plunged his legs into the pool, splashing me.

I wiped water from my eyes and he said, "Sorry about that, doctor. Joyce, baby, where've you been?"

"I did a little shopping and decided to take in some sun. How are you feeling my little honey bear? You were out cold when I left the room."

"That nap did me wonders. I'm ready to rock. So, doctor, where do you practice?"

"Right now, I'm in between engagements."

"Really? Well if you ever have any inclinations to move to upstate New York give me a call. Hoosick Falls is a helluva town. We have a movie theatre and a bowling alley. Lots of stuff to do and I could always use a hero on my staff."

"Even if I don't have a tuxedo?"

He was in a downright jovial mood and laughed. "Water under the bridge, doctor. Water under the bridge."

I asked, "So, how's the financial situation at your hospital? I know times are tight." I thought that was a reasonable question since he just offered me a job.

"That they are. We're stressed out to the max, of course, like everywhere else, but we're holding our own, squeezing out a small profit, managing to pay the bills. It's a struggle, but I'm lucky. I have a good team in place and we're all pulling together for the first time in a long time. I think we'll be okay at least for the next few years, but who knows what will happen now that we're on the government's radar."

Joyce stood up. "I've heard this story before. I'm going to get myself a drink from the bar since Brad didn't bring me one."

Brad said, "Hey, as long as you're up would you mind getting me another scotch? This one is almost done."

Turning to me she asked, "Doctor, would you like anything?"

"No, thank you, Joyce."

She sauntered away, one hip at a time, her thong leaving nothing to the imagination. Continuing the conversation, I said, "You mean all the new regulations?"

He nodded. "Yeah, they're breaking our balls good, but the bottom line is this: people always get sick and they'll always need doctors and nurses and that means they'll always need hospitals. You may have to work for free but at least you'll have purpose. There's something to be said for job security."

I noticed he didn't include hospital administrators in the 'you may have to work for free' line. "What about you?"

He smiled and took a sip of scotch. "If I can run the place efficiently and keep everybody's head above water, I'll be okay."

"If not?"

"Scorched earth."

"What's that mean?"

"I dismantle the place. Sell off assets, piece by piece. Reduce staff, cut services, turn off the lights, bring everything down to barebones operation and if that don't work I release pheromones."

"Pheromones?"

"Yes, you know what they are, right?"

"Yes, of course. Chemical substances released into the environment by animals and insects to attract the opposite sex."

"That's right only in healthcare it means when the financial sheets start to glow red, I send feelers out to the larger hospitals."

Nodding slowly, I said, "To sell the hospital to the highest bidder."

"Wrong. It's to sell *me* to the highest bidder. You got to see it. These guys and their lawyers start wining and dining me like no tomorrow. The one that puts his hand up my dress the highest gets the prize."

I was appalled at his frankness and said, "The golden parachute."

He raised his glass. "Salute."

"You don't care who gets hurt, fired, downsized, or what's best for the community, do you?"

"Survival of the fittest, doctor."

At a loss for words, I was quiet for a moment, and then asked, "You weren't really offering me a job, were you?"

"Hell no. Why would I do that? I don't even like you. I was just trying to be nice in front of Joyce. I'm sorry if you misunderstood."

"Why don't you like me?"

"Oh please. I'm so sick of doctors, I could puke. Nothing but whiny ass bitches. They're like little children. Always crying about something. There's not enough nurses. There's not enough gauze. The equipment's old. I can't see this many patients in one day. I need more time off. I need more money. There's too much work. When will you guys understand? Healthcare is not about the doctors and their patients anymore."

"What's it about?"

"It's about me showing the board of trustees that I can turn a profit. You and everybody else are just pawns, interchangeable cogs in the machinery. For people who claim to be smart, it amazes me that none of you have figured it out yet."

"The people of Hoosick Falls are very lucky to have you."

"Damn right about that." He finished his scotch and continued, "But with you, I have a separate axe to grind."

"What's that?"

He looked over his shoulder. Joyce was returning holding two drinks but was still out of earshot. He hissed through clenched teeth, "This was two days in a row I caught you staring at my wife's tits. One more time and you're going overboard, understand?"

I didn't have time to respond. Joyce handed him his drink and said, "Here you go, Brad."

He stood, taking the glass. "Thanks, Joyce. C'mon babe, let's go lay out and you can put suntan lotion on me before I become toast. It was nice talking to you, doctor. Think about my offer."

"I will."

Joyce said, "Goodbye, doctor. Maybe we'll see you tonight.'

"You never know."

Chapter 8

At 5:00 p.m., I shaved and showered. My clothes were laid out neatly on the bed and I was feeling great. An hour-long massage followed by an hour-long nap and I was ready to face the world. Pasquale was a real mensch. He had managed to tailor both tuxes in time and they fit perfectly. Donning the white tuxedo jacket, I stood in front of the full-length mirror, adjusted the black bowtie and admired the view. Needing one more accessory to complete my look, I went to the vase on the coffee table, plucked a red carnation from the arrangement and inserted it into my lapel. Back at the mirror, I stood in awe of my image.

I said, "Bond…James Bond."

Definitely!

I found Katarina sitting at the bar in the Golden Lion smoking and sipping a gin martini. The bar was a replica of an English pub from somewhere in London. It was dark with leather stools, wood tables, and dart boards. It was early and there were only a handful of guests. Taking a seat next to her, I said, "You look nice."

She wore a knee length blue dress with matching blue heels, gold necklace, and earrings. Her makeup was a tad more aggressive than last evening. Her eyeliner was much darker, her lashes much longer, and she chose red lipstick tonight. It made her look older and I suspected that was the idea. She was beautiful, but I wasn't going to tell her that. She was like an outdoor grill that you had to constantly monitor the temperature of or it would get out of control.

"Thank you. Look good too. Hair stick up in back. I fix." She reached behind me and gently brushed her hand down the back of my head. "Better."

"Thank you. So, how is Berislav?"

"He is overjoy. Want I marry quick but I say no. This is last vacation as virgin. I want enjoy every minute. He no happy but say fine."

I chuckled, and she said seriously, "Not funny."

"I'm sorry, but I'm glad it worked. This will give us some breathing room."

"Give you some breathing room maybe. I suffocate. Old man want dinner with me tomorrow night. I want vomit."

"Well, I'm sorry, but you can understand that, can't you? You're his bride to be."

"Please…"

The bartender came up to us and I ordered a Manhattan up with Basil Hayden bourbon. "Okay, let's talk about these gangsters who are harassing you. Do you know how many of them there are?"

"I only saw two, but who knows?"

"Does Berislav know?"

She sipped her martini and twirled the olive with the toothpick. "I don't know. He no talk too much about gangsters. Afraid scare Katarina."

I nodded. "Well, since you know what they look like I suggest that we take a walk around the ship after dinner. Maybe you'll spot them. I'd like to know who they are."

She smiled. "You want know who they are?"

"Yes, of course."

"One sit right behind you. Drink beer."

I raised my eyebrows but didn't turn around. "One's right behind me?"

"Yes, Berislav call them. Tell about wedding plans. Ask them watch me. Make sure no man try take me some place quiet…to talk."

"Man, you got a tough life."

"You telling me?"

The bartender placed my drink on a napkin in front of me. I thanked him and took a sip. "Okay, I'm going to the men's room."

"One sip and you have to pee? Weak bladder, no?"

"No, I want to get a good look at this guy."

"Turn around and look. He no care, and already see you. Been watch for ten minutes."

She had a point so I turned slowly as if I was just looking around the room out of curiosity. It was just my nature to be furtive. Maybe espionage was in my blood. Katarina shook her head in frustration, stood, and dragged me by the hand over to the guy's table. On the way she said, "His name Niko."

Shaved head and thick neck like a linebacker, he wore a tight black suit and sipped beer from a frosted mug. He looked up, and Katarina said, "This John. He no take me some place quiet for to talk, okay?"

I couldn't tell his exact size sitting down but he seemed pretty big. The guy nodded and said something nasty in Croatian. Katarina gave him the finger and we walked back to the bar.

She said, "You get good look?"

"I did."

"Now what?"

"We finish our drinks while I think."

"I teeny bit pissed off at you."

"Why?"

"Is birthday and you no say anything."

"I'm sorry. I forgot. Happy birthday. Are your really twenty-one?"

She hesitated, "I was…once."

I couldn't help myself and chuckled. "Is it really your birthday?"

Nodding vigorously, she said, "Yes, it is. Twenty-five like I told you the other night."

"Why do you lie so much?"

She shrugged and I sighed. She gave me a funny look and I asked, "What?"

"No kiss?"

I nodded in the direction of Niko. "He may not like that."

She shrugged. "Keep pants on."

I thought it over for a second. This was really weird. Yes, it was normal to give kisses on birthdays, but she wasn't really my friend and having a thug nearby watching us made me feel very uncomfortable. On the other hand, how could it hurt?

I said, "On the cheek, okay?"

Shaking her head in exasperation she said, "Fine, on cheek."

She turned her head and I leaned in close. At the last second, she suddenly reached up, grabbed my face, and kissed me on the lips. I pulled away quickly but not before she groped me with her tongue.

I said, "That's what I mean about you."

She laughed, "Oh please. You like. I know it."

"I no like and you don't know anything."

She looked past me and put her hand up. I turned and saw that Niko had started to rise from his table. She said, "Is okay, Niko. Just birthday kiss." He sat back down.

Still smiling and happy with herself she said, "We look good together. You in tuxedo and me in dress."

"Look if you want me to help you, you have got to stop acting like a silly schoolgirl."

"What mean silly schoolgirl?"

"Forget it."

"You want schoolgirl? Is disgusting. Even more disgusting than old woman. Maybe you need psychiatrist?"

"Can you shut up for a minute. I can't think like this."

"You need go someplace quiet?"

"No, I don't need go someplace quiet…Hey, I got an idea. What I really need to know is in which room these gangsters are staying. Can you move freely about the ship?"

"With Niko follow me."

"After dinner, tell Berislav, you feel like walking around the ship, maybe go for a night swim or to the casino. Niko will follow you but then you go back to your room. I'll follow you and Niko and then after he drops you off I'll follow him back to his room."

She thought about that for a few seconds. "Maybe work."

"Unless Berislav comes with you for the walk. Then he won't need Niko. Would he do that?"

"Maybe yes. Maybe no. Probably not tonight. He say he have business meeting after dinner."

"You mean he's scamming somebody, already?"

"He try."

"Do you know who?"

"Man at table last night. Big American who own hospital. Wife is whore."

"Really?"

She nodded and finished her martini.

"Do you know the scam?"

She shook her head, "No."

"You share a suite with Berislav?"

"Yes, big with two bedrooms, balcony. Is on Deck 8."

"Would you mind giving me the key to your room?"

She raised her eye brows. "Not safe there. Berislav might find us talking quiet."

"That's not what I want it for. I'd like to take a peek around Berislav's stuff when he's not around."

She shrugged. "Sure, I no care, but I not know what you find that help."

"Thanks. You never know with these things. Every little bit helps and since I can't talk to him directly about this matter this is the next best thing."

"Fine. What about old lady? You make her scream again tonight?"

"That's a definite possibility. So, no dawdling when you go for your walk."

"Is disgusting. Make me scream like that. I no tell."

"Find me in ten years and we'll talk."

"Ten years?! I be old woman too."

I laughed. She was killing me. "The key please."

"How I get in my room without key?" she asked.

"Tell Berislav you lost your key. Either he'll give you his or the ship will issue you another one."

"What if they don't?"

"What do you mean? 'What if they don't?' Of course they will."

"It's late. They may not, and Berislav go out tonight. He will not want give me his key in case I fall sleep. Besides, how I get in room after I take walk tonight?"

"This is ridiculous."

"No, is not."

She was right. How would she get in the room after her walk? Berislav would simply tell her to skip the walk and go straight to the room after dinner where he would let her in and then go to his business meeting.

She saw me thinking and said, "See, no make sense."

I nodded. "Okay, keep the key for now. I'll follow the guy to his room and then tomorrow we can meet somewhere and you can give me it."

"Why not come search Berislav room tonight after follow gangster. Berislav no return until much late."

I digested that. It made sense. "That's not a bad idea."

She folded her arms. "See, I very smart…and sexy."

"Yeah, okay. Well, let's get out of here. It's almost time for dinner."

"Wait one minute. I want see something."

She got off the barstool, went over to Niko, and asked him something. He had a nasty look on his face as he answered her. She returned, grabbed her purse off the counter, and said, "C'mon, let's go."

I asked, "What was that about?"

"I ask him his room number."

"What did he say?"

"He say if I speak to him again he take me somewhere quiet to talk."

"Seriously?"

"He is hole in butt."

"You mean asshole."

"That too."

Chapter 9

The grand dining room had been transformed almost miraculously from stiff and formal last night to almost whimsical this evening. The white tablecloths and napkins had been replaced with lavender ones and the centerpieces were made of long stem white roses. Cherubic angels hung from the walls and the jazz band had been replaced by a massive harp, cello, and grand piano in the center of the room. Several violinists in tails walked the room serenading the guests. Off to one side, an ice bar had been set up with about forty different brands of vodka sitting on shelves carved into the ice. I wasn't sure what the theme was but I was pretty sure I didn't care. I'd already been told by someone in the know that the main course was lobster thermidor and that was all the information I needed.

Seating arrangements were slightly different than last night. The captain sat at a different table and we got, Sven Jorgensen, the ship's doctor who sat to my left. Betsy sat to my right and Roger to her right. Berislav and Katarina sat across from me next to Joyce and Brad.

I hadn't seen Betsy all day and wondered what she was thinking. She wore her necklace again and I couldn't help but wonder how much something like that cost. I loved the way the big diamond fell into her cleavage.

She must have read my mind because she whispered in my ear. “It’s five carats.”

I raised my eyebrows. I had never seen a diamond so large or so beautiful before. The colors of the other jewels spanned the spectrum of the rainbow and, just as last night, I found them mesmerizing. I assumed you didn’t just walk into any store and pick a necklace like this out of a case. “Is the necklace an heirloom, Betsy?”

“Yes, indeed. I’ve traced it back ten generations. My great, great, great, great grandfather on my mother’s side was a scalawag and a smuggler. He ran around in circles that were less than seemly by today’s Bostonian standards to say the least. They believe he came across the stones in Barbados where he was trading illegal rum with thirst-starved pirates who had just come across a Portuguese treasure ship loaded with gold, silver, and gems recently plundered from the Brazilian jungle. Legend has it they traded him a bag full of jewels for his entire hold and he had them made into this necklace. It’s valued at twenty million dollars but if the backstory were ever taken into account the value would be higher by tenfold. I would pay ten times that myself to recover it if it ever went missing. My great grandmother died in a house fire because she refused to leave the burning building without her necklace and her great grandmother put it up as collateral to help finance weapons for the abolitionist movement. The women in my family have worn it on our wedding days for over two hundred years.”

“I didn’t know diamonds were part of the loot of treasure ships?”

“Certainly, diamonds have been around forever, but didn’t really take off in value and popularity until the African mines were discovered in the late 1800’s, but they were mining diamonds in Brazil for a hundred years already by then. The best part of the story is that the pirates thought they took my ancestor to the cleaners on that deal."

I looked at her. That was a valuable piece of jewelry to be lying around the bathroom like I saw it last night. "Do you have a safe in your room?"

"Yes, but it really isn't necessary. My whole room is essentially a safe."

"How is that?"

"We've had special locks installed in the doors to my room and that of Roger's. There is a chip embedded in the metal of the room key that emits a certain frequency. Similarly, the locks on our doors are computerized and emit their own frequency. The two frequencies match up and temporarily neutralize each other. If the door were to open for any reason without that key in the lock, an alarm would be triggered in the ships central security office. If you want the exact science behind it you'll have to ask the captain or ship's chief engineer. Needless to say, they are not ordinary doors and are made of reinforced steel."

I nodded. We carried on our conversation in lowered voices. "That's interesting. How do staff get in to clean your room?"

"They always come in pairs, never alone, and always accompanied by the ship's security who stay with them the whole time. Why do you ask? Did you feel awkward when you saw the necklace lying around in the bathroom last night?"

She surprised me with that because I hadn't mentioned that I had gone to her room. I hesitated and she explained, "The lock mechanism records every entry and at what time it took place. Since the alarm didn't trigger, the person who entered my apartment at just after midnight must have had a key. You were the only one I gave the key to so it had to be you."

"What if I had lost the key or had given it to someone else?"

"Then my necklace would not have been there when I returned."

The way she said that seemed very cavalier and I furrowed my brow trying to sort it out. The necklace was much too valuable both monetarily and personally for her to be so flippant.

I rubbed my chin and then it came to me. Looking at her, I said slowly, "It was a test…for me."

She smiled. "And you passed marvelously."

"The necklace I saw…?"

"Not real. I always leave a fake one out just in case."

"You didn't trust me?"

"I didn't know you, but now I do. Not every young man I give my key to passes like you did. It always hurts. I'd much rather know what's in a man's heart before I give myself to him."

Suddenly feeling very self-conscious, I asked, "Cameras?"

"No, unfortunately cameras are a double-edged sword for me."

"Because it documents all the traffic to and from your room?"

She nodded. "Exactly. It would be too easy for someone to use that against me."

Geez. "You have a tough life."

"You're telling me?"

I sighed and she said, "Are you upset with me?"

"No, just caught off guard a little." I felt like a mouse in a scientific experiment.

Smiling she said, "I did try to make it up to you afterward."

I grinned. "And you succeeded with flying colors. Will there be an encore performance tonight?"

"Tonight, I will rest. I'm afraid I'm not as young as I think I am, but tomorrow night is a definite possibility if you're still interested."

"Count me in."

"I pleased you?"

I leaned close to her ear and picked up her scent. "I've been thinking about you all day."

She liked that a lot, and inches from her lips, I was tempted to kiss her right there in front of everyone. Out of the corner of my eye I caught Katarina glaring her disapproval from across the table. Betsy sensed my incipient weakness and cleared her throat, whispering, "We should spend time with the other guests."

I nodded and sat back in my chair, turning to the ship's doctor on my left who was busily engaged with a flight of three shot glasses in front of him filled to brimming with clear liquid. Sven was about forty, overweight but not fat, glasses, and a pointy nose. I spotted a wedding ring and he reeked of tobacco, probably pipe or cigar.

I said, "What's in the shot glasses?"

He replied in stilted but grammatically correct English with only the slightest trace of a Norwegian accent. "Vodka, man's best friend."

I chuckled and wondered how many he had at the bar before dinner. I said, "I thought that was a dog?"

"A dog cannot keep you warm on a cold night in the north Atlantic. A dog cannot take away the pain of a broken heart when your slut of a wife leaves you for your best friend. Only vodka can do this for you." He hoisted a shot glass in the air. "Here's to vodka!" He downed it and winced.

He was soused all right and I watched him polish off the other glasses in short order. After he was done he ordered another round and asked me if I'd join him. I politely declined.

"I understand you're a doctor back in the states?" he asked.

"Actually, I'm a doctor right here at this table as well."

He smiled. "Of course, and what is your specialty?"

"Gastroenterology."

"Hmm, a good specialty for a cruise ship. I am a general practitioner."

"Do you see a lot of GI illnesses on board?"

"It depends on what you call a GI illness. There are occasional outbreaks of food poisoning, a smattering of appendicitis, diverticulitis, toothaches, and given the average age of the guests, chest pain once in a while. Hangovers and sea sickness are probably the most common reasons people come to see me."

The lobster was served with steaming sides of roasted potatoes and sautéed green beans. It only took one bite for me to realize that I wanted to live on this ship forever.

Betsy asked, "How is your meal?"

Jokingly, I replied, "Not bad. A little heavy on the garlic in the green beans perhaps but I'll survive."

She laughed politely. "You're an expert on green bean preparation?"

"I'm an expert on that…and many other things."

Nodding she said, "I know. You seemed very knowledgeable the last time we…saw each other."

I chuckled and lowered my voice. "Not fair. I thought we flirted enough for one night?"

"You started it."

"I know but I'm trying hard to not get worked up over here."

She lowered her voice. "I don't think I heard you correctly. Did you just say you're getting hard?"

I laughed and whispered back, "Jesus, you're as bad as Katarina."

Grinning broadly, she denied any culpability, "I didn't do anything."

She was having fun playing with me. I glanced at Sven and watched him down yet another flight of vodka shots in rapid succession. I said, "I don't mean to interject, Sven, but you may want to taxi at the gate a little before taking off for another flight."

His speech was clearly slurred now and his eyes glazed. We had almost reached the tipping point. "Have you ever been in love, John?"

Here we go. I loved it when guys got drunk and waxed philosophical. I said, "Many times."

He gave me a funny look. "I didn't mean have you ever had an erection."

"Oh, then just a couple of times."

"Martina was my whole world. She is beautiful, caring, gentle. I don't know how I will survive without her. What will I do?"

He suddenly burst into tears and leaned his head on my shoulder sobbing. I put an arm around him and patted him consolingly. "There, there, Sven. We'll get through this."

The waitress dropped off another round of vodkas for him and I took one in a quick gulp as I held him. Betsy asked, "Is he all right?"

I said, "He'll be fine. It's man stuff."

She chuckled as the rest of the table stared. I put my hand up to reassure them that everything was okay, and they resumed their dinner conversations pretending not to be interested.

I looked at my watch. It was almost 10:00 p.m. Sven was babbling and drooling on my tux. If the captain saw, it could be the end of Sven's career. Katarina caught my gaze and nodded ever so slightly. She would head to the casino black jack tables after dinner with Niko in tow. I would track her down there and when she spotted me she'd meander for a few more minutes before returning to her room. But first things first. I had to get Sven out of here.

I waited for the dance floor to be cleared and the lights to grow dim. When the music started, I said, “C’mon, Sven. I know where we can find some Grey Goose.”

I hoisted him up and with his arm around my neck he said, “Grey Goose? What do the French know about vodka? Real men drink Vikingfjord vodka. They use water from the Jostedalsbreen glacier. Very healthy for you.”

“That’s great. I’ll have a bottle sent to your room. Now come with me.”

“You are very nice for an American.”

Chapter 10

Sven wasn't big, but he wasn't small either, and I struggled under his weight assisting him to his room. Several of the crew saw us and offered to help but I waved them off. No point in having anyone get close enough to witness just how badly drunk he was. The crew were lodged in low deck 2. His room was midship and when we arrived I was sweating profusely and he was barely conscious. Using the key I found in his pocket, I opened the door and walked him in, plopping him down on the bed.

I sat next to him, catching my breath. Rousing a little, he said, "It's just not fair, John."

"Welcome to the real world, Sven, where you don't always get what you want."

"You are a good man." He sat up slowly, staggered to his feet and started to undress. I thought to myself that he should be okay.

"You look like you can take it from here. Get a good night's rest." I didn't really want to be there when he dropped his trousers. I heard European men had even stranger ideas about what constituted acceptable underwear than they did about swimwear.

"I've embarrassed myself terribly. I'm sorry."

"Take it easy with the embarrassed yourself stuff, all right? Everybody has been dumped once or twice by someone they thought loved them."

"Have you ever been dumped, John?"

"I could practically set my watch to it."

I didn't reach the door fast enough and watched his pants hit the ground. For God's sake! A red thong. My eyes burned at the sight. Too uncoordinated from the alcohol, he couldn't quite get his feet out from his pants and stumbled forward into me. I caught him and walked him back to the bed and pushed him onto it, dragging his pants off. He wiggled under the covers and said with eyes half-closed, "Thank you. What should I do? What would you do? I can't bear the thought of losing her."

I shook my head. I shouldn't get involved but what the hell. "When did this all happen, Sven?"

"She called me just as the ship was leaving Venice, knowing I would be trapped like a rat for the next three weeks."

I let out a deep breath. "Do you really love her, Sven? I mean, really, with every ounce of your being and every breath you take?"

He looked at me, and with desperation in his voice, said, "I do. I really do."

"Then start acting like a man and go after her. Find her and tell her that you love her and that she is the ying to your yang, that she fills a void in your soul in a way no other can. She married you, didn't she? That means she loves you. Find out what's wrong. Fight for her."

"But John, I can't leave the ship. That's desertion. We are governed by maritime law. I could be imprisoned. I'm not sure, maybe even executed."

"You asked me what I would do, and if I loved someone that much, then I wouldn't let anything stand in my way to win her back. Sober up overnight, go to the captain first thing in the morning, and tell him you have a family emergency. He might let you go but he may not. Just remember, a man's got to do what a man's got to do. Don't let anything or anyone keep you from the woman you love."

He nodded. "Who are you?"

"Just a guy from the Bronx who's watched one too many sappy movies on the Hallmark channel."

"A man's got to do what a man's got to do. I will not forget."

I watched him fall asleep and left to go find Katarina in the casino. She was at a ten-dollar table nursing a cocktail. She saw me and nodded. I walked by without stopping and took up a position about twenty feet away, mingling in with the crowd.

Five minutes later, she threw a chip at the dealer as a tip, and wandered off slowly and nonchalantly, winding around the casino toward the exit. Niko was about ten feet behind, committed to her surveillance but giving her some space. I was ten feet behind him. The thought crossed my mind to race up to her room and wait there hiding somewhere in the hallway but that had two disadvantages. First, loitering in the narrow hallway for a prolonged period of time might cause one of the passengers or crew to alert security. Second, it would be nice to know what this guy's strengths and weaknesses were; did he have a limp, was he right or left-handed, was he carrying heat? I was not planning on a confrontation, but you never knew with this kind of stuff, and the longer I spent observing him the better I would get to know him. Right now, all I knew was that he was a hole in butt. I smiled. Damn, I was even starting to talk like her.

At the exit, she hesitated, looked back briefly, and left the casino. She was quite a sight. Six foot three in heels and a skin tight dress. I pictured her on a runway sporting Christian Louboutin shoes and a Valentino handbag. I liked what I saw. He followed her casually, but sped to catch up just as she reached the elevators. I quickened my pace and pressed the up button on the car next to theirs just as their door closed.

My elevator came just a moment or two later and I boarded, my excitement growing. Arriving a minute after they did, I spotted them half-way down the hall walking slowly in tandem. The corridor was narrow; no more than eight feet wide with little to conceal myself should he turn around. I doubted he would remember me from our brief encounter earlier in the evening, but you never knew. The corridor lights had been dimmed and that would help. His night was winding down and he was probably bored and tired of babysitting her. I tried to put myself in his mindset.

As they walked ahead, I heard him engage her in Croatian. Whatever he said drew her ire and she responded in an irritated tone. He laughed and continued. She didn't say anything this time, and whatever vulgarity he may have insinuated, she obviously felt the best tactic was to ignore him. Reaching her stateroom, she said good night to him in English and put the key in the door. I stopped twenty feet behind and across the hall from them, turning toward the nearest door and fumbling for the key in my pocket.

Suddenly, the sounds of a commotion startled me and I turned abruptly. He was just supposed to drop her off, but apparently, he had other plans. As soon as the door unlocked he reached in and shoved it open, pushing her into the room ahead of him. I heard her call out in surprise. What the hell was he doing? Making a snap decision, I sprinted to the door and before it could close completely stopped it with the edge of my foot, listening. I heard her cursing him half in Croatian and half in English. Then came a slap and the sound of a zipper.

That was enough for me. I flung the door open and charged into the room. His back was toward me and Katarina was on her knees in front of him. He held her roughly by the hair. I tackled him from behind and he fell forward, grunting, with me on top. He let go of her hair and Katarina slid off to one side. Before he could recover, I punched the back of his head repeatedly with rights and lefts stunning him. He was still moving when Katarina came over with a glass vase.

She said, “Here, let me.”

I leaned away and she smashed the vase on the back of his head. Day lilies and water doused him and he stopped moving. I lay back against her coffee table and caught my breath.

She sat next to me. I said, “Jesus, what the hell was that all about? I thought he was supposed to guard your virginity?”

Shrugging, she said, “What he have in mind not affect virginity.”

Still panting, I asked, “Are you all right?”

She nodded. “I fine. Thank you.”

“No problem. Well, let’s see who this guy is.”

I got on my knees and searched him, finding a black semi-automatic .45 pistol, model HS2000 in a shoulder holster. I took out his wallet and was dismayed when I saw an official-looking badge that had the word *Policija* written across it. I showed it to Katarina and said, “Please tell me this isn’t what I think it is.”

“Police? So what?”

“He’s Croatian police? I thought you said he was a gangster?”

“In Croatia it same thing.”

Oh God. This was really bad. I rubbed my forehead and my temple started to throb. Katarina was a little confused. “I no understand. You no rescue me if know he is police?”

“Of course, I would have rescued you. It’s just that this makes the situation even more complicated than it was before.”

“I don’t think so. One less gangster to worry about.”

“Katarina, he’s going to wake up.”

“Says who?”

I looked at her. "Don't even think it, okay?"

"I think it right now."

"I'm not killing him, Katarina."

"Is mistake. He kill us. So what do? Wait for him wake up? I no want to be here for that."

"Give me a second to think about it?"

She was right about one thing. When he woke there was going to be hell to pay and most of it was going to be directed at her and Berislav assuming she didn't throw me under the bus. There must be something we could do. I looked down at him as I thought over the dilemma. He was carrying a handgun on a cruise ship. That had to be against the rules somewhere, but he was a cop and may have been given permission to keep his weapon. I wasn't sure how that worked. If, however, he smuggled the weapon on board somehow, he would be in extremely hot water. We could call security and let them sort it out. The trouble with that was he might be able to talk his way out of it. One call to the Dubrovnik police force might clear it all up and then he would be twice as mad.

There were too many ifs in this line of reasoning for my comfort. I needed him off the ship without any further discussion, but if I tossed him overboard unconscious, he would drown and I wasn't quite that upset with him.

What to do? What to do? What to do? I looked at my watch. It was approaching midnight. I said, "I have an idea, but first, let's clean this mess up so Berislav doesn't see it."

Pocketing Niko's room key, I went to the balcony and threw his wallet and badge overboard. In the living room, she handed me a towel to dry the floor while she swept pieces of glass into a dust pan. Done, we dragged Niko into the hallway hoping no one would see us. It was well after midnight by now and we didn't see anyone so I took a chance and hauled him over to the elevators and pressed the call button.

I said, "Go to your room and when you hear gunshots, call security and direct them to the elevators on this floor. Go now and wait for me."

For once she did what I told her without arguing. The elevator came and I prayed no one was on board. If there was I would tell them he was drunk and get out of there as quickly as possible. The doors opened revealing an empty car and I dragged him half way in. I took his gun, and quickly fired two shots into the wall across from the elevator. I wiped my prints off with my shirt and placed the gun in his right hand. Putting his index finger on the trigger, I fired one last shot into the carpeted floor. I stood up just as an alarm went off throughout the ship and an overhead announcement blared loudly warning people to stay in their rooms. I smiled as I watched the elevator door hit him in the head repetitively as it tried to close.

I ran back to Katarina's suite. She was waiting for me with the door cracked open. I reached in and pulled her out. "You're coming with me."

"Where we go?"

"My room."

We ran down the hallway until we found a fire escape. Adrenaline surging, we charged down the two flights of stairs to my deck and found my cabin. Inside, we both fell onto the bed staring up at the ceiling fan, our pulses racing and breathless. She kicked off her shoes, and after a minute of complete disbelief at what had just happened, she said, "We in big trouble for sure now. Why come here?"

"We can't be sure what the other gangsters will do when their partner doesn't return. They might come looking for you."

"Good thinking. So, this guy, what will happen?"

"It all depends on how the captain reacts to having a passenger, police officer or not, discharge a weapon on board his boat. My guess is he won't react well at all. Captains are funny like that, but I have a feeling it won't matter. From the way the elevator door was slamming into his head, I think he's going to be in need of an urgent CAT scan."

She turned suddenly and climbed on top of me. Grabbing my wrists, she held them pinned on the bed over my head. "This is two times you save Katarina. Is time for reward."

"Katarina, haven't we had a long enough night already?"

"When Niko slap me and grab hair. I no care. When he pull down zipper. I no care. Want know why?"

Curious I asked, "Why?"

"Because in my mind, I pretend it was you and I not scared anymore."

Having no idea how to respond to that, I was speechless, and just stared at her. I had never been in a situation of complete helplessness like that, and couldn't even fathom what it must be like. She leaned down and kissed me for a long time. Then she let go of my wrists and we locked onto each other's gaze.

She reached down to her hemline and hiked her dress up and off, shaking her head to restore her hair. As I watched her reach behind and undo her bra, I tried to decide what to do. My brain was frazzled, and pushing her away right now, somehow just didn't seem like the right thing to do. Not after what she just said. In fact, pushing her away at this moment could possibly be the mother of all wrong things to do.

"Well, you like?" she asked showing off her breasts to me.

Why were women obsessed with what men thought about their breasts? I cleared my throat. I wasn't even a breast guy. I said, "I like them a lot."

"Then touch."

I reached up with both hands and held them. As I fondled her, she made a soft cooing sound of approval.

"Now say something for me," she said and then hesitated.

"Say what?"

"Say, happy birthday, Katarina."

Chapter 11

The next morning, I strummed my fingers on the table as Katarina sat across from me sipping black coffee wearing my terry cloth robe, her hair wrapped up in a white towel. I was getting used to this look. She held the cup with two hands as if it were a bowl. I glanced at my watch. It was 10:00 a.m. She smiled at me contentedly and said, "Is best birthday ever. Beat up gangsters. Make love to boyfriend. How you say in America? Damn hot!"

I smiled at her. "*Hot damn* is the expression."

"Hot damn!"

She'd been going on like this for the last hour. I sipped my coffee and took a bite of toast thinking things through. I said, "You know, Katarina, in America making love just once wouldn't mean I was your boyfriend."

"What once? We do four times. That even more than you do with old woman. I can't believe I make even more noise than she did. Amazing. How you do that? Maybe we do again before go out?"

I shook my head. I was exhausted. I wasn't old but I wasn't twenty either. Plus, she was rough. I've never been so sore in all my life. "We have a lot to do today."

"Okay, maybe in afternoon."

Changing the subject, I said, "The ship pulls into Dubrovnik tomorrow morning, doesn't it?"

"Yes, first port of call. You know I think I should be one to tell her."

"Tell who? What?"

"Tell old lady you don't need her anymore. Have new girlfriend."

I put my cup down and let out a deep breath. "Katarina, please don't talk to Betsy…ever, and if for some reason you can't help yourself, don't bring up this subject…ever. I think it might be best if we kept what happened last night our little secret."

"But I so happy. Want to tell world."

That's what I was afraid of. "I understand how you feel."

"No, you don't. It took so long to get you into bed. Never work so hard in all my life for man."

"We just met three days ago."

"Seem like forever." She looked around. "Maybe I bring my stuff down here for rest of cruise. Tell Berislav wedding off. I have boyfriend now."

"No, that's not a good idea at all. There are still people out there that want to kill you and Berislav. It's best if we stick to the plan, okay? Look, last night was fun. I have no regrets, but I think there's a very slight chance you're getting carried away."

"Why you so grouchy this morning? Thinking about old woman?"

"Could you please forget about her for a minute. We have a lot to do and I need to concentrate."

"Fine, what we do today?"

"First, we have to come up with a story for you to tell Berislav about where you spent last night."

"Is no problem. I tell him that Niko walk me back to room. Five, no six men attack me for sex with virgin. Niko fight them off but too many. I scared and run away. Hide all night in ship laundry room."

I chuckled. Man, she was an Olympic-class storyteller. "And what happens when Niko wakes up?"

"You think he remember anything?"

I thought about that. I punched him multiple times, she smashed a vase on him, and when I last saw him an elevator door was smacking him in the head. He had a thick skull. I could tell by the way my knuckles hurt this morning, but still, there was a good chance that he had a significant concussion. I said, "Maybe not."

"What he going to say anyway? That he was the one attack me and someone stop him? I don't think so."

She had a point. Besides, this story was for Berislav not the police. It didn't have to be perfect.

"Okay, next thing on my list is to go search Niko's room. I held onto his key last night."

"You forget search Berislav room last night."

"I didn't forget. I didn't have time, but I will do it tonight when everybody is eating. You leave me the key now. Berislav should be home and he'll let you in. Tell him in all the excitement last night you lost your key."

She handed me the key and asked, "You no come dinner tonight?"

"I've got too much to do. If I finish searching Berislav and Niko's rooms in time, I might make it for dessert."

She nodded. "When we…you know?" She glanced over at the bed.

"Right now, I have no idea, so relax."

She narrowed her eyes and pouted. "Fine, I come here after Berislav go sleep. In Croatia, real woman take what she want anyway."

I chuckled. "Same in America."

"Really? I thought in America man in charge."

That made me laugh. "Of what?"

She furrowed her brow thinking about that and decided to drop it for another day. "So, what next do on list?"

With mild irritation in my voice, I said, "Then I have to take my tuxedo to the dry-cleaning service. It got all wrinkled and sweaty from fighting with Niko last night. It's a mess."

She didn't like my tone. "What? So is my fault? Just like man. Blame woman for everything. You should learn how to fight without sweating."

There was a knock on the door. We looked at each other. I said, "Quick, under the bed."

She folded her arms defiantly. "I no go under bed. I girlfriend now."

"Fine, the balcony then."

Rolling her eyes, she said, "Fine."

She quickly went outside and I threw her clothes and shoes after her. The knock came again only louder and more insistently. As I walked to answer the door, I paused to throw a cloth napkin over Katarina's coffee cup to hide it. Through the peephole, I saw an unhappy Berislav.

I opened the door partially and he pushed it open the rest of the way, forcing me to take several steps backward. "Where is she?" he asked angrily scanning the room.

"Where is who?"

"Daughter. Where is daughter?"

"How should I know?"

He was a big man, but pushing seventy, and I wasn't too concerned for my physical well-being unless he was armed. I doubted that. Con-men were generally not violent types. They devoted all their energies into the art of persuasion. Nonetheless, I made a mental note not to turn my back on him.

He looked haggard, and I suspected he was up late or worrying a lot.

He searched the room in frustration, and abruptly wagged his finger in my face saying, "I know what you are up to. I watch American television. Katarina is good girl. You leave alone. No take someplace quiet, understand?"

"I don't know what you're talking about."

As we spoke, I spotted Katarina's thong on the floor by the bed. He said, "I check bathroom."

He marched over there, and I walked quickly to the bed, kicking the thong underneath. He returned even more upset and stormed toward the balcony. Before I could intercept him, he swung the doors open, and I closed my eyes waiting for the explosion that was sure to come.

Nothing happened. He said, "You are slob."

I joined him at the balcony door and saw my robe and towel on the floor. Looking in both directions, I guessed she hopped the balcony railing like she did the other night. She was pretty athletic, but just to be safe I walked to the railing and looked down into the water half wondering if I'd see her floating around. No, she made her get away safely, albeit panty-less, which made me smile.

He turned to me, his cheeks colored red with anger. "I go now but I know something up with you. Stay away from daughter."

"Hey, that's fine with me. I'm just here on vacation."

"Bullsheet. I see the way you look at old lady. You are gigolo. Is disgusting. Daughter mean nothing to man like you with no honor. She is plaything only for you, but I tell you now, she is engaged be married to eligible bachelor, Dubrovnik. Man of great integrity. Something you know nothing about, so stay away. I no say again."

"I thought you said she was going to enter a convent."

"She change mind. Is none of your gigolo business."

He slammed the door on the way out and I plopped into a chair. At least he didn't ask me to pay him back for the tux. Man, was there anybody on this ship who wasn't insane?

Probably not.

Chapter 12

At noon, I brought my tuxedo to the dry cleaning service and ran into Pasquale. He looked at me and then at the tux. "What a you want now?"

"I need the tux cleaned by three so I can wear it later."

"Why not wear the other one?"

"I like the way I look in this one."

He shook his head in frustration. I might make it to dinner. I wasn't sure, but it couldn't hurt to be prepared. He looked down his nose and over his glasses at me. "Everything a rush rush rush with a you. You know a that? Didn't your mama ever teach a you patience, she is a virtue? What a you do anyway? I give you beautiful brand a new tuxedo just a yesterday."

He took it from me and examined it, scrunching his nose in disgust. "What a you do to my tuxedo? It was a so beautiful when I give you. Forget it. I don't even want a know what happened. You think a I'm a you personal servant? You think a my job easy? You want a do my job? Here, I give a you my measuring tape."

He held out his measuring tape. I didn't take it. Letting out a deep breath, I said, "I'm sorry about the tux, Pasquale, and I don't think your job is easy. Can I have it by three?"

He waved his hand in the air, made a disparaging comment under his breath, and turned around with the tux. Apparently, I was dismissed and left.

I had nothing to do for a couple of hours and went to the promenade deck to enjoy the view from the bow. It was a beautiful, clear day, seventy-five degrees, and a gentle breeze. The peaks of the Apennine mountain range of Italy on one side of the Adriatic and the Dinaric Alps on the other, were beautiful and serene. The wood flooring of the deck was buffed and immaculate. Many benches and telescopes graced the perimeter and of course there were several traditional shuffle board courts. A fair number of people milled about enjoying the sunshine. A waiter walked around with a large silver tray loaded with finger food.

I spotted Betsy chatting with another woman who was about her age and she waved as she saw me approach. I said, "Hi Betsy."

"Hi John." She turned to the woman, gave her a polite kiss and said goodbye.

"You didn't have to do that," I said.

"It's okay. That was Mrs. Williams. This is her tenth voyage with us. We're old friends. Come let's take a walk. I'm so glad we ran into each other."

She slid her arm through mine and I glanced over my shoulder to see if anybody was watching. Old habits die hard.

Picking up on my paranoia, she said, "We're just talking, John. It's not a federal crime."

"I beg to differ. Where I come from, touching another man's wife even as harmlessly as this, is most definitely a federal crime, usually associated with the death penalty."

She chuckled, "Would you rather we held hands?"

"No, this will be fine."

"Did you hear about all the commotion last night?"

I shook my head. "I must have been asleep. What happened?"

"A man fired a pistol several times on deck 8 last night on the other end of the ship from my quarters. No one knows for sure what happened. He was found unconscious with a serious head injury. Apparently, he scuffled with someone, fired his weapon, and fell in such a way that his head became wedged between the elevator doors which kept opening and closing on it. The doctor was beyond drunk and almost useless. Anyway, the man didn't fully regain consciousness so the decision was made to airlift him to a hospital. At that point, we weren't too far from Pescara, Italy so they called for a medical helicopter to pick him up. Oddly, he had no ID on him. We don't even know which stateroom he was staying in."

"A helicopter landed on the ship last night?" I asked.

"Yes, there's a landing pad on the uppermost deck. I'm not surprised you didn't hear it. The ship is quite large and the rooms are well insulated."

"Wow! Pretty exciting cruise. Are they always like this?"

"Hardly, and now we have a new problem."

"And what is that?"

"Drunkenness on board the ship is not only unacceptable behavior for a crew member, whether in private or public, it is against maritime law. The captain had no choice but to confine the doctor to his quarters."

"I'm sorry to hear that." I really was.

"The poor man was babbling something about his wife and love and all that. It's a terrible situation."

"What happens if he leaves his quarters?"

"He'll be arrested for real and thrown in the brig below ship. There's a four-cell prison down there. It could potentially ruin his career."

"What happens in the meantime if somebody gets sick?"

"The doctor will be escorted to the infirmary to care for his patient and then escorted back to his room. In the event that his behavior requires that he be thrown into the brig, arrangements will be made to obtain the services of another physician at the next port of call. Looking for a job?"

I smiled at that. "Let's hope he falls in line."

"Or at least sobers up. I went to see him this morning and the man was still reeking of alcohol."

We reached the bow and took in the vista. She still held my arm and asked, "May I come see you tonight?"

I thought about Katarina's threat to come to my cabin and said, "How about I come see you instead?"

She smiled, "It's a date. Have you had lunch?"

"I was going to pass. I had a big breakfast."

"Roger is expecting me at one o'clock in the *Black&Blue,* a steakhouse on deck 4. If you decide you'd like to get something to eat don't hesitate to join us."

"Thank you, but steak for lunch might be overdoing it a bit for me."

She chuckled politely. "You don't *have* to get steak. They make wonderful salads and of course all the seafood is as fresh as it gets."

There was a bench nearby and we sat down. I asked, "What's Dubrovnik like?"

"Magnificent and old. As old as the ancient Roman empire itself. You're going to like it, and the food. I've been there many times."

"A friend of mine from New York will be joining the cruise there. It was a late decision for him."

"How nice. Well, better late than never. I'm sure we'll enjoy his company if he's even half as charming as you."

"Trust me. He's not even a quarter as charming as me, but I promise to keep him under control, and if I can't then I want to apologize in advance."

Laughing she said, "I can't wait to meet him. I'll notify the wait staff that he'll be sitting with us."

"You don't have go to any trouble for him. I can bring him table scraps. Believe me, he won't know the difference."

Still laughing. "My oh my, I haven't been this amused in a long time, but I insist he sit with us. Now I have to meet him."

"Thank you. So, when exactly, do we reach port?"

"In the early morning, sometime. It takes a couple of hours to moor the ship and register with the Croatian port authority. Everything should be ready to let the passengers off to their excursions and tours bright and early so they can return in time for dinner."

I was sort of a night person and asked out of curiosity. "Do the ships ever dock at night or stay overnight?"

"Some do, but the vast majority don't. Most depart in the evening for the next port."

"Why is that?"

"Part tradition, part common sense. Having thousands of drunk passengers roaming around a strange city at night has proven to be too risky in the past. It's best to let them explore the port in the morning and afternoon, and then round them all up before they get out of control. The fact that there is a deadline for the ship's departure in the evening is highly motivational."

I nodded. That made sense. We sat quietly for a moment staring at the coastline slowly drifting by. She inched her hand over to me and rested it on mine as she looked straight ahead. I didn't move but wondered where we were heading with this. I looked down and saw a three carat diamond engagement ring resting next to a gold wedding band. Her skin was just starting to become worn with age and loss of collagen. Her nails were polished and neat. Without turning her head she said, "I'm dying to kiss you right now."

I glanced around. There were many passengers milling about chatting and looking out at the vista. Two groups of four were playing shuffle board. One or two crew members performed various tasks. No one seemed to be particularly interested in us. I wasn't worried about the guests, but the crew might possibly recognize her. I said, "I'd rather not spark a scandal for you."

"That's very considerate of you; although, sometimes I think I'm past that stage of my life where I care about what others think. I've always thought how marvelously romantic it would be to get kissed right here watching the ocean with the breeze in my hair and the taste of salt on my tongue. Am I being silly?"

"No, you're not."

"You know, John. You remind me of someone I knew a long, long time ago when I was just a girl. He was handsome and athletic like you, but most of all, he made me laugh like you do…"

I turned to see her better. She suddenly looked sad. I thought about what she said about not caring what people thought. I had my own share of scandalous liaisons with nurses at the hospital where I worked. True or not, it was never fun to be the object of malicious gossip, and it was exhausting always wondering what others were saying about you.

Moving close, I wrapped my arm around her shoulder and kissed her long and passionately. I stuck my tongue into her mouth and was surprised when she stuck hers back into mine.

When we pulled apart, I saw a solitary tear run down her face. Touching my cheek gently, she said, "Thank you. I needed that."

Removing my arm, I slid discreetly away and looked at my watch. "You're going to be late for lunch."

"Yes, I should get going. I'll see you tonight?"

"Unless a meteor, five miles in diameter, traveling at 200,000 miles per hour hits the Adriatic in the next five minutes, but even then, I wouldn't count me out."

Chuckling, she walked away, and I sat there alone for the next few minutes contemplating recent events and enjoying the view. Eventually, a large man wearing obnoxious Bermuda shorts with black dress socks stepped forth from behind a group of people. Carrying a back pack, he wore a straw hat, dark sun glasses and had zinc oxide smeared on his nose which was why I hadn't recognized him. Looking ridiculous, he walked with determination in my direction. What did he want?

Without greeting me, he sat down. "Aah, what a beautiful day it is? Wouldn't you agree, doctor?"

"Hi Brad."

He wore a silly grin on his face. "Good afternoon, doctor."

I nodded. "Where's Joyce?"

"At the spa getting some sort of treatment. She likes to keep herself in good shape for her Braddy Bear."

Braddy Bear?

"She looks like she's keeping up pretty well."

"Oh yeah and she'd better. I keep on top of her about that stuff. That's for sure. I like them lean and mean."

"You deserve the best."

He chuckled. "That's the way I see it."

Continuing our inane chit-chat, I said, "Doesn't anybody eat lunch on this ship?"

He chuckled. "I noticed the same thing. It makes sense though. You have a five course meal that goes on until eleven every night, go to bed drunk, wake up at ten or eleven and stuff yourself at the breakfast buffet. Who needs lunch?"

I agreed. It was a pretty good assessment of the routine here. "Well, as much fun as I'm having catching up with you,

Brad, I really have things to do. So, I guess I'll be on my way."

I started to rise and he grabbed my arm with a mighty paw and pulled me back down. I was startled, but not enough to crush his larynx. He said, "Not so fast, doctor. I haven't even had a chance to tell you why I'm in such a jolly good mood."

Now I was truly curious. I gave him a not-so-friendly, get your effin' hand off me look, and he let go of my arm. I said, "And why would you want to honor me with your good news? When last we spoke, I got the feeling that we weren't exactly hitting it off."

"Water under the bridge, doctor. Water under the bridge."

I raised my eyebrows at that. "Again?"

"Sure. Doctor, I'm a straight-up businessman. One day, we may be competitors, but then the winds suddenly change and the next day we're on each other's side. As the saying goes, it's nothing personal, just business."

"So the winds have changed?"

"Dramatically. Besides, *you* are the reason I'm so happy"

"How so?"

"Here, let me show you."

He retrieved an iPad from his back pack and turned it on. I asked, "What do you have there?"

He smiled. "Be patient, doctor."

The screen lit up and he tapped a few icons. When he was ready, he held it so I could see pictures of Betsy and me walking arm in arm, sitting on the bench touching hands and then kissing tenderly with my arms around her. I didn't say anything and he chuckled. "I'm no doctor or anything, but isn't that your tongue?"

I still didn't respond.

"C'mon doctor, what are you thinking?"

"Have you ever heard the expression 'hole in butt'?"

"No."

"I didn't think so."

He'd gotten under my skin and knew it. He slapped his knee, guffawing, "Don't be a sore loser. I wouldn't be CEO if I couldn't outsmart guys like you in my sleep. You have to admit. This is pretty sweet. I mean, holding hands, kissing, staring into each other's eyes. This is great stuff. I'm surprised you didn't pull down your pants and let her have it right here on the promenade."

"What do you want, Brad? You already own one hospital. I don't have anything to give you."

"Ah, but there's the rub. You may not have anything I want, but the old lady does. It's very expensive being me, and as you said before, I deserve the best. You know, I always had a taste for the good life even as a kid. Just couldn't afford it. I used to ask my parents all the time if maybe I was accidentally switched at birth with the child of some rich family. Did I mention that I also videoed the entire encounter with you and the old broad. The sound is a little distorted but I know a guy who can fix that. Lovely tabloid shit. Who knows, maybe even television. I heard she's a Lady or something like that. You know, some sort of big deal."

I was getting angry but controlled myself. "Brad, why would you want to hurt an old woman and her husband?"

"Me? I wouldn't hurt a fly, but you, that's a different story. You're going to do all the hurting, and lots of it. That is—if you don't do exactly as I say."

"So, what's your game plan here?"

"Not sure yet, what's yours?"

"What's that supposed to mean?"

"C'mon, game's over and you lost. You're on this cruise to bag a wealthy old lady for her dough. Anybody with half a brain could see that. I just want to wet my beak. Who knows, maybe you're planning on snatching that necklace she wears every night. It's got to be worth millions. Either way, you've been busted. Now you have to pay the consequences. Brad one, Cesari zero. Get used to that score. I must say though, I thoroughly misjudged you. I thought you were just trying to get as much snatch as possible. It never occurred to me until a few minutes ago just how low a guy like you could sink."

If I wasn't so upset, I might've laughed. The day wasn't half over and I'd already been accused of being a gigolo twice. I said, "I don't suppose it would change anything if I told you I'm not trying to scam her out of her money, and that I really like her."

He snorted. "That's a good one. Save it for the paparazzi or the police. I'm sure the captain and her husband will be thrilled to see these pictures too. I'm going to have to check, but I think there are laws about stuff like this. So, what do you think about when you're doing it with her? You know, to get it up. Some porn movie you watched? You know what?" He chuckled and continued, "I don't really care. I just thought I'd let you in on what I got so you can start adjusting your attitude. I'm going to think it over how best to use this and then I'll get back to you. Now, now, don't look so sullen. Uncle Brad will cut you in on a little piece of the action if you're nice."

All he needed was a sign on his forehead that read, *Douche.* I said, "Brad, you don't want to do this."

He grinned broadly.

"But I do, doctor. I really do."

Chapter 13

"Bond...James Bond." I said to the mirror, adjusting my bow tie and cummerbund. It was ten of seven and Berislav would be sitting to dine with Katarina. She was going to make sure that he wasn't late or dawdle on the way. I planned to search their suite first and then Niko's room. Hopefully, Niko's cabin didn't have any surprises in it like another gangster. Betsy would be disappointed when I didn't show up but it couldn't be helped. I couldn't let her in on what I was doing and if all went well, I'd show up toward the end of the meal.

Then, there was Brad. The head of some picayune hospital in Podunk, New York. He thought he was a real bad boy. There was a special place in hell for CEO's. I was sure of it. He was under the impression that because he was able to use weak-kneed physicians and powerless nurses like mere pawns on a chess board, that he was ready to throw a saddle on John Cesari. Well, he was about to find out the hard way this mustang wasn't ready to be broken in. I gave him the chance to back off but he chose to stay in my jungle. So be it, but first things first.

I left my stateroom and went to Berislav and Katarina's suite. There was one other couple walking down the hall toward me engaged in heated debate about politics. They didn't even nod in my direction and I brazenly entered the room, making a beeline to Berislav's quarters. I looked in all the drawers, the closet, the bathroom, behind the TV, pictures on the wall, and under the bed. There was a safe in the bathroom linen closet which I couldn't access because Katarina didn't know the code. I searched his luggage thoroughly and found nothing helpful. I sat on the edge of the bed frustrated. Not even a weapon for self-defense? That I found very surprising.

Finished, I put everything back in its place and admired the fact that without professional forensics, you couldn't even tell I'd been there. I casually glanced around the living room and kitchen, but they spent very little time in their cabin and I discovered nothing interesting. I hadn't intended on searching Katarina's bedroom but figured as long I was here I might as well.

I didn't look around quite as aggressively as I did in Berislav's room but everything seemed more or less in its place and ordinary. She had one more suitcase than he did but that was to be expected. Women always packed more clothes and personal items than men. Her bathroom was filled with shampoo, hair conditioners, scented soaps, candles, hair brushes, body lotions, and a curling iron. In the medicine chest, there were a couple of prescription bottles, nothing serious. I didn't read Croatian but I was sure one of them was for sea sickness and the other I wasn't sure about but hoped it was for birth control. I smiled. If I ever met a girl who needed birth control, Katarina was it. I left her room key on the night table for her.

Satisfied there was nothing more I could do there, I looked at my watch. I had spent just over an hour and had come up with nothing. Still, something irked me. I just couldn't figure out what. Niko's room was one deck down and I reached it in five minutes. Standing outside, I fumbled for the key and hesitated. What if he was sharing the room with the other gangster or cop or whatever? What story could I possibly come up with to explain why I was unlawfully entering using his friend's key?

I decided to knock first. If someone responded I could always say I was looking for a friend and confused the room number. That would work. I rapped on the door three times and waited. No one answered and I knocked another three times.

This time the door opened a sliver and a woman with short, dark brown hair, and a round face answered. Maybe thirty or a little older, she was cute and really, really short. An inch or two shorter and I might have thought she was sitting. She checked me out up and down with large brown, intellectually curious eyes and said curtly with a Croatian accent, "What you want?"

I surmised she was Niko's girlfriend or wife. Deciding to change my approach and rather than say I knocked on the wrong door said, "I met a man named Niko last night in the pub, and after he left I noticed that he dropped his room key. I just thought I'd return it. Are you his girlfriend or wife?"

I showed her the key and she hesitated as she looked at it. "Yes, I girlfriend Niko."

"Well, here it is."

She opened the door a little more to take the key and I saw she was slender and dressed sharply in a navy blue pant suit. Looking down, I was surprised to see she was wearing two-inch heels. A quick calculation in my head put her at just under five feet without shoes and maybe a hundred pounds dripping wet, if that much.

She thanked me but made no move to close the door or take her eyes off me. I stood there trying to think of a way of getting her to invite me inside to chat without appearing creepy or aggressive.

I said, "I hope Niko's feeling okay. He was pretty drunk last night."

There was no change in her expression.

"My name is John."

She looked concerned but not overly worried or stressed. What did that mean? Maybe she was used to Niko staying out all night without calling. I hated to involve civilians like this but it was Niko's fault. He shouldn't have attacked Katarina. I was running out of ideas and was on the verge of trying the creepy approach when she suddenly smiled and said, "Is rude of me. No sleep well. Thank you for return room key. Please come in. My name Antonela. Niko not here right now but I sure he return soon. I just make pot of coffee. You have some with me?"

That was easy. I really couldn't have asked for a better opening. "Well, I never turn down coffee, but I really don't want to put you out."

"No, I insist. Niko will be very happy see you. Thank in person."

She opened the door and I stepped past her into the living room. It was a large one bedroom suite just like mine. She said, "Please have seat. I return one moment."

I sat on the sofa, my mind preoccupied with what kinds of questions to ask her. She stepped behind me and I glanced into the kitchen. I didn't see a coffee pot or any cups. What did that mean? Before I could answer that question, I felt a sharp pain in the back of my head and heard the unmistakable sound a gun cocking.

Whispering in a menacing voice she said, "Lean forward and put hands behind back…slowly. Move very slowly. Gun is hair trigger."

I did as I was told and she slid a plastic hand restraint over my wrists and tightened it. In as innocent a voice as I could muster I asked, "What's this all about?"

She came around in front of me, the pistol trained on my chest. It was a .45 just like Niko's. "That is what we find out. Now stand up…slowly. Do everything slowly."

I stood and she searched me, removing my wallet and room key, placing them on the coffee table. Then she lifted my cummerbund, undid my tuxedo pants and pulled them down to my ankles. This brought a smile to her face. "You wear silly underwear."

"You don't like tighty whitey's?"

"Is for children. Now sit…slowly. Everything do slowly."

Realizing I wasn't going anywhere for a while, I said, "I'd like sugar in my coffee, please."

She smirked and tapped the side of my head with the barrel of her gun. "Would you like one lump or two?"

I shook my head. "That won't be necessary. Just a little joke."

"Where is Niko?"

"I really don't know. So, I guess he's not your boyfriend?"

Ignoring me she asked, "How get key?"

"I found it on the floor in the pub like I told you. Who are you anyway?"

I was such an idiot. Just then it dawned on me. She was the other gangster Katarina had told me about. Being the massive chauvinist that I was, it never dawned on me that the other corrupt cop might be a woman. Underestimating the other gender was going to bring me to ruination one day.

"Question is who are you?"

"You have my wallet with my ID."

She picked it up and studied its contents for a minute. "It say you are American doctor, but who are you really?"

"What makes you think I'm anything else?"

"Last night, Niko tell me he meet American wearing tuxedo in bar with girl. Now Niko missing and American in tuxedo show up in Niko room with key. In Croatia, we call that suspicious."

"In America, we call that being nice. I met the girl and her father at dinner. I saw her in the bar and went over to say hello. She introduced me to Niko. We hung out for a while, and after he left, I found his key. That's all. You know, you didn't have to handcuff me. I would have told you all this."

"Learn long time ago that man much easier to talk to if tie up first."

"Well, I'm not giving you any trouble so maybe you can free me. My wrists are hurting. The restraint is too tight."

Ignoring my plea, she took a step toward me, and placed the tip of her gun inside the elastic band of my underwear. Pushing down hard enough for me to wince, she said, "What you want with girl?"

"I don't want anything from her. I was just being nice. Look, if you let me go you'll never see or hear from me again. I swear."

"If go near girl again, you never make children. Understand?" She wiggled the gun to make sure I got the message.

I nodded and grunted, "I get it."

With the gun still pressing against me, she sat on my lap, straddling me. I looked at her. She was inches from me now, staring, her eyes examining my features. She said, "Do you?"

"I do. Please take the gun away before an accident happens. Remember, it has a hair trigger."

"Maybe I shoot anyway."

I caught my breath. "Why would you do that?"

She smiled revealing perfect, white teeth and whispered, "Maybe it turn me on."

Great. I was handcuffed with a lunatic on my lap. It seemed like crazy women were the story of my life. Gently rocking back and forth, she ground herself into me like a lap dancer would. I didn't say anything and was afraid to even breathe. She pulled the pistol out from my underwear and pressed the muzzle against my temple.

Leaning in close, our noses touched and she whispered, "Don't move. This is the most dangerous time." The way she said it made me wonder how many times she had done this.

She kissed me hard and long and grabbed my upper lip with her teeth. She bit down and pulled on my lip until I groaned in pain and then she let go. I was sweating now and thoroughly concerned about my immediate future. After what seemed like forever, she took the gun from the side of my head and released the hammer, saying, "You better hope nothing happen to Niko or I finish what I start today."

She got off me and put the gun in her bag. Leaving my wallet and room key on the table, she walked to the door and opened it. She turned and blew me a kiss. "Goodbye, doctor. For your sake, I hope we never meet again."

After she left I let out a deep sigh of relief. I was drenched in perspiration but happy that I hadn't wet myself. Damn! I made a mental note to scratch Croatia off the list of places I was thinking of getting a mail-order bride from. Looking around, I considered how best to get out of my current predicament. The plastic restraint holding my wrists together was quite taut and digging into my flesh. I wiggled and pulled my wrists apart forcefully without any success at loosening it. I stood and shuffled into the kitchen, impeded by my pants hanging down around my ankles.

There was a tray with a dirty plate and cutlery on the table and may have been Niko's dinner last night before he went to keep an eye on Katarina. Backing up to the table, I lifted the knife from the tray and manipulated it so the serrated edge pressed up against the plastic handcuff. With great care and little by little, I began sawing the restraint. It took a while, and a great deal of sweat, but I felt it eating through the plastic. Having weakened it considerably, I dropped the knife and strained my muscles, bursting the bond apart.

Rubbing my aching wrists, I noted red welt marks around them and hoped I had the opportunity to repay her. This was obviously not her room, but I would find her. I picked up my pants and hightailed it out of there.

Given what had just happened, I decided to bail on my rendezvous with Betsy and hoped she would understand. It wasn't that I couldn't perform, it was that I wasn't in the right frame of mind, and didn't feel I would be any fun. As a rule, when I came to play, I liked to come with my game face on, and right now I was irritated.

I went to the casino, had a couple of drinks to bring myself down and thought about what had just happened. This was a new and unanticipated wrinkle. This Croatian gangster, Antonela, was the real deal. Diminutive, feminine, a tad psychotic, and genuinely dangerous, I'd better not take her for granted. Two bourbons became three and three became four.

It was almost 1:00 a.m. when I opened the door to my room. There was a night light on and I saw Katarina sleeping under the covers on my bed. I walked over to her and watched the sheets rise and fall with her gentle breaths. She was wearing a black velvet ribbon around her neck that she had tied into a bow. I liked it.

How did she get in here? What was I going to do with her? Good questions. The word no or stop didn't seem to be in her vocabulary. On the whole, she was harmless if not just a tiny bit over-enthusiastic. Despite myself, I was starting to like her, but I wasn't going to like her tonight.

I was tired and had a pounding stress headache. It was a king bed and quite large but if I disturbed her she'd be on me like a barn cat in heat. I went to the bathroom, dropped my clothes to the floor, and popped a couple of ibuprofen. Then I took a spare sheet and blanket from the linen closet, grabbed a pillow from the bed and quietly went onto the balcony. It was a beautiful, balmy evening with a warm gentle breeze coming in from the west. I stretched out on one of the recliners, snuggled under the blanket and looked up at the starry sky.

It was almost like camping.

Chapter 14

I sipped my coffee and inhaled the fresh aroma wafting off the surface of the steaming cup. It was good and I was deeply contented. My headache was gone and I felt refreshed. Sleeping outdoors like that was an unexpectedly pleasant experience. Looking up at the towel on Katarina's head, I started to wonder if I was going to wake up to this sight every morning for the rest of the trip. It was only 7:00 a.m. and she was already pissed off at me. She had woke early to an empty bed, found me on the balcony and had been raising Cain ever since.

She scowled and strummed her fingers on the table glaring at me. "Maybe you are fag and just don't know it."

"You mean gay. We don't use words like fag anymore. It's not considered nice."

"Why not nice?"

"I don't know."

"So, are you?"

"Just because I didn't have sex with you last night?"

"That's right."

"No, I'm not. It's just that the situation is complicated."

She snorted with contempt. "Is no complicated. Boyfriend either want Katarina or boyfriend is gay. Is very simple."

I wished I could package her self-confidence and sell it. I'd make a fortune. I said, "Well, I'm a little more complicated than most of the men you know."

"Oh please..."

"Katarina, I was tired and so were you. When I came into the room last night you were snoring."

"Is no right what you did. I not getting any younger. In Croatia twenty-one year old girl is almost old maid."

"You're twenty-five years old, remember?" I asked, wondering if she even really knew anymore.

Ignoring my jab, she continued her tirade. "You are lucky man. If I no find you on balcony this morning I almost go to old lady's room and give her a piece of my brain."

I chuckled.

"And what is so funny?" she asked.

"You mean give her a piece of your mind, not your brain, and we need to clear the air on this once and for all. You must promise me right here and now that you will never—ever confront Lady Harrington about us. If you do, I will never speak to you again."

She pouted but didn't respond.

I said, "Promise?"

After a long pause she said, "Fine, I promise."

"You know, Katarina, in America, girls never lie to their boyfriends."

"Same in Croatia."

We looked at each other. Then she smiled and then I smiled. Then I laughed and then she laughed.

She said, "That was good one."

"Yeah, I know. Say, how did you get in my room last night?"

"Is easy. I borrow room key I see in bathroom last time I here."

"You stole my spare room key?"

"No steal. Borrow boyfriend's key. You had my key and I have your key."

I shook my head, exasperated. She was the motherload of trouble my mother had warned me about. "And what about Berislav. How'd you get out this time? The balcony again? Because, I'm getting a little nervous about that. I know you're athletic but sooner or later you're going to be swimming in the ocean."

"No balcony last night. I just walk out. Berislav no come room. Out late making deal with fat American hospital man."

"Hmm, so whatever that deal is seems to be progressing?"

"Probably. Berislav very convincing. He can sell sand to people in desert."

That made me smile. I was very curious as to what kind of deal they were working on. "So, what find in rooms last night?" she asked.

"I didn't find anything in Berislav's room but in Niko's room I found the other gangster. Why didn't you tell me she was a woman?"

She shrugged. "You no ask. Is midget with nasty temper. I no like."

"I don't like her either." I looked at my watch. "You never told me. How did Berislav handle the story about what happened to Niko?"

"He very scared. Doesn't like but doesn't know what means. Wait for midget to come today to talk."

"What do you think she is going to do?"

"Not sure, but Berislav think she probably call for more gangsters from Dubrovnik for to help unless more already on ship."

"From what I could tell she has no idea what happened to Niko. It's going to come as a surprise to her when Berislav tells her your story."

"Is better that way. Women like surprises, even midgets."

I laughed. "You are incorrigible."

"What mean incorrigible?"

"It's American for trouble."

She sat back and folded her arms. "I told you. I no trouble. Don't make me pissed off."

"The midget may want to talk to you herself so keep the story straight in your head. I doubt that she'll go to the captain on a fact-finding mission though. I'm quite certain she's not going to want to answer questions about why Croatian police are on board in the first place."

She nodded. "I ready for her."

"Good, are you going to leave the ship today? We're in port."

"No, where I go? No money, no car. Besides, I live Dubrovnik. Already see everything there is to see. Even more gangsters off ship than on. No, I stay."

"I have a friend who'll be joining us on the cruise today. His name is Vito."

"Is he gay too?'

"Hardly."

"Good, because apparently I need new boyfriend."

She made me laugh again. "I'll introduce you."

Furrowing her brow she said, "You don't even care?"

"I'll be devastated, maybe even join the priesthood."

She shook her head in exasperation. "Is not funny. This is no laughing matter. My baby clock is tick-tocking."

"Your biological clock is ticking."

"That's what I say."

A knock on the door interrupted us and I gave her the you know what to do look. She rolled her eyes and whispered, "I go balcony."

"No, Katarina, I don't won't you climbing over the balconies. It's dangerous and somebody might see you. Please get under the bed."

"So, you do care?"

Whoever it was knocked again.

I whispered, "Of course I do. I don't want you to get hurt."

"Then say it."

"Say what?"

The knocking became more urgent and louder.

"That you care."

Son of a bitch. I couldn't believe she was doing this. I gritted my teeth and said, "I care about you, Katarina."

She smiled and scurried under the bed dragging her undergarments and high heels with her. I called out, "I'll be right there."

I ran to the bathroom and scanned quickly for any leftover hints of her presence, found none and scooted to the door. It was one of the crew. I opened the door and greeted him.

"Dr. Cesari?"

"Yes, how may I help you?"

"Seaman Marty Rook, sir. The captain has requested your presence in Lady Harrington's stateroom, sir. He told me to tell you it's a matter of urgency. Would you please come with me?"

"Yes, of course, is everything okay?"

"I'm not at liberty to say, sir."

"Okay, please give me a moment and I'll be right there."

I closed the door and went to the bed, kneeling down to see her. "You heard?"

"Yes, what happen?"

"I don't know but I have to go. I'll see you later and once again, try not to be seen when you leave. I have a hoodie in one of my drawers. Use it, okay?"

She nodded and I left the room accompanied by the seaman, walking in silence to Betsy's room. We took the stairs up to deck 8 and, and found two more crew standing on either side of her stateroom door. This wasn't good. They were wearing sidearms.

Seaman Rook stayed outside as I entered and found Betsy sitting in a large Queen Anne wingback chair, the captain on one knee beside her, his hand on her shoulder, consoling her. She was crying and he appeared very upset. Sprawled on the floor in the middle of the room in his tuxedo with a bullet hole in his chest was her husband, Roger. He was quite dead.

Shit!

Walking quickly toward her, I paused for a brief moment as I passed Roger to study his blood-soaked white dress shirt. It looked like a pretty big hole and I guessed it was probably a .45. I'd seen enough of them to know. Kneeling down on her other side, I held her hand, nodded to the captain who was tearful, and asked, "What happened, Betsy?"

She put her arms around me. Distraught and almost incoherent, she sobbed, "It was so terrible. I still can't believe it."

I looked at the captain who also seemed in shock and I doubted that anything like this had ever happened before on a ship he commanded. The fact that he was close with the Harringtons only compounded the pain and confusion he was undoubtedly feeling.

I repeated softly, "What happened?"

She sniffled and caught her breath. "Last night, an armed man was waiting for us when we came in. He was wearing a mask, the kind that is used at the ship's masquerade ball…" She broke down and simply couldn't get the words out as she wept uncontrollably into my chest.

The captain finished for her. "A masked man was waiting for them. He demanded Lady Beth's necklace. When she refused to give it to him, he got rough and Roger went to her defense. You can see the result."

I nodded. "When did this take place, Betsy?"

She had regained some of her composure and said, "We returned to our room shortly after midnight."

It was now close to 8:00 a.m. I must have looked puzzled because the captain added. "After the villain took Roger's life, Betsy put up a struggle and he pushed her to the ground. She hit her head and passed out just regaining consciousness less than an hour ago."

"Where's the doctor?"

"That's a good question," the captain said wryly. "He wasn't in his room and can't be found so I sent for you to tend to Lady Beth while we hunt him down. I didn't think you'd mind."

"Of course I don't mind." I turned to Betsy. "Betsy, did he hurt you in any other way?"

She shook her head. "No, and thank goodness the floor is carpeted."

I examined her head while she spoke. "Well, I don't see any cuts or lumps so I suspect you'll be all right. No headache or problems with your vision right now?"

"No, I feel fine, just drained. Oh my God, Roger deserved better than this and my necklace...I can't believe it."

I said consolingly, "I'm so sorry, Betsy."

The captain stated with great resolve, "I promise you, Elizabeth, we will find whoever did this and return your necklace to you."

Betsy slumped forward onto my chest weak and exhausted, emotionally spent. I said, "Betsy, you need to lie down."

She nodded, "I know, but where? I can't here, and in his room would be even worse."

I said, "Do you feel strong enough to walk? We can go to my cabin."

The captain said, "You may use my room Elizabeth. I'll have my belongings moved into the first mate's quarters."

"Thank you, Bjorn, but that won't be necessary."

"But I insist."

"I won't allow it, but we'll talk later. Right now all I want to do is lay down somewhere before I faint. Doctor, please assist me to your stateroom."

She stood and put an arm around me. As she stared down at Roger's body, I felt a shiver run through her and I held her close.

Under her breath she whispered,

"Goodbye, Roger."

Chapter 15

We reached my room, and I hoped Katarina had cleared out, but braced myself for the worst. In her present condition, I wasn't sure what Betsy's reaction would be, although I suspected that she wouldn't care, and might even be a little amused. My concerns were unfounded however, as the room was empty, and she had even straightened out the bed for me.

After drinking a glass of water, Betsy laid down and closed her eyes. She slept fitfully and called out unintelligibly several times. I sat in a chair close by trying to sort things out. This was just an awful situation and I wondered what the procedure was.

We were in Croatian waters. Was this a matter for the Croatian police or were we still under the jurisdiction of maritime law? Is there a morgue on board the ship to keep the body on ice or do you call the local Dubrovnik funeral parlor? I had no idea but was sure I would soon find out.

An hour later, there was a gentle knock on the door and I went to answer it. It was the captain. I stepped out into the corridor so as not to wake Betsy.

"Hi Captain. Betsy's sleeping."

He nodded. "I just came by to check on her condition. I won't disturb her."

"She's been resting and seems okay. So, what's going to happen now?"

"Well, I've sealed the ship for starters. No one is allowed on or off until we've performed as thorough an investigation as possible. Roger will be kept in the ship's morgue facility below deck until we return to England where the ship is registered. The Croatian authorities want nothing to do with this sort of situation."

I thought about that. "Is that typical?"

"Yes, in general, crimes on a ship are generally dealt with by the country in which the ship is registered, unless circumstances merit immediate intervention. It would be tricky business if Roger or the perpetrator were Croatian nationals, but since Roger isn't and we haven't apprehended the killer that is not an issue."

"So, the passengers won't be allowed to go sightseeing in Dubrovnik?"

"I'm afraid not. I can't have the killer just wander off into a crowded Croatian street with Elizabeth's necklace."

That made sense. "Is anyone at all allowed on or off?" I was thinking about Vito.

He shook his head. "The crew will tend to some routine maintenance and re-supply issues and so there will be some necessary interaction with the Croatian dock-workers, but other than that we are in full lock down."

"What's going to happen to the doctor when you find him?"

"Well, I'd like to skin him alive and then make him walk the plank like back in the good old days, but I'm not allowed to mete out well-deserved justice anymore. There's no room for this kind of behavior on a ship, doctor. Without strict discipline, an ocean-going vessel is doomed."

I winced. Man, he was very angry.

He let out a deep breath and continued, "To answer your question, he will be arrested and placed in the brig below. He will be formally charged with insubordination, dereliction of duty, and conduct unbecoming an officer." He seemed to soften up as he spoke. "It's a shame, really. He joined the crew about two years ago and has an exemplary record. Until now, he seemed well grounded. This will be the end of his cruise ship career at the very least. He may well have to serve time in prison, but that won't be for me to decide."

"That's too bad. Sven seemed like such a nice guy. I hope he's okay."

"He'll show up sooner or later. I mean, where could he possibly be?"

"Exactly."

"Anyway, doctor, thank you for caring for Elizabeth. I assume you know she means a lot to me and my family." He hesitated for a second and cleared his throat. "We are in a bit of a crisis at the moment as I'm sure you realize, and being short an AWOL doctor is only adding to my headache. Could I possibly burden you with the responsibility of acting in the capacity of ship physician until such time we can find an adequate replacement for Sven? I assure you, you will be well compensated for your trouble and of course have my deepest gratitude."

What could I say? "Would I get to steer the ship sometime?"

He smiled, "I'm sure we can work something out."

"Then I'll do whatever's necessary to help."

"Thank you. I'll notify the crew and staff in the infirmary that I'm giving you full authority to act as the ship's chief medical officer. That will include supervisory discretion over the medical personnel and include access to the pharmacy. I'll have someone show you around the sick bay as soon as possible and introduce you to our nurse practitioner."

He left and I went back into the room. Betsy stirred and I sat next to her. Her eyes fluttered open and she asked, "How long have I been asleep?"

"About an hour and a half. Not too long. Bjorn just came by to see how you're doing."

"The poor man. The stress he must be under. He and Roger were very close almost like father and son."

"He seems like a good man and he's very concerned. How are you?"

She took a deep breath. "Devastated. I feel like I'm free falling off a cliff."

"I'm sorry. Can I get you some water or…a stiff drink?"

"No, I'm okay. There'll be time enough for that later."

I nodded. "Bjorn just requested I act as the ship's doctor until they find a replacement for Sven. I agreed. I can prescribe you a sedative if you would like. There are going to be some rough days ahead."

"Thank you but no. I've never been one for medication." She paused and touched my arm. "John, I just can't believe it."

She was going to be saying that a lot, for a long, long time. I said, "I know what you mean."

"What did Bjorn say he's going to do?"

"Well, for starters the ship is on lock down. No one can leave or come on. I assume there's going to be a massive room to room search of the ship for your necklace."

"How dreadful. The publicity will be horrendous."

"Unfortunately, that can't be helped. The important thing is to catch the animal who did this and bring him to justice."

"Yes, of course."

"Is there anything about him that you found memorable? You know, his voice, was there an accent, tall or short. That kind of stuff."

"It all happened so quickly, I can't be certain of anything. We were so frightened. He wore a tuxedo and one of those ornate Venetian masks with white gloves and a top hat. He looked fiendish."

"Could you tell me how tall he was or what his race was?"

"About your height I would say and white for sure. The mask didn't cover his ears and neck."

"He spoke English I presume. Did he have an accent?"

"Not really, his voice was deep and brutish like a wild beast."

"That narrows it down a bit unless he was masking his voice. That's possible. Well, that was helpful, Betsy. I'll let the captain know so they at least have a starting point for their search."

"John, do you think this had anything to with the shooting last night?"

That made sense to try to connect the dots, but I knew better. "You never know, but I doubt it."

She reached out for me to hug her and I did. "Thank you for allowing me to come here. Would you mind very much if I stayed for the next few days?"

I was taken aback by this. Concerned I said, "Betsy, how would that look?"

"I don't care how it looks. I just don't want to be alone right now."

When I didn't answer right away she added softly, "Am I being an old fool?"

Hesitantly, I said, "No, you're not, and of course you can stay, but..."

"Yes, John?"

"I don't know. Bjorn may have...concerns."

She thought about it for a few seconds. "I'll explain to him that I would feel more comfortable having a physician nearby in case I have a panic attack or something of that nature. He knows I have had heart problems in the past. I'll have him bring a fold up cot for you to sleep on for appearances sake. We can set it up at the foot of the bed. Only you and I will know the truth."

I must have looked apprehensive maybe even a little shocked. She said, "John, don't be dismayed and try to understand. I cared for Roger, but more like a good friend than anything else. We hadn't been intimate in years."

I understood where she was coming from, kind of, but still, it didn't sit right. Her husband was just murdered and she moves in with a guy, thirty years her junior. Even if the captain bought her story, no one else would. Especially the women on board. You can't try to fool women with stuff like this. They're the ones who invented lying. Before women came along there was just a bunch of guys walking around telling the truth. I would be made a pariah on the ship, a gold-digging gigolo just like Berislav had accused me of being. He would feel vindicated, even worse, so would that prick, Brad. It might even embolden him. Then there was Betsy. I liked her and we were just starting to become friends. Could I really turn my back on her in her time of need? Her logic resonated with me, and since when did I ever care what anyone thought. There were only two things I needed to be worried about. One was named Katarina, and the other, Vito.

She watched me thinking and said, "I would find it very comforting to have you near."

I nodded slowly and let out a deep breath. "All right, but when you explain it to Bjorn please let him know with no uncertainty whose idea it was. I don't think he's going to take kindly to it. I'm pretty sure I wouldn't if the shoe were on the other foot."

"Thank you and I'll take care of Bjorn. John…?"

"Yes, Betsy?"

"I promise to be discreet, and if perchance you meet someone else on the ship that you would like to spend time with then I encourage you to do so. I don't want you to feel like you're stuck here with a withering flower when there is a fresh young bloom beckoning to be plucked."

I grinned politely, wondering what I had just gotten into. "I only want what's best for you, Betsy. This is going to be a difficult journey for you."

"Thank you. I know that you care."

"I do. Well, it's almost noon. You must be hungry. I know I am."

"I don't have any appetite, but I suppose I should try to eat something. How about we order room service?"

"That would be great. Betsy, I'm going to try to phone my friend, Vito. He's stuck in the port and can't board the ship. I just want to see how he's doing. Would you order for us while I did that?"

"Of course. What would you like?"

"Whatever you're having just tell them two. You don't mind if I step outside for a minute?"

"Go make your call. I'll be fine."

While she dialed room service, I retrieved my cellphone from my suitcase and walked out of the room as it powered up. I hadn't even bothered turning it on since the ship left Venice, but now that we were in port it occurred to me that I might be able to reach Vito.

Walking down the hallway as Vito's phone rang, I found a bench and sat down. He didn't answer and the call went to his voice mail. I waited a minute and tried again. Three, four, five rings this time.

"Cesari, what hell is going on out there? They won't let anyone on or off the ship."

"What's the word on the street?"

"Nothing but speculation. Everyone's thinking terrorism or some sort of viral threat like maybe Ebola. Maybe both."

I chuckled. "Ebola? Really?"

"It's not funny. Lot of people are upset. They want the ship to clear out as soon as possible and take whatever plague is onboard with it. This is Croatia, Cesari. They still believe in vampires here. So what's the skinny?"

I glanced both ways down the corridor to make sure no one was within earshot. I wasn't sure if the captain had made an announcement to the passengers or not. I said, "A guy was murdered last night in one of the staterooms and his wife was robbed of millions of dollars of jewelry."

"You're kidding?"

"Nope. They figure if they don't let anybody off the ship then whoever did it can't get away. Meanwhile, they're going room to room searching for the rocks and the killer."

He laughed. "What are they, the keystone cops? Whoever did it isn't going to keep the ice in his room."

"Where's he going to keep it then?"

"I won't know until I get on board and get a feel for the layout, but there's no way in hell it's going to be in anybody's room. No one could be that stupid. So who's the guy that got sent to meet his maker?"

"That's another thing. His name was Roger Harrington, and he and his wife are the majority owners of this ship."

He whistled through his teeth. "Oh boy. This is good."

"Yeah, you can imagine the kind of heat this is going to bring down."

"Somebody's going to fry for sure."

"And there's one more tiny thing you should know before you come on board…"

"And that is…?"

"I'm banging his wife."

Chapter 16

It took all day to search the staterooms and at 10:00 p.m., frustrated and thwarted, the captain called it quits. There was no sign of the necklace or of the murder weapon. After consultation with Betsy, he decided the show must go on and informed all the passengers that the ship would be leaving port without disembarkation. The next stop was Corfu, Greece, two days at sea away. His hope was that this would give him more time to catch the murderer. It made sense. His explanation to everyone was that if he stayed another day in Dubrovnik, the ship's timetable would be upset, and for many reasons he couldn't allow that. Eventually, he knew he would have to let people off the ship, but for the time being everyone was a suspect. Many were outraged, but most were just frightened. I mean, who was next? The mood was palpably subdued and people eyed each other anxiously.

Most of the day, my room had a long line of visitors who came to console Betsy and in hushed tones inquire about me. With furtive and distrustful glances in my direction, sanctimonious women offered her sage advice about ship board hustlers such as myself. By nightfall, Betsy was exhausted and fell asleep.

I went to the promenade to watch the crew prepare for departure, and to call Vito again. He could catch a flight to Corfu and meet us there. I hadn't thought about that when we talked earlier. Inconvenient, yes, but there was nothing more to be done on this end. The die had been cast. Katarina had come by the room, saw all the commotion and left with steam coming out of her ears. God only knew what she would do. She didn't strike me as being the sympathetic type.

It was a beautiful night and the dock was busy with crew members scurrying about in the dark preparing the ship for departure. Only one passage way was open and it was busy with crew and shore workers loading routine supplies onto the lower deck and removing the ship's refuse. Large dumpsters with wheels, loaded with black plastic garbage bags lumbered slowly down the ramp toward Dubrovnik sanitation trucks with their engines idling. An armed security guard stood at either end of the ramp in case the killer tried to make a break for it. So this is what went on when we were all drinking.

I took out my phone and dialed Vito. It went to voicemail. I tried two more times unsuccessfully before I gave up. He'd figure it out. I hoped. I felt a presence next to me and turned.

"Hello doctor. Lovely night, isn't it?"

It was Brad and he was holding a scotch glass. I let out a deep breath. "What can I do for you, Brad?"

He smirked and then chuckled. "Interesting you should say that."

"Want to let me in on the joke?"

"You really amaze me you know that? I didn't think you had it in you to go the distance with the old lady, but you…wow, I just don't know what to say."

"Just say it anyway."

"All right, if you want to hear it in plain English. You got balls. That's for sure, doctor. The old woman's husband gets eighty-sixed. He's barely blue, and the word is out you're already plowing grandma's corn field. Jesus, you're a cold-hearted bastard."

He took a long slug of scotch and winced. I said, "That's one interpretation."

"It's the only interpretation possible. Let me float a few scenarios out there for you and you tell me when I'm warm. One, somebody kills the old man and steals the necklace. By that time the old woman is already smitten by Cesari charm and goes to you for consolation. That's the romantic version. Yes, it looks bad to the public, but I suppose it's possible. Two, you killed the old man, stole the necklace, and now you're stuck with the old woman because she's already in love with you. You didn't count on the effect your sausage would have on her but what are you going to do? And three, the old man caught you with your banana in her fruit salad and went nuts so you killed him. To protect you, the old bag came up with the story about being robbed and hit on the head. How's that for deduction?"

"What do you want, Brad?"

"First off, I want you to know that I'm sympathetic to your, shall we say, delicate situation. I've been known to wine and dine old ladies too."

"Really?" Despite myself I was curious.

"Of course, romancing old women is an occupational hazard for every CEO in healthcare."

"Why is that?"

"What did Willie Sutton say when he was asked why he robbed banks?"

"It's where the money is."

"Exactly. Their husbands die and they want to do something good with all the loot they're left with, like leave it to a deserving hospital, but there's a catch. There's always a catch with women. If you want their money, you have to be willing to go the distance with them. It's risky business, and competitive, and sometimes unexpected things happen."

"They do?"

"All the time. Once, I went to call on some rich widow. I got all spiffed up, fresh haircut, a dozen roses, get the picture? I walked into her parlor and there were three other CEO's from competing hospitals all waiting there holding bouquets of flowers. Well, she picked me. Great, right? Wrong, she was eighty-five and had all sorts of medical problems. To make a long story short, she took me to her bedroom for an audition. She was on her knees in front of me bobbing for apples, if you get my drift, when suddenly she looks up at me and her eyes roll back in her head. She keeled over dead on the spot from a stroke. I left her there, running as fast as I could, and didn't call 911 until I was safely home in my own bed. By the time I did, I almost had a heart attack myself."

"You're a sweetheart."

"The point I'm trying to make, doctor, is that I did what I had to do. Old women like that leave millions and millions of dollars to hospitals and charitable institutions. In that particular case, things didn't quite work out because she died before I could convince her to change her will. But that's the way life is. Sometimes you're the bug and sometimes you're the windshield. So, you see doctor, I see what's going on here very well."

I sighed and shook my head. He was a very exasperating human being. I asked, "Okay, now what?"

"I want that necklace. I know you have it so let's cut through the bullshit. I'll let you keep whatever else you took or plan to take, including that rock I saw on her finger at dinner. That had to be at least three or four carats. Not a bad night's work."

"You can't be serious?"

"But I am, doctor. I really am. You see, the CEO business hasn't been doing so well lately. The hospital's hemorrhaging money, the government's crawling over the books, union negotiations are torture, the insurance companies are a constant headache…Doctor, I'll be honest with you. I'm just plain tired. I got a five bedroom house on the lake, two boats, a Porsche, another house in Boca Raton…"

"An expensive girlfriend."

He smiled, "I'm glad we're on the same page, doctor. Anyway, it's time to get out. Well, a business opportunity has just come up on this very ship that will make my future so bright I'll have to wear sunglasses at night. I can get in on the ground floor but only if I act quickly. I need collateral in a hurry to make it happen, so I want that necklace you have. I'll give you a couple of days to think it over, but I want it before we dock at the next port of call. I wouldn't want you making a hasty getaway."

"What if I really don't have it?"

He laughed. "What if every star in the sky was an angel? What if every drop of rain a teardrop from heaven?"

"What's that supposed to mean?"

"It means I don't believe in unicorns and I don't believe you. You're boning the old woman. You know it, I know it, and everybody knows it. Think about this. We're talking about murder on the high seas, not just theft, not just scamming a rich, married woman. If I show the captain pictures of you kissing and fondling the old broad the day before her husband gets murdered in cold blood, just how angry do you think it will make him and everybody else on board?"

He was right. "Pretty angry, I would guess, but that doesn't make me guilty of anything."

"Maybe it doesn't but it's quite possible that one of the guests and his wife might tell the captain, anonymously of course, that they overheard you plotting to go to her room to steal the necklace."

The color rose in my cheeks and I felt like he had just taken one too many steps over that invisible line we all have. I said, "You would perjure yourself?" I was incredulous.

"What are you, some sort of boy scout? Of course I would, and I've been doing it for years. Filing false accusations of misconduct against physicians with the state of New York is a favorite tactic of mine to get your type in line, and it works every time. True or not, they start peeing in their pants at the thought of a state investigation, and Brad comes to their rescue...as long they agree to do what I tell them. Kind of like…well, kind of like what we're doing here. Don't look so shocked, doctor." He finished his scotch and threw the glass over the side. Letting out a deep breath he added, "Lovely night, isn't it?"

He walked away as I shook my head watching him. He had to be one of the most morally bankrupt human beings I'd ever met. I headed over to the casino needing to get a drink and blow off some steam. The black jack tables were packed and the room was crowded. It seemed that everyone on board needed to decompress. Taking a seat at the five-card draw poker table, I threw a hundred dollar bill at the dealer and he pushed some chips in my direction. I ordered a Manhattan with two cherries from a passing cocktail waitress and settled in.

After four or five hands, I bought more chips and was working on my second Manhattan. The seat next to me opened and a slight figure sat down. I glanced over and almost gagged on my drink. It was Antonela. She sipped white wine as she ordered a couple of hundred dollars' worth of chips and smiled politely at me. Barely up to my shoulder, I stared down at her with my mouth open.

She said, "Hi."

I whispered, "What do you want?"

"I play poker like everyone else."

"Yeah, right."

I signaled to the dealer that I was leaving and Antonela touched my arm. "Wait, don't go. I want talk." She raised her arms in the air. "Go ahead, frisk. No gun."

I looked around to see if anybody was watching and said, "Put your arms down." Relaxing a little, I threw a chip into the pot and signaled the dealer that I had changed my mind. "Talk about what and why aren't you watching Katarina? I thought that was your job?"

"Is my job, but no can do all the time by myself. Must eat and sleep."

"And gamble…"

"Is bad habit I pick up in Dubrovnik."

She was a whole lot friendlier tonight for some reason. "So what happened to Niko?" I asked, curious if she had figured anything out yet.

"Not sure. Girl say eight or nine men attack her for to have sex and Niko protect. Get beat up. Now in hospital in Italy."

"You seem awfully calm if that's what happened."

Shrugging, she replied, "Is tough business."

Damn, she was cool. I nodded, "Okay, what do you want to talk to me about?"

"I hear about old man get killed and old wife move into your room."

This was ridiculous how fast the news had spread. "How'd you hear about that?"

She made a face and said, "Oh please. Everyone talking about it. I hear from crew man."

I let out a deep breath. "So?"

"Antonela think about what that means and come to conclusion that you kill old man. Not for jewels, but for love. Anyway, I lie in bed thinking about man who would kill another man for to take his woman. It kind of turn me on. You know?"

"No, I don't know and I didn't kill him, so you can turn it off."

"Of course you must say this way. I understand, but I admire you. Think maybe I make mistake about you. At first, I think you just weak American man. No spine. Chase after volley ball slut. Now I know better. You forgive?"

I was incredulous. "You admire me? Because you think I killed an old man to steal his wife? How crazy are you?"

"No crazy. Is very romantic and very manly. Woman in Croatia respect man who is strong like bull. Take what he want. I lie in bed thinking of you killing old man in fit of passion. No mercy. Very sexy. I no can sleep. I wonder what it would be like you push me down and do things…nasty things."

I looked at her carefully and said, "The girls in Croatia aren't quite right, are they?"

"What mean?"

"Nothing. Look, I got to go. Thanks for the interesting conversation."

"Wait. Wait. I come with you." She grabbed her chips and swung herself onto the floor. "It noisy here. How about we go someplace more quiet to talk."

I blinked several times. This couldn't be happening. She handcuffed me and nearly neutered me and now she wants to go someplace quiet…to talk. I must have missed something about girls when I was growing up because no one ever taught me about this.

"You threatened to kill me the last time we met."

"Yes, of course, was my job. Am sorry but if go near girl I still have to kill you. But doesn't mean you can't go near Antonela."

She finished that thought with a seductive smile and a cock of her head. I said, "Thanks, but I'm really tired. I'm going straight to bed."

She put her arm through mine. "If you nice to Antonela, then Antonela be nice to you. Tell you something interesting."

"What's that supposed to mean?"

"I don't know for sure but I have good idea who might have necklace."

This was getting interesting. "If I killed her husband then wouldn't I have the necklace too?"

She smiled. "Is two different crimes. I no believe you would steal jewels."

"Why not?"

"I think you care about old woman. Is why you kill husband, and if you care about old woman then I think you care about her jewels."

"So, tell me. Who has them?"

She smiled mischievously.

"We talk in my room."

I thought it over for a few seconds. She was a trained police officer and I was curious as to what she knew or speculated. "Tell me your room number. I have to do something first. I'll meet you later."

Chapter 17

Arriving at my cabin close to midnight, I found Betsy sleeping peacefully, and I quietly rummaged through my clothes looking for the room key she had given me. Eventually, I discovered it in the pocket of the trousers I had worn to that first dinner on the ship. I had decided to take a closer look at the crime scene. Not that I didn't trust the captain to perform an adequate investigation. He was a competent officer but I was a criminal or at least I used to be. I had one felony conviction and a long list of near misses but that was all in the past. Medicine had saved my life. The net effect was that I had a unique way of looking at things.

I whispered good night to Betsy and just as quietly left her. A few minutes later, I let myself into her suite. She had left her stuff in her room for the time being and except for the carpet being cleaned of any bloodstains everything was just as it was the night of the murder. The bed was made and everything was in order. I tried to put myself in the mindset of the killer. He was waiting for them in the room when they came home from that night's revelry. Wait a minute. That was the first rub. She told me that the lock was specially designed to trigger an alarm if not accessed properly. Did the assailant have her key and how did he get it? How many keys were there anyway? Housekeeping had a key. What about the ship's security? Was there a master key somewhere? Good questions.

Okay, next. Where would I hide? Betsy wasn't sure where he was when they entered the room. She and Roger were tired and had been drinking. The room was dark...pitch black. They turned the light on and he was on them it seemed, almost instantly. The room was big but not that big. The closet was an option. Under the bed? No. Maybe he was just standing behind the door? Possibly. The bathroom? Yes, that made sense, especially if he was going to have to wait for an unspecified period of time for them. He'd want to be comfortable and at least he could sit down in there.

I walked over to the bathroom and flipped on the light, searching for any clues, a cigarette butt, gum wrapper, anything to suggest a human presence other than Betsy's toiletries. The counter was empty and suddenly I wondered where the fake necklace was. Did the thief take that too? Of course he would have. He wouldn't have known it was fake.

Then it hit me. If I entered someone's room illegally to rob them and found a necklace like that fortuitously sitting out in the open, would I still sit around waiting for the occupants to return? That wasn't an ordinary necklace. Any moron could see it was worth millions. Even the fake was of extraordinary quality and would be worth thousands in its own right. He would have snatched it and run as fast as he could unless he knew the real one would be along any minute, but how would that be possible? Why would he take the fake one too? Or did he? Betsy never said and I didn't think to ask.

Coming here had raised a lot of questions in my mind about what happened that night. My cellphone buzzed breaking my concentration. It was Vito.

He whispered, "Cesari, where are you?"

"Where do you think? On the boat."

"I know that but where? I need help."

"Where are you?"

"I'm on the ship somewhere. I don't know where exactly."

"Slow down. What do you mean you're on the ship? It's on lock down and we're about to leave port."

"I was on the dock waiting to see what was going to happen. They started offloading these gigantic garbage containers when I noticed that two of the crew pushed one off to the side and just kind of left it there in the darkest part of the port. I thought that was strange so I went in closer for a better look when all of sudden the top pops open and a sailor climbs out with a duffle bag. He took off at a run and I made a snap decision."

Sven, the ship's doctor, going to fight for his wife. I was proud of him, but wondered what the legal ramifications would be for me if my involvement ever came out. I said, "You thought if he could get off that way then you could get on…?"

"You don't have to be a genius to figure out that somebody was going AWOL and had paid off his buddies to help him. I figured that sooner or later they'd come back for the container, so I hopped in quick. Trouble is they locked the cover and I can't get out. It stinks in here."

"Hang tight. I'm coming."

"Hurry."

I clicked off and went to the main deck just as the lights of Dubrovnik faded slowly in the distance. There were quite a few passengers out and about strolling hand in hand or leaning against the railing with cocktails and wine. I ran into a crew member emptying a trash container and asked some reasonable questions about garbage disposal onboard and was told that the main collection of refuse was on the lower level not far from the engine rooms. The ship was basically a self-contained floating city and they got rid of as much trash as they could at each port to prevent build-up.

I took the elevators to the lowest level and noticed the temperature rose by at least ten degrees and the noise level by several decibels. The roar and grinding of the engines filled the sub-compartment and scattered, sweaty crew members working the night shift busied themselves with their tasks. Oddly, there were no security measures for preventing wayward or overly curious passengers from looking around the ship. It was easy to keep out of sight though, and I did my best, sticking to the shadows and slithering behind large machinery and pipes as I made my way toward the garbage hold.

Eventually, I found a garage-sized door with a sign reading *Waste Management* overhead. I looked both ways and entered slowly. Relieved that it wasn't locked and there was no one around, I turned on an overhead light. The room was quite large, filled with dozens of over-sized dumpsters on wheels. Each was ten feet long by six feet wide by five feet tall. The covers had simple latch engagement locks on their sides. With over a hundred containers, this could take a while to find him.

I pulled out my cellphone but had no reception bars. Whether this was because of our location below deck behind the steel hull of the ship or because we were now beyond the reach of Dubrovnik's cell towers I wasn't sure. A metal broom for sweeping up debris leaned against the wall. I picked it up and started walking around rapping on the sides of each container, calling out his name as I did. Halfway through the room I got lucky and he banged from the inside and called to me.

Opening the top he stuck his head out gasping for air, I noticed he was red-faced and drenched in perspiration. I realized then how much hotter it must have been inside.

Sucking wind, he said, "God damn, it's hot in here. Help me get out."

"Do I look like I have a ladder on me? How'd you get in?"

"I just hopped over it like it was a fence."

"Well, do the same thing."

"Thanks. How about giving me a break? I've been sitting in a ninety degree can covered in stench for the last two hours."

"Oh please, spare me the whining. C'mon you're wasting time. Jump up and throw your leg over and I'll help you on this end."

He grabbed onto the edge of the container and leapt upward throwing his leg over the side. Being hot, irritable, and impatient by nature, he flung his 260 pounds over the side with too much force and too quickly. I didn't have the chance to stabilize him and because of his size, I was forced to step out of the way or risk serious injury. He hit the floor with a thud and a grunt. He rolled once and lay there staring at the ceiling.

"You are such an asshole, Cesari."

"Are you all right?"

He held his right hand out and grimaced. "No, I hurt my finger. Help me up."

I grabbed his extended hand and I pulled him up. He reeked. "Next time give me a chance to brace myself."

"There ain't going to be no next time. Damn, I'm bleeding. I'm going to need a doctor."

"I am a doctor, remember? Let me see that."

He showed me his index finger. He had the tiniest of cuts with maybe half a drop of blood oozing out of it. I pushed his hand away dismissively. "It's nothing. You'll be fine. Anyway, what's the idea behind this little move? You had a legitimate ticket and now you're a stowaway."

"Do I look like I give a rat's ass? Besides, why should I have to pay to go to some freakin' Greek island to catch the ship? I paid to get on in Dubrovnik and that's what I did. Besides, who knows if they'll even let anyone on there?"

He had a point. There was no telling what was going to happen when we reached the next port. "Where's your luggage?"

He gave me a funny look and then glanced back at the dumpster. I said, "How stupid can you be? You couldn't just hand it to me first?"

"I was hot."

I shook my head in exasperation as I stepped near the container to peer in. His suitcase was lying flat in the middle of it, out of arms reach. I said, "You're a piece of work. Did you know that?"

Hopping up, I hoisted myself to straddle the side of the dumpster and grabbed his hand. "You better not let go."

With a mischievous grin he said, "Why would I do that?"

Leaning over one side with Vito acting as a counter balance, I stretched down as far as I could and was able to just grasp the handle of his suitcase. It was heavy and I guessed it weighed at least fifty pounds. I dragged it up, handed it to him and jumped back down. I was a little winded, and scrunched my nose. The smell in the dumpster was ferocious.

I said, "C'mon let's go."

"Do you have an extra bed or cot for me to sleep on."

"You can't sleep in my room. I have a guest."

He smiled. "Are you kidding? You're unbelievable. People are getting knocked off, diamonds are being stolen, but nothing slows you down. So who is she?"

I hesitated for second as we left the garbage room and looked around. We kept walking and I said, "The wife of the dead guy. The one I told you I was...you know."

He was incredulous and rolled his eyes. "You have got to be joking. She's in your room? Like for the night? I mean the guy just croaked. I know you told me you were doing her but I just assumed his death would have put a damper on that."

"I know, but she insisted."

"Wow, that's pretty weird. Is she hot, at least?"

"She's very attractive in an..." I cleared my throat, "...an older sort of way."

He raised his eyebrows. "Older? How much older?"

I was dreading this moment. "I told you she and her husband owned the ship or at least most of it."

"So what's that mean?"

"Well, you don't get to own ships like this when you're in your twenties. He was in his late sixties, maybe early seventies."

"Fine, but from the way you phrased it, I just assumed that she was a twenty-five-year-old bimbo who married him for his money. How old is she?"

Sighing deeply, I said, "Well, she's not a twenty-five-year-old bimbo. She's old enough to..."

"To what...?"

"To be your..."

Catching on to where I was heading with this he dropped the suitcase and put his hands over his ears, suddenly very agitated. "Don't say it. I swear to God if you say it I will effin' kill you. This is so sick...even for you."

"Will you relax? She's in her sixties and she's really nice."

He shuddered. "I can't believe you. You are so twisted."

"Look, get it out of your system because we have to think about where you're going to stay."

He picked up his bag and shook his large head. "Fine, I was counting on staying with you but I didn't realize you had necromaniac tendencies."

I counted to five so as not to let him get to me and calmly said, "Put it behind you, all right?"

"Fine. Where am I going to stay?"

"I have the key to her room. No one will expect anyone to be staying there, and since I don't have a better idea..."

"Oh, that's just great."

"It will be fine. The bloodstains have been cleaned up. She still has her stuff there though, but I'll offer to bring it all back to my cabin so she doesn't make any surprise visits and find you."

He reluctantly agreed to my plan although I didn't see that he had any other option. By the time I settled him into Betsy's room it was almost 3:00 a.m. and I was wiped out physically. I decided it was too late to visit Antonela even though I was extremely curious about who she thought had the necklace.

Chapter 18

I sipped my coffee and looked across the table at Betsy who nibbled on a fresh-baked blueberry muffin. Her hair was up in a white bath towel.

"Did you sleep well?" I asked.

"I did indeed. Like a rock. I didn't even hear you come to bed. When did you get in?"

"A little after midnight. I played a little black jack at the casino."

"Did you win anything?"

"No, I'm pissed. Lost twenty dollars."

"That's not bad. I lost about twenty million in jewelry."

I grinned. "So you know how it feels."

She chuckled and nodded.

"What's on the agenda today?" I asked.

"I think I should go make the rounds and thank people for caring. Quite a few of the guests are regulars on this cruise and have socialized with Roger and me often. They will be worried and come here anyway. What about you?"

"Just whiling away my time. Maybe I'll start off the day with a massage, then caviar for lunch, and then a Grey Goose martini with a twist. Now that I'm thinking about it, maybe I'll just skip the massage and caviar and head down to the bar for an after breakfast martini. I'm not sure yet."

She grinned. "You do a great imitation of the idle rich in the *Great Gatsby*."

I poured more coffee into my cup. "Are you a fan of F. Scott Fitzgerald?"

"Who isn't? He was a great man."

"Good point. Although if you read about his life it's hard not to feel that he was a bit of a hypocrite."

"How so?"

"Well, *The Great Gatsby,* Fitzgerald's magnum opus as it were, was a harsh critique, even a rebuke, of American wealth and decadence in the1920's and yet he wrote the bulk of it while living it up, sipping champagne, and dining on foie gras every night along the French Riviera."

She seemed fascinated by this revelation. "Did he really?"

"Yes, and although *The Great Gatsby* is now widely accepted to be a literary classic and generally considered the quintessential, "Great American Novel", it wasn't always so. In fact, when it was first published it did very poorly both in sales and critical reviews. So poorly, in fact, that at the time of his death in 1940, Fitzgerald considered it a failure."

"My oh my, but you are a fountain of information."

I smiled. "Well, I cling to stories like that just in case I ever decide to become a writer."

She liked that. "Is that a possibility?"

"Everything's a possibility."

"What kind of book would you write?"

"I'm pretty sure I have a great sex novel inside me somewhere desperate to spill out onto the pages."

Laughing, she said, "No, I think you're a Great Gatsby kind of guy."

"Maybe. When I get home I might start wearing my tuxedo every day for inspiration."

"Your patients will love that."

"I'm sure. I'm a bit eccentric as it is and I tend to attract eccentric patients."

"Do you?"

"I collect nuts like a squirrel."

Laughing again, she put her cup down on the table. "You have a delightful sense of humor."

"Thank you for pretending to find me amusing."

"I'm not pretending. You really are. Well, if you ever do decide to write a book, you must let me know. I have many contacts in the publishing industry."

"Thanks, but that would kind of be like cheating. If I wrote a book, I'd like it to be recognized because of the quality of its content, not because of who I know."

She gave me a patronizing look. "You're charming but incredibly naive."

"Am I?"

"It's just not the way the world works."

"But it's the way I work. I believe that the cream will always rise to the top and that a society that is not built upon merit will crumble on its foundation."

Looking wistful, she stared at me for a long moment and said, "It's been a long time since I met someone as idealistic as you." She let out a deep breath. "Well, I should get dressed and get an early start."

"Are you sure you want to do this?"

She nodded and sighed. "If I don't go to them, they're going to come to me. So…"

"It could get uncomfortable."

"You mean because of you?"

"Yes. Women can be cruel. I know what they're whispering behind my back and in front of my face."

She smiled and nodded. "They are opinionated creatures, aren't they? I know about women's cruelty better than anyone, but I'm not a frightened schoolgirl and you shouldn't be either. If I want the company of a male friend for support then they'll just have to deal with it. Besides, those who really know me well are already aware of my distant relationship with Roger."

"All right then. I'll finish breakfast while you get dressed. I'll walk you to your first stop."

She smiled. "That's sweet, but my first stop will be the captain's quarters. That might not be the best place for us to show up together. He's very understanding but I'd rather not push his compassion to the limit."

I agreed. "Then I'll head to the ship's infirmary and say hello to the staff and see if there are any patients for me to see. It's about time I earned my keep on this bucket."

"That's the spirit."

"Maybe later I can go to your room and get the rest of your belongings and bring them here?"

"Would you do that for me? I'd just as soon not go there myself just yet—maybe never. I can't even imagine being in that room again. The memory is so strong."

She got all choked up thinking about it and I said, "I wouldn't mind at all. I'll bring everything here. I assume you have luggage there I can use. I'll be as neat as I can."

"Just throw everything in the suitcases that are in the walk-in closet. I'll sort it all out here. Thank you. I appreciate your concern, John. You're such a dear."

"My pleasure, Betsy. If there's anything else I can do, don't hesitate to let me know."

"Thank you."

She finished her coffee and went to the bathroom, closing the door behind her. I finished mine too, dabbed my lips with a napkin, and straightened my hair in the mirror. I was tucking my shirt in my pants when I heard a gentle rapping on the balcony door. Turning with a start, I saw Katarina peering through the glass. I glanced quickly toward the bathroom door to make sure it was closed and then raced over to Katarina with my index finger over my mouth to hush her.

Stepping outside I whispered, "What are you doing?"

She threw her arms around me and kissed me passionately. "I miss my boyfriend."

I pushed her away. "I understand, but you need to be sympathetic. The woman's husband just died. This is a delicate situation. I don't want to hurt her feelings and create anymore controversy for her. If somebody sees you climbing over the balconies to come here the rumor mills will be working over time."

"What means rumor mills? Never mind. I don't care. She is whore. Everybody on ship knows it."

"Stop that. You're making me angry. Now, you have to go. I'll meet you for lunch somewhere. There's a salad place on the same deck as the casino. I'll see you there at noon, okay?"

"Not okay. I need more than just salad."

"Well, that's all you're getting today. My dance card's all full."

I heard a sound from inside the room and heard Betsy call out for me. I pushed Katarina to a corner of the balcony out of sight from the room unless you came right up to the door. She slipped her arms around me and hung on tight, preventing me from returning to the room, and not wishing to make any noise, I stood there paralyzed.

Betsy called for me again and guessing that I had left, returned to the bathroom. I peeked inside and saw that she had left the door open this time.

Shit.

I looked at Katarina. "She left the bathroom door open."

"So?"

"If I go inside now, she'll see me and know I was hiding out here from her and then she'll wonder why."

"Who cares? Tell her you with girlfriend."

"Stop. I don't want to hurt her. Got that?"

She rolled her eyes. "But you don't mind hurting Katarina?"

"You can handle it. She's grieving."

"Humph."

Letting out a deep breath, I looked around thinking through the problem at hand. Betsy wasn't going to stick around much longer, but that could mean upwards to half an hour or more in women's time. Too long for me to be in a clench with Katarina, and there was always the possibility she might come onto the balcony for one last breath of fresh air before she left. I whispered, "We have two choices. We can either wait for her to leave or climb over the balconies. I don't like the idea of waiting."

"Then we climb balconies together. Is very romantic."

I looked over the side and wondered what it would feel like to land in the water from about eight or nine stories up. Probably not pleasant assuming I didn't hit one of the lower decks on the way down.

Sensing my hesitancy, she said, "Is very easy."

"Yes, of course," I said wryly.

"But is easy. Just do as I do."

"I'm not as lithe as you."

"What mean lithe?"

"Nimble, flexible."

She nodded, "I go first. I help."

Without waiting for my approval, she hoisted herself onto the four-foot metal railing and balanced herself against the supporting pole bracing the divider between my balcony and the next. Swinging one leg around the pole she obtained a foothold on our neighbors railing and jumped onto their balcony. She made it look effortless.

Leaning around from my neighbor's balcony, she said, "Hurry. I help."

She extended her hand and I climbed awkwardly onto the railing wondering what would happen if the people in the next stateroom suddenly came out to sunbathe. They'd probably call the ship's security.

Clinging nervously to the support pole, I glanced over my shoulder at the water below, shuddered and closed my eyes for a moment before proceeding. I wasn't big on heights and except for my bedroom escapades rarely embraced new experiences.

I looked at Katarina and realized my heart was racing and I was holding my breath. She stood there waiting patiently her hand outstretched. I would have to step around the support pole and lean in her direction before I could jump down. My brain told me it was a very short distance and I had nothing to worry about, but my anxiety told me I was stepping off a cliff.

She whispered, "Give me your hand. What wait for?"

Frozen in place, panic starting to creep into my consciousness, I stared at her with a blank look and didn't say anything. She repeated with some urgency, "Take my hand. Don't be scared."

Too late for that. Why'd she have to say that anyway? The last time a girl told me to take her hand and not be scared I was fifteen, and Gina Louisa Rigoletto, a seventeen-year-old senior in my high school, invited me up to her room to show me a "new game". When her alcoholic father burst into the room cursing me in Sicilian, I nearly broke my neck when I fell down the stairs trying to get out of there. I limped for a week from a sprained ankle and had a headache from getting hit in the head with a bible my mother threw at me when she found out.

Yeah, I was scared and hugged the pole in front of me tightly. I was almost to the point of stepping back down and taking my chances with Betsy when Katarina grabbed my hand, and started tugging on me insistently. The thought of struggling with her on such a precarious perch made me even more anxious. Our eyes met, and for the first time, I thought I saw a hint of maturity in her empathetic gaze.

Very softly she whispered, "It will be all right. I no let fall."

Nodding, I looked down at the water one more time, and grasped her hand firmly. With her encouragement I curled around the pole to the other balcony and clumsily jumped down almost knocking her off her feet. I stood breathless and trembling, my heart pounding in my head. My neighbor's balcony doors were closed and their blinds drawn. We quickly went to the other side and hid in their blind spot. I tried to regroup while Katarina held me. My legs were jelly and I didn't think there was any way I was going to be able to do that again.

Shaking my head, I said, "I can't do it."

"Just one more and there is ladder."

"A ladder?"

"Yes, goes up and down for emergency. We go up. Find my room."

We looked at each other for a full minute before I said, "One more?"

"One more."

I took a deep breath. "One more and I go to the hospital infirmary, not your room."

Using the same technique, but with slightly less trepidation, we made our way to the next balcony and eventually onto a narrow metal ladder which appeared to run all the way from the top down to the main deck. Probably used for maintenance, I surmised. We clambered up to her deck and much to my dismay found out that I still had to climb across an additional two balconies until we finally reached her room. Once there, I threw myself down onto one of her recliners, breathless and drenched in sweat as she walked toward the door.

Suddenly, I didn't think that was such a great idea and whispered, "Don't open it. What if Berislav is inside?"

She looked at her watch and shook her head. "Berislav drink again last night. No wake up until noon. Always same thing."

I sat up in anticipation. She continued, "I go in. If his room closed, I signal you and we leave quick, yes? Maybe go promenade? Play shuffleboard?"

"I told you I have things to do."

She didn't answer me and opened the balcony door, disappearing inside. A moment later, she returned and waved for me the coast was clear. I entered the room and made a bee line for the door and just as I reached it saw the handle jiggle in frustration and heard a male voice curse from the other side.

Turning to Katarina, I saw her eyes go wide with apprehension. She whispered urgently, "My bedroom, quick."

We both raced to her room, closing the door behind us, just as Berislav entered the living room calling out for Katarina. She turned to me. "Under the bed. Quick."

I went to one side of the bed and slid myself underneath. To my surprise she slid underneath as well from the other side. We scrunched up next to each other and I glanced at her with a puzzled look.

She said, "I leave note for Berislav I spend morning at spa. If find here, he know I lie."

I shook my head but didn't have time to worry about her incessant lying. The door to her bedroom opened and from under the bed I saw two men walk in. Berislav said, "Katarina?"

Brad said, "This is her room, huh?"

"Yes, but she at spa. Get massage. We can talk freely. Come let us sit."

They walked back to the main living area, leaving the door open a crack. I wiggled to get out and Katarina grabbed me, shaking her head and hissing, "No. Stay."

I got real close to her ear. "I want to hear what they're talking about."

She relented and let go of me. I quietly slid out from under the bed and on hands and knees crawled over to the door peering furtively around it. They were sitting on the sofa facing away.

Berislav had poured them something to drink and they clinked highball glasses. He said, "Here's to new friends and business partners."

Brad concurred and they took a sip from their glasses. Brad said, "I'll have the buy-in for you in just a day or so. I'm working on something but I have every confidence it will turn in my favor."

"I hope. I like you very much and think you will make good partner for Berislav, but unfortunately I cannot hold off other investors for more than a day or two. Already, they breathe fire down my neck."

"I understand. I'm a businessman as well. So, tell me, if all goes well, when will the project begin?"

"Yes, once final approval comes through from Croatian government, we break ground for new private cancer treatment center in Dubrovnik maybe less than six months. Take one year to build and then we roll in dough, yes?"

"Sounds great, but I can't believe they're letting you compete against the state run hospitals there."

"Is loophole in law of Croatia. As long as no call ourselves hospital and no apply to government for aid then can do anything we want. People sick of cockroach-infested government hospital, come to Dubrovnik Cancer Center. Beautiful marble floors, pretty nurses, we hire only models. Put on pretty uniforms, yes? Everybody happy."

"But I run a hospital. It's expensive. Doctors, supplies, chemotherapy, CAT scans, MRIs, etcetera. The profit margin is minuscule."

"No need for all that. Is Europe, not America. People here expect to die when get sick. So, instead of spend money on expensive tests and medicines, give money Berislav and I make last days happy ones."

Brad thought over the implication of that and then grinned broadly. "I like your style and you're right. But I do have a question though…?"

"Yes?"

"People have expectations. When they come to your center aren't you going to have to do tests, give medications, and you know...treat them?"

"And we do…sort of…maybe. Buy old machines, cost less, maybe no work too good. Find doctors who say what we want. Nothing more to do. Give sugar water, charge for chemotherapy. Is easy. Pretty nurse, short skirt, clean rooms, good food. No one know. No one care. People die. Is unfortunate, but have cancer, yes?"

Brad slapped his knee. "Berislav, you are my kind of guy. You would have made a great CEO."

"Maybe even make you CEO of center, million dollar a year salary. Why not?"

"Why not indeed? Who would know better than me how to cook the books? I've been doing it for years anyway for peanuts. Might as well get paid what I deserve."

"You are right. Is settled. You will be CEO of new Dubrovnik Cancer Center. Best part is this. Once build, start making money, we sell to big corporation. Make fortune, maybe ten times investment. Take three year, maybe four year, tops."

"And you've done this before?"

"Many times. All over Balkans and eastern Europe."

"Man, I can't believe how lucky I am that I met you when I did. I'll come up with the capital for you. I promise. I have a deal going down and I should know soon. One thing though, I may not have access to that much cash but something just as valuable to use as collateral. Will that be all right?"

"Collateral? What kind of collateral? Deal was for cash."

"Trust me Berislav, you'll be very pleased, and if it's worth more than what you need, you can keep the rest."

"What is?"

"It would be best if I kept that my secret for the moment."

"I am very disappoint, but I trust you."

So that's what Brad wants the necklace for. He was smart enough not to try to keep it for himself. I sensed a presence next to me and saw that Katarina had crawled up close and was listening. She looked very apprehensive. I put my finger over my lips and she nodded. I had to admit, Berislav was smooth as silk. After listening to him for a few more minutes I was almost ready to buy into his scheme myself. I needed a plan. We couldn't just sit there the rest of the day. It was almost 11:00 a.m. and I heard Berislav pour Brad another round. They were settling in. They must have cast iron stomachs to drink this early in the day. Either that or I needed to train harder.

Katarina inched close and whispered, "What we do?"

I looked around the room for a way out. There was a decent-sized window with pretty curtains. "Does that open?"

"Of course, but you no like where go."

I grabbed her hand and we crawled closer to it and I said, "Why not?"

"Because look."

Glancing quickly toward the living room, I stood and peered outside. The window didn't open onto the balcony as I had hoped. We were at least ten feet from the railing. I looked straight down the side of the ship into the water. There were small metal projections from the ship that could possibly provide sturdy foot and hand holds, but I wasn't sure that I had the stomach for it. I sighed deeply.

Katarina read my mind. "Not sure I like odds."

"Me neither. Under the bed. We need to talk."

We slid under the bed together where I felt marginally more relaxed. Side by side, we looked at each other. She was smiling and I whispered, "I hope you're having fun."

She suppressed a giggle and nodded.

Great.

"Look, we have to create a diversion. The way they're drinking out there, they might be there for hours. Do you understand?"

She snuggled in real close. "Kiss me."

I was shocked. "No, this isn't a game. They're plotting serious crimes."

Smiling seductively, she persisted. "Never make love under bed before. Might be fun."

I couldn't help myself and let out a soft chuckle. "You're crazy. Did you know that?"

"Kiss me or I scream."

"You're not going to scream."

She leaned her face close to mine and kissed me. Gently, with passion, not rough like she had the other night. She looked me in the eyes and I said, "That was very nice."

"Is that how old woman do it?"

"Leave her alone."

"I have idea."

"I'm listening."

"First make promise."

"What kind of promise?"

"If idea work then you make love Katarina tonight."

"Will you stop. I'm not going to promise that. Do you have any idea how stressed I am?"

"Then fine. We stay here all day until Berislav pass out."

She turned her gaze to stare up at the bottom of the bed. I said, "You can't be serious? That is not a reasonable request."

"Is what I want."

"Fine, then we'll stay here all day."

"Fine."

We both lay there staring at the bedsprings. After a few minutes, I let out a deep breath and turned toward her. "I don't like being ordered around especially when it comes to that."

She turned to face me and without any remorse said, "Then just do what I say."

Unbelievable!

I felt my face turning red with anger. "Fine. Tonight then, but only if your idea works."

Thoroughly pleased with herself she smiled. "Okay. This is plan. I call concierge and ask deliver message to Berislav to meet midget in casino. Is urgent. He much too afraid of her to refuse."

"Midget? You mean that gangster, Antonela?"

"Yes."

I thought it over. It might work. "The concierge would do that? He won't ask questions?"

She suppressed a giggle. "Of course not. Is how married men get away from wives all the time; have concierge call them. Must be your first cruise?"

"It is my first cruise, but how do *you* know so much about how married men evade their wives?"

She was quiet for a moment, and I thought she was blushing. She shrugged and said, "I watch American TV?"

She was killing me. "Yeah, I bet. Okay, get the phone off the night table and make the call, but very quietly, all right?"

Chapter 19

It worked like a charm. Berislav and Brad left in a hurry as soon as the message arrived.

"Man, he really is afraid of her." Having met Antonela, I didn't blame him.

Katarina looked proud of herself. "Is what I say."

"Are there a lot of girl gangsters in Croatia?"

She shrugged. "Don't know, but know this; they are much meaner. At least with men, I can smile, talk, you know? Girl gangsters—forget it. All business."

I smiled at that. For a woman like Katarina, not being able to flirt her way out of trouble had to be very frustrating. "Interesting. Well look, I have to go now. We'll catch up later."

I had many things to do starting with going to the ship's infirmary to see if they needed anything. Katarina had wanted to come with me to make sure the female employees there knew I was taken, but I put the kibosh on that even going so far as to threaten to renege on my promise. Reluctantly, she decided to go to her spa treatment albeit a few hours late for her original appointment. There was still a good chance I was going to renege, but that was life in the fast lane. If she wanted to be a Cesari girl, then she was going to have to start learning the rules. Smiling as I walked, I tried consoling myself with the notion that she could possibly be tamed, but I had the sneaking suspicion that it might not happen in my life time.

The ship's medical center was located on deck 2 and was relatively small with just two exam rooms. There was a curmudgeonly, middle-aged receptionist who looked at me over her glasses and a pleasant forty-year old male nurse named Erik. The nurse practitioner was in a room seeing a patient when I got there so I introduced myself and wandered around the facility checking things out. Eventually, I settled into a leather chair in the nurse practitioner's office playing with a pen on her desk. A few minutes passed, and hearing a sound, I looked up.

A gorgeous woman with shoulder length soft brown hair and stylish, black framed eye glasses walked in. In her early thirties, she wore a white lab coat, stylish shoes, and a stethoscope tucked in one pocket. She entered the room like a model on a runway, one foot in front of the other.

With a mild French accent she said, "Allo, you must be Dr. Cesari. The captain told me you would be coming by. My name is Aimée."

I stood to greet her, and was mesmerized by her beauty. Only the French would wear short skirts and high heels to see patients. When I didn't say anything, she added, "Are you all right?"

Recovering, I said, "Yes, I'm fine. I'm Dr. Cesari. It's a pleasure to meet you, Aimée. Forgive me, I was expecting someone…"

"Older?"

I smiled. "Different."

She liked that and smiled back. "Well, as long as you are here, may I ask your advice?"

"You can ask me whatever you want."

She took a step toward me, offering her hand. I took it and quickly checked for a wedding ring. There was none. She said, "Thank you. There is an older woman in the exam room complaining that the skin under her right breast is burning but I see nothing. Except for hypertension, which is under control today, she is in good health."

She was close enough now that I could feel the pull of her electromagnetic field. Trillions upon trillions of electrons spinning around their orbits at 2200 kilometers per second or just over 1366 miles per second, fast enough to circle the earth in 18 seconds. Each one of them pulling at my electrons. I said, "How about we go see her together. The captain didn't ask me to take care of patients long distance."

"Let us go then."

The exam room was just across the hall from her office and was an efficient ten by ten room. Sitting on the exam table was a gray-haired woman, Graciella Lourdes, who was in her mid-seventies and carried it well. She had a cloth exam gown draped around her and Aimée introduced me.

"I'm sorry you're not feeling well, Mrs. Lourdes. Could you please tell me in your own words what's bothering you and for how long?"

She was American and spoke with a slight south-western twang. "I feel a burning sensation that wraps around from my back to the front underneath my right breast. It's been getting worse ever since we left Venice. It feels like my skin is on fire and even the touch of my clothing hurts."

"May I take a look?"

"Certainly, but please don't touch. It hurts. I'll point to where the pain is."

"That's fine. I'll be very careful."

She lifted the gown, raised up her breast, and using her index finger and thumb gently traced a two-inch band that swept around from back to front. She watched me guardedly as I inspected the area. There was nothing there.

I thought it over for a moment and said, "Mrs. Lourdes, you can cover up now. I think you probably have shingles. Have you ever heard of that?"

"Yes, I have. In fact, a friend of mine had it last year, but she had a rash. It was terrible."

"Yes, the rash will probably appear in a day or two, but it frequently starts just like this. This sensation you're experiencing is referred to as a painful paresthesia, which is an irritation of the nerve ending. The nerve comes out of the spinal cord and wraps around to the front in what we call a dermatome. You described it perfectly. It is caused by a virus known as varicella which is the virus associated with chicken pox."

"Chicken pox? The childhood illness?"

"Exactly. We acquire the virus as a child but as the illness clears the virus can remain dormant in our nerve endings, and then, unfortunately it can re-activate many years later as shingles. We'll check the pharmacy but I'm sure they'll have a medication which should help. It's called Acyclovir."

She let out a deep sigh and seemed apprehensive. "How long will it last? My friend was in pain for months."

"Unfortunately, that can happen sometimes. More commonly, however, the rash usually resolves after two to four weeks. As you are already aware, there can be a fair amount of pain involved, but shouldn't get much worse than it is now. If it does, we can prescribe analgesics for you."

She nodded and said wryly, "Nice way to begin a vacation."

"I'm sorry for that."

"It's not your fault. Thank you. You're very nice. Say, aren't you that doctor friend of Betsy's?"

I hesitated slightly. "That would be me."

"I don't know if you're aware of this, but people are saying all sorts of nasty things about you."

Glancing sideways at Aimée, I saw her raise her eyebrows in surprise. "Why would anyone say anything mean about me?" I asked innocently.

She narrowed her eyes and smiled. "Please, doctor, I've been around too long, and I don't really care. God bless her is all I can say. Why should the young girls have all the fun?"

I grinned. "Why don't you get dressed, and Aimée will get your medication for you."

Aimée and I walked back to her office. She said, "Thank you for your help. I am impressed. The captain told me that you were a gastroenterologist but that was a nifty piece of primary care you just performed."

Smiling and thoroughly pleased with myself I said, "It was nothing. I'm really looking forward to working with you. How many patients do you see in a day?"

"Not many at all, five or six usually. Some days none at all. Remember, it is a cruise ship. Most of the older patients check in with their doctors before coming on board. It's the diarrheal outbreaks that keep us the most busy when they occur. Fortunately, it has not happened this season at all." She hesitated and seemed uncomfortable before adding, "What was she talking about in there?"

"Oh that. You know how people are. If you talk too much with one person over dinner everybody starts spreading rumors about it."

She laughed and accepted my sidestep of the question. "Yes, that is very true. People love to gossip. It is a cross-cultural, multi-racial phenomena. In all my travels, I have never been to a place where people did not engage in gossip."

"How long have you been working on this ship, Aimée?"

"This is my third season and I really love it." She became sad when she said that and continued. "So did Sven. I hope he is all right."

"I think he'll be fine."

"No one knows where he is. There is speculation, he may have jumped overboard. He was very upset over his wife. I feel so bad for him. He was such a nice man."

"Let's keep our fingers crossed he didn't do anything rash. So…when you're not on duty do you ever socialize? Like eat or drink or take walks around the promenade with tall, dark, and ruggedly handsome men?"

She smiled, "Sometimes. In fact, a man who fits that description exactly was here just an hour ago and invited me to dinner. He was a big tough man, but was such a baby. He had the tiniest of cuts on his index finger and made such a big deal about it. All he needed was a band aid. I almost did not accept his offer for dinner, but I found him somewhat irresistible in a roguish sort of way. Interestingly, he sounded just like you. The accent, I mean. Plus, he was such an odd sight, wearing a silk suit and tie in the early morning on a cruise ship."

Vito!

"I see. Well, if you're occupied this evening then some other time perhaps?"

She sighed uncomfortably. "Maybe it would be best if we kept our relationship strictly professional? Otherwise, working together may be difficult."

"Of course. You're right. That was silly of me."

"You do not mind?"

"Not at all. It makes perfect sense."

She seemed genuinely relieved. "I'm glad. You seem very mature. I like that quality in a man."

I heard the whirring sound of her electrons. "That's me. Very mature. Well, I guess I'll be going then, I have a patient to take care of elsewhere on the ship."

"You do?"

"Yes, I'm afraid that this trip wasn't one hundred percent vacation for me."

"Can I be of any help?"

I hesitated and said, "I…I'm not sure if I should say anything."

"Please, I do not want you to betray anyone's confidence."

I sighed deeply as if the weight of the world was on my shoulders. "No, it's okay. It will do me good to get it off my chest. I'm actually on this ship to keep an eye on my cousin. My mother's only sister's son. He's in the late stages of tertiary syphilis, which he contracted from a prostitute back in New York. He's failed all treatment and it's beginning to affect his mind. In fact, he frequently forgets he has the disease. My aunt Norma asked me to keep him company on the cruise not just for his sake, but to make sure he doesn't, you know…infect anyone. It's not that he means any harm, he just can't help himself. The doctors think he's a victim of sexual addiction. He'll have sex with just about anyone or anything. It's a terrible burden on his mother. Her neighbors complain that their pets act strange around him as if they're afraid.

"One of the reasons I agreed to fill in for Sven as the ship's doctor was so I could treat his victims discreetly in case he ever got out of my sight." I covered my face with my hands. "It's actually quite exhausting chasing him around. He goes after every girl he sees. It doesn't matter to him what they look like or what kind of person they are. By the way, I should have asked. Do we have penicillin for injection? We'll need quite a bit, I expect. The last cruise we were on, we ran out in the middle of the Atlantic."

She saw how distraught I was and moved close, placing an arm around me. "Don't worry. We have plenty of penicillin, but how awful to put that kind of responsibility on you."

"I don't mind. I would do anything for family and Vito is like a brother to me."

She stepped back aghast. "His name is Vito?!"

"Yes, my cousin, Vito."

"Oh my God. Is he a big man?"

"Yes, he's a gigantic man, with black, wavy hair, sharp features, a big nose…very Italian looking, always wears a suit…Oh no! You said that man who asked you to dinner wore a suit and tie."

"That was him. He is the one with the cut on his finger. I cannot believe it. He looked so healthy."

I looked shocked. "Maybe it wasn't him. My cousin always wears a fake diamond Rolex watch and other gaudy costume jewelry to impress inexperienced women."

"Yes, there can be no doubt. He was dressed just as you describe."

I looked down in shame. "That's why he fools so many women. I can't believe he targeted you. I just warned him last night to try to remember how contagious he is, but he can't help himself. It's the disease eating away at his brain. I'm so sorry. I'll talk to him. He didn't mean any harm. I swear it. Please don't report him to security."

"Oh my. I won't. How terrible this has to be for you."

"It is. It really is. I'll go find him. You don't have to say anything to him. I'll handle it. In fact, if you see him again don't bring it up. Don't even go near him. As his mental condition has deteriorated over the last year he has been prone to fits of intense rage when he doesn't get his way."

She let out a deep breath. "I feel so sorry for you."

"It's okay. Every family has their deep, dark secrets."

She nodded, "Yes, they do."

As I turned to leave she gently touched my shoulder and I felt a shock run through my body. Electrons shifted and protons bounced in excitement. She said, "You are such a tragic figure. Like out of a French novel."

I looked into her eyes. "Whatever do you mean?"

"I mean that I think I would like to get to know you better. Maybe we can have a drink later."

"But I thought…?"

She put a finger over my lips. "Shh…Seven, in the Golden Lion?"

I tried hard to suppress my joy. I said, "Seven it is."

We chatted for a few more minutes, but she had paper work to do so I took my leave, and went to find Vito. Poor guy. He had no idea how badly he had been torpedoed, but it was his own fault. I had told him to lay low. Hitting on one of the medical staff the minute you get on board hardly fit the description of laying low. Besides, she was out of his league by about a thousand miles. I was glad I was there to save her.

An hour later, I found him in Betsy's room eating lunch. "I see you discovered room service?"

There was a 20-ounce T-bone on a plate with a trio of dipping sauces, a pile of fries, and an urn of coffee. I found a mug in the kitchen, poured myself a cup and grabbed a handful of fries as I sat opposite him. He had a shit-eating grin on his face.

He swallowed the food in his mouth and asked, "So how's your day going?"

"Pretty good although I haven't had a chance to eat yet."

"Well, that's a shame because the food on this ship is pretty good."

He wore a gray suit, white shirt, and solid red tie. "I see you're all spiffed up."

"Yeah, I went to the tailor first thing and had him press my shirts and suits. Little Italian guy. He's a trip. Practically took my head off when I told him I needed it done in a hurry."

I noticed a band aid on his finger. "Where'd you get the bandage?"

"Oh, that?" He raised his finger to show me. "Yeah, there was stuff like that in the bathroom."

He was always lousy at lying. "Glad you're making yourself at home."

"I'm trying to. It's a little hard figuring things out without an orientation. I hope the old lady won't mind me charging lunch to her room."

"She won't mind, but do me a favor, use your credit card or cash from now on. The real question is how are we going to legitimize your being here if you're discovered?"

"Relax. The ship docks in Greece in a couple of days. I'll just pretend to board from there."

I thought about that. "That should work. Can you keep a low profile until then?"

"Of course I can."

"That means not going to the tailor anymore or any other place. Just sit tight and watch TV."

"Look, Cesari, the tailor was a necessity, but that's all I had planned anyway."

"Good, because I would prefer it if you left the room as little as possible until you're formally registered as a passenger. Remember, there was a murder on board. If you're discovered stowing away someone could easily jump to the wrong conclusion."

He nodded and I saw a light flicker on in his brain. "That makes sense. Don't worry. I won't take any chances."

"By the way, I forgot to ask you if you brought any weapons with you."

He smiled. "Of course. A .45 caliber. Picked it up in Dubrovnik. They practically sell them on every corner."

"Great. Can I see it?"

"Sure, it's in the front pocket of my suitcase."

I finished my coffee, retrieved the gun and looked at it. It was an HS2000, the same gun Niko and Antonela had. There was a ten round clip in it. I walked out onto the balcony as Vito watched with curiosity. I looked back at him, smiled and flung the gun as far as I could, watching it make a tiny splash when it hit the water. He jumped up with bewilderment as I returned and poured myself more coffee.

"What gives? That cost me a thousand bucks."

"Sit down and relax. You're not in America, Vito. An illegal weapon on the high seas will get you in more trouble than you could possibly handle and no high-priced lawyer will get you out. By the way, did I mention there was a murder on board possibly using a weapon just like that one?"

He sighed and sat down. "You could have warned me."

"About what? That you're your own worst enemy or that you couldn't survive in the wild for a day without me?"

"Geez, a little cranky today, aren't we?"

"You could have offered me a piece of your steak. You know I'm irritable when I'm hungry."

"Fine, get a plate from the kitchen." When I returned, he cut off a small portion and shoveled it with some fries onto my dish.

He said, "So bring me up to speed."

Chapter 20

I watched him work on a molar with a toothpick and said, "Do you have to do that? It's sort of a disgusting habit."

"My dentist says I have to take better care of my teeth."

I don't know why that surprised me. "I didn't know you went to a dentist."

"I never did, but this one's into me for fifty G's. He's a real degenerate and has no luck with the ponies so he's working it off with free dental care for me and my crew."

I didn't know how to respond to that. "And he told you to clean your teeth in public? At least go into the bathroom."

In response, he ignored me and belched loudly, but he did throw the toothpick down onto the tray in front of him. "So let me see if I got this straight, Cesari. You're on this cruise less than a week and you're shacking up with some old broad whose husband got murdered. There are at least two other guys on board, Berislav and Brad, who would like to see you dead or at least seriously injured, but you say you didn't do anything."

"Don't forget the little Croatian cop."

"Oh yeah. The midget. How could I forget? And, as long as we're not forgetting anything, there's her partner, who is now in an Italian hospital." He chuckled softly. "And you didn't want me to come along because you were doing just fine on your own."

I crossed my legs and sipped my coffee. "I was doing just fine. Thank you."

"You're a piece of work. Did you know that? You should be kissing my ass right now. I'm like the U.S. cavalry coming along to save you."

"Then why am I worried that you're going to make things ten times worse?"

"Because deep down you're a weak human being. There are some guys who hide under their bed at night trembling at the sound of the wind and other guys who howl at the moon. Guess which one you aren't?"

I snorted. "Spare me your philosophy, please."

"Fine, so how can I help?"

"Not sure yet, but if you don't bring a lot of attention to yourself you could work in the background. First thing you need to do is buy some real clothes. Waking around a cruise ship in a silk suit and tie makes you stand out like a sore thumb. There are multiple stores on decks 2 and 3. You can buy almost anything you want."

"I want to wear a suit and a tie."

"Do you want to help me or not?"

"I'm not wearing shorts."

I sighed, "I don't care. Just don't come back looking like a secret service agent. While you're at it, pick up a camera with a decent zoom lens."

"Why?"

"I haven't fully thought it out. Just do it."

He shook his head. "Is there a gym around here? I'm going to need something to do while I await your orders."

"It's on the main deck. There are signs posted everywhere. There's also a pool, a sauna, a jogging track, and a place to get a massage."

He smiled. "Is there a place to get laid?"

"Yeah, it's called the bathroom. You go in there, close the lights, and pretend you're with a beautiful woman or in your case a beautiful goat. Now listen carefully. We're not here to party right now. There's some heavy stuff going down and I need you to stay focused. Can you do that?"

"Jesus, Cesari, a guy can't even make a joke around you."

"No, a guy can't. I want you to go shopping, go work-out, and then come back to the room and lay low. If you're starving there are pizzerias and sub shops scattered around the ship. Try to stay away from the fancy restaurants and high-end bars. You'll only get in trouble."

"You're making me feel like the hunchback of Notre Dame. Maybe I should just find a church belfry to hide in? What am I supposed to do if some hottie throws herself at me?"

I chuckled. "Take a picture of her with the camera because I won't believe it without seeing it."

"And what are you going to be doing while I'm laying low."

"I have a million things to do beginning with packing up all of Mrs. Harrington's clothes and personal effects and hauling them back to my room. Why don't you be a good Vito and help me do that? Then I have a whole bunch of leads I have to track down. I'll be very busy so don't expect me back any time soon."

We shoved everything we found in the closets, drawers, and bathroom into three huge suitcases. With a modest degree of difficulty I was able to transport the luggage back to my room in just one trip where I found Betsy taking sun in a lounge chair on the balcony. She wore a one piece swimsuit, oversized sunglasses, and a straw hat. She looked pretty good. I always liked women's hats. It was 4:00 p.m.

Smiling when she saw me, she rose and helped me wheel the bags over to the closet. "Thank you so much, John."

"Don't thank me just yet. There are some nice dresses getting crushed in there."

"Don't worry about that. That's why we have dry cleaning services."

"How'd it go today?"

"Wonderful, if you like to hear hens clucking for hours on end. Goodness gracious. You would think I was the first woman on earth to lose a husband. It took two martinis and all my strength not to tell them all to shut up."

I was taken aback by this. She and Roger undeniably weren't the poster couple for the ideal marriage, but that seemed a little cold. On the other hand, she was undoubtedly very stressed and didn't enjoy being reminded constantly, as people were prone to do, of how unfortunate she was. That could be pretty annoying. I also reminded myself that people grieved in different ways. I had no doubt the floodgates would open sooner or later.

"Sorry to hear that, but I suppose they meant well."

"I guess." She sat on the sofa and patted the space next to her. "Come, sit next to me."

She definitely looked sad and exhausted. Perhaps she just wasn't the crying type or maybe all those stereotypes of emotionless northeastern bluebloods were true. I sat next to her and she took my hand. She said, "I was going to visit Roger in the morgue later. Would you come with me? I haven't gone to see him since that night and I feel bad about it. I'd rather not go alone."

"Of course I will. What time were you thinking?"

"Maybe around five, five-thirty. The captain invited me to his private chambers with several other prominent members of the crew and guests for cocktails and dinner at six. It's going to be more of the same all evening. He extended the invitation to you as well but I didn't want to bore you. I do hope you'll come back to the room before I pass out. I could really use some hugs tonight."

I leaned over and kissed her gently. She pulled me close and I smelled alcohol on her breath. I said, "I'll do my best."

"I wish I could keep up with you. What do you do all night anyway?"

"Mostly, I drink heavily and hit on fat girls."

She laughed. "Just as I expected, and how is that going?"

"Pretty good. I almost got one last night, but just as we were leaving the casino to go to her room we passed an all-night, all-you-can-eat buffet and she lost interest in me."

Giggling, she glanced at her watch and said with resignation, "I'd much rather stay here and let you entertain me, but it's after four already, and I must get ready."

"Okay, I'll just hang out."

She disappeared into the bathroom, and when she was gone from view, I went out onto the balcony and lay on one of the lounge chairs. The ocean was a little choppy today. The smell of the air, the breeze, the glow of the sun, a guy could get used to this. I needed a cocktail. I let out a deep breath. Okay, enough daydreaming. It was time to come up with a battle plan.

There were many things going on in many fronts and I needed to narrow down the playing field a bit. I shouldn't have agreed to meet Aimée for a drink later. I really didn't have time to spare. That was a mistake driven by compulsive womanizing over the years. In my defense, I would need to eat something anyway. It might as well be with my beautiful nurse practitioner. What harm could come of that? Besides, it was kind of fun keeping her away from Vito. Cancel that; it was lots of fun keeping her away from Vito. I smiled. So much for my plan to learn self-restraint with the fairer sex. How did that saying go? The road to hell was lined with good intentions.

Vito was something else. Stowing away and barely acclimated, he hits on the nurse practitioner within hours of his arrival. Plus, he must think that I'm a moron to believe that he was going to stay put in his room. I just wanted the moral high ground when I caught him roaming around. I couldn't wait to see the expression on his face when Aimée didn't show up for dinner.

Okay, back to business. Problem number one was Brad. He was breathing fire down my neck and I didn't like it. Plus, he had the ability to sully Betsy's reputation with those compromising pictures he took of us. I wasn't going to allow that, but how to best neutralize him was the question. Brad was like a blunt weapon and guys like him didn't understand or respond to subtlety. I snapped my fingers suddenly and chuckled. A great idea came to me, and one that could keep Vito busy for a while too.

Betsy called from the bedroom interrupting my line of thought. She had cleaned up and put on a smart knee length navy dress. She needed help zipping it up in the back. I got behind her, tugged the zipper up and fastened it at the top.

"Thank you."

"At your service, Lady Beth."

She giggled. "Stop, you'll make me feel older than I already am. How do I look?"

She turned to face me and I studied her. "Sophisticated."

"Not sexy?"

"You're in mourning. It would have been uncultured of me to say that, but yes, very much so."

"Thank you. Well, I'm ready. Shall we go?"

The morgue was on low deck 2, and we found it without difficulty. Despite having been on many cruises, Betsy had never actually been to the morgue before, and held my arm tightly as we neared. Standing in front of the door, I asked, "Are you ready?"

She nodded. "I think so."

I turned the knob and we entered. There was an attendant crew member waiting for us. Betsy had called down earlier to let him know she was coming and he courteously led us to Roger's drawer. The morgue room was a fourteen-by-twelve-foot refrigerated, rectangular room, which housed four metal drawers built into the walls. The attendant pulled the drawer out, unzipped Roger's body bag, and then politely retreated back to his desk in the other room. He closed the door behind him and the sound echoed loudly in our chamber.

We looked at each other and then down at Roger. This was becoming increasingly more difficult for her and she shuddered as she looked at his corpse. Holding me tightly, she started weeping softly. I didn't say anything and thought it would be best for her to let it out.

After a moment, she collected herself and leaned over him whispering, "How could you, Roger?"

I looked at her. What did that mean? I said, "Betsy?"

Ignoring me she continued speaking to him, "How could you? You bastard." And then suddenly before I could stop her, she spat on his snow white face.

I pulled her back as I sensed her growing anger. "Betsy, what are you doing?"

"Don't worry, John. I'm fine. I just needed to get that off my chest while I still had the chance. Come, let us go. The captain will be expecting me soon."

Speechless, my mind reeled. What the hell was that? We thanked the attendant and walked out in silence a moment later. She didn't bring it up and I was too overwhelmed with astonishment. I'd heard of women grieving in peculiar ways at the loss of a loved one but this took the cake, and my mind swirled at the implication. Was she mad at him for leaving her alone to fend for herself? Or did she just plain hate him and was only now letting it out? I had a lot to think about. Emotions were running high and I needed to tread lightly. I reminded myself that I had just stepped into the middle of a fifty-year-old movie and barely knew what was going on.

I walked Betsy to the captain's quarters as if nothing at all unusual had occurred and then headed over to the Golden Lion to meet Aimée. Arriving a little early, I decided to pregame it with a Jack Daniel's Sinatra Select whiskey, neat, and pondered about what I had witnessed. There was no easy answer. Women were complicated no matter what the age. That was the only thing I knew for sure. It was always better to suck it up and not piss them off.

I sat in the same wood booth that Niko had. It commanded a great view of the room which was starting to fill up. My drink came and I sipped the amber liquid, savoring it for a moment. Smooth as silk. Well-heeled men and women gathered at the bar and the surrounding tables for libations and revelry. They all seemed so innocent. I was a little jealous. Somehow my vacation had turned on its head.

Just as I was finishing my drink Aimée walked in and I stood to greet her. Dolled up, she looked even more stunning than earlier in the day. She wore tight jeans and a peach top, gold earrings and necklace. She had swapped her black-framed glasses for a red pair. I loved Europeans and their eyewear. To them, eye glasses were just as important as the jewelry or clothes they wore. Many had literally dozens of pairs for almost any occasion. I found them very sexy and made a mental note to ask her to keep them on should we ever take this to the next level.

I said, "Hi."

"Bonsoir."

To my surprise, she came right up to me and gave me a polite kiss on both cheeks. I had forgotten about that French custom. God, she smelled great.

We sat opposite each other and I signaled the waitress. "You look really nice."

"Thank you."

The waitress approached and Aimée ordered champagne and I stuck with Jack. "How is your cousin, Vito?" she asked.

"He's fine. I medicated him heavily, and when I left the room he was sleeping comfortably with one of the stuffed animals he brought along. He was adorable lying there hugging his giraffe. When I spoke to him earlier he didn't even remember meeting you, so please don't give it any further thought."

She smiled. "A giraffe? How sweet."

"I should have taken a picture for you."

"Please do not do that. You are so amazing the way you watch out for him."

"Thank you, but I don't feel amazing. I wish…"

I choked up and she reached across the table to touch my hand. "What do you wish?"

"I wish that I could find a cure for him. I would give up everything I have…even my own life."

"Mon dieu, how much you are suffering."

"It's been a long painful journey these last few years watching him descend into the abyss. He drools now when I try to feed him."

The waitress set our drinks down in front of us and she raised her champagne to toast me. "Here is to good men, so few and so far between."

I raised my glass also. “Here’s to my cousin Vito, a restless soul who I hope one day finds the peace he deserves.”

She sipped her champagne and studied me for a long time. She had long lashes and full lips. Her features were soft and compelling and I had no doubt she could bring any man down to his knees with desire. I let the silence sit there as we appraised each other.

Finally she said, “I am at a loss for words. I have this need to throw my arms around you right now. I almost cannot control myself.”

“I don’t know why.”

“Because you are one of the most selfless men I have ever met.”

“Thank you but I don’t feel that way. In fact, I feel very selfish. I shouldn’t even have left him alone, and I almost didn’t come here tonight because I worry about him so much. But I thought it would be rude to you to just not show up.”

She thought for a long moment and said, “Have you eaten?”

I shook my head. “No.”

“I have left over broccoli pizza in my room.”

Gag me. Broccoli on pizza? I couldn’t believe the lengths some people went to ruin good food. I said, “Sounds delicious and broccoli is so good for you.”

“It’s two days old.”

I said, “Aged pizza is my favorite.”

“We can go there if you would like? I have a microwave.”

“I love microwaved pizza.”

She smiled, “That settles it.”

This was going better than expected. I said, “First promise me something.”

She looked puzzled. “What?”

"That no matter what happens, you'll leave your eye glasses on."

"What could possibly happen?"

"Promise?"

"Oui, oui."

Chapter 21

I staggered out of her room, panting, several hours later, my shirt half out. She stood at the doorway wearing almost nothing but her eyeglasses and a provocative smile. She wouldn't let go of my arm and had one leg wrapped around one of mine. Her eyes were glazed and she had completely lost it. Pulling me down for another kiss, she almost convinced me to go back in for another round.

"I really have to go check on my cousin, Aimée. If he wakes and I'm not there, he'll be scared."

"I understand. You will come to the clinic tomorrow?"

"Yes, I will. I promise."

She smiled and kissed me once more before letting go. I walked away, tucking my shirt in. It was almost 11:00 p.m. and I had gotten side-tracked again. I had planned on having one, maybe two drinks tops with her and nothing more, but here I was once again, sore and exhausted. At the rate I was going, the thought occurred to me, I might be the one who needed a shot of penicillin.

By the time I reached the casino, my head cleared and I was able to focus again. Much to my surprise, I saw Vito at the five-card draw poker table. So much for laying low. I walked up to him and ordered bottled water from a passing waitress.

Aimée had dehydrated me. Vito was bluffing on a pair of eights. I rolled my eyes at him and all he did was nod back.

I said, fairly loudly. "Should you really bet that much on a pair of eights?"

One guy folded and two others raised him by throwing in hundred dollar chips. He threw his cards down in frustration and shook his head at me. "You trying to be funny?"

I smiled. "Who me?"

He threw a chip at the dealer and stood. "I'm having a bad night, Cesari. I needed to blow off some steam. That's why I left the room."

"How bad of a night?"

"It's hard to explain."

"Try me. I'm a good listener."

The waitress walked by with two whiskeys on her tray. I grabbed one and Vito grabbed the other. She said curtly, "They weren't for you, gentlemen."

I said, "I know. I asked for water."

He placed a twenty-five dollar chip on the plate and said, "Well now they're for us."

She frowned but the chip soothed her, and she walked away. I said, "Let's get something to eat. I'm starving. All I had was a couple of bites of two-day-old broccoli pizza and that was three hours ago."

"Broccoli pizza? Who the hell eats something like that? Don't even say it again. It'll make me puke."

Next to the casino was a café where we ordered hamburgers and fries. Not ordinary burgers and fries mind you. The burgers were eight ounces of perfectly charbroiled Kobe beef on toasted brioche buns with a garlic aioli dressing and the fries were covered with shaved white truffles. We had no choice but to order a bottle of cabernet sauvignon to go with the meal, so we chugged the whiskeys down and launched into our food.

He looked at me noticing something amiss. "Are you all right? You look a little…disheveled."

"I'm fine. Did you get the camera like I asked?"

"Yes, I did, a Canon Powershot with a 40x optical zoom. It should handle most things. Four hundred bucks you owe me."

"Thanks because I think I know what I want you to do with it."

"Yeah and what's that?"

"Remember, I told you about that jerk, Brad, the CEO of the hospital back in New York?"

"I remember. He's got some pictures of you and the old broad."

"Well, the whole story is that he's married, but his wife is back in the states visiting her sick mother. He's here with his girlfriend, Joyce."

Vito chortled. "Good for him."

"No, good for me. Two can play at this picture game. I want you to follow them and take pictures."

"What do I look like, a private dick?"

I could have hit that one out of the ball park blind folded but I decided to take it easy on him. "You want to help or not? I need this guy off my back. He's got compromising pictures of me and I want compromising pictures of him. Get it?"

"You've got to be kidding? I don't even know what they look like."

"I'll find out their room number and you stake it out."

He took a huge bite of his burger and said, "Man, this is good."

It was. "Okay, so what are you pouting about? You said you were having a bad day."

He looked down. "If you promise not to get angry, I'll tell you."

"I promise."

"I know you told me to lay low, but I met a real babe and asked her out. She was supposed to meet me for dinner and...."

"And what?"

"And she stood me up, and I'm really bummed out. She was all over me one minute and now I got blue balls."

"Look, pal, I'm sorry but maybe it's for the best. You know? Having no girl is better than having one that will break your heart. Capeesh? Besides, it's really best if you don't make a lot of noise around here until you get officially registered as a passenger." He was giving me a sad-sack look, so I added, "You'll always have your best bud, Cesari. Don't ever forget that."

He nodded. "Thanks for not being angry at me for going off the reservation and you're right. Who needs her anyway? Although I have to tell you she was really hot, and French, a nurse or doctor or something. I went to the ship's medical unit and she bandaged my finger for me. That's how I met her. She was gorgeous and had this cute little accent. I was looking forward to tapping that action."

"I wish you hadn't told me that."

"Why?"

"Because that guy you saw jumping out of the container going AWOL last night was the ship's doctor. His wife left him high and dry for another man and he was distraught and took off after her."

"No shit, but what's that got to do with anything?"

"The captain asked me if I would fill in as the ship's doctor until they got a replacement in a couple of days. I'm supposed to go down to the infirmary to see patients and supervise the staff for a couple of hours each day. I really couldn't refuse."

"So what?"

"So what? Now when I meet this person who hurt your feelings I'm going to be pissed off because of the way she treated you. How the hell am I going to work with her? We're BFFs, dude, one for all and all for one. Capeesh?"

"Cesari, take it easy. I don't know what happened to her tonight but don't let it get in the way of your professionalism, all right? I'm a big boy. I'll get over it. She probably just changed her mind about dating a passenger and didn't have the cojones to tell me."

I shook my head. "You're probably right. It just annoys me when people act like that. You sure you're okay?"

"I'm like a cat, Cesari. I always land on my feet."

I glanced at my watch. "Good. It's almost midnight. Let's get some shuteye."

We parted company and I went back to my room. The lights were out and I quietly went to the bathroom to take a quick shower. I had Aimée's scent all over me and needed to scrub it off before I got into bed with Betsy. Some things were just wrong and coming to bed after sex with another woman without bathing was one of them. A short while later, I gently slipped under the covers so as not to wake Betsy, but she woke any way and snuggled close, wrapping her arms around me.

"You're home early. What happened? She turn you down?"

I smiled in the dark. I kind of liked her attitude. "Yeah, something like that."

She giggled. "Well, you always have me."

Our lips found each other and we kissed for quite some time. She sniffed me several times and said, "That's Chanel. She has good taste."

Jesus.

I dodged that and kissed her again more passionately. She turned away and backed into me, saying, "Hold me tightly."

I put my arms around her and kissed the back of her head and shoulders. She was half asleep and I was dog tired. Spooning was just fine with me. She said, "This is nice."

"I agree."

"Did she wear you out?"

I hesitated. It was an unwavering Cesari code never to discuss one woman with another, but I decided, that in view of the extenuating and highly irregular circumstances, to make an exception. "A little."

I could feel her chuckle quietly. She said, "I'll bet you never realized how demanding a cruise could be on a guy."

That made me smile. "I won't need a stress test after this. That's for sure." Since she felt like talking I asked, "Hey, Betsy, can I ask you something?"

"Considering the position we are now in I'd venture a guess and say yes."

I loved her sense of humor. "It's something about the night of the murder. I don't want to upset you by bringing the subject up."

"Go ahead, dear. In case you hadn't noticed, I'm not a shrinking violet."

"The intruder waited for you and Roger to come to your room to steal your necklace, right?"

"Yes."

"Did you have your fake necklace lying out that night?"

"Of course I did. I always leave it out. Why?"

"Did he take it?"

"No, it was still there. When I woke that morning, after I called the captain for help, I staggered to the bathroom where I found it. I dropped it in my bag for safe-keeping. It's been there ever since. I intended on putting it away in my safe, but there's been so much going on it slipped my mind, and to be honest, I really haven't given it much thought until now. Why do you ask?"

I was troubled by this. "Don't you see what that means, Betsy? The thief knew the necklace in the bathroom was a reproduction. That's why he didn't take it. There's no other possible explanation. That narrows down the list of potential suspects considerably. How many people knew about the fake necklace?"

She was very quiet and after a minute said, "Why do you want to talk about this?"

That startled me. "I was thinking about it. I know how important the necklace is to you, and I'd love to help you get it back."

"John, this is probably not the best subject for you to start speculating about."

What on earth did that mean? "I don't understand. Why not?"

She let out a deep breath. "John…except for Roger and me, you were the only one who knew about the faux jewels."

I almost jumped out of my skin at the implication of that statement and turned on the night light, sitting up in the bed. My eyes wide open I said, "What are you saying? I hope you don't think I killed Roger and stole your necklace?"

With a quizzical expression on her face she said, "I never said that."

Still indignant I said, "Betsy, I would never kill Roger, and I'm not a thief. I can't even believe we're having this conversation. For God's sake we're sharing a bed. What kind of person would that make me?"

She sat up in bed and looked at me. In a consoling voice she said, "John, first of all I never accused you of anything. You brought the subject up and I simply answered your question. I don't believe you killed Roger or stole my jewelry, but I can't explain how the thief knew about the phony necklace. He must have seen it that night. It was lying right out in the open. How he could have known is anybody's guess at this point. As far as sharing a bed, I need the comforting embrace of someone I like and trust right now so…"

That was nice, but I wasn't done. "What about housekeeping and the security people who came with them. Would they have seen it lying around and guessed its true purpose?"

"No, they always scheduled their appointments with us and I would lock everything away in my safe until after they left. If it had been lying around all the time they almost certainly would have suspected something was fishy about it."

"So you're willing to put your concerns about me to the side?"

She smiled and touched my face. "You're being silly. I don't have any concerns about you, John. I know for a fact you didn't do it, but as long as we're having this conversation, you might as well know something else."

She hesitated and I prompted her. "I'm listening."

"According to the captain, there was no sign of forced entry. The electronic record in the security office shows that my room was accessed by a legitimate key thirty minutes before Roger and I arrived."

"Okay, and…?"

"I gave you the only other key to my room."

Chapter 22

I couldn't sleep after that disheartening news so I left Betsy to get some fresh air and think things over. No matter how many times she tried to placate me, there was no hiding from the obvious fact that I had to be viewed as the number one suspect. In fact, as far as I could tell, I was the only suspect. Only a fool would think otherwise. The circumstantial evidence was overwhelming. Of course, she didn't say it quite like that, and in fact, she was extremely supportive, but it was just a matter of time before all eyes turned on me. I felt sick to my stomach. This was supposed to be a get-away-from-it-all vacation.

It was well after midnight and the promenade was mostly deserted. Storm clouds loomed over the horizon, hiding the moon, and cooling things off considerably. A breeze coming in from the north chilled me as I sat on a bench overlooking the bow. Betsy hadn't told the captain yet about me having a key to her room, or else I'd probably already be in handcuffs, but she planned on having a frank conversation about me with him soon. She felt that the best approach with him would be complete honesty, and that she would vouch for my innocence. I couldn't wait for that discussion.

A sinking feeling told me that I wasn't getting off this boat until that necklace was found and Roger's murderer was caught.

I was depressed. I had been accused of a lot of things in my life but the idea that I might kill a man and then bed his wife made me very upset. It was one thing for a low-life like Brad to make an accusation like that but if an honorable person like the captain started thinking it, I'd be in trouble. What kind of pond scum would do that? I was getting worried that soon everyone onboard was going to start thinking that I was that kind of pond scum.

Sensing someone approach, I looked up. "Katarina, what are you doing here?"

"I follow you."

"You followed me?"

"I was on balcony when you have fight with old woman."

"We didn't have a fight."

"You hug, kiss, turn on light, argue, and leave room. Look like fight to me."

"You were there? The whole time?"

"Couldn't see much. Too dark. Lucky for my eyes."

I shook my head. "We didn't have a fight. We had a miscommunication."

She slid close to me on the bench, purring, "You made promise to Katarina, remember?"

"I know I did, but I'm tired. I've had a very long day and now…"

"Now, what?"

I let out a deep breath. "I need a place to sleep."

She picked up my arm and placed it around her shoulder as she snuggled next to me. "I have a room and a big bed as you know. I will even let you sleep on top."

Smiling at that, I asked, "On top of what? The bed or you?"

"Whichever you prefer."

"Where's Berislav? Won't he be annoyed if he finds me there?"

"Who knows? Probably drinking in bar with fat American. They are best friends now. Maybe even go to his room to drink. Other night he so drunk I had to go to fat man's room to help him walk home."

"You know which room the American is in?"

"Yes, is 5028. Why?"

"Nothing, I was just curious. Say, where is your bodyguard, Antonela?"

She frowned. "Midget walk me to room an hour ago. As soon as she leave, I go out balcony to find you. Is disgusting watch you with old woman."

"We were just hugging. Besides, I thought you couldn't see anything?"

She blushed and hesitated. I said, "Don't answer that. It doesn't matter. I'm tired is all you need to know."

"Is not fair. You lie."

"I'll tell you what. I'll take you up on the offer of sleeping in your bed, but no sex. I need to sleep."

"No sex? Then you can sleep out here on deck. Nice big bench. I hope you are comfortable. Sleep with your lies."

I thought about going to Vito's room but the sofa was small there and the idea of sleeping on a floor where a man had been murdered didn't appeal to me. Plus, he snored like a wounded buffalo. I couldn't bring myself to go back to Betsy. That was too weird for me. I'd get over it eventually but not tonight. Aimée was a possibility but it was almost 1:00 a.m. She might think I was a freak if I woke her up at this hour and what would I say?

I looked at Katarina. "If you let me sleep then maybe we can do it in the morning."

"We do it tonight or you sleep here."

Damn, she was hardcore. I said, "You don't understand. I don't think I physically can do it right now."

"Why not?"

"I told you I'm tired. I just can't. Men have their limits."

"Kiss me now and I check."

I chuckled softly. She didn't give up. "No, we're not going to start making out here in public. C'mon be reasonable."

"Kiss me or I scream."

"You're not going to scream."

"How do you know?"

"Because I do. That's how."

She smiled. "Fine, in morning then."

That wasn't unreasonable so I nodded. "In morning, maybe. If you let me get some rest."

As we walked to the elevators holding hands, it occurred to me that Betsy might be feeling pretty bad over the way I had left her. My ego had been bruised at the idea that she would even remotely consider me culpable, a notion she adamantly denied, but how could she not? I wondered how the captain would react. Betsy owned the ship but it was his boat. After she told him I knew about the diamonds and had her key, throwing me in the brig might be the only choice he had until we docked in London.

We stepped off the elevator but had to walk the length of the ship to her room. She was feeling pretty chipper and was humming a tune I didn't recognize. "Don't you ever get tired?" I asked.

She shook her head. "Being tired is for old people like your girlfriend, old lady. Katarina young, healthy, stay up all night."

That's what I was afraid of. Suddenly, I thought this might be a bad idea after all. Vito's room wasn't that far away and I made up my mind to go there instead. As she opened the door, I touched her shoulder to let her know there was going to be a change of plans. Misinterpreting my intention she spun around and threw her arms around me, planting a big kiss on my lips.

I let it run its course, and when she came up for air, said, "Katarina, that was very nice..." Her eyes went wide with fright as she looked past me.

Puzzled, I started to turn to see what caused her concern, and found myself staring down the barrel of a .45 caliber pistol with the hammer cocked. Antonela did not look happy.

She nodded at Katarina. "Go in room, beetch, and lock door."

Katarina was practically shaking and stepped inside the room without making a sound. I heard it lock from inside. She hissed at me, "Turn around and walk slowly. Don't make sound."

I did as I was told and felt the muzzle jammed into the small of my back. We reached the stairwell at the end of the corridor and went one flight down.

I said, "Antonela, it's not what you think."

"Oh really? What is it I think?"

"I was very tired and locked myself out of my room. I just needed a place to rest." Probably, the lamest story I had ever told but I was exhausted and was having trouble thinking straight.

She laughed. "So where you rest? Between her legs?"

"No, absolutely not. I was going to sleep on the floor or the sofa."

"Keep walk."

She jabbed me in the back again with the gun. "Where are we going?"

"Some place safe. No bother girl no more."

When we reached her room, she opened the door and waved me in. When I reached the side of the bed and could go no further, I said, "Now what?"

"Pull down pants to ankles."

"Oh c'mon. Really?"

She poked me hard in the back. "Do."

Unfastening my pants, I slid them down around my ankles. She said, "Underwear too."

She waited for me and continued. "Now remove shirt and lay face down on bed. Extend hands to corners."

I crawled on the bed and stretched my hands toward the bed posts. Without taking the gun or her eyes off me, she grabbed the wrist nearest her and quickly slapped a pair of metal handcuffs on attaching it to the metal frame of the bed. After that she seemed to relax a little as she walked to the other side, restraining that wrist in similar fashion.

I said, "So, what are you going to do? Keep me here for the rest of the cruise?"

"Is idea."

She walked to a bureau on one side of the bed and I turned my head to watch. With her back to me, she rummaged through a drawer and said, "You promise to come visit Antonela last night."

I let out a deep breath. "You can't be serious? That's what this is about?"

"Very serious. You hurt feelings of Antonela."

I could tell from her tone that this was no laughing matter. In a contrite voice, I said, "I'm sorry, Antonela. A friend of mine got sea sick and needed my help or else I would have come."

She found what she was looking for in the drawer and turned around, sniffling. Her eyes were red and she practically shouted at me. "You lie. You prefer volleyball girl to Antonela. Is obvious."

This was just great; jealousy and anger, my two favorite female emotions. Even without the handcuffs, I would be smart enough to be alarmed. I've been around angry women before and was starting to get really nervous. I needed to tread cautiously, and defended myself as best I could. "Absolutely not. I just felt sorry for her. She doesn't seem to know how to make friends easily. I don't even like her."

She sensed the desperation in my voice. Smirking, she wiped her eyes, blew her nose, and sat in a chair next to the open drawer as she lit a cigarette. "I warned you not to go near girl. Now what I supposed to do?"

"I'm sorry about that. I swear. It was unintentional. We both just happened to be on the promenade at the same time and started talking."

"Do you know what makes me more angry than anything?"

She blew a puff of smoke in the air, and I didn't like the glazed look in her eyes, or the way her voice had become just a little throaty. I shook my head no.

She nodded slowly, saying, "When man disobey me."

I didn't like the sound of that and didn't say anything. She stood, reached for something in the drawer and came out with a red rubber ball in one hand and a pink, zucchini-shaped object in the other. My eyes went wide as she came close to me, and putting the red ball next to my mouth, said, "Open up, beetch."

Oh shit.

Chapter 23

She blew a smoke ring at me and then sipped her coffee as she sat curled up in a chair wearing a bathrobe, her hair wrapped up in a white towel. I sat quietly, watching her and waiting, my coffee and cheese danish untouched on the plate before me. It had been one helluva night, and I doubted I would ever forget it or talk about it…with anyone…ever.

She looked at me with curiosity, and asked as if nothing was wrong, "Why you no eat?"

I grinned politely. My hands were cuffed tightly behind my back and I was naked, but she knew that. I said, "It's a little difficult, my Shwimbo." She had taught me to call her that during play time. It was the pronounced form of the eponym, SWMBO, She Who Must Be Obeyed.

Smiling, she said, "Oh yeah. You want I should release your hands?"

I nodded. "That would make it a little bit easier to hold my coffee cup."

"Maybe you eat food off floor like dog?" She got all excited. "You do that for Shwimbo?"

Without hesitating I replied, "I'll do whatever pleases my Shwimbo."

She liked that. "You are fast learner. For that, I release one hand."

"Thanks."

I had come to realize after hours of torture, sexual sadism, and sodomy that she was the worst kind of sociopath, and that my only chance was to play along with her. There was no sickness she wasn't capable of. In fact, the more perverted the act the more pleasure she derived from it. My key to surviving the night was to submit unconditionally to her domination. Even the slightest resistance was met with blinding white fury and a 'time-out' with the pink zucchini.

Picking up the gun from the table in front of her, she walked behind me. She unlocked my right hand and said, "Cross right leg over left and put other end of handcuff on ankle." To make sure I understood, she pressed the tip of the pistol into the base of my skull and cocked it.

After she was comfortable that I was thoroughly secured, she uncocked the weapon and resumed her seat across from me. I sipped my coffee and took a bite of the pastry. She asked, "How do you feel?"

"Like I never want to make my Shwimbo angry again."

She stretched like a cat. "Is good for man and woman to understand each other."

Why was it always the little ones, man or woman, who were the meanest? "Did you really have to do that?" I asked.

"Do what?"

She knew exactly what I was talking about. "That thing you did."

"Why?"

"Because it hurt…a lot. Haven't you ever heard of lubrication?"

"Oh please. Be man already. Besides, now you know how girl feel. Last night no for your pleasure was for mine. Last night also was for to teach you lesson. Did you learn anything?"

"Yes, I did."

"Shwimbo is good teacher, no?"

"Shwimbo is very good teacher, yes."

"Then no problem."

Changing the subject, I asked, "So how do you feel?"

She squashed the remains of her cigarette in a saucer. "Much better. Very relaxed. Was all…how do you say…pent up."

"That's good, isn't it?"

"Is very good…for me anyway."

"Will Shwimbo let me go now that she is feeling so much better?"

She thought about that. "I think so, but I catch with girl again I no take it so easy on you."

I nodded. I was in agony and couldn't wait to go somewhere and take an hour long bath. "Thank you for your mercy."

"Hmm. You have no idea. Part of my brain tell me to cut you into pieces and throw overboard when gets dark."

"What's the other part tell you?"

"Tie you up and keep you as slave until cruise finish and then cut you into little pieces and throw overboard."

I was silent, thinking that over, and she continued, "But another part of brain, maybe something else, maybe my heart, admires you for killing old man. Can't help but like that." She sighed deeply. "Shwimbo getting soft."

Great. Cold-blooded murder had earned me a place in her heart. I said, "I'm not worthy of Shwimbo's kindness."

She smiled, "No, you're not, but I show mercy anyway. I no kill or keep as slave…For now, I think I let go."

I let out a deep breath. I could feel the conversation beginning to normalize and said, "Thank you. Well, as long as we're friends again, would you mind finishing that discussion we started the other night about who you thought might have the necklace?"

She stood and walked to the bed dropping her robe to the floor. Naked, she bent over and started putting on her panties. "Is Berislav. In Dubrovnik, he is famous…hmm, not sure how say in English. He sell stolen things."

"A fence. He's a fence? Really?" This surprised me.

"Yes, he is fence, among other things. Specialize in jewelry, not little things like TV or camera, so this right up his, how you say…sidewalk."

"Alley…it's right up his alley." I thought about that. "But would he have stolen the necklace himself?"

"Is good question. Right now he is desperate for money. So, is possible, but if he has necklace and no tell me then he in big trouble even more than you. I don't even like him. He, I definitely cut up and throw overboard."

Curious about Berislav, I asked, "So back in Croatia he was a career criminal? You know…his whole life?"

"No, he was schoolteacher but decide he need more money."

I chuckled, "A schoolteacher?"

"Yes, teacher for the deaf and hearing impaired."

"Seriously?"

Nodding as she buttoned up a pair of jeans. "Yes, he was even head master at school in Dubrovnik. Teach sign language and lip reading at university and government. He even train police force. I know him long time."

I'll be damned. She went into the bathroom before I could ask another question. I guessed the conversation was over as I heard her brushing her teeth. I thought about making a run for it but realized how stupid I would look in the hallway butt naked one wrist handcuffed to the opposing ankle. Besides, I'd probably break my neck like that. I elected to wait and trust that she was going to let me go as she said.

Returning a short while later, wearing a cotton top and sandals, she literally looked like the girl next door. Brushing her mostly dry hair, she smiled, "Glad you no try escape. I watch from bathroom. It would have been bad for you."

"Why would I want to escape Antonela?"

Her eyes flashed angrily and I realized I forgot to call her Shwimbo. She said, "Maybe you need another time-out?"

I caught my breath, but before I could apologize and beg for forgiveness, she chuckled, "Is all right this time, but only once."

She sat on my lap and wrapped her arms around my neck holding the hair brush in one hand, the handle pushing up against the back of my head. It was a little uncomfortable with my wrist and ankle cuffed but she was so light I could deal with it. She looked into my eyes and I was tempted to grab her with my free hand. She said, "I like this. Maybe I change mind. Keep you here. We do like that every night." She waited for a reaction from me but got none. Then she laughed and admonished me, "Smile, I joke. No be so serious."

I didn't trust her but had learned to fear her, so I smiled like she told me to. "You are right. I need to relax more."

She said, "Is right…Why you no try grab Antonela with free hand? You have big muscles. I no can fight."

I hadn't moved my right hand, not even an inch, and had no intention of doing so. Behind my head I heard a metallic clicking and the sound of metal scraping. She brought her hair brush around to show me the five inch stiletto blade sticking out from the grip. I let out a deep breath. That would have been a nasty little surprise had I made a move against her.

"You good boy. I let go now, but remember what Antonela say."

She gathered up all my belongings and stuffed them into a large garbage bag. Then, dropping her gun into her handbag, tossed the handcuff key onto the floor nearby. "I put clothes in stairwell outside room. Leave handcuffs and key on table, understand?"

I nodded. What a piece of work. Couldn't just let me get dressed in peace. She walked out the door with my things and I retrieved the key, freeing my hand and ankle. Standing there in the raw, I stretched and…finished my breakfast. Looking around, I decided she was going to have to pay a little bit and I decided to cause as much mischief as I could.

If she thought I was cowed, she was sorely confused. Wounded, humiliated, but not defeated, I searched her room and found two large suitcases, opening them on the bed. I emptied her closets, drawers, and bathroom cabinets into the valises minus one teeny tiny lace thong I found. This I placed strategically on a pillow for her to see when she returned. Satisfied that there was nothing left to pack, I hauled the two heavy suitcases out onto her balcony. Dark clouds loomed overhead and the water looked rough. It wouldn't be long before the dam broke. I heaved her luggage overboard and watched them hit the water. That felt very satisfying.

A middle-aged blonde on the balcony next door peeked around the divider, saw me and smiled. She held a coffee cup in her hands. "Housecleaning?" she asked as she checked out my equipment.

"My divorce just came through so it's out with old and in with the new. Time to move on if you know what I mean?"

She chuckled. "Oh my. She's not going to be happy when she comes home. I do hope you saved something to wear."

I looked down and laughed. "I'm afraid not. I wanted to make a clean break."

"Wait there, okay?"

She left for a moment and returned with a man's bathing suit. "My husband has dozens of them."

She tossed it at me. I caught it, and to thank her, I put it on while she watched. It didn't fit too badly. I said, "Well, I have to run. Thanks, I'll drop the suit off later."

"Don't bother yourself. It's old anyway and I've been dying to get rid of it. We'll survive. Hope you have a better day. Ta."

"Ta."

Leaving quickly, I half-ran, half-limped, to the stairwell, dressed and made my way back to my room to shower and shave. Betsy was already up and gone and I made it my first order of business to apologize to her for being so peevish last night. The fact of the matter was that she believed I was innocent when most people probably wouldn't have. I should have been grateful not offended.

I thought about Berislav being a jewel fence and an expert in sign language. Could he have read Betsy's lips the night she told me she kept a phony necklace on display? He was sitting opposite us at dinner so it was possible, and who had better motivation than he did? But how would he have come across Betsy's room key? I had no answer for that one.

As I dressed, there was a knock on the door. It was Captain Bjorn and I let him in. He said, "Good morning, doctor."

I nodded, "Same to you, captain."

He looked around the cabin. "Lady Beth's out?"

"Yes, how can I help you?"

"May I sit?"

"Of course."

We sat opposite each other at the kitchen table. I said, "I'm sorry I don't have anything to offer you."

"Perfectly all right. I came to talk to you about Sven."

"The ship's doctor?"

"Yes, well, it seems that he managed to get off the ship with the help of two of his friends. They confessed just hours ago. He fed them some story about his young wife running off with another man and they felt sorry for him."

"I'm sorry to hear that but love and passion are very strong emotions and very difficult ones to control sometimes."

"Yes, if only that were the case."

"What do you mean?"

"What I'm about to tell you is very embarrassing, doctor."

I waited patiently as he let out a deep breath and continued, "We have no record of our good doctor, Sven, being married at all, and..." With raised eyebrows, I waited for the other shoe to drop. He said, "…we searched his cabin and found Lady Beth's room key."

"What are you saying?"

"It's pure speculation of course, but it's possible he staged that whole drunken sailor exhibition to deflect attention from himself and his true plan."

"Which was?"

"To rob Lady Beth of her diamonds."

"And kill Roger?"

"Collateral damage. He didn't plan on Sir Roger putting up a fight like he did."

I thought it over and said, "I don't believe it."

Startled he said, "Why not?"

"The night he was drunk, I helped him walk to his room. I'm very familiar with the condition of being intoxicated, and he was, without a doubt, totally soused. I'd stake my reputation on it. He also told me about his wife running away. I believed him and I still do. He was as honestly distraught as anyone I had ever met. Why would he have told me that story? We had just met for the first time. I'm nobody to him. Look, captain, I'm a pretty good judge of people and Sven is definitely not your man. I suggest you keep looking."

He let out a deep breath and nodded. Bjorn was a contemplative man and right now he was contemplating me. After a while he said, "Perhaps you're right, doctor. I'll keep it under advisement, but he still has a lot of explaining to do when we catch up with him, and we most certainly will. I've notified the Croatian and Italian authorities as well as the home office."

"Is that why you came here? To tell me about your concerns about Sven?"

"Partly, and partly to see what your reaction would be."

"Why?"

"Well, if you were the guilty party, I think you would have been eager to throw Sven under the bus with that information. After all he's not even here to defend himself; instead, you argued on his behalf. So either you're the most brazen criminal I've ever encountered, or you really have nothing to worry about."

"That's a heck of a way to let someone know he's a suspect, but I understand how it must look."

"I'm glad you understand. You're sleeping with a very wealthy woman, doctor. Betsy and I spoke over breakfast this morning, and she told me everything." He made eye contact with me and held it. "She may vouch for you until she's blue in the face, but make no mistake, I'd have to be the biggest fool on the planet not to consider you a suspect. However, you spoke well just now and I must admit I am greatly assuaged by the feeling I get from you. Also, Aimée, the nurse practitioner told me how well you handled yourself in sick bay yesterday. She was quite impressed."

When he mentioned Aimée, I instinctively looked at my watch. I was supposed to go there now to see if she needed me.

I said, "Speaking of sick bay, I need to get going. Aimée might need help. Thank you for not prejudging me."

He nodded, "I won't keep you any longer, doctor."

I stood to leave and said, "You're not upset about Lady Beth and me?"

He shrugged. "I've known the Harringtons for a long time. Theirs was a long and involved relationship. Roger was a notorious womanizer and I'm afraid he hurt her terribly on more than one occasion. Why she never left him has been something of a quandary for me for years. In the past, I suspected it had to do with the times and social norms of her generation, and now that his health had been declining, I'm sure she felt duty-bound to stick it out with him."

"What was wrong with his health?"

He stiffened up, and I saw I wasn't going to get much more on that score. "I shouldn't have said anything. Suffice it to say that Roger wasn't always on the same page as everyone else in the room."

I nodded but didn't say anything, so he continued, "Please don't bring it up with Betsy. Anyway, despite what I just told you, I know she had feelings for Roger, but I doubt those feelings even came close to what we would call love. So no, I'm not upset that Lady Beth has turned to others to fill the void in her life. It saddens me how things have turned out for them both. Treat her well, doctor. She's a great woman and deserved better than to have this happen."

I suddenly felt like shit. "I'll do my best."

Chapter 24

I stepped into the elevator to go down to the infirmary, and just as the door started to close Brad stuck his big hand in, stopping it. He stepped inside and said, "Hi, doctor. Fine day, isn't it?"

I took a deep breath and braced myself. "It's going to rain, Brad."

The doors closed behind him. "May do a little more than that from the look of it."

"What do you want, Brad?"

"Just wondering where my necklace is."

"I told you I don't have it."

"Yes, you did, and I told you that I didn't believe you. I just want to remind you that if I don't have the necklace in my hands by midnight tonight then I go public with the pictures and video of you and the old broad. I'll start with the captain first thing in the morning."

"I don't think I would do that if I were you, Brad."

"And why is that?"

"The captain is quite fond of Lady Beth and already knows that she and I are friends. He might take offense at your intention to hurt her."

He smiled. "How sweet. Well, if he wants to ignore evidence in the middle of a criminal investigation, that's his business, but I doubt anyone else will be that compassionate. My understanding is that the British press can be quite vicious. It will be bad news for you and her highness, and whether I get a rise out of the captain or not, I'll hit the tabloids hard and fast with the story. I've got a friend back in the states who works for one of those morning gossip shows. I'll email him the pictures and video and we'll take it from there. What fun. You'll be famous."

I was close to the breaking point. "Tell your friend it's C-E-S-A-R-I."

The elevator stopped on my floor and the doors opened. As I stepped out, he grabbed my arm and snarled, "If you're not on the promenade at the stroke of midnight with the jewels, I go straight to the business center and push the send button on that e-mail, and then it's breakfast with the captain in the morning. Understand?"

I looked down at his hand on my arm. He was really making me angry. I took a deep breath and said, "I heard you."

"That's good, doctor. I'll be waiting for you."

The clinic was busier than yesterday and I found Aimée running back and forth between exam rooms. I rolled up my sleeves and pitched right in. She looked at me and smiled knowingly. The way people do when they share secrets. She was wearing black and white tiger stripe framed glasses today to match her black and white heels.

"Good morning, Aimée."

"Good morning to you as well, doctor," she replied with pretend formality.

"So, what do we got…nurse?"

"The patient in room 1 has lower abdominal cramps, not too bad. No vomiting or fever. She seems well enough, probably a little constipated. I have already started with her. There's a middle-aged man in room 2 complaining of dizziness. Would you mind seeing him? This is his third time here, and I don't know what to do. I already put him on anti-vertigo medication. His blood pressure's normal and he seems fine otherwise."

"For you, anything."

I knocked on the door and entered. A fifty-year-old man graying at the temples lay on his back with his dressing gown half open. Surprised to see me he sat up abruptly covering himself up. I raised my eyebrows at the sight and introduced myself.

He said, "Where's Aimée?"

"She's tied up with another patient. I'll be taking over your case now. I'm Dr. Cesari."

We shook hands and he looked disappointed. "But I like Aimée."

"That makes two of us, but she asked me to see you because she didn't feel she had anything more to offer. Give me a chance and I'll do my best to help you. So tell me what's been going on..." I looked at his chart. "...Ryan?"

About my height, in decent shape, clean-shaven he mulled over the question for a minute. "I was feeling dizzy but you know something. I think it's gone now."

"Really, just like that?" I was starting to get the hint now. This may have been more of a social call for Aimée than anything else.

"Yeah, maybe it's the medicine Aimée gave me the other day."

"But you just told her a few minutes ago how awful you were feeling."

"What can I tell you? I'm one hundred percent better now."

"Okay, but why don't you turn onto your side, I'd like to check your prostate while you're here. You can never be too careful with these things."

He jumped off the table. "I'd rather not if you don't mind. I think I'll be going now."

"No problem, Ryan, but look, I think I'd like to check on you tomorrow just to make sure you're okay. It says here that you're in room 5521. Maybe I'll bring Aimée along and we can meet your wife...I glanced at the chart again. "...Ashley? Maybe we could have a spot of tea or something?"

He turned pale. "That won't be necessary. I'm sure whatever it was won't be coming back."

After he left, Aimée joined me as I charted the encounter for the ship's record. "He left in a hurry. What happened?" she asked.

"I don't know, but he said he was feeling much better." I smiled. "All's well that ends well."

Puzzled, she said, "I agree. C'mon there are two more patients and then we can get lunch if you can stand being with me."

She was standing next to the door and I waved her to come more fully in the room. I walked behind her and looked out. The nurse was in one of the exam rooms with a patient and the secretary's desk was not visible from where I stood. I closed the door and locked it. She turned to face me and I put my arms around her. She did likewise and we kissed for a long time. She smelled great.

I said, "Say it, please."

"Say what, Jean?"

I loved the sound of my name in French. "What you said last night."

She smiled. "Je te veux Jean, tu me remplis de désir."

"Yeah, that's it. What's it mean again?"

"I want you so much, Jean. You fill me with desire."

"I think I love French."

The color rose in her cheeks and she touched her upper lip with the tip of her tongue. A knock on the door caused us to jump apart. She opened the door and told the nurse that we'd be right out. We laughed and went to see the two remaining patients.

We finished at 11:30 a.m. and took a stroll up to the promenade. There were no patients scheduled for the afternoon and she could pretty much do what she wanted as long as she was available. The wind was picking up and we could feel the boat roll a little. Light drops of rain annoyed us more than got us wet. A few people stood about watching the waves. The sky had darkened considerably and it felt more like dusk than noon.

"You are limping, Jean. Why is that?" she asked noticing I was having trouble keeping up with her.

I wanted to tell her that a diminutive Croatian cop performed an unsedated colonoscopy on me but instead, said, "It's an old sports injury from college. It acts up when the humidity is high. I'll be fine."

"Oh, I am sorry."

We went to the railing and looked over the side. "I've never been at sea before. How bad can one of these storms get?"

"Not too bad usually. Some people are more sensitive than others though. Even this slight movement will bring in a few patients feeling sick. Hopefully, there won't be any…"

A gigantic lightning bolt lit up the sky followed by a deafening clap of thunder which took our breath away. I looked at her and said, "Oh my…"

She giggled and said, "I was just going to say that hopefully there won't be any lightning. Oh well, there will be quite a few patients coming in this afternoon looking for valium and sleeping aids. You do not have to stick around for that."

The rain started to pick up and we took shelter indoors. There was a café on our level and we ordered Caesar salads and white wine. She said, "Too bad about the lightning and rain. I was hoping to take you back to my room."

I grinned. "I see. You're that type of girl."

"What type is that?" she laughed.

"The type that thinks she can just drag a guy to her room whenever she feels like it."

She nodded her head enthusiastically, "Yes, I am definitely one of those types."

"Well, maybe we can get together later. I have a few things to take care of this afternoon too."

The romaine lettuce was crisp, the dressing made fresh, and anchovies dotted the surface. Perfect. She said, "What is your room number? Maybe I will come visit you?"

I shook my head suddenly alarmed. "That wouldn't be a good idea. I have a roommate." I hesitated and added, "I should have mentioned it."

Taken aback she said, "No, no, that is fine. I did not mean to be so forward."

I didn't want to say anything that was going to come back and bite me. "It's not what you think. I'm not married or anything like that."

"Really, it is fine. There is no need to explain. My room will be fine."

I had obviously knocked her out of her comfort zone with that. Even worse, the clear implication was that my roommate was female or else I would have immediately declared otherwise, right? I had already told her that my cousin Vito had his own room, so I couldn't play that card. I thought it over and came to the conclusion that the less said about Betsy the better. I offered her an olive branch and said, "You should still have my room number now that I think about it. You may need me in the clinic for some reason. If I'm not there you can always leave a message."

That seemed to make her happy. "Yes, of course. That makes sense."

"It's 6092."

We chatted and flirted for about thirty minutes more. The mood had changed, of course, with the news of me having a roommate, and I knew she was dying to ask who it was but she was too polite. Toward the end of our lunch, a gentle tap on my shoulder caused me to look up.

It was Betsy and I stood to greet her. "Hi."

"Hi John. I see you have company. Please sit and finish your conversation with the lovely young woman."

She extended her hand to Aimée and said, "Hi, I'm Elizabeth. It's a pleasure."

"Hello, I am Aimée. It is also my pleasure. Would you care to join us?"

Betsy looked at me for a long second and said to Aimée, "How kind. Thank you, but no, I am expecting a guest. I just wanted to say hello to John. I'll be going now."

She walked away and sat alone at a small corner table. I sat and looked down at my empty plate. Aimée patiently waited for me to explain. Eventually, I said, "That was my roommate."

She smiled. Genuinely happy, she said, "How sweet. You share a stateroom with your mother. Now I understand why you were reluctant to tell me who it was. You were embarrassed." She was greatly relieved. "Between caring for your cousin and now this…I am at a loss for words. You may be the noblest man I have ever met. I must think of a special way to reward you later."

I wanted to tell her the truth, I really did, and was just about to when her beeper went off. She jumped to attention and said, "It begins."

I knew what that meant. Many nights in busy city hospital emergency rooms began in the same fashion. I said, "You go back to the clinic. I'll drop by later to help out if you're swamped."

"Thank you. You are almost too good to be real." As she stepped past me she leaned down and gave me a polite kiss and looking into my eyes whispered, "I think we will share a bubble bath tonight with a bottle of champagne and lots of candles."

My heart skipped a beat and I wondered how I was going to make it through the rest of the afternoon with that thought on my mind. "I can't wait."

She walked away and I went over to Betsy. She had just finished ordering a ham and cheese quiche.

Smiling politely, she said, "Hello, stranger."

"Are you really expecting someone to join you?" I asked.

"No, please have a seat. Are you limping?"

"I bumped my knee on the desk in the sick bay this morning."

"I'm sorry."

"No, Betsy, I…I'm sorry about the way we left off last night. I was childish."

She smiled. "It's okay. After you left, I thought about our conversation and realized how strange it must have sounded, and even harder to accept from your point of view. I do hope that you believe me when I say that I emphatically do not consider you a suspect."

"Thank you because I've been discovering that just about everyone else does."

"Really?"

I nodded. "I'm the hands down favorite to go to the gallows."

She chuckled, "I'm sorry for that."

"Not your fault. It's human nature. Thankfully, not everyone on board knows me."

"Well, at least at the masquerade ball tonight you can hide behind your mask."

"Masquerade ball? Really? After all that's happened?"

"Yes, the show must go on. People have paid a lot of money for the right to be on this ship. It wouldn't be fair to turn it into a funeral. Besides, the masquerade ball is a tradition on most cruise lines. Some people consider it the highlight of the trip."

"I didn't know. I don't have a costume."

"You don't need one, but certainly you should wear your tuxedo, and purchase a venetian mask from one of the shops onboard."

"A venetian mask? So this isn't going to be like a Halloween party."

"Heaven's no. No ghosts or goblins. Mostly tuxedoes, cute masks, tipsy matrons in long, period gowns and lots of bling. The younger women generally like to sex it up a bit with daring outfits showing lots of leg and cleavage. You will definitely be entertained. I have no doubt. Under ordinary circumstances, I would have loved to attend."

"Aren't you going?"

"No, I'm afraid that would be pushing my nerves to the limit. I'm physically and emotionally exhausted and can only put on a brave face for so long. I couldn't possibly spend another evening with everyone telling me how sorry they are for me. I've more or less reached the end of my rope with that so I'll just curl up with a good book and a glass of sherry."

"I could curl up with you…just saying."

She smiled broadly as lunch was set down before her. "That's sweet, but I insist you go. Maybe you can have Aimée accompany you. A doctor and his nurse practitioner are an ideal couple."

I looked up in surprise. Aimée was dressed nicely, but in ordinary clothes. She left her white coat with ID badge in the sick bay. "How'd you know she was a nurse practitioner? Have you been to see her?"

"Aimée? It is my ship, remember?"

"But she didn't seem to know you."

"That's because we've never met. The captain reviews all of the dossiers of the crew with me and the head of our human resource department back in London. Given Roger's and my ages, I pay special attention to all the medical personnel we take on. Aimée was particularly qualified for the position in addition to being stunningly attractive as I'm sure you noticed."

"I see. Still, you have an outstanding memory."

"And outstanding hearing as well which brings us to our Croatian volleyball virgin, Katarina."

"I raised my eyebrows and grinned. "What about her?"

"Would you be a dear and ask her not to climb onto the balcony tonight? I'm getting worried about her. Sooner or later she's going to slip and we'll have yet another tragedy on our hands."

I smiled. "I'll see what I can do. Not much gets past you, does it?"

"Not much. For instance, Aimée wears Chanel. I smelled it on her immediately when I came over to your table and I smelled it on you last night despite your having showered before coming to bed. Ergo you and Aimée must have been…how do I say this delicately…very close to each other. Would you like dessert? I feel silly eating by myself."

How awkward was this? I cleared my throat.

She giggled. "John, you should see the expression on your face. It's priceless."

"I don't know what to say."

"Please don't be parochial. You don't need to say anything. You're young and healthy and I already told you I totally approve."

"It doesn't bother you?"

"Not at all. It's not like she's scratching at the balcony door for you like a cat in heat."

I laughed. "I've told her to stop doing that, but I think it's ingrained in her at this point. I'll tell her again."

"You really are an interesting man, Dr. Cesari."

"I am?"

"In barely a week you've managed to make half the women on this ship ovulate. That's pretty good by any standards."

I smiled. "Well, it's nice to be good at something."

"Don't be modest. There's still the other half of the women you haven't met yet."

"You're making me blush now."

She was enjoying making me feel uncomfortable and continued, "It's funny how some men are so naturally adroit at charming women and others are like sledge hammers in a glass museum."

"There was a country song called "Tequila Makes Her Clothes Fall Off." We could change that to *Cesari Makes Her Clothes Fall Off*."

She nodded in agreement. "You'd make a fortune."

"Betsy, can I change the subject? The captain paid me a visit this morning."

"For what purpose?"

"Well, for one, to let me know that I ought to be a suspect although he thinks it unlikely." I raised my hand as she registered surprise. "It's okay, he was very pleasant and told me you spoke to him. He also told me that you vouched for me and that went a long way with him. Thank you for that."

She nodded and added slowly. "Well, it does make sense under the circumstances, John. I guess he would be remiss if he didn't consider it no matter how much I protested to the contrary. He's much too intelligent."

"Yes, I know, and I expected no less."

"And what else did he want?"

"He told me Sven wasn't married."

"That's true. We have no record of that."

I let out a deep breath as I came to the uncomfortable part. "He also told me that they found your stateroom key in his cabin."

Placing her fork down, she gently strummed her fingers on the table. "I guess that would make Sven a suspect, wouldn't it?"

"Yes, it would, but I don't believe it for a minute. It's too convenient. I'm a good judge of character and he didn't kill anyone. He went AWOL because he loves a woman neither you nor the captain knew anything about."

"You are a romantic one, aren't you?"

"Extremely so, but the question I have is how did your room key get in his cabin?"

"How do you think?"

"Betsy, were you having an affair with Sven?"

She chuckled, "Heaven's no. John, you are so funny. I love the way your mind works."

"Well then…?"

Thoroughly amused, she mocked me, "Am I a suspect too? Should I have a lawyer present before I answer any further questions?"

"I'm just trying to help."

"I just told you moments ago that I took a special interest in the medical staff hired for this ship because of Roger and my health issues. I gave Sven a key to our room so he could have emergency access in case something untoward ever happened to one or both of us. Roger had high blood pressure and suffered a minor heart attack several years ago. He wore a medical alert bracelet that sent a distress signal directly to Sven's beeper."

Egg on my face, I let out a deep breath. "I'm sorry, but last night you told me I was the only other person with your room key."

"You're right, I did say that. I hadn't considered Sven's key because I had given it to him so long ago when he joined the crew."

I sat back in my chair and sighed, "Betsy, I have an idea how we can flush out the thief, but I'll need your help."

"I'm listening."

Chapter 25

I bought a venetian mask at one of the shops, and afterward, met Vito in the casino at the craps table. It was raining hard outside and the place was packed. He ordered a whiskey and I looked at my watch. I said, "Let's go sit somewhere private."

There were multiple chairs and small tables scattered around the room and we picked one discreetly off to the side. I looked at him. He had traded in his suit for khakis and a solid blue long sleeve dress shirt with two buttons open at the top allowing dark chest hairs to flow out. His diamond and onyx pinky ring and gold bracelet on one side balanced the twenty-five thousand dollar Rolex on the other wrist. Of course, nothing shouted *I'm from the Bronx* more than the thick, braided gold chain around his neck with the Italian horn dangling from it. Pure muscle swimming with testosterone, he was well over six feet and at least 260 pounds. He reminded me of a great white shark. He didn't really think through life the way most people did. He more or less reacted to various internal and external stimuli. If you threatened him, he attacked. If he was hungry, he attacked. If a fecund female swam by, well, you know the rest.

He sipped his bourbon and said, "I won three hundred bucks already."

"Hey, that's great. Now shut up and listen. Brad's room number is 5028. Forget about gambling, and start staking out his room. His girlfriend's name is Joyce and she's about five-seven, with blonde hair out of a bottle, and a thirty-eight chest courtesy of modern plastic surgery. I'm supposed to meet him on the promenade at midnight or he goes public with the tabloids immediately. He's going to email the video and pictures to a friend back in the states. He also plans to make noise with the captain; although, I'm not sure how far that will get him. The captain's pretty tight with Betsy. If I can get something on him before then to slow him down it would be helpful."

"I don't know what you think you're going to get, Cesari. I mean it's three o'clock in the afternoon. It's not like they're going to get naked and start doing a waltz in the hallway at this hour."

"It doesn't matter whether they're naked or not although that would be icing on the cake. He's married and his wife doesn't even know he's on this cruise. Pictures of them holding hands, kissing, hugging, anything like that should work."

"Fine. I'll see what I can do. What if I don't spot them? Then what?"

"I don't know. I guess I'll just have to buy more time. I'll tell him something. Just do your best, all right? Remember, I need it by midnight."

"Midnight, got it."

He sat there looking around sipping his whiskey and I kicked his leg. "Go!"

"Jesus! You're not going to let me finish my drink?"

"Take it with you."

He left in one direction and I left in the other. Brad had me worried. He was a braggart and a bully and I didn't like either attribute. He wouldn't hesitate to hurt innocent people if it gave him even the slightest advantage. I could deal with him but I needed to know if Joyce was complicit too. If she was then she could easily pull the trigger on that email for Brad which made this doubly complicated. He also implied that she would be willing to perjure herself with him about overhearing me plot to steal the necklace. I had trouble believing that, but you never knew. Money was, after all, the root of all evil.

It was a big ship and the ball didn't begin until 8:00 p.m. It was too early for dinner and I hadn't seen her in the casino. Where would someone like Joyce be on a lazy rainy day? Brad would be off somewhere drinking and plotting his future for when he was done milking healthcare. She would be...getting her nails done?

Maybe.

I ran down to the spa, and walked through, scanning around. Several women were getting pedicures and manicures but no Joyce. There were various other treatment rooms and I entered several but didn't find her. The massage rooms were a different story. Entering those would raise a few eyebrows even if I pretended I was looking for my wife; however, an attendant told me that there was a log in book for all the guests at the entrance so I went to check it out. Skimming through the pages I came across the name Joyce Dombrowski.

A Polish girl.

It said she checked in half an hour ago to use the whirlpool and sauna. The attendant asked me if I'd like to check in. I nodded, signed the book, and asked where the sauna was. He handed me a towel and robe, pointed to a locker room and said there were signs inside that would direct me. I changed, wrapped a towel around my waist, and followed the arrows. There were three saunas, one for men only, one for women only and a coed one. Knowing Joyce, it wasn't too hard to figure out where she was, and I made a bee line for the coed sauna.

Looking through the small glass window of the door, I found her on the bottom bench, her hair tied back in a pony tail, busting out of her towel. It wasn't a bad look. It was time to turn on the Cesari charm. Two much older gentlemen in swim suits with towels folded around their necks oozed sweat as they sat on the top bench chatting. The room was stiflingly hot and dry and as I entered one of the men asked me to pour some water on the briquettes to give the air some moisture. Joyce smiled and waved exuberantly when she saw me.

I finished pouring the water and said, "Hi Joyce. What a coincidence meeting you here."

"Lucky me."

I noticed she was drenched with perspiration. "Where's Brad?"

She frowned. "Who knows? Probably drinking in one of the pubs. He's been celebrating nonstop about this deal he's about to make. I've never seen him so happy…or so drunk."

"That's good for him, I guess. Not good for you. May I sit with you?"

"Of course."

I sat next to her and she boldly ran her eyes up and down my form, appraising my physique. I said, "It's too bad some guys obsess about business and money so much."

"I'll say. That's Brad for sure."

"Say, do you know anything about this deal he's drooling over?"

She shook her head. "All I know is he said it has something to do with that Croatian guy."

"That's all?"

"That's it. He don't tell me much when it comes to his financial dealings, and I don't really care. I'd rather not know anyway. So how are you? I don't get to see you as much as I'd like."

"Well, you're seeing me right now."

"Yeah, but you have that towel on. It's blocking the view."

"I could take it off."

She giggled. "I thought you didn't even like me."

"Why would you think that?"

We were on the loud side, and one of the old guys cleared his throat. "Hey, why don't you two just get a room?"

I looked up and Joyce retorted, "Why don't you take a picture, grandpa, it'll last longer."

I said, "Okay everybody. There's no need for unpleasantness. We were just leaving anyway."

Joyce said, "We were?"

"Sure, I heard there's a jacuzzi around here somewhere."

She smiled, liking that idea. "Let's go."

I never liked saunas anyway, so we left and found the jacuzzi. In fact we found several of various sizes and selected an unoccupied one that could easily seat four. "Are you limping?" she asked.

"A little. Shuffleboard got a little rough yesterday."

"You gotta be careful. Are you wearing anything under that?" she asked pointing at my towel.

"Not much. I was a bit unprepared."

"That's fine with me."

She suddenly dropped her towel to the floor revealing a skimpy bikini bottom. I helped her climb into the tub where she waited for me. I hesitated and glanced around. No one could see me but still, this was a little strange.

She chuckled, "C'mon, no one cares. This is a grown-up cruise."

She had a point. There were no children on this ship at least none that I saw or heard, but would anyone object? I didn't know. Besides, I wasn't really naked. I was wearing my underwear. I let out a deep breath, dropped my towel and quickly climbed into the tub, sitting next to her. She cooed watching me and turned on the jets. The warm current felt good and I started to relax.

Chuckling, she said, "You're too funny. Are those Fruit of The Looms or BVDs? Who wears those anymore?"

"I like things snug."

"I'll bet. From the size of that bulge, I wouldn't want it floating in the breeze either. You ever think of getting a holster for that thing?"

She was funny. I liked that. "I applied for a conceal and carry permit for it, but I haven't heard back yet."

She laughed. "So what do you do with that anaconda besides frighten innocent women like me?"

"Don't worry. He would never hurt you."

"The day's not over yet. So how come so friendly all of a sudden?"

"I'm not sure what you mean. I'm always friendly."

"There's friendly and there's friendly if you know what I mean?"

"Which one am I?"

Our eyes met, and she locked on trying to read me. Finally, she said, "Why do I feel like you're dangling a piece of candy in front of me."

"Me? I think you're reading too much into a chance encounter."

"Oh yeah?"

"Yeah."

Her hand crept over and she rested it on my thigh. When I didn't push it away she smiled and said, "Hmm."

In reply, I blew her a kiss.

She said, "All right. I get it."

I said, "Do you?"

"I think so."

"Good."

She looked around feeling more confident and said, "Here? Right now?"

Still exhausted from last night, I hoped it wouldn't come to that, but braced myself. Glancing around, I said, "Maybe, but I'll be honest Joyce. I need something."

"I knew it," she chuckled. "You really were dangling candy in front of me. Okay, I can live with that. I'm used to bartering with guys. What do you want?"

Smiling I said, "I want a piece of that deal Brad's involved in and I'm willing to do anything for it."

She pursed her lips thinking about that. I reached up and gently touched the side of her face. She liked that. "Really? Anything? Because I know a lot of things."

"Anything."

"And just how can I help you?"

"I know Brad has been sending and receiving emails from the states concerning the details of the venture. I'd like to read some of them so I can make an appropriate offer without losing my shirt."

I leaned over and kissed her. She in turn slid her hand from my thigh up and between my legs whispering, "I think that that is entirely within the realm of possible."

Pushing her hand gently away before things got too out of control I continued, "The situation is rather time sensitive. I need to access his email as soon as possible."

She put her hand back on me and I started throbbing. She whispered, "I need something accessed as soon as possible too."

I looked around again. "Wouldn't we be more comfortable in a bed?"

She undid her bikini top and let it float in the water. "I need to know you're serious. In my business a lot of guys try to get away without paying the agreed upon price."

"And what price did we agree upon?"

"Once here, and then again in a real bed after I deliver what you want. I name the time and place."

She wiggled her bottoms off and tossed them with the top into the raging water. "Deal?"

I studied her carefully and suddenly remembered what a nurse friend had said to me once when I was in training. A female superior was harassing her and the other nurses in the OR, and my friend asked me to run interference for them by romancing the woman in order to distract her. She was hideous and I had refused. My friend told me that if I didn't, she and the other nurses would make my life a living hell. It was one of those shit rolls downhill situations. Nothing personal. When I pouted, she proclaimed, *"Look, Cesari, sometimes you have to take one for the team."*

I looked at Joyce, all botoxed, collagenized, dyed, implanted, only God knew how many men had come along before me. I blocked it all out and said, "I'd love to take a peek at his iPad too."

She climbed on top of me and put her arms around my neck. Nibbling on my ear, she murmured, "I'm sorry honey, but that'll be extra."

"Fine."

Chapter 26

I showered and scrubbed as hard as I could in the locker-room, letting hot water run over me for an extended period not just to cleanse me of chlorine but of my sins as well. I wringed out my soaking underwear and then threw them in the trash can out of frustration. Leaving the spa commando like that made me feel awkward and self-conscious and the chafing from my jeans annoyed me to the point of distraction. For the first time in my life I felt like a whore. Harlot, strumpet, slut, that was me, all of the above. I was now officially for sale. I was going to have to reform my ways. I didn't like this feeling at all. After this cruise, I was going to practice celibacy. Maybe I would join a monastery. That was it! Pope John Cesari the first. Would they take me? Good question.

As I walked toward the infirmary, the ship rolled vigorously, and I braced myself against the nearest wall. The vessel steadied itself and I proceeded to the door leading out to the promenade. Looking through the glass I could see that the rain was driving hard and the wind had picked up considerably. I wondered again just how bad a storm could get here on the Adriatic. Aimée had reassured me that they were usually not too severe, but I guessed things like this were relative. I mean, maybe her idea of severe wasn't the same as mine. Did they get hurricanes here? I had no idea and smiled inwardly. One strong wave and I was already talking myself into a panic.

There were two patients left in the sick bay to tend to. Both looked like they were suffering from anxiety. Aimée looked frazzled and I guessed the wind and the rain were causing the land lubbers a great deal of stress.

She smiled when she saw me in the doorway to her office. "How's it going?" I asked sympathetically.

Looking exhausted she said, "Mon Dieu, we are going to run out of sedatives for sure at this rate."

"Take a deep breath. There's only two more patients out there. I'll see one and you see the other."

"Thank you."

Thirty minutes later, we closed up the clinic and walked to her cabin. It was after five. I cleared my throat and said, "Aimée…?" She waited politely for me to finish. "Would you do me the honor of accompanying me to the masquerade ball tonight?"

She leaned back against her door, smiling coyly. "Are you asking me out on a date, Jean?"

I chuckled, "Yeah, I guess I am. I know it seems kind of silly considering…"

"That we have already made love?"

"Yes."

"Not silly at all. It is amusing the way modern relationships are evolving. It used to be that you went on one, two, three dates before you even started to touch in an intimate way, but now you have sex one, two, three times and then you ask the girl out on a date."

She made me laugh with her analysis but she was pretty close to the mark. "You should write a book."

"I might just do that, but first I will have to get ready for our date. Shall I meet you in the ballroom or will you come here first?"

"I would love to escort you there, but I'm afraid I have too many things to tend to."

"I understand. Between your sweet mother and sick cousin I am surprised you have any energy for anything else."

"Yes, it certainly has been taxing trying to keep up with them, but once they're tucked away, they are usually good for the night. I'll meet you at nine, all right?"

Just then the ship lurched and I fell into her, pinning her against the door. The air squished out of her, she looked up at me smiling and wrapped her arms around my waist. She said, "I want to just bring you inside and keep you there."

I kissed her. "A lovely thought but I really must go. I'll see you tonight if the ship doesn't capsize."

Laughing she said, "Have no fear. I will protect you."

She kissed me again and with great reluctance I pulled away from her. "I'll see you later."

As I walked back to my room, I was feeling pretty bad. All of a sudden, I was becoming acutely aware of all the times in my life I had lied just to get inside some girl's pants. Why did I do it? Were all guys as bad as I was? I hoped not. Maybe I needed some spiritual counseling. I snapped my fingers and looked at my watch. I had a few minutes. Why not?

I found a crewman and he directed me to the chaplain's office which was one deck up. Overwhelmed with these new feelings of remorse and self-reflection, I went there and knocked on the door.

A female voice bid me enter and I walked into a moderate sized room with a wood desk, two consultation chairs, and a sofa. I thought it odd that I saw no overt evidence of religion on the walls. A not unattractive forty-year-old woman in a crisp white sailor's uniform sitting behind the desk stood to greet me. She wore the tiniest of gold crucifix pins on her lapel. Her short brown hair was in a bob and she gave off a very business-like demeanor.

Extending her hand, she introduced herself with a distinct English accent. "Allison Trevor."

I shook her hand, "John Cesari. Is it reverend or…?"

"It's Allison if you don't mind. I don't believe in titles. Please have a seat and what can I do for you?"

Sitting down opposite her, I tried to think how best to sum up my dilemma. "Can I ask what religion you belong to, Allison?"

"Certainly, I was raised Anglican but consider myself non-denominational these days. Just for the record, I have a master's degree in theological studies from Oxford and spent two years in Israel and another year in Saudi Arabia studying Judaism and Islam respectively. I'm also well-versed in Buddhism, Hinduism and Shintoism. What about you?"

"Marginally Catholic and mostly ignorant."

She smiled. "You have something on your mind I gather? How can I help?"

I nodded. "Do you mind philosophical discussions?"

Siting back in her leather chair, she folded her hands. "I'll do my best. Go ahead."

"Is there a heaven and by extension is there a hell?"

"That's a theological question, not a philosophical one, but certainly one of my favorite topics." She paused for a moment as she collected her thoughts. "You want the party line or the truth?"

I liked her already. "The truth."

"The truth is nobody knows for sure about any of it not even the pope himself. It's all a matter of faith and how you view our existence. Did I mention that I also studied physics at the University of Zurich for two years with specific emphasis on the origins of the universe?"

I was impressed. "What do you think?"

"Did you just find out you have some type of terminal illness?"

I laughed. "No."

"Okay, because I just want to make it clear that if you need a medical doctor that's who you should go see. Okay, so what do I think?" She took a deep breath and began slowly. "I have pondered this very question almost since the day I became conscious of it. It drove me as a child and young adult and has consumed most of my life to this day. Thousands of hours of theological study across the globe have done nothing to satisfy my need to know the truth. I have come to believe that there are two types of people in this world: Those that believe everything can be explained through science; that x's and o's are the answer to everything, and there are those who believe that the shear improbability of our existence; the inexplicably complicated nature of even the simplest of one-celled organisms begs the existence of a higher authority. Those people simply cannot accept the randomness of our presence here on the third rock from the sun. The flip side of that argument says that if there is a God and we are his children then why are there literally billions, maybe trillions of other suns, planets, galaxies and universes, an equally good observation. Notice I didn't even bring up the question posed by the discovery of the dinosaurs, which lived millions of years before man even became a twinkle in God's eye.

"Then there is Jesus, whose birth, life, death and teachings have been the single most important seminal event in western culture for the last two thousand years. As a Christian, I have spent countless days and nights trying to unravel the events of two millennia ago in Jerusalem, trying to understand what happened in historical context. The question that faces every Christian is trying to decide if the story of Jesus rising from the dead is simply an unadulterated hoax perpetrated by his well-intentioned but perhaps deluded followers. For me, it boils down to this; why would twelve otherwise rational men and select others such as Mary Magdalene and notably, St. Paul, go around preaching sedition and blasphemy when they knew that not only would their own people put them to death but the Romans would as well. A most unpleasant, agonizing, and thoroughly humiliating death I might add in case you're unfamiliar with the Romans' talent for inflicting pain upon enemies of the empire."

She looked past me for a moment lost in reflection as I contemplated that. I said, "Still, just because you can't answer the question of why they would do that doesn't mean what they said actually happened."

"No, it doesn't, but you asked what I think, and I think it goes contrary to human nature for even one person to die proclaiming something happened when he knew for a fact it didn't let alone multiple people. Remember, they stood to gain nothing. No monetary reward, no fame, nothing, only extreme pain and misery. They dispersed across the globe even reaching as far as India, on foot mind you, living as paupers and dying as martyrs because they believed in something so big, so momentous, that they would rather suffer and die than deny it. Think about that. Well, until I can explain why anyone would do something like that for any reason other than their absolute certainty that they spoke the truth, I choose to believe, and that is what faith is all about after all…choice.

"So I believe because, after many years of study, travel, research, and reflection, I cannot do otherwise. My senses tell me this is the right thing and I am at ease in my belief. I don't deny science. I just don't accept it as the ultimate source of all we desire to know. To your original question; if there is a God, then there is a heaven and there is a hell. What lays ahead for us we'll just have to wait to find out. Was that helpful?"

"Very. Do you do confession?"

"Is there something weighing heavily on you, John?"

"Yeah, sort of, but it seems silly after what we just spoke about."

"You don't have to tell me if you aren't comfortable, but you should know that I am bound by oath and protected by law to keep in strictest confidence any conversations within these walls."

"I'm worried about going to hell."

She smiled. "We all are or should be, but why in particular are you so concerned?"

"My relationships with women lean toward the…shallow side."

"I see. You have a tendency to…sleep around?"

I nodded. "Thank you for being delicate. Yes, something like that. Some lying is involved too."

She remained dead-panned and I thought she would make a great psychiatrist. "You lie to women to get them in bed?"

"Not always."

"Often enough?"

"Maybe lying is too strong a word."

"Misleading, half-truths, deception, insincerity, partial disclosure, they're all euphemisms for the same thing, and if you have to qualify it, then you're only kidding yourself." I nodded, and she pursed her lips. "Do you think you have sexual addiction, John?"

"Don't all men? To be fair, I'm not always the one who starts it. I just don't seem to know how to turn off whatever needs to be turned off."

She thought about that for a minute. "Women are attracted to you?"

"Yes, unusually so."

"This bothers you because...why?"

"It's not always good for me to say yes."

She seemed puzzled by that. "Do you mind my asking what is it exactly that women find attractive about you? Are you funny? Tell a good story? I mean it can't be your looks? Please don't take offense. I'm just trying to understand."

I raised my eyebrows. It never hurt to get smacked down once in a while. Reality checks were good. I just didn't expect it to happen during confession. "No offense taken, and I can't really answer your question. Somebody once told me that I give off sexual vibes that women pick up on. I'm not even sure what that means. I don't do it consciously whatever it is."

She nodded politely almost as if she was having trouble believing me. "Would you mind standing up for a moment?"

I stood up and looked at her with bewilderment. "What is it?"

"Turn completely around, please."

"Turn around? Why?"

"I just want to get a feel for what you're saying. Maybe there's some physical issue I can help you address to keep these women at bay. Maybe it's not spiritual guidance you need so much as a fashion consultant."

I twirled around slowly and she shook her head, "I still don't get it. You can sit down."

For crying out loud. She was pushing my buttons and I felt the color rise in my cheeks. That last comment was a bit unnecessary and even kind of mean.

Perplexed, she sat there thinking about my problem with furrowed brows. Suddenly, her demeanor changed as she raised her head, gently sniffing the air. "What is that?" she asked.

I sniffed once and shook my head, "I don't smell anything"

She looked around her office, zeroing in on the air vents and then back at me. "It's cinnamon…" Looking at me strangely she added. "You're not carrying cookies on you or candy?"

"No, of course not."

Letting it drop for the moment, she returned to our conversation, saying, "Okay, John, what would you like me to tell you?"

"I'm just kind of nervous is all. Thinking about things. You know what I mean? Like maybe I've been doing the wrong things."

"I see, and you think that maybe you've committed a sin that could land you in the fiery pits many leagues below?"

"I was wondering what God might think about me."

"Well, I don't pretend to speak for God, but on behalf of women everywhere, you're kind of pissing me off."

Surprised, I watched her take a deep breath. She said, "All right, it's like this. Sex isn't necessarily a sin in most of the earth's religions, but lying is definitely a sin in every one of the earth's major belief systems so…knock off the lying and you should be okay. The fact that women come after you isn't really your fault. I'm not sure you're required to say no in order to gain access to heaven. That's a bit old fashioned and a very Catholic way of thinking about it. Now, go in peace and lie no more."

"That's it? No Hail Mary's and a bunch of Our Fathers?"

She chuckled. "No amount of praying and or punishment will help you if you're not truly repentant, and only you know what is in your heart. Make yourself a better person and then pray. Don't pray because you think it will make you better. John, you're not a bad person because you like sex, okay? But lying is a bad habit for any reason…and lying to a woman for sex can be very hurtful. Is that what you want to do? Hurt someone you care about?"

I shook my head and looked at my watch. It was time to go. "Thank you rev…Allison, but I lost track of time. I have to leave now."

"It was a pleasure meeting you, John. Stop by anytime. I enjoyed our little chat. Services are held every Sunday at nine and the chapel just down the corridor is open 24/7. It's a great place to meditate. Let me show you out. I was just about to close up for the day anyway."

She came around from her desk and walked past me to the door, placing her hand on the knob. I followed and as I neared her she took another long sniff and said, "What are you wearing?"

"What do you mean?"

"Your after shave, does it have cinnamon in it?"

"I'm not wearing any aftershave."

Almost as if she couldn't control herself she sniffed again which I thought was kind of rude. "I find that hard to believe. Well, whatever it is, it's very nice."

We stood there awkwardly for a moment as I waited for her to open the door. Eventually, I said, "Thank you, Allison. I really appreciate your time and if it's all the same to you I think I'm going to say a few Hail Mary's tonight."

"Whatever floats your boat."

I looked at her. She smiled and pointed a finger at me, saying, "We're on a ship. Get it?"

Almost reluctantly, she stepped out of the way and opened the door for me. As I passed she said, "Are you sure you're not wearing any aftershave?"

Chapter 27

Not sure if I felt better or not, I left the chaplain's office and made my way back to my stateroom to get ready for the ball. Betsy sat in a chair reading. There was an empty short-stemmed martini glass with an olive at the bottom next to her on a small table.

"Gin or vodka?" I asked. She looked up and I could see she'd been crying. The ice was finally starting to thaw.

"Gin. How was your day?"

"Busy. Are you all right?"

She nodded. "I'm fine. Just coming to grips with everything. It was a long journey Roger and I had been on. I think it's just starting to dawn on me that it's over."

I smelled cigarette smoke and noticed an ash tray with several spent butts that had been dashed out. "I didn't know you smoked."

"A well-guarded state secret. I've cut way down from the good old days, but the recent stress is getting to me."

I smiled. "As a physician, I'm not supposed to condone such behavior, but as a realist, whatever gets you through the night..."

"Tonight that will be gin, and maybe a Cesari chaser depending on when you return from the ball."

"I'll do my best."

Hearing the wind howling at the balcony door, I walked over to look out. Rain was coming down in sheets and lightning lit up the ominous looking sky though the boat held its own and I didn't feel much motion.

I said, "It's really coming down now."

"Yes, it is. I find the rain peaceful for some reason. I always have." Perking up she added, "So are you taking Aimée to the ball?"

"She's going to meet me there, but yes, we'll be together."

"If she invites you to her room, please feel untethered. I was just teasing about the Cesari chaser. At the rate I'm downing martinis, I'll probably be asleep anyway. Besides, I like the way you and Aimée look together. You fit."

I had decided to come clean with Aimée about Betsy and Vito and was quite sure the evening would end with a glass of champagne being tossed in my face if not something worse. "To be honest, I'm not sure at all what's going to happen."

Misinterpreting my concern, she said reassuringly, "Don't sell yourself short. I can't imagine she doesn't find you attractive."

"Thanks, I appreciate the vote of confidence." I hesitated, and changing the subject, said, "Did you think about my proposal?"

"Yes, I did." She reached down into a bag by her chair and handed me a rectangular leather jewelry case. "I do hope it works. It would be nice to bring whoever it is to justice."

I opened the case and examined the imitation necklace folded in place. It glimmered in the light and was of such high quality, the casual observer would never know the difference. I said, "Thank you for trusting me, Betsy."

She smiled, "With what? Fake emeralds and rubies?"

"Still, I don't like gambling with other people's property."

"Trust me. These mean nothing to me. The real ones, however, are a different story. If using these as bait can bring whoever it is to justice, then I'm all for trying. I do hope your plan works, John, but please don't be disappointed if it fails. I have a feeling you are up against a very clever individual."

"Thanks. Well, I'd better get ready. Cocktail hour will begin soon."

I went into the bathroom to clean up and dress for the ball. I was about to splash on some after shave and thought about what had happened in the chaplain's office. I opened the bottle of Drakkar Noir by Guy Laroche. It was my signature scent. Placing my nose at the opening I searched unsuccessfully for any hint of cinnamon. Putting that memory behind me, I splashed some on and looked in the mirror. I almost made the Bond comment again and checked myself. Maybe that was my problem with women. Perhaps, I was too self-confident and that caused the release of some sort of man-scent that only women could detect. I glanced at the bottle of Drakkar. Maybe it was too potent and some women just couldn't resist it. Well, I wasn't going to find an answer tonight, and for the moment I was in up to my eyeballs so there was no point in going against the current. However, I made a vow not to accept any new passengers on the Cesari train.

I put my tuxedo on and straightened myself out as Betsy watched, thoroughly entertained. "You look pretty sharp, doctor."

Before I could stop myself, I turned to her and said, "That's Bond, mum. James Bond."

She laughed. "You are too funny."

I smiled. "I try."

"Well, have a good time."

"Thank you, Betsy." I leaned down and kissed her, adding, "Take it easy with the martinis, all right? Remember, no more than one an hour or you'll blow over the legal limit."

Smiling, she nodded and I slid the box with the necklace into my jacket's inside pocket. It just barely fit and made a slight bulge. In my world almost everyone would have assumed it was a pistol. My mask was mostly black with ornate red and gold trim. I tied it loosely around my neck so that I could put it on easily when necessary. I wasn't sure how strict they were at these affairs, never having been to one.

After saying goodnight to Betsy, I wandered off to find Vito still staked out down the hall from Brad's room. He was leaning discreetly against the corridor wall behind a potted fern. He was five doors down and near a stairwell.

"Anything interesting yet?" I asked.

He checked out my tuxedo and mask. "Where are you going?"

"A masquerade ball. You didn't answer my question."

"Are you actually going to wear that thing?"

"Yes, and you still didn't answer my question."

"The hooker came to the room about two hours ago and I haven't seen the guy yet. I took a few pictures of her. Man what a sight. She was classic. You could have warned me."

"Her name's Joyce, and yeah, I suspect she's addicted to cosmetic surgery."

"She was wearing a skimpy bathing suit and sandals with heels. Jesus! She doesn't care who sees what."

I looked at my watch. It was getting close to 8:00 p.m. "Are you sure you didn't see him go in? Cocktail hour starts in a few minutes and I can't believe he would miss it. He's been perpetually sloshed ever since he boarded."

He gave me a nasty look. "I'm telling you I didn't see him go in. All right? Now, do you have something else to say?"

“Fine.”

Just then the door opened and Brad and Joyce came out in their evening attire. He looked sharp in his tux and she wore a long, flowing red evening gown. They wore their venetian masks which covered the bridge of their noses and eyes. Her mask had a long feather sticking out and she held a blue Gucci bag. The bag was for me and in it hopefully was the iPad and the password to Brad’s email account. When the time was right, she would casually leave it lying somewhere for me to pick up. Vito busily snapped photos.

After they were out of ear shot, I nudged him. “Nothing gets by you, does it?”

He shook his head. “He must have been in his room all afternoon because I’ve been standing here for hours.”

“You didn’t leave your post, not even for a minute?”

He grew quiet and looked down. I said, “I thought so.”

“I had to go to the bathroom. Give me a break.”

“If this were the army you’d be shot for dereliction of duty.”

“Shut up.”

I looked at him and he became uncomfortable and asked, “What?”

“Why are you still standing here? Go after them and don’t stop at the bar on the way.”

Jesus Christ! I had to stay on him like a hawk. He followed Brad and Joyce to the elevator and I took the staircase down to the ballroom. Repeating in my mind over and over, red dress, blue bag, red dress, blue bag.

I reached the ballroom at 8:30 p.m. and it was brimming to overflowing with partygoers. I estimated at least a thousand people had turned out. To a man, all wore tuxedoes with slight variations. I wore a black cummerbund, many wore vests both black and white. Some had tails and cravats instead of bowties.

There were top hats, walking sticks, and occasional monocles. The chandeliers sparkled in the light and the orchestra played a romantic tune. The ladies were the highlight of the show as always in their beautiful gowns, shoes, and bling. Champagne flowed as if somebody had decided to outlaw it tomorrow. I looked around to see if Aimée was here. I was a little early and didn't see her. Not realizing what a mad house this would be I hadn't thought to pre-arrange a meeting spot but figured the bar would be a likely place, so I headed there, grabbing a couple of cocktail shrimp from a passing waiter.

I ordered a Southern Comfort Manhattan with two cherries. I was feeling kind of sweet. The bartender looked at me like I had two heads until I upgraded to a premium bourbon. It was already paid for, so he made a good point. Looking around, I discovered Katarina walking slowly with an old man using a walker. He was well into his eighties. She was so out of control. She wore a very pretty black sleeveless evening dress with a slit up the side practically to her waist. Her reddish hair was layered and recently trimmed. She wore a gold mask that she held up to her eyes with an attached stylet. With three inch heels, she towered over the old guy.

The bartender handed me my drink and I thanked him. It looked right. There was a twist of orange and two cherries at the bottom. I sniffed it and took a sip. Nice. He knew what he was doing. Katarina reached me a step ahead of the old man.

I said, "Who's your friend?"

She took her mask off and frowned. "Is Edvard, my fiancée, most eligible bachelor in all Dubrovnik."

I nearly snorted bourbon from my nose and suppressed a laugh. Edvard eventually reached me and I proffered my hand. "Hello, my name is John."

He looked up over his thick glasses and scrunched his nose. He said something in Croatian and I realized he spoke no English, but he took my hand. His was bony and pale and I started to wonder what all the fuss was about. I doubted he would make it much past the wedding night under any circumstances. Katarina said, "He says is pleased to meet you. He will have vodka martini two olives."

She smiled. He thought I was a waiter. This was hysterical. "Maybe you should find him a table so he can sit and I'll bring him a drink. He won't last long standing around like this. What would you like?"

"I am no allowed to drink in front of Edvard. He is old fashioned and would disapprove." It just kept getting better and better. She steered Edvard toward an open table and I was startled by how low cut her dress was in the back. It went all the way down to her panty line if she was wearing any. I didn't put anything past her. As they crept along slowly, I chuckled softly to myself at the scene and then ordered a martini for him.

When it came, I deftly navigated the throngs of guests with the two drinks and made it safely to their table spilling not one drop. Pleased with myself, I set down Edvard's drink in front of him and sat next to Katarina, subtly positioning my drink between us so she could sip it if she desired. I nodded at the drink and she smiled in understanding. We sat facing the dance floor which was just starting to warm up. People weren't quite lubricated enough yet.

Watching Edvard sip his martini with a shaky hand I said to Katarina, "He just spilled more of his drink than I did walking across the room with it."

"Don't pick on fiancée."

I shook my head laughing which made her smile. She poked me. "Is not funny. We are in love."

Oh brother. "Fine, you're in love. So what is this all about?"

"Is all your fault."

"Why?"

"Midget tell Berislav she catch you kissing me. She tell him I can no leave room without be watched. I tell Berislav you are animal, force yourself on me for virgin sex. Midget say I lie. Berislav very angry. He and midget agree fiancée should spend time with me. Here we are… spend time."

She was pissed. I could feel it in her tone. Pissed but trapped. I said, "Don't worry, I have a plan."

"What plan? Old man already want take me some place quiet to talk."

She was killing me. "Relax, he's harmless."

"Pfft, is easy for you to say. You know what he wants me to do later?"

"Please don't tell me. I'd rather not have that visual."

"If you have plan, better start soon before I jump overboard."

The old man turned to her and said something. She turned to me and said, "He go bathroom. I must help."

"Okay. We'll have to try to talk alone later, all right?"

"Is all I try to do whole trip is talk alone with you, and all you do is run away."

"I understand. This is different. Take him to the bathroom and we'll talk more when you return. I don't want him wetting himself here."

She was indignant as she chastised me, "Be nice. Is future husband and love of my life."

They shuffled away slowly, and I spotted Aimée at the bar looking around for me. I waved and went to greet her. I had finished my Manhattan and left the glass on the table. She was stunning in a deep blue evening gown with a bit of a ruffled, flared bottom. There was enough cleavage to distract me and a beautiful emerald pendant dangled from a gold chain allowing me to hold my gaze without feeling like too much of a creep. Women had this stuff down to a science.

She held a small evening bag in one hand and her white venetian mask in the other. Her hair was done up in gentle waves which flowed around her shoulders. I leaned down to kiss her on the cheek and she turned abruptly catching my lips. She said, "You smell nice, Jean."

She was going to hate me before the night was over, so I might as well enjoy myself while I could. "Thank you, and you look so beautiful I am without words."

Smiling, she said, "Thank you. You look very handsome in a tuxedo."

"I am the darkness and you are the light."

"You are very romantic."

"You mean for an American?"

Chuckling, she said, "I mean for anyone."

"May I order us a cocktail?"

"Champagne will be fine."

I caught the attention of the bartender, placing the order. I stuck with another Manhattan. Drinks in hand, we meandered around the room people-watching. Not unexpectedly, she unconsciously studied many of the women's ensembles, an instinctual ritual since the beginning of mankind. These subtle differences between men and women always amused me. For instance, I wore a tuxedo and thought I looked pretty good, but I really didn't care what the other men in the room were wearing.

We eventually wound up near a marble column at the periphery and chatted amiably about nothing and everything. She had been a nurse practitioner for six years and liked to paint with watercolors in her spare time. French politics drove her crazy. She'd like to have children someday but not now. She had way too much on her plate at the moment. Traveling the world was her passion and she hoped to spend an extended period of time in New York when her financial situation permitted.

Antonela walked by looking for something or someone. Even with heels on she was barely over five feet. I quickly donned my mask and turned away. Aimée was amused, "Did you see the bogey man?"

"No, nothing like that, but it is a masquerade ball. Aren't we supposed to wear masks?"

"Of course." She put her mask on as well. Venetian masks were cool. You could breathe, eat and drink with them, and in a crowded, dark room they served to adequately conceal your appearance. Antonela continued walking and was soon lost in the crowd. The little troll was going to get hers.

Aimée noticed me observing Antonela out of the corner of my eye. She grinned. "An old flame?"

"Hardly."

"You seem frightened of her."

I didn't say anything and she let it drop. "They are playing a waltz. Dance with me."

A slow waltz wasn't very intimidating and I agreed. We put our glasses down and stepped into the middle of the dance floor. She placed her right hand in my left and her left hand on my right shoulder. I gently rested my right hand on her waist. Not too close and not too far. Sensing my trepidation, she said, "Don't be nervous. It's very easy. I will lead. Just follow me and remember it's 1,2,3; 1,2,3, like that. Now on the top of the beat we go."

We were off to the races. After a clumsy, flat-footed start, I started to get the hang of it. She smiled, "Now, we move around the room, slowly, following the rhythm and losing ourselves in the music. Get ready, I am going to twirl."

She stepped away, spun around gracefully and was back in position before I could even register surprise. I smiled. "That was beautiful."

"Merci. Now, if you desire to be beautiful as well you must show some feeling in your movement. Shift your weight from your heels to the ball of your feet almost as if you are leaning forward. Then anticipate the beat, and just before it comes, bend your knees slightly, dip down, and rise to full height upon its arrival. Here let us try. That is it. Now, with feeling and passion. The waltz is for lovers."

We danced around the room a bit more gracefully and I was starting to have fun. We passed Katarina's table and I saw that Berislav, Brad, and Joyce had joined them. Antonela stood discreetly to one side keeping an eye on the room. Katarina and Joyce spotted me on the dance floor and watched me intently clearly wondering who Aimée was.

We circled the room two more times as the orchestra played an extended version of Anne Murray's "Could I Have This Dance," a slow country waltz. As luck would have it the song finished right in front of Katarina's table and as everyone clapped, Aimée put her arms around me and said, "You are a fast learner."

"That's because you're a great teacher."

She pulled me down for a kiss and out of the corner of my eye, I saw Katarina, Joyce, and Antonela giving me the death stare.

I felt like a marked man.

Chapter 28

Aimée and I ate raw oysters and caviar from a buffet set up to one side of the room. We shared a crème brulee and danced some more. After my Manhattan and her two glasses of champagne, we decided to do hits of absinthe in the traditional way using an absinthe spoon, sugar cube, and ice cold water dripped in until the liquid turned a pretty opaque green. For a French girl, she was a light-weight, and by 10:30 p.m., she was pretty toasty and starting to get randy. I had been tracking both Joyce and Katarina, waiting for the right opportunity. I'd lost Antonela in the crowd.

Preoccupied like that, I hadn't noticed Aimée gradually moving her chair closer, and she was near enough now that I could feel her breathing on me. She slipped her hand onto my thigh and I looked at her.

She whispered, "I am ready."

"For what?"

She giggled. "It's so noisy here. Let's go someplace quiet to talk."

I laughed. I thought I had made up that line. "Oh yeah?"

"Yes, and I can teach you to dance better in the privacy of my room."

"Very tempting, but I'd like to stay a little while longer if you don't mind. Not too much longer. I'm enjoying watching everyone dance."

She gave me a little pouty smile but agreed. Brad had moved to a corner to talk privately with Berislav, and Joyce took that opening to nod at me to follow her. She stood up and headed to the bathroom with her Gucci bag. Good girl.

Aimée said, "Jean, are you listening to me? I need you…"

I hadn't been listening because I had been so focused on the room. I kissed her. "I need you too. I'll be right back, Aimée, and then we'll go to your room. I promise. Please excuse me for a moment. I have to go to the bathroom."

I walked hastily and caught up with Joyce just outside the entrance to the lady's room. We were hidden from the dance floor by a privacy wall. Nonetheless, she glanced around nervously and reached into her bag coming out with her room key.

She said, "I couldn't grab the iPad. He was playing on it right up until we left. It's on the coffee table. Here's the key to our room. Leave it on the kitchen counter."

"What about his email?"

"It's bradsimmons, all one word, at gmail.com, and his password is letsdoit69."

"You're kidding?"

She smiled, "He can dream, can't he? Okay, hurry. I don't want him to catch us like this. He'll go through the roof if he sees me talking to you. For some reason, he hates you."

I went to grab the key from her and she pulled back. "A quick kiss first and do it like you mean it, like the way you kissed that girl on the dance floor. Who is she by the way? She's beautiful."

Glancing both ways, I leaned down and kissed her. I was glad she was on my side. "She's just a friend."

"I bet." She relinquished the key and added, "Don't forget our deal."

"I won't, but can I ask just one more teeny tiny favor."

"Jesus Christ! How much more can I do for you?"

"I'm willing to pay for it."

"Oh yeah?"

"Yeah."

"Hurry. What?"

"When you leave the ballroom later please kiss Brad very publicly like you adore him, and remember to take the masks off."

She looked confused. "Why?"

"I leaned down, kissed her on the ear, and whispered a few words of encouragement.

Smiling she said, "You're pretty wild. You better not break that promise."

"I won't."

Racing out of the ballroom, I hoofed it up the stairwell to her room. The corridor outside was empty and I quickly accessed it. The iPad was exactly where she said it was, and I snatched it, tossing her room key on the kitchen table. I bolted from the room and made a bee line to the ship's business center on the main deck, thoroughly pleased with myself. I was perspiring by the time I got there and took a seat, firing up one of the laptops.

I was alone and tapped nervously on the desk in anticipation. I looked at my watch. It was after 11:00 p.m. Hurry. After what seemed like forever the login screen came and I accessed the internet.

I pulled up Brad's email account and logged in successfully. I deleted every file in his inbox, outbox, and draft box. Then, just for fun I went to his settings and changed his password. I grinned and powered off the laptop, breathing a sigh of relief.

As soon as I disposed of the iPad, he could kiss my ass. The sound of the door closing behind me echoed loudly in the small room and I turned abruptly.

Shit!

Antonela stood with her back up against the door pointing her .45 at me. She was out of breath and her hair was a bit tousled. She was a strange sight in high heels, a short black dress, pearls and handbag. If she wasn't so damned nasty, she'd be cute. Where did she get the clothes? I guessed she'd had a busy day shopping.

She seemed curious and said, "What you do?"

Thinking quickly, I replied, "I needed to send an email back home. I meant to do it earlier, but I forgot and the business center is always so busy I figured this would be a good time."

She nodded and smirked. "I see. Is that why you steal iPad from fat American's room?"

I caught my breath as my brain raced. She read my mind and smiled. "Don't bother lie. You left ballroom in such big hurry. I was suspicious and follow. You go in room with nothing and come out with iPad. Why is important?"

For lack of any good response I asked, "How'd you know whose room it was?"

"Anybody go near Berislav and girl I follow."

She was good. I nodded and she added, waving the gun menacingly. "Answer question."

"He took pictures of me and Mrs. Harrington and was threatening to use them to hurt us."

She liked that and grinned. "He don't like you."

It wasn't a question. Apparently this was common knowledge throughout the ship. "No, he doesn't."

"So what you really do here?"

I sighed. "He told me that he had already prepared an email with the images to send to some tabloid paper in the US that would use them to embarrass Mrs. Harrington. I just hacked his account and deleted his email."

She raised her eyebrows. "Seriously?"

I nodded and she seemed to relax. "I guess that is okay. As long as has nothing to do with girl."

Starting to breathe easily again, I said, "Absolutely nothing to do with her."

She made a humming sound as she stared me down for a full minute. Suddenly she snapped to attention and with an edge in her voice demanded, "When I return to room everything gone. Where is?"

I shrugged my shoulders and shook my head innocently. My heart skipped a beat. "I don't know what you're talking about. Were you robbed?"

"You lie."

I could tell she was starting to work herself up again. "No, I didn't. I swear. Why would I take your stuff?"

"I don't know. You no seem stupid. Get Antonela angry again."

With genuine alarm in my voice, I said, "Trust me. I would never do that."

Fear turned her on and she sneered at me. "Maybe I take you to room and interrogate?"

"Please don't."

She pursed her lips thinking it over. I could practically read her mind. It was a long way to her cabin from here to walk with a gun pointed in my back. Even at this late hour, we would undoubtedly be seen. I didn't like the look in her eyes or the way she was breathing; shallow with quick respirations. She appeared to come to some sort of conclusion.

"Stand up, turn around, and put hands behind back."

"Antonela, please…"

In response, she cocked the gun. "You say wrong."

Oh no, here we go again. "I'm sorry. I meant Shwimbo."

She waved the gun. "Remember, is hair trigger. Now do as I say."

I stood slowly and turned around as she fished a pair of handcuffs from her bag. Desperately trying to get her to reconsider, I said, "The door doesn't have a lock on it."

It was solid wood, however, and would block us from view. She said, "Is late. No one come."

"I came. Someone else might."

"Put hands behind back. Danger make it more exciting."

She approached me cautiously. She was a trained law enforcement officer, but was well aware I was much larger than her, and no amount of training could mitigate against that reality. That's what guns were for. The great equalizers.

Up close behind me, she pressed the muzzle hard in the small of my back and said, "We have fun right here."

She deftly snapped one cuff onto my left wrist, and just as she was about to do the same to the other one, the ship suddenly lurched and rolled violently from the effects of the storm raging outside.

I stumbled backward, knocking her down and landing on her. The gun went off loudly in the small room. The round lodged harmlessly in the wall and the pistol went flying from her hand across the room. I spun around quickly, pinning her down as she gasped for air. A 220 pound man had just landed on a 100 pound woman without any preparation on her part, and I wondered if I broke any of her ribs. She writhed in pain as I frisked her for any other weapons. She had none on her person but I found the deadly, stiletto hairbrush in her bag, along with the key to the handcuffs.

I secured the .45, expelling the chambered round and unlocked the cuff on my wrist. She was red in the face, but eventually settled down as she looked at me seriously concerned for her safety. Physically, she was fine just winded.

Coughing, she whispered, "What you do?"

"More than you would do for me."

I toyed with the idea of handcuffing her to the leg of the desk naked for the crew to find in the morning, but my mother raised me better. Besides, she was no threat to me anymore. I took the gun, knife and cuffs, shoved them into her bag and tossed her room key at her.

Grabbing the iPad, I left her lying there on the floor without another word. Out on the promenade, the driving rain drenched me instantly and I was barely able to fight the wind and tossing of the ship as I made my way to the railing. I hurled the iPad and her bag overboard. It was almost midnight and I would have loved to taunt Brad with his inadequacies, but I had left Aimée in the lurch and felt bad. He was no longer a serious concern of mine anyway. Things were falling into place. I would find him in the morning and tell him the good news. I hoped he had a hangover when I ran into him.

I liked CEO's of hospitals.

I really did…

Not.

Chapter 29

It was after midnight and I must have looked a mess, dripping wet and hair mussed up. I still had my mask and placed it on as I searched for Aimée in the ballroom. In the low lighting with ninety percent of the guests drunk or tipsy, I was doing fine but I couldn't find her.

Katarina tapped me on the shoulder. "Shall we dance?"

How she always managed to find me no matter where I was completely baffled me. For a second, I considered that she had planted some type of tracking device on me. Remembering I needed to talk to her, I said, "Sure."

She put her arms around my neck for one of those slow swaying dances and flinched as she touched me. Stepping back she said, "You're all wet."

"Yeah, I had to go outside for a minute. Do you want to dance or not?"

She hesitated but only for a second and put her arms back around me. "Sure. So where is new girlfriend?"

"I don't know. I was just looking for her."

"She find another man already? I would never abandon you like that."

The dance floor was jammed and we accidentally bumped into another couple. Excusing ourselves we moved in a different direction. I said, "How can you say that when you're here with your fiancé?"

She snorted derisively, "Oh please. You are only man for me."

"Where is he anyway?"

"He sleep at table. I take back to room soon."

"Should you be out here with me like this?"

"Berislav drunk, old man sleep, midget go somewhere, no one care. So what did you want to talk to me about?"

"I think I figured a way out of your marriage dilemma."

She slid her hands down and grabbed my butt, saying, "I'm listening."

"Are you?"

"Yes, talk already before I get bored."

"I have something very valuable, worth many millions of dollars. It will easily pay off your debt to the gangsters. I'll give it to you and Berislav."

She looked at me suspiciously. "Old lady necklace?"

I nodded and she added, "So you did steal like everybody say?"

"How I came across the necklace isn't as important as the fact that I would like to use it for a good cause."

Studying me as if for the first time she asked, "Did you kill husband? I no believe."

I shook my head vigorously to reassure her. "Absolutely not. You have to believe me on that."

"I believe. You would give up millions of dollars to help Katarina?"

"Yes, I would."

She grabbed me around the neck and kissed me long and ardently. When she came up for air there were tears in her eyes. "Is nicest thing anyone has ever done for me."

"If it'll work."

"Even if no work. Is still nicest thing anyone has ever done for me. Thank you."

"You're welcome."

"I have the necklace on me. I'll give it to you as soon as the dance is over. The question is how to handle this in such a way that Berislav and Antonela don't realize I'm helping you. They'll get suspicious if they find out I gave the jewels to you."

She thought about it for a minute and said, "Is easy. I tell Berislav I get angry at you for trying to sex me in hallway last night." I raised my eyebrows. "I go to your room to yell at you. He knows I have temper and will believe me. No one there but door open. I go in and see old lady's necklace on table and take. She still staying with you, right?"

I nodded. "That's the most ridiculous story I ever heard. No one in their right mind would believe that."

"Except for one thing…"

"What?"

"I really do have necklace. How else explain? Is more believable than you give me."

I considered it for a few moments. It was preposterous in its premise but…it just might work. Especially since Berislav's desire for the jewels may outweigh his common sense. It certainly couldn't hurt and she really would have the necklace. The real benefit was that if Berislav was the thief and already had the real necklace as Antonela suggested he may have, then he would freak out at seeing a second set of gems. This would throw him into panic and confusion. That is of course, unless he already knew there was an imitation necklace because he read Betsy's lips over dinner when she told me.

So if he becomes upset, then he has the real jewels but didn't know about the reproduction. If he is nonchalant about the whole thing then he has the real jewels and knows Katarina stole the phony set. If he is overjoyed and excited then he wasn't the thief in the first place and thinks he just came into a massive windfall.

I thought about Katarina. God, she was a natural born liar. I said, "Have you ever thought about going to law school?"

"Why?"

The song ended and people clapped. "Just a thought. Okay, here they are. Go put them in your bag and take the old man to his room. One more thing, when you give the necklace to Berislav, I want you to study his reaction carefully and tell me about it, but other than that you should stay as far from me as possible for a while."

She made a face. "I no stay away. You are my hero. I must give reward." She glanced around furtively. "Is dark. I could give reward right now if want."

She reached down to my crotch but I caught her with my hand and chided her. "Stop. This is serious. Now get going."

I handed her the box with the necklace, and pouting, she turned to walk away. Watching her, I wondered how I had let her ruin my vacation like this. Maybe I should just walk away? I shook my head and knew I couldn't. Chicks in a fix were my kryptonite.

The party was still in full swing but I gave up finding Aimée there and decided to try her cabin. At almost one, I gently knocked on her door, once…twice…three times and waited. A hushed voice said, "Who is it?"

"It's me, John."

She opened the door and let me in, wiping sleepies from her eyes. Wearing a pink flannel robe with fluffy slippers, she looked adorable. "What happened, Jean? You never came back." Her eyes widened as she got close. "Mon dieu, you are soaked to the bone. Come in and dry off before you catch your death of cold. Why did you go out in the rain?"

Sidestepping the question, I said, "I'm sorry about leaving you like that, Aimée."

She went to the bathroom and returned with a bunch of towels. "Undress and dry off. I will make us coffee."

I threw my clothes to the floor and patted myself down. We had already seen each other naked so I wasn't shackled by concerns about modesty. Not that I had ever been accused of that before. When I was done, I wrapped a dry towel around my waist and sat next to her at the small kitchen table as the coffee brewed.

"I am sorry too," she said simply.

"For what?" I asked.

She hesitated. "I got drunk and acted silly. I am very embarrassed. I thought that maybe…"

"What?"

"Maybe you found that unattractive and ran away."

If she wasn't so serious I might have laughed out loud. How did I answer that? I could tell her that drunk girls were my favorite, but I knew that validation of her feelings was required at the moment. I said, "I didn't even notice. Were you drunk? It doesn't matter. I didn't think you were acting silly and that's not why I left."

Well, here comes the part where I tell her I lied about Vito being a mental patient and Betsy being my mother. Might as well throw in Katarina, Joyce, and the midget for completeness. Instead of drinking coffee I'd be wearing it but I liked her too much to continue the deception. You see, when you like a girl a lot, you have a need to be perfectly open and honest with her. It just feels right that way. This wasn't about the ship's chaplain talking about heaven and hell. This was about doing the right thing.

She looked puzzled, "So why did you leave?"

I studied her face as I got my story straight in my head. She had large brown eyes, a delicate dimple of a nose, and full lips which I wanted to kiss so badly right now. Determined to lay bare my soul about what an unadulterated womanizer I was and how I didn't deserve her friendship, I galvanized myself and cleared my throat. If she wanted to slap or punch me I would simply close my eyes and let it happen. I deserved whatever venom she spat at me, but then, as we sat there, her robe slipped open accidentally, revealing one of her nipples. In true European fashion, she made no attempt to cover it up and I stared at it helplessly. Even worse, it was aimed right at me like a canon waiting to fire. It was as if it was trying to speak to me; to tell me something important. I wanted to get close to it and let it know how much I cared about it.

My conscience roiled with indecision and a bitter civil war erupted internally between good and evil. A little angel on my right shoulder nudged me to tell her the truth and take my lumps. A little devil on my left shoulder poked me with his pitch fork and whispered, "I'll be right back." Suddenly, with great violence, the little devil, who had snuck up behind the little angel, dragged him away, kicking and screaming.

I said, "Aimée, when I went to the bathroom, I…"

"Yes, Jean…?"

I couldn't do it. I couldn't tell her the truth. I mean how could I? She'd been feeling hurt and rejected by me and now on top of that I was going to tell her I'd been lying to her since the very first minute we met. She'd kill me of course. That went without saying but she'd also be crushed. I let out a deep emotional breath and went with what I thought was the lesser of two evils. "I discovered my cousin Vito in one of the stalls playing with himself with the door open." Her eyes went wide in surprise. "Needless to say, I was appalled. I tried to get him to stop and he became combative. It took all my strength and ability to reason with him but finally he agreed to return to his room. On the way, he insisted on stepping outside on the promenade for a moment which is how I got wet, and then you know what he wanted before he agreed to get into his Batman pajamas?"

She was in complete shock. "I can't even imagine."

"A strawberry lollipop. Can you believe that? Fortunately, I keep a bag of them in my room for just such an occasion. I'm just thankful no one saw him."

"Mon dieu, he is mad."

"Like a hatter."

"I feel so bad for you, Jean. I can see you are in misery. How much longer can you go on like this?"

I shook my head. "I don't know…I think the coffee is ready."

I don't think I ever hated myself as much as I did at this moment. I deserved to be flogged; no punishment could be too severe. She stood and retrieved the glass pot pouring us both a cup. I said, "Thank you. Anyway, that is why I left without telling you. I feel terrible about it. I'm sorry. I hope you can forgive me."

Pouring cream in her cup, she said, "Please, don't fret another moment over it. Family is the most important thing. I am so glad you came here tonight to explain. I was worried that I may never see you again. We were both able to clear the air and now I feel much better." She paused and then added. "I was feeling so inadequate."

"You? Inadequate? How is that possible? You are so beautiful and so intelligent."

The little angel had climbed back onto my shoulder and hissed, "Knock it off, and tell her the truth." I reached up and flicked him away.

She giggled, "Merci beaucoup. You are so kind, but I think you may need glasses."

I cleared my throat. "Speaking of glasses, I see you're not wearing yours."

She gave me a sultry look and cocked her head. "You want that I should put on my glasses for you like the other night?"

"Only if it's not too much trouble...The blue ones were kind of cool."

"Sure, why not? But I find it interesting that you ask for that. Most American men think that because I am French I must have closets full of lingerie."

Hmm.

"Do you?"

Grinning from ear to ear she said, "Of course I do. Should we take a look and pick something out together?"

I said, "Vive le France!"

Chapter 30

I woke up with a start at 3:00 a.m. as the ship rocked violently. Aimée lay snuggled in the crook of my arm, snoring softly, the way beautiful women do. The ship settled itself again and I wondered how long the storm could go on like this or if it could possibly get worse. I had gotten used to the gentler undulations and even found them relaxing. It was the infrequent surges that I found unsettling. Like sudden turbulence on a jet, your stomach shot up into your mouth and even the most stoic allowed their worst fears to creep into their thoughts. Thank goodness, I wasn't prone to sea sickness. Betsy was all alone and I decided to return to my room to check on her.

I shook Aimée gently, whispering, "Hey there…"

Without opening her eyes, she answered, "Yes, my darling."

Darling? I loved it. "I have to check on my mom. Do you mind if I leave?"

"No, by all means. Will you come back?"

"I'm not sure. It's pretty late."

"Then, I will see you in clinic tomorrow. I am sure it will be packed."

Gently, removing my arm, I leaned down and kissed her goodbye. She said, "Go quickly before I wake up fully and ravage you again."

Now there was a thought. I dressed in a hurry and went back to my cabin. When I went to place the key in the door, I noticed it had been jimmied opened with resulting damage to the lock mechanism. My pulse quickened as I sensed danger. I opened the door slowly and entered the pitch black room illuminated only by a solitary bolt of lightning flashing briefly through the window and balcony door. It was enough to see her body on the floor as thunder shook the room.

I turned on the light and saw Betsy lying prone on the carpet, one of my belts wrapped tightly around her neck. I ran to her, removing it, and turning her on her back. She was alive but unconscious. There was a red bruise mark around her neck. I checked her quickly for any other injuries and found none so I picked her up and placed her on the bed.

Shaking her gently I said, "Betsy, can you hear me?"

She murmured almost inaudibly and I felt her pulse. It was strong and she was breathing well so I decided she needed a little more time before I pressed the panic button. I was the ship's official doctor for the moment and we were in the middle of a violent storm. What more could I do at this hour anyway?

There was an empty bottle of gin on the floor that had toppled off the coffee table perfuming the room with Beefeater. That and her smashed martini glass suggested a brief struggle. Otherwise, I found no other clues. The balcony door was locked from the inside. She was weak but I surmised she would make it. Sitting vigil next to her, I watched her chest rise and fall with her respirations wondering who would do such a thing.

Twenty minutes later, her eyes fluttered open and she looked at me puzzled and confused. "John, what happened?" she asked weakly, her voice hoarse.

"You don't remember?"

"No, I don't…wait…yes…maybe. The storm was making me nervous. I had one too many martinis and fell asleep in the chair. That's all, and now this. My throat hurts."

She swallowed painfully. I said, "Somebody broke into the room. They pried open the lock. They…they strangled you."

Her eyes went wide in horror. "Oh my God. They strangled me? But why?"

"That's a good question. How do you feel?"

"Awful…and sick, like I'm going to throw up. Oh no, I am going to throw up. John, quick, help me to the bathroom."

I helped her stand up and assisted her on wobbly legs to the bathroom where she collapsed onto her knees, clutching the toilet bowl, and then suddenly began retching violently. The putrid smell of gin mixed with partially digested food filled the air. I ran a small washcloth under cool water and handed it to her to wipe her face. I felt really bad for her. She'd been through so much.

After ten minutes of uncontrollable vomiting, she looked up at me pale as a ghost. "John, I don't feel good."

"I'm sorry Betsy. I'll take you to the sick bay and hook you up to an IV with fluids. They have anti-nausea medications there. It will help."

She nodded and I noticed she was perspiring. Suddenly, she put her face back in the toilet bowl and vomited a massive amount of bright red blood.

I exclaimed, "Holy shit!"

She continued to throw up blood while I stood by helplessly. Just as suddenly, she passed out and slumped into my arms. I laid her down flat and placed a pillow from the bed under her head. My brain raced. I couldn't drag her to the sick bay like this. Without the ability to transfuse her, at her age, her chances of survival were diminishing rapidly. I made a snap decision and raced to the clinic leaving her there.

The ship rocked mightily again and flung me against the wall in the hallway outside the sickbay. Recovering, I winced from a pain in my shoulder. Inside, I searched frantically for supplies, and finding what I needed hurriedly retraced my steps. I carried several liter bags of saline, alcohol swabs, IV tubing, a tourniquet and an 18 gauge IV needle and a few other essentials stuffed in my pockets. It was the best I could do. I moved as rapidly as I could but the intensity of the boat's rocking had increased and I stumbled several times. My apprehension reached peak intensity just as I entered the room.

Betsy was sitting up covered in blood, leaning back against the bathroom wall. She was white as a sheet. I wiped the blood from her face with a wet towel. "Give me your arm Betsy."

She looked at me with resignation. "Am I going to die, John?"

"Not if I can help it. Now make a fist." I grabbed her arm and wrapped a rubber tourniquet around it. Waiting impatiently for a vein to show up I massaged her skin, trying to coax one to the surface. She had lost too much blood and all her superficial veins were deflated.

I said, "Betsy, this is going to hurt. I'm sorry." I swabbed alcohol on the inner aspect of her forearm near to her elbow, took a deep breath, and plunged the large bore needle blindly into her flesh. She grimaced and moaned. I dug around searching for a large vein as sweat covered my brow. After thirty seconds, I was rewarded with the flow of dark red blood from a deep blood vessel. I taped the IV in place and hung the saline bag to a hook behind the bathroom door. I ran the bag wide open and watch the life-saving volume expander flow into her arm. I had several more bags of saline and would let the first couple fly at top speed.

Betsy watched me with curiosity. "Thank you, John, but this doesn't look like my night, does it?"

"You're not the first girl to ever throw up on me. Remind me some time to tell you about a blind date I went on in medical school." She smiled and I continued. "Hang in there Betsy. It's always darkest just before the dawn."

"You're a good doctor, aren't you?"

"That depends on what your definition of good is."

"You inspire confidence in your patients."

"That may be the case, but I could still be a quack."

"Somehow I doubt that."

"Any abdominal pain or chest pain?"

She shook her head, "No."

"Good."

"What's going to happen?"

"My goal right now is to get us through the rest of the night. One step at a time."

She nodded, "I understand."

"Do you think I'll be able to clean up in the bath. I feel disgusting."

"In a couple of minutes, okay? I'll help you into the tub as soon as all the fluid runs in. No hot water though. The vasodilation could cause your blood pressure to drop and you would pass out again. So room temperature only."

"Fine. It will be better than nothing."

As the second bag of fluid finished, she was starting to look a bit more chipper and I asked, "Feeling better?"

"I am. Very weak but not like I'm going to keel over. So why am I bleeding?"

"You might have an ulcer or sometimes when people vomit excessively they can actually tear their own esophagus causing it to bleed. It's called a Mallory-Weiss tear and it's not that uncommon. Have you been taking any aspirin or medications like ibuprofen?"

"I've been on a baby aspirin every day for years for stroke prevention at the advice of my doctor, and I take one or two ibuprofens daily for arthritis. Did that cause this?"

"Maybe. They're notorious for causing ulcers in the older population. As soon as we reach port I'm taking you to a real hospital for proper medical attention. You're going to need blood and an urgent endoscopy."

"You mean a scope?"

"Yes, have you ever had a colonoscopy?"

"Several."

"Smaller instrument but the same idea."

She nodded. "I'll do whatever you tell me I have to do."

I helped her undress and get in the tub. As the water ran, I threw her clothes in the hamper and on hands and knees cleaned up the floor and toilet as best I could with a towel.

I said, "Try to keep the IV out of the water."

"I will."

With the tepid water covering her up to the waist, I turned the faucet off and began to wash the blood and vomit off her. She touched my hand. "Thank you so much. What did I ever do to deserve you?"

"I don't know, but you must have been pretty bad in your previous life if they sent me."

Chuckling she said, "Don't you ever stop joking?"

"Never." I ran a wash cloth down her neck. "I was awkward and shy growing up. Making people laugh was how I overcame my anxiety."

"You seem to have done just fine."

"That's a matter of opinion."

"Oh, hush. You're being silly." She washed her face and said, "What should I expect now?"

"Hopefully nothing, but it might not be over, and you may throw up blood again so brace yourself. I don't want you taking anything by mouth except for sips of water or apple juice for now. Your next bowel movement will most likely be black and tarry from digested blood passing through your intestines, and until you get a blood transfusion you will be very weak. Even walking around the cabin will exhaust you."

Nodding she said, "You saved my life."

"Well you're a great kisser and I wasn't quite finished with you."

She giggled. "How do you do that? I may die tonight and I'm laughing my head off."

"I'm not going to let you die, and laughter is the best medicine, they say."

"Sex works pretty good too."

Now I chortled. She had game. "You're almost cured. C'mon let me help you up. We'll shower you off, put on fresh clothes and get you in bed."

After we were done, I wrapped a towel around her and she brushed her teeth. Gastrointestinal bleeding like that was a horrifying experience and I kept my fingers crossed that the worst was behind us. Helping her put on her embroidered pajamas, I couldn't help but notice how frail she suddenly seemed. After I tucked her under the sheets, I hung another bag of saline to the end of the curtain rod of the window nearby. I took her pulse. It wasn't racing nearly as hard as before and I slowed the IV rate down to a steady drip. Stabilized for the moment, I sat next to her, with my feet propped up on an ottoman deciding what to do next as she fell asleep from exhaustion.

I needed to tell the captain what was going on so he could arrange for an ambulance to meet us as soon as we reached port. I called the operator who politely informed me that one doesn't just call the captain in the middle of the night, and that he was probably on the bridge anyway dealing with the storm. I didn't want to leave Betsy alone, and dialed Aimée's room to ask her to watch her while I sought out the captain. It would require a full confession on who Betsy really was, but I should have done that already anyway. The chaplain was going to have a field day with me if she ever found out. Aimée didn't answer after numerous rings and I assumed the alcohol had taken its toll on her. I was frustrated but relieved that I didn't have go through a long explanation and suffer through her reproach.

I dialed Betsy's stateroom hoping Vito would pick up but he didn't. He was a sound sleeper and I wasn't surprised. He would only have been slightly less than useless in this situation anyway so I took a chance and headed out to the bridge, leaving Betsy sleeping comfortably.

Chapter 31

The bridge was awash with activity and tension. It was a modern luxury liner and walls of computer monitors lined the room with busily engaged crew. I found the captain in deep conversation with the first mate as they stared straight ahead into the dark sea, rain and waves splashing vigorously on the horizon.

Bjorn turned to me and asked sharply, "Doctor, what is the meaning of this, and how did you get in here?"

"Please excuse the interruption. I know you're busy, Captain, but this is something of an urgency." The sailor who let me in was young, and I told him that since I was the ship's physician, I was technically part of the crew. It sounded right to him and would probably hold up in court.

Pinning my ears back, he barked, "More urgent than trying to navigate a ship with three thousand passengers through gale force winds, torrential rain, twenty-foot waves and zero visibility?"

Stress lines were etched in his face. I replied calmly, "It's about Betsy."

Easing up a bit and suddenly appearing concerned, he asked, "What happened?"

I glanced uneasily at the first mate and then back at him in the universal signal for privacy. He turned to the man and said, "Karl, you know what to do. Give me a moment."

Karl left us to another part of the bridge. "Be direct, doctor. I don't have time."

"Someone attacked Betsy in my stateroom while I was elsewhere. Following the assault, she began vomiting blood. She's okay now but needs urgent medical care which we cannot give her on the ship. We need to get her to a hospital as soon as possible."

His eyes went wide and he let out a deep breath. He suddenly looked exhausted. He had that, *what more could go wrong tonight*, look. "Where is she?"

"In my room. I placed an IV in her that I got from the infirmary and am giving her fluids. For the moment, she's stable and resting comfortably, but that could change at any time."

"Doctor, the storm is much worse than had been predicted, and we won't be able to bring the ship into port under these conditions. I may even have to divert back out to sea."

I looked blankly at him, not knowing what to say. This was the worst possible situation to be in. Trapped at sea with a serious medical condition. Reading my mind, he said, "The weather forecasts and satellite images suggest the storm may lighten up in a few hours. Not enough for us to dock but possibly enough to get a medical helicopter out here."

I nodded. "That would work."

"Dawn will break in about two hours. A lot can happen with weather patterns at sea in that time. Go tend to Lady Beth and prepare yourselves for transport. I'll call for the med-evac helicopter. If the weather calms down they'll get here."

"I'm going with her?"

"Of course. She trusts you and since I can't go with her, you will. Do you have any idea who attacked her or why?"

I shook my head. "No, I don't, and she doesn't remember anything."

"Well, I have to carry on with business up here. Please return to your cabin now, and we'll sort things out in due time."

Back in the room, Betsy was still sleeping. I threw some of her clothes in a small suitcase purely guessing what her needs might be. I did the same for me and fell asleep, overcome with exhaustion. Two hours later, a loud knock on the door jolted me from my slumber. It was two crew members and two emergency medical technicians in heavy, brightly-colored rain gear wheeling a stretcher to transport Betsy.

I hadn't had a chance to give her a head's up, and when she woke she was quite startled. I filled her in quickly and her fears were allayed when she realized I was coming with her. I was given a rain slicker and a life preserver. Betsy was bundled up and strapped securely in the gurney. On the upper most deck, the wind and the rain pelted us, and seemed even worse than last night, when I had gone out on the promenade. It was after 6:00 a.m., but the dark clouds and inclement weather gave no indication there was a sun fusing 620 million metric tons of hydrogen each second behind them.

I had never seen a helicopter up close before and was impressed at the size and power of this one. It was a monster with two massive rotary blades, and landing gear resembling that of a jet; two front wheels and four in the back. There was a cabin with four windows behind the cockpit. It looked like it could lift a tank. The stretcher, two crew members, pilot, copilot and myself fit with room to spare and we took off.

Buckled in near Betsy, I leaned over, wiped rain off of her face and held her hand. She said, "Thank you," over the whirring of the blades and grinding of the noisy engine.

I nodded, "No, I should thank you. I was starting to wonder if this was just going to be another boring cruise."

She smiled. "Promise me you'll stay with me. I'm old enough to know when things don't look good and mature enough to be comfortable with it, but being alone at the end is something no one ever plans on or wants."

I squeezed her hand gently. "It's not the end, and you're not alone, but I promise. Now try to relax. It might be a bumpy ride."

That was the understatement of the century as the chopper careened unsteadily from gusts of wind pushing it back and forth and up and down. A fifteen mile trip to Corfu felt like a slalom ride down Mount Everest, and when we touched down at the heliport in Corfu, Betsy was white as a sheet. I was green and clammy and fighting the urge to upchuck. The crew politely pretended not to notice my discomfort.

We boarded an ambulance and a short drive later we were in the emergency department of a local hospital waiting for a physician. Other than being on an island called Corfu, I had no idea where we were. The emergency room was small and clean with maybe eight beds in total, and seemed relatively new and modern. I felt reassured by that. The nurses spoke broken but perfectly understandable English. They cleaned up Betsy's IV site, took her vital signs, performed an EKG and hung anti-ulcer medications up. Blood samples were drawn and she was typed and crossed in anticipation of a transfusion. They interviewed us both extensively about the events of last night. Thirty minutes later, a beleaguered, older man wearing a white coat pulled the curtain aside and greeted us looking through thick old-fashioned spectacles. I noticed a pack of cigarettes in his breast pocket.

Smiling he said, "Welcome to Corfu. I am Dr. Kastropolis, but please call me Constantine." He turned to focus on Betsy. "I am so sorry you are not well, young lady. This is no way to spend your vacation."

I stood as he took Betsy's hand, embracing it warmly. I informed him that I was a gastroenterologist and gave him a detailed rundown on what had happened. He asked her a few basic questions to get to know her and bring himself into the loop.

He jotted down notes in a chart, examined her and said, "Well, Mrs. Harrington, it sounds as if your friend, John, has taken good care of you. So this is plan. We have special medications running in your IV to help control nausea and for to treat the ulcer. Blood is on the way and I will call in our GI specialist to perform an upper endoscopy on you to see where the bleeding is come from. He should be here within the hour. In the meanwhile, a bed is being prepared for you. If all goes well, I would anticipate you will be with us no more than a day or two. Unfortunately, you can take nothing by mouth until after your procedure."

Betsy nodded. "I understand, doctor and thank you."

I said, "Doctor, I know this is irregular, but would it be possible for me to come into the operating room to observe the procedure? I'm very experienced and I'm sure Mrs. Harrington would find it very comforting. I might even be of some help although I'll be quiet as a mouse if that's what you want."

He hesitated and said sympathetically, "I don't think that will be possible but I will ask person in charge. I know you are doctor in America but here you are just friend of patient. Please try understand."

I nodded and he left the room closing the door behind him. I said, "And now we wait."

"I'm sorry to do this to you, John, and thank you for offering your medical expertise to the doctor. You didn't have to do that."

"Don't be silly. This is what I do every day."

"Yes, but you're on vacation."

"Doctors are never on vacation. Didn't you know that? Besides, this is kind of fun. I got to go on a helicopter ride for free."

She smiled broadly. "And what a ride that was. I'm not sure which was worse. Being sick last night or the ride in the helicopter."

I nodded in agreement. "I give those guys a lot of credit. Talk about real heroes. You couldn't pay me enough to do stuff like that."

"You're heroic in your own way."

"Just because I don't wet the bed when it thunders outside doesn't make me heroic."

She chuckled, "There you go again making me laugh."

Thirty minutes later, the doctor returned with two OR nurses. He politely informed me that he was sorry but his supervisor said I couldn't join Betsy in the operating room. I thanked him for at least asking. The nurses wore green scrubs and were carrying a bag of blood. They smiled, introduced themselves, and checked Betsy's ID bracelet. After taking her temperature, they began the transfusion. One said in a very thick accent. "We take operating room now."

Betsy asked, "We're not going to meet the doctor first?"

"You meet in operating room. He is preparing now."

Betsy looked at me uncomfortably, and I said, "It's okay, Betsy. That's not unusual. I'm sure you're in good hands." I leaned down to kiss her. "You'll be fine, okay? I'll see you in your room later."

As they wheeled her away, the other nurse said, "We take room 302 after test. There is elevator down hall outside emergency room."

"Thank you."

I found the cafeteria in the basement, they were always in the basement, got myself coffee and an omelet with feta cheese while I waited and hoped everything turned out all right. After breakfast, I went to her room and sat in a chair by the bed, looking around. It had the appearance of any hospital room anywhere in the world: antiseptic colors and furniture, nondescript and easily forgettable wall coverings, and no window. I was depressed already, and exhausted. With barely two hours sleep, I was ready to drop, and I did, sitting upright, legs in a manspread and head at an awkward angle.

Gagging and choking on my own saliva, I woke several hours later to find that someone had placed a blanket on me. Betsy was nowhere in sight and my neck hurt from the uncomfortable position I had been sleeping in. I yawned, stretched and went to the nursing station where I was informed that she was still in surgery. I looked at my watch. Damn, she'd been in the OR more than three hours. That was a long time for an endoscopy. Either there was some delay in starting the case or something untoward happened.

I asked the nurse if she knew what was going on and she shook her head no. I rubbed my neck, went back to the room, and an hour later was getting really concerned when a middle-aged doctor wearing scrubs and a long white coat entered the room.

We shook hands and he introduced himself. His name was Kosmos. "I am surgeon who operate on mother. She is do fine in recovery room."

I put my hand up, raised my eyebrows and was clearly agitated. "What are you talking about?"

He seemed genuinely surprised. "No one tell?"

"No, no one tell. What happened in there?"

"Please sir. Is sorry. Have seat and I explain."

I sat and he pulled up a chair next to me. "GI specialist scope mother and find big ulcer which start bleed. He cannot stop bleeding and call me. He try very, very hard but cannot stop bleed."

I nodded. I'd been there myself on a few occasions. He continued, "Mother very sick, blood pressure drop, he transfuse. I come in and operate, remove part of stomach. Mother in recovery room. Do well but still sleep. She go ICU afterward. I am sorry."

Oh brother. I said, "Thank you. When can I see her."

"Maybe twenty, thirty minutes, okay?"

"Okay."

Chapter 32

By early afternoon the deluge had let up somewhat and the major thrust of the storm had shifted back out to sea leaving us with heavy rain and manageable wind. The ship had docked uneventfully, and those who weren't in their rooms praying or popping valium to calm their nerves, disembarked to tour the island with umbrellas and ponchos.

The captain arrived in Betsy's room in the early afternoon and we shook hands. I gave him the news and he thanked me for staying by her side, worry lined his countenance. Betsy was still sleeping both from the effects of the anesthesia and from the narcotics dripping into her IV for pain control. She had done well post-operatively so far, but that was all relative and she looked awful to Bjorn's non-medical eyes. She was pale and receiving blood in one arm and antibiotics and morphine in the other. There were tubes in her nose and her bladder, an oxygen mask on her face and various wires and gadgets attached to different body parts. Various machines recorded her blood pressure, pulse, and oxygen level with eerie beeps and even eerier multicolored tracings on a monitor overhead.

I noticed his concern and said, "She'll be all right, Bjorn, this is typical post-op stuff, but she's not going to be able to go back to the ship anytime soon."

He nodded. “Clearly. What are we to do?”

“Does she have family? If she does we should give them a call. There’s no telling what the future will hold.”

He seemed to hesitate which puzzled me. It was almost as if he was deciding whether to tell me something he shouldn’t. “She has a daughter who lives in Italy. They weren’t close and Betsy hardly ever spoke of her. I’ve never met her, and I don’t know of any other family.”

“Well, Betsy’s going to be here for a while, and there could be complications. An operation like this, in someone her age, will require an extensive recovery period with rehab and visiting nurse services after discharge. My guess is that we are looking at least one full week before the doctors let her leave the hospital, and probably another four to six weeks before she starts feeling like her old self again. At some point she may feel well enough to travel back to her home in London or Boston to finish her recuperation.”

He sighed. “It is what it is. At least she’s alive and doing well.”

“Yes, she is.”

Being a practical person he said, “But now we have yet another crime to consider, and quite frankly, I am at a complete loss at how to proceed.”

I sympathized with him. When the ship returned to London, every aspect of his handling of the crisis would be scrutinized and he would be judged harshly. Such was the way of these things, but I truly believed his first concern was for Betsy’s well-being. I said, “I feel for you Bjorn and I’ll do whatever I can to help, but first things first. Betsy can’t leave this island, and the ship can’t stay in port indefinitely.”

“I know. We’re going to have to leave her here. I hate to do that but I must follow maritime law and it would be unfair to the thousands of passengers to do otherwise.”

"And Betsy wouldn't have it any other way."

He nodded. "No, she wouldn't. I know I have no right to ask this, doctor, but will you…stay with her?"

Without hesitation, I nodded. "Of course. I've already been googling hotels."

"I have no doubt Lady Beth will cover your expenses, but if she doesn't, I will."

I smiled. "That won't be necessary, but I appreciate your offer. I'm quite solvent."

"You really are an extraordinary man, doctor…John. I can't thank you enough for all you've done. If you hadn't been there when you were, she might have died. I can't get over anyone trying to harm her. I mean, it's one thing what happened to Roger, a robbery gone bad and all, but what was the point of this? What kind of wild animal are we dealing with?"

I furrowed my brows somewhat confused and then it dawned on me. He thought her ulcer was the result of the assault. "Bjorn, I know it's an amazing coincidence but the ulcer had nothing to do with the attack on Betsy last night and was more likely the result of the ibuprofen she was taking for joint pains. It's an exceedingly common occurrence in her age group and was probably brewing underneath the surface. Believe it or not, the ulcer would probably have blown at one point or another regardless of the attack."

He stood there considering that, and I could see from his expression that he found it hard to accept. "Really? Well, I'm sure you know more about these things than I do but to any non-medical person it would seem related."

"Yes, it would. I can see that, and it's possible that the stress of her situation exacerbated things, but from what the doctor told me about the size of the ulcer and its nasty appearance, I'm convinced it had been there for quite some time and would have become a problem sooner or later."

"Still, I don't understand why anyone would want to hurt her."

"Agreed and neither do I, unless they didn't come to my room to hurt her. Maybe they didn't even know she was there. Maybe they came to rob me and found her there by accident."

He said, "Not trying to muddy the waters too much but maybe they came to hurt you, not rob you. Would anyone want to hurt you?"

I almost laughed. Only half the women in New York, and maybe a third of the men. "Me? Not that I know of."

Then, I thought about Brad. He was very pissed off right now, but he didn't seem the type. He was a bully and gave me the impression he would run at the first hint of a physical confrontation. Antonela and Katarina were both very jealousy prone women and each a little crazy in their own right but I had a hard time picturing them hurting Betsy. What about Berislav? Did he see me as a threat? Yes, he did. Anyone that went near Katarina was a potential threat to his future well-being; enough of a threat to come to my room to hurt me and wind up hurting someone else? Once again, I didn't see it. How about Joyce? No way. She was harmless, and probably the most straight-forward person I had met on the ship so far. Besides, I had promised her further sexcapades so she had something to look forward to. Why ruin a good thing?

On the other hand, I learned a long time ago never to underestimate a woman once they got their claws into you. What if she had come to my room looking for some unscheduled nocturnal entertainment and found Betsy there instead? Suddenly a quote appeared in front of my mind. Something about hell hath no fury…

Bjorn interrupted my chain of thought, saying, "Well, that is good. Anyway, keep thinking about it. I must return to the ship now. When she wakes please let her know I came by."

"I will, although I may go check into a hotel soon and crash for a few hours. I'm beat and I need to shower."

He grinned politely. "I'll bet, and I feel the same way. It was a long night for everyone."

After he left, I waited another thirty minutes for Betsy to wake, but she was still out cold and receiving more blood when I finally decided I had to sleep myself or pass out in place. There was a small boutique hotel nearby called the Siorra Vittoria which had an availability, so I reserved a room and let the nurses know how to reach me.

A short cab ride later I stood in front of a gorgeous, restored 19th century aristocratic mansion in the heart of the old part of Corfu. Named after one of the island's founding matrons, and still owned by the original family, the restoration of the building was performed with extreme care to preserve its authentic style. The interior transported me back to another era, one that had been greatly influenced by a blend of Venetian architecture from when that city ruled the Adriatic and Corfu's native cultural heritage.

I checked in, was given a room on the fifth floor and was told there was a rooftop bar and café completely enclosed in glass with a dance floor and hot tub. On the main level was a five star restaurant and spa. There were also several night clubs and bars within walking distance of the hotel as well. It was almost like I had never left the ship. I went to the room threw my duffle bag on the floor and fell face forward onto the king bed, asleep almost immediately.

I slept and I slept and I slept. I didn't hear my cellphone go off and I didn't hear the house phone either, but I did hear a loud knocking on my door. Waking with a start, I went over and looked through the peephole. It was Vito.

"How on earth did you find me?"

"It wasn't very hard. The captain told me you were staying in town so I just called a few hotels asking if an ugly American had recently checked in."

I was very groggy and not ready for him. Sitting down on the edge of the bed, I wiped my eyes and yawned loudly. "What time is it?" I asked.

"It's after eight. Time for dinner." I nodded breathing heavily from sleep. I belched and stretched. He said, "Beautiful."

"Okay, so tell me again. You met the captain?"

"Well, we docked and I pretended to just come on the ship so I registered with the steward and told them what happened, you know, how I couldn't board in Dubrovnik and took a train and ferry to Corfu. They were okay with it, in fact, apologetic. The captain came down in person to welcome me aboard. I told him you were my friend and here I am."

"But he didn't know where I was."

"Cesari, wake up will you? He sent me to the hospital and the nurses told me."

I nodded "Did you see Betsy?"

"No, but I heard all about it. Man, she's really getting slammed. I'm sorry. I know you like her." He took a deep breath and let it out. "Well, c'mon, rise and shine, and for God's sake, take a shower. You're ripe. Then let's go eat."

"All right, but I have to check on Betsy first so control yourself."

"C'mon Cesari, it's late and I'm starving. She's probably asleep anyway."

He had a point, and I was starving too, not having eaten since breakfast. I called the hospital and they put me through to the nursing station. They told me there had been no change in her status and that although she had woken briefly an hour or two ago she was sleeping comfortably again now. The doctor had just checked on her and was satisfied with her condition.

We went up to the roof top bar and café, ordered a couple of gin martinis, and sat at a table watching the dance floor while perusing our menus. Vito lit up a camel and blew a puff ring at nowhere in particular. He wasn't the only one. There were quite a few people smoking. Greece was a few years behind the times in that regard and didn't really have any national consensus on smoking etiquette. Even at the hospital, the emergency room doctor had a pack of cigarettes in full view. That would have been a major no-no back in the states.

Vito glanced around, taking it all in. There were couples frolicking in the hot tub positioned toward the edge of the roof where they could view the city lights down below. They sipped champagne and cuddled unabashedly. Others grinded on the dance floor to American R&B.

He looked up at the ceiling and said, "This is pretty cool," as he observed the rain beating down on the glass canopy. It was indeed not like any glass enclosed room I had ever seen before. Rather than being square in nature it was the shape of a dome like you might see on one of the great cathedrals of Europe. Potted plants dotted the room and multiple ceiling fans circulated the air. Air conditioning kept the humidity down.

I nodded in agreement. "Very different."

"I don't know much about Greek food, Cesari. What should I get?"

The menu was casual and had English translations next to each item. On one page, there was a brief history of the hotel and of the island itself. For the first time, I realized that I was in the city of Corfu, which was also the capital of the island of Corfu. I said, "You've never had a gyro or souvlaki?"

"Of course I have, but I want to try something authentic."

"They are authentic, but if by authentic you mean something you've never had before, try the moussaka with eggplant. It's a meat dish and sounds delicious."

He tapped his cigarette into a hastily placed ceramic ash tray. Looking up at the waitress he thanked her, apparently oblivious to the fact that she had just saved him from damaging the tablecloth. She was cute and dark, like she spent a lot of time in the sun. Her name was Charmaine. "Are you gentlemen ready to order?" she asked.

I said, "Give us another minute and thank you."

She gave me a big smile. "For what, the ash tray?"

"That, and I haven't been called a gentleman in a long time."

She chuckled and walked away.

Vito frowned. "Are you some sort of compulsive flirter, Cesari? You know what? Please don't answer that. So what are you going to have?"

Ignoring his barb, I said, "I think I'll have the pastitsio. It sounds like the Greek version of lasagna."

"I can't make up my mind. Can I have some of yours if I don't like mine."

"What are you, my wife? No."

"Aw, c'mon?"

"C'mon nothing. Be a grown-up and eat your own food." Every now and then I had this nightmare that someone asked me to babysit their very difficult child and then refused to take it back. It felt just like this.

"You can't be serious? Just a few bites."

"Fine. Then say it."

"Say what?"

"Say it."

"Bite me."

"Say it."

"Please."

"Fine."

I laughed and he suddenly got very serious. "And the waitress is mine, okay? I've been cooped up in a room for the last couple of days running errands for you. I need to unwind a little."

"I'm not interested in the waitress. I was just being friendly."

"Spare me, Cesari. This is me you're talking to. I know how you operate; a little smile here, a little joke there. Just back off this one time, will you?"

"I resent that."

"Resent whatever you want, but stay away from Charmaine. From now on I do all the talking."

I made a face and said, "I don't care about you or her."

"That's fine with me."

"She's probably a lesbian anyway."

"Shut up."

Charmaine approached the table and looking directly at me, smiled, and asked, "May I take your order?"

I didn't respond, and Vito said, "I'll have the moussaka and my friend will have the pastitsio…and cut the portions in half in case we want to share."

I shook my head as she wrote the order down, took his menu, and then reached for mine. Coming close to me she hesitated, and with a puzzled look, gently sniffed the air. She looked at Vito and then back at me, asking, "What is that you're wearing? It's very nice."

"I'm not wearing anything," I replied casually.

"Do you mean that…nothing?" she asked, smiling mischievously.

The temptation to flirt back was overwhelming but I restrained myself. "I meant I'm not wearing any after shave or cologne."

Vito tried to seize the initiative. "I'm wearing Dolce and Gabbana."

She looked at him deadpanned. "I recognized your scent right away. Many women like it although I had no idea a man would consider wearing it as well. It's too fruity. No, I smell something else here." She turned back to me. "Something I cannot place, something earthy, something that is familiar and…comforting…"

I said, "Cinnamon?"

Her eyes opened, "That's it. Cinnamon. How did you know?"

"A wild guess."

She stood there for a moment and then said, "I will go place your order," but she didn't leave.

I cleared my throat. "We're kind of hungry."

Embarrassed, she said, "Yes, I go now."

She left and Vito roiled, "I absolutely, from the bottom of my soul, hate your guts."

"What are you talking about? You should be thanking me. I softened her up for you."

"Softened her up? She practically accused me of being homosexual."

"Well, who told you to wear Dolce and Gay-bana. This is Greece, dude, home of the Spartans, the Three Hundred, the Olympics, Zeus, Alexander the Great, Zorba the Greek. Men are proud of their chest hair and Greek women wouldn't have it any other way. The bar for men is set pretty high in this part of the world, and you waltz in smelling like sunshine on a spring day in an open meadow surrounded by butterflies. Jesus, I'm surprised she didn't ask you to leave. Why don't you go wash that off before she gets angry?"

He was stunned and getting irritated. “Me?! You smell like pumpkin pie and you’re criticizing me? How much more of this do I have to take?”

“Go wash that stench off your face in the bathroom and I’ll order us another round of martinis. You need to cool off. With your bad attitude, you’re going to be celibate for a long time.”

He threw his napkin down on the table and went to the men’s room. When he was gone I let myself have a well-deserved chuckle. I loved baiting him. It was just so easy. I ordered another round of drinks from a passing waiter and they arrived just as Vito returned to the table.

Sitting, he took a long swallow. I asked, “Hey, you never told me. Did you get any pictures of Brad?”

His face brightened up. “Boy, did I ever. After they left the party, they were all over each other. I’d swear she was posing for the camera.” He shook his head smiling at the memory. “I got some great shots of him grabbing her ass. He even did a nose dive into her cleavage.”

I laughed out loud. “No way. That’s great. For that, dinner’s on me. Do me a favor though. When you get the chance see if there’s some place on the ship you can have prints made.”

“Prints? What size?”

“Wallet size will be fine.”

“I’ll get it done, but why?”

“Not sure yet. I just want to be prepared.”

We raised our glasses and toasted good health as Charmaine placed our dinners before us. Charmaine’s eyes lingered on me a fraction longer than they should have and feeling compassionate, I said, “Charmaine, my name’s John and this is my friend Vito.”

She smiled politely and I clocked her at twenty-five to thirty, no more and no less. I continued, “I was wondering what would people do for fun around here on a rainy night?

I don't mean the tourists but the people who live here like yourself."

Looking down shyly, she said, "Well, there are night clubs where men and women can dance, like here, and get to know each other better. Bar *GREC* is one of the better ones downtown, but the old city has a beautiful shore walk by the sea. It is very romantic when the moon is full. You can get wine or gelato and walk barefoot in the sand, but it would not be that enjoyable on a night like this. Tonight I would recommend visiting one of the medieval castles that are scattered throughout the city. They are dark with narrow, cobble-stoned streets lit by gas lamps that shed just enough light you do not trip. There are numerous cafés to buy coffee, dessert, or a cocktail. In the rain, the castles are that much more romantic."

Vito watched me in awe, the way you might imagine the audience watched Mozart conducting *The Marriage of Figaro* in 1786. She bit her lower lip in anticipation and it was time to let her down easy.

I looked at my watch. "I'm meeting my wife after dinner. She is with the children right now exploring your lovely city. Once she tucks them in the room with a good movie I was thinking we might go for a walk around one of those castles. The trouble is my friend, Vito here, is all alone. I was wondering if you would consider joining us. Three is such an awkward number, isn't it?" I hated to bait and switch her like that, but all's fair in love and war.

She seemed disappointed, but thought it over, looked at Vito, sized him up, and said, "Three is an ugly number. I agree…" She hesitated still not all in but then suddenly smiled. "Why not? I would love to join you. I will be free at eleven. I meet you in the lobby."

She left and Vito said, "You're amazing, but what do I tell her when you and your *wife* don't show up?"

He was frustrating me. “Just make up something, my wife had a headache, one of the kids was sick, I was horny. I mean, really, do I have to do everything here?”

Vito beamed his admiration, “I owe you one. That was smooth.”

I made a quirky grin. “Who’s your daddy?”

“You are.”

“Good, because you’re paying for dinner.”

Chapter 33

Vito went on his playdate with Charmaine, and I went to see Betsy, arriving in the ICU shortly after eleven. It was late but the staff was understanding of the extenuating circumstances and let me in. She was groggy and weak, but alert, and I took a chair next to her, gently squeezing her hand.

"How are you doing?" I asked softly.

Managing a smile, she said, "Exhausted, although the pain's not too bad."

"Narcotics are wonderful drugs when used correctly."

"So when do I get out of here?" she asked jokingly.

I chuckled. "Are you in a rush to go somewhere?"

She shook her head no and I added, "Then don't be impatient. You're going to be here for a while so let's put on a brave face. Bjorn told me you have a daughter. We should call her."

She nodded. "I do have a daughter, Veronica, although we haven't spoken in years. I doubt she'll be interested in my condition."

I decided not to pry, but trying to encourage her, said gently, "I wouldn't bet on that. Situations like this tend to bring people together. Does she know about Roger?"

"I don't see how she could."

I said, "I don't mean to insert myself into your family dynamics, but don't you think she should? You know, Betsy, if all goes well, in about a week, you might be able to travel. Bjorn told me she's in Italy. That's a short plane ride away. You could finish rehabbing there with her. Nothing wrong with that. I hear there's some pretty good food over there."

She managed a little grin at my attempt at humor. "John, there's a lot you don't know. Suffice it to say that I don't think she'll have me…now…or ever."

"I find that hard to believe. Her father just died. I don't know what transpired between you two, but this is probably as good a time as any to mend fences."

Looking even glummer she said, "I'll think about it. In the meanwhile, I can afford home nursing care whether I stay here or travel to Italy or wherever. Either way, I'll be fine. I don't mind being alone."

"You're not going to be alone. I'm going to stay here with you."

Raising her eyebrows, she said, "Absolutely not. I will not allow it."

"The decision's been made."

Suddenly animated she sat up and winced from pain. Whispering through gritted teeth she said, "You can't. Please try to understand. I need you on that ship, now, more than ever."

"Why? The necklace?"

"Yes. I told you how important it is to me. I don't care so much about the money, but it has been in my family, passed on from mother to daughter, for generations. I would rather die than lose it, and whether my daughter wants me in her life or not, that necklace belongs to her. That's her legacy."

"You don't think Bjorn will recover it?"

"Bjorn is a wonderful man and there has never been a better captain of any seaworthy vessel, but mystery solving is not his strong suit."

"I didn't realize it was mine."

"Trust me when I say that it is. You have a clever, quick mind and pick up on things that would fly past Bjorn and most other men in a heartbeat."

"What about most other women?"

With a half-hearted chuckle, she said, "No, you're not that good."

I chuckled and then was silent for a moment, not sure of what to say. I sat there looking down. Finally, I said, "Betsy, I hope you realize that despite your confidence in me, there is a more than likely chance I may not recover it either."

"Nonsense. Don't sell yourself short, John. I trust you more than an army of Pinkerton private investigators."

I smiled at that. "Thanks, but I'm not sure you got the right guy. Nor am I convinced it's a wise idea for me to leave you alone."

"Is this my life or yours, Dr. Cesari?"

Jesus, she was feisty. Combative women were the story of my life. Maybe I brought that out in them. "I'll think about it."

"You'll do more than think about it. I'll have you barred from my room if you do not board that ship tomorrow."

"Betsy…"

She was getting agitated. "You heard me."

I was stunned but didn't want to work her up any further so I acquiesced and dropped the subject. We chatted about nothing for the next fifteen minutes, and eventually, at close to midnight a nurse walked in to take her vital signs. She politely asked me to leave so Betsy could rest, and I bid her good night with a gentle kiss, promising to see her in the morning.

By midnight, the rain had slowed to a light drizzle and the people were spilling out into the old town. The historic center of the city bustled with tourists, cafés, pastry shops, and night clubs. I had a lot to think about as I strolled along the narrow, wet sidewalks and glittering lights. Betsy was a determined woman for sure and there was a whole lot going on that I was just barely scratching the surface of. I really couldn't do anything about it if she didn't want me here, and she was right in that she could afford an army of nurses to care for her. Heck, if she wanted she could rent out the entire hotel I was staying in for however long she needed. All that she really cared about was getting that necklace back. I thought about that. It was unlikely, but I would try my best. It was the least I could do.

I was saddened to hear about her relationship with her daughter but that happened sometimes. Rich or poor, it was never good to dig your heels in when it came to people you loved. I learned a long time ago to always leave a little wiggle room for reconciliation. I smiled. Look at me; the doctor of love.

Proud of myself, I decided to step into a club in the center of town for a nightcap before heading back to my room. It was called *GREC* and it was near the water. During the daylight, it probably commanded a great view of the mainland. Waiters were busy drying off outdoor tables and setting up large umbrellas just in case the rain picked up again.

Loud euro-pop-rock piped from outdoor speakers, and a crowd gathered, ready to make up for lost time. I'd been soaked enough in the last two days and went inside the club where the noise increased to near deafening level. The humidity was about ten points higher than outside and after only a couple of minutes I was already tired of bumping into sweaty people.

Hundreds of mostly young men and women milled about in the dark room sipping drinks and chatting as woofers pounded and strobe lights blinded them. I was surprised to see a couple of topless girls in bikini bottoms and high heels go-go dancing in hanging cages. That was a very sixties thing. No one tried to approach them with cash. This wasn't that kind of bar and most people paid them no attention. They were part of the background like a vase or floor lamp.

There was a sudden opening at the bar and I grabbed the seat. The counter was long and made of wood with a large mirror and rows of spirits arranged neatly behind. Two bartenders worked busily mixing cocktails, beads of perspiration on their foreheads. One guy was cool, in his late twenties with a long ponytail, the usual tattoos up and down his bare arms and black plugs in his earlobes. The other was more corporate with shaved head, a nose ring which made him look like a bull, and a black t-shirt that said *Eat the Rich.* Lovely. I felt like I was in a Starbucks.

I ordered a negroni which was a combination of gin, Campari, and sweet vermouth served in an old-fashioned glass usually with a half wheel of orange. My cocktail came and I took a small sip to test the waters and was thrilled. My boys knew what they were doing.

Looking around casually, I noticed something familiar. I scanned the room and at a corner table, not too far away saw the back of Berislav's head. As he spoke, he moved slightly and opposite him and facing me was Antonela. I turned away quickly and hoped he was pitching her the necklace as an adequate substitute for the cash he owed. Betsy had told me it was of the highest quality and even the best of jewelers would be fooled by it. Certainly low-level cogs such as these two wouldn't know the difference.

Jesus! I couldn't get away from these people. I didn't want any trouble tonight so I threw twenty euros on the counter, and asked the ponytailed guy to pour my drink into a red solo cup. He handed it to me and I went to the bathroom for a quick pit stop before going back to the hotel. Skirting around the periphery to stay out view of their table I entered the bathroom unseen. The urinals were taken so I placed my cup on the sink and entered a stall, closing the door behind me. As I unzipped to do my business, a cellphone in the stall next to me went off and Brad answered.

For crying out loud; the bathroom too? But then I remembered this was a local hot spot recommended in all the guidebooks and by the hotel. Even Charmaine our waitress had mentioned it.

He answered in his usual blustery tone. "Yeah, Milo, how goes it?...No, really?...Well, screw him...Besides, I'm working on something here...Yeah, it's big. That's right...Hey, do me a favor, will you? There's some prick named John Cesari on the ship with us. He's a real wise guy and I'd like to put him in his place. He says he's a doctor. See what you can dig up on him, all right? C-E-S-A-R-I, that's it. The nastier the better...hold on." He made a grunting noise, expelled gas and sighed. "Okay, look Milo, my email account's been hacked and there's some other funky stuff going on so try to call me before we depart tomorrow afternoon. Once we're at sea the phone reception can be sketchy and expensive. Look, I got to go. You caught me in the can trying to drop a duke and you're distracting me...All right, bye."

This guy was unbelievable. I zipped up, flushed and washed my hands. Just as I was about to leave, I chuckled to myself and thought I'd have some fun. I dumped my drink out in the sink and filled the cup with warm water and soap from the dispenser, mixing them real well. I returned to Brad's stall and glancing around to make sure no one was watching, bent down and gently released the greasy contents of the cup on the floor in front of his door. I tossed the cup away and crossed my fingers. As I left the bathroom, the little devil on my shoulder jumped up and down with joy as the other guy sat cross-legged with his face buried in his hands in shame.

Outside, the clouds were starting to clear up and I could see the moon. I wondered where Vito was and even more importantly, what the hell I was going to do tomorrow? Would I stay or would I go? Entering the hotel lobby, I waved at the girl at the desk who smiled in return. It was midnight, but I wasn't quite ready to sleep, and I still hadn't had my night cap.

I asked the girl at the desk, "Is the bar still open?"

"Of course."

I thanked her, went to the rooftop and was mildly surprised to see it was even more crowded than before. The dance floor was jammed with people gyrating and grinding against each other and the hot tub was filled to capacity. The glass dome's retractable windows had been opened allowing in a nice cool evening breeze. I had my heart set on a negroni until Brad intervened so that's what I ordered. When it came, I was again impressed. The cushioned seat was more comfortable than the other bar and I settled in, minding my own business and making sure my eyes didn't linger too long on anybody's breasts. Most bar fights usually started that way. A casual glance in the wrong direction, a meaningless smile back, one too many mixed drinks, and before you knew it you're getting cold-cocked by some drunk half your age.

I wasn't a very reflective guy generally speaking. I tended to eat when I was hungry and drink when I was thirsty without thinking a whole lot about it. George Bernard Shaw once said that some men see things as they are and ask why. Others dream things that never were, and ask why not. I didn't fall into either category. I didn't have great thoughts, but I did have one quality even a lot of great thinkers didn't. I wasn't afraid to stand up for what was right. The question here at the moment was what was right?

A man had been brutally murdered in front of his wife's eyes. Her relationship with him was complicated to say the least, but I had no doubt she cared for him. The killer had apparently gotten away with the deed, and there were no clues. Betsy was old and now sick. Too sick to pursue the investigation herself, and so had commissioned me to act on her behalf. She wouldn't be fully healed until long after the ship reached its final destination, and all the passengers had disappeared to the far corners of the globe from whence they came. The captain would do all he could of course, but he had a ship to manage and the responsibility for thousands under his watch. He was far from a detective anyway. Betsy's beloved necklace was missing and some bastard would profit from his crime.

Well, not if I had anything to say about it. I finished my negroni, and determined not to go to bed sober, signaled the bartender for another, saying, "Double up on the gin if you don't mind." He nodded, and as he turned away Katarina sat next to me and called out, "I'll have whatever handsome man is having."

Looking at her in surprise, my mouth dropped. "How on earth…?"

She crossed her legs and hiked up her skirt, revealing a healthy dose of thigh. She said, "I see you in bar *GREC* and follow here."

Of course, she was with Berislav. "You followed me?"

"Was not hard. You seem preoccupied. Did you know you talk to yourself?"

I smiled. I did know that. An odd habit I had inherited from my mother. "I have a lot on my mind. What about Berislav?"

"He negotiate with midget about necklace you give me. Tell me he thinks all go well."

"So Berislav was happy when he saw the jewels?"

"Very much so. Jump up and down, dance, sing, everything."

"He didn't seem alarmed or concerned?"

"Not at all. Why would he? He very happy. Call midget right away. Arrange meeting."

I thought about that. It pretty much ruled him out as the thief. If he had the real set, then he certainly would have been deeply dubious if another, exact set, suddenly appeared. I asked, "What about Antonela?"

"She is just messenger for big gangster back Dubrovnik. She will have to check with him before agree."

"So you don't have to marry the old man?"

"May marry anyway. I find out he is even wealthier than I thought. He tell me. Better yet, he is even sicker too. Not live long. I make special honeymoon for him. By time over, I wealthy widow. Wear black." She gave me a devilish grin.

I chuckled as the bartender placed our drinks down in front of us. Raising my glass to hers, I said, "Here's to true love."

She gave me a big toothy smile and winked. "Here is to rich husbands…and sexy boyfriends."

"Well, you look very nice," I said. She was all made up, red lipstick, long eyelashes, gold earrings, the whole nine yards.

"Thank you. Is celebrate tonight."

I asked, "What's that you're wearing? It's very…alluring."

"Is Dolce and Gabbana."

"Really?"

"Yes, you like?"

I nodded. It was a lot nicer on her than Vito. "I do. So is this your celebration? Following me to my hotel?" I sipped my powered up second negroni and was starting to feel not unkindly toward her.

She noticed my relaxed demeanor, smiled, and rubbed my calf with the side of her shoe. I looked down at her leg next to mine and felt a tingling. She said nonchalantly, "I am engaged to be marry. I have no interest in you anymore."

I snorted, "Okay, you're right. It's for the best."

Downing the rest of her drink in one long swallow, she placed her glass loudly on the counter and said, "Come, let's dance and I explain to you all the things I am going to do to old man instead of you."

She stood and grabbed my hand, pulling me with her onto the teeming dance floor. Placing her arms around my neck, she pressed her hips into me and locked onto my gaze. Swaying back and forth slowly, I saw a hungry look in her eyes.

She said, "Why you no take Katarina seriously?"

"I disagree. I've taken you very seriously."

"Hmm. I like you, John."

"And I like you, Katarina."

She smiled. "Then show."

"You're engaged."

"Is excuse."

"I thought you were going to tell me all the things I was going to miss out on."

Smiling, she pulled me close and kissed me long and tenderly. "First I kiss him like that over and over and over."

"He's a lucky man."

She twisted around and facing away put her right arm behind my neck and tugged me forward as she squirmed her bottom into me. She took my left hand and placed it under her breast, not caring who saw or what they thought. Turning her head back she said, "I do that to him next."

"I hope his pacemaker is working."

"Is no laugh. He will like and you will die with jealousness."

"You mean jealousy."

"I no care, and when he get excited real good I…" She turned back to face me, leaned into my ear and whispered what could only be described as verbal pornography.

I looked at her. "Now that's going to require a demonstration."

A big grin across her face signaled an end to the foreplay. "We go room."

"We definitely go room."

Chapter 34

We woke up late and hung over. Katarina showered quickly, chugged a cup of coffee, and bolted from the room to get back to the ship, hoping Berislav would be too drunk to realize she'd been AWOL all night. She was in such a rush, she almost left with the bath towel on her head.

I looked at my watch. It was almost eleven. I dressed and headed over to the hospital to visit Betsy. She looked very depressed when I arrived, but that was to be expected. The anesthetics were wearing off and the gravity of her situation was starting to sink in. All alone in the world at an advanced age with an acute medical problem, and looking forward to an extended recovery period was a grim and depressing prospect for even the most stoic of individuals.

Placing my styrofoam coffee cup down, I gave her an encouraging kiss and sat next to her. "Good morning."

She smiled. "Good morning."

"I see they're starting to take some of the tubes away." They had removed her naso-gastric tube and nasal cannula. She also looked as if she had washed up and brushed her hair.

"Yes, and they even let me go to the bathroom to pee."

I chuckled. "It's the little things in life..."

"Isn't that the truth. The doctor was in here this morning and spoke with me at length."

When she didn't expand I asked, "And what did he have to say…?"

She hesitated and then said, "I can have some clear liquids today, but only if I pass gas."

I smiled, "Well, you have something to look forward to."

"Lovely. They'll advance my diet depending on how well I do after that."

"He say anything else?"

"Nope. That's it."

"Okay, that's sounds about right at this point. I'll talk to him later before I leave."

"No, John. I don't want you to talk to him," she said emphatically. "You've done enough and I want you to focus your energy on recovering my necklace for me. I'm a big girl and I can handle my own healthcare."

That took me aback, but I nodded in agreement. It was her right, of course, but I had never met anyone before who didn't want their own personal physician friend to run interference for them if only to clarify the medical jargon. I saw the determination in her face and said, "Whatever you want, Betsy."

"It's what I want."

"How's your pain today?"

"Still there, but manageable. I use the morphine pump on a regular basis but they have ordered me pills to try to switch me over to oral medications as quickly as possible."

"The rehab people will probably start showing up soon."

"This afternoon, a physical therapist is coming by to assess me."

Nodding, I said, "They seem to be on the ball here."

"They really are. I believe that I am in good hands. Bjorn was here earlier to say goodbye. He has to get the ship ready for departure. It leaves at three. I told him you will not, under any circumstances, be staying behind. He was upset but agreed it was my right. He will have the appropriate people contact the best nursing services on the island and make all necessary arrangements for my care moving forward. He will also reach my attorney and financial people in London to let them know what happened and where I am. Before sun down, I should be inundated with phone calls from lawyers and accountants."

I chuckled. "Don't overdo it."

She smiled, "I'll be fine. I've been through a lot in my life. This is nothing."

As she said that, a tear came to one eye. She wiped it and I said, "Betsy…I'm so sorry…about everything."

She shook her head, refusing to let her emotions get the better of her. "No, don't be. I've had a wonderful life. I have no regrets."

"I'd really like to stay with you Betsy."

"I appreciate that, but I won't allow it. I'm fine. I want you to give me a kiss and then…I want you to leave."

"But I just got here."

"Kiss me."

I stood and leaned down, kissing her gently. She began to cry softly. I too was starting to get emotional. "Betsy, talk to me, please."

"Leave. Please, don't ask any more questions. Just go. I've already spoken to Bjorn. He will gather all my belongings from your room and place them in storage."

I was confused and at a loss for words as I studied her face for a clue as to what she was thinking. Like most women, the more I tried to understand her, the more confused I got. Reluctantly, I said, "I'll go now."

She breathed a sigh of relief. "Thank you, John."

At the door, I turned. "If it's the last thing I do I'll find your necklace and bring it right here to you."

She said, "I'd expect no less."

I nodded and left the hospital to check out of the hotel and find Vito. By 2:00 p.m., we were on the gangplank boarding the Queen Boudica. The sun was peeking out and he was in good spirits. I was deep in thought and barely registered his chatter until he nudged me.

"You have nothing to say?"

I looked at him. "About what?"

"About what? Haven't you heard a word of what I just said? Charmaine, the waitress. I was just telling you about her."

I sighed deeply. "Tell me again."

"We went to one of those castles she told us about, walked around and had a drink in one of the cafes."

"Sounds nice."

"Yeah, it was until the walk back to the hotel. We passed a church that was open all night."

He caught my attention with that. "A church was open all night?" Maybe that wasn't as strange as it sounded.

"Yeah, and people were in it praying. There was a service going on. Some patron saint festival is going on this week and they're all getting ready. Apparently, they take this stuff pretty seriously in the Greek Orthodox religion."

"So what happened?"

"What happened? She goes to the front row, kneels, and starts praying."

I grinned. "Get out of here."

"I kid you not."

"And then what?"

"I waited in the back of the church for about half an hour for the service to end. When it finally did, she came back and told me she was going to take a cab home. Now that she'd been praying and reflecting on her sins and all that bullshit she didn't feel right about going to my room with me and whatever."

"Damn. What a stroke of bad luck."

"You're telling me? Before that, she was all over me. I thought I had struck gold. I can't believe what's happening to me. That's the second time I got left at the altar if you'll pardon the pun. These European chicks don't seem to be into casual sex."

"Sorry, bud. It's a different moral compass here. You'll get used to it, but the good news is, your pal, Cesari, always has your back. And as long as you're not distracted by women you can help me."

He laughed. "That's some consolation, I guess. So how's the old lady?"

"She looked good physically, considering her age and all she's been through. Emotionally is a whole different story."

He nodded. "And you?"

"I'm upset. I didn't want to leave her but she insisted. She wants me to do whatever it takes to get her necklace back. It's an heirloom, and besides being worth a small fortune, it has great sentimental value for her."

"What are your chances of doing that?"

"Slim to none, but there might be some clues I've overlooked. I'm going to retrace my steps and take a fresh look at things, your basic gumshoe stuff."

"And what am I supposed to do?"

"Keep me supplied in Manhattans and make sure no one sticks a knife in my back if I get too close to the truth."

"I can handle the Manhattan part but the other will cost you. Bodyguard fees are outrageous just so you should know."

I smiled. It felt good to have him on board. One of these days I was going to have to let him get laid, but for now, I needed him to stay focused. I said, "No problem."

"Is that it? Just watch your back?"

"How about calling one of your guys back home and see what they can dig up on that CEO guy, Brad. That would be helpful."

"I thought he's been neutralized?"

"Slowed down is all. A deleted email is never really gone. The video and pictures are still in cyberspace and there's always a chance he might figure out how to recover them. I need to discourage that."

"Aren't the pictures I took enough?"

"They're priceless, but I've been thinking about it. He's such a loser. He might turn around and say he doesn't give a crap and that he was planning on getting divorced anyway."

"Good point. Okay, I'll make the call and tell them to light a fire under it."

We parted company, agreeing to meet for drinks in the Commodore's Lounge on deck 10 at 6:00 p.m., and from there head to dinner at the Princess Grill.

In my room, I discovered that Bjorn hadn't wasted any time, and all of Betsy's belongings had been removed. There was no trace that she had spent the last few days with me. My natural cynicism wondered if they had wiped the room down for prints. All of my things seemed to be pretty much as I had left them. I was getting paranoid. It was always an uncomfortable feeling knowing someone else had been in your room.

I laid down on the bed and wondered why Betsy had been so adamant about me leaving. There was something about her affect that bothered me. Initially, I thought she was just down in the dumps over her condition and lack of control over events. That was common, but by the time I left, I felt that there was something more going on. She seemed…resigned to whatever it was she was resigned to. More puzzles.

I was soon asleep.

Chapter 35

Arriving in the Commodore's Lounge at just after the agreed upon time, I found Vito looking out the massive window at the sea trailing behind. We were on the stern side of the ship and could still see the lights of the receding coastline as darkness descended. He was sipping scotch and I ordered one for myself, a double, Talisker, neat.

"You look good," I commented as I nestled into a large leather chair next to him. He wore a black silk suit, white shirt, solid red power tie, diamond cufflinks and tie-pin, and spit-shined leather Italian shoes. Very casual for him.

"Thanks, you don't look too shabby yourself."

I wore dark gray dress pants, blue and white striped shirt open at the top, and a navy blazer with gold buttons. I said, "Thanks."

My drink arrived and I sniffed it. Good stuff. Very smoky. We clinked glasses and sipped, staring outward. It was very peaceful right now and hard to imagine just how ferocious the weather had been the night before.

We talked over the situation examining it from various angles. He was good at this kind of stuff. In fact, it was right up his alley. In the mob world, unexpected things always happened and had to be dealt with on the fly. Crisis management occupied most of his time. He whistled, "Damn, Cesari, for a guy who was supposed to be meditating, you've been pretty busy."

He didn't know the half of it. Except for Betsy, I had deliberately left him in the dark about my other amorous adventures. "Yeah, it's been a struggle."

"Okay, let's do a threat assessment first and then run down the list of likely suspects, assuming of course it wasn't that love-struck doctor who skipped out in Dubrovnik. If it was him, then I'm afraid those jewels are gone forever."

I nodded. "It wasn't him, I'm sure of it, but we'll find out soon enough. If he was really in love like he told me then he should be in custody any day now. His plan was to return straight to his wife and win her back. The captain told me the authorities will be staking out his apartment in Oslo. If he lied to me then that would be the last place he would go."

"Fine, let's start with this Croatian cop, Antonela. She sounds a little crazy and possibly dangerous."

I interrupted him, "Definitely dangerous."

"Fine, she's dangerous. Then there's the CEO, Brad. Dangerous or no?"

"My guess is that his first instinct is not to use physical violence like Antonela would. He's more of a strategy kind of guy. Likes to lay traps and landmines and then steer you into them. He's got no leverage on me now but he needs cash and thinks I can help him so who knows what his next move will be. And like I said before, it may dawn on him that those pictures of Betsy and me are recoverable. At this point, I think he would publish them out of pure spite."

"Yeah, but now we're the ones with the compromising pictures of him and Joyce. Granted, he may not give a shit but they're pretty embarrassing nonetheless. In addition, I called my guys like you said and they're doing research on him and that hospital he runs. They're tracing all his financial records, personal and professional. They should have something for us later tonight."

I sipped my scotch. "Thanks, I need to think over the Brad situation some more. It would be nice if I could give him a compelling reason to leave me alone. I've tried appealing to his decent side, but he doesn't seem to have one. Let me know if and when your guy comes through with anything."

He nodded. "I will. Berislav?"

"Good question. He thinks he hit a home run with Antonela and the Croatian mob and he may just well have. Sooner or later, however, somebody is going to fact check those diamonds and realize they're phonies and then all hell is going to break loose. I don't really care what happens to Berislav. All I want is time to make sure his step-daughter is out of harm's way when the shooting starts."

He finished his drink and ordered another. "So the only real maniac on the ship is this four foot Croatian cop and she seems to be busy for the moment with the diamonds and Berislav?"

"Yeah, but don't underestimate her. She's pathologic and has issues with anger and right now she's angry at me. That sums up my cruise experience so far."

He smirked at me. "If I didn't know better I'd say you were scared of her."

I hadn't told him the whole story and most likely never would. "Just watch out for her, all right?"

"Fine. Well, it seems to me that if anyone of that rag tag bunch stole the necklace then they wouldn't be so excited about having come into possession of the phony set. Ergo, none of them are in possession of the real necklace. Ditto for the fat CEO guy who thinks you have it."

"I agree, so who else could possibly have had not only knowledge of the phony necklace's existence but access to her room as well?"

We sat there contemplating that thought for a moment. He said, "Just how well do you know this Captain Bjorn character?"

"Bjorn?" I looked at him. "Not a chance."

"Why not? Because he looks squeaky clean? Those are usually the worst ones."

I didn't have an answer to that and he continued, "Let's examine the facts. Bjorn was a close friend of the Harringtons and has known them for a long time, right?"

I nodded. "Yeah, but…"

"But what? Whether you were aware of it or not there's a good chance he may have known about the phony necklace, and who would have had access to any room on this ship any time he wanted?"

Damn, he was making sense. I was starting to feel uncomfortable. I was generally a very good judge of people, almost clairvoyant in fact. If I was wrong about the captain then my sixth sense had let me down in a big way.

I said, "I just find it hard to believe."

He swirled his scotch and sniffed it. "Who said that once you eliminate the impossible, whatever remains, no matter how improbable, must be the truth?"

Jesus Christ! A guy who took six years to finish high school was quoting literature at me. I said, "That was Sherlock Holmes."

"And that would explain why he tried to strangle her in your room. She knew him too well and sooner or later he knew she would have put two and two together."

"Yeah, but my room had signs of forced entry. He wouldn't have had to do that. As you just said, he's the captain. He can go anywhere he wants at will."

"Don't be stupid Cesari. Use your head. He could only play that card once or else suspicion would naturally fall on anyone with universal access, so this time he makes it look like a break-in or something more mysterious. You know, a rich old lady with many enemies or something like that. Who knows? Maybe even…"

He was suddenly quiet and I asked, "Maybe even what?"

"You know who the number one suspect on this ship ought to be?"

The waitress came by and I paid for our drinks. We stood and I said, "Who?"

"You."

I rolled my eyes. "Of course I know that, but I don't have the necklace or the murder weapon. Besides, I've been through this already. Bjorn doesn't even consider me a suspect...not seriously anyway."

"That don't mean anything. He could just be trying to lull you into a false sense of security."

"That's ridiculous."

"Still, if I were Bjorn and I wanted to pin this on someone to deflect attention from myself, you'd be the perfect scapegoat. You said she was strangled with one of your own belts, right?"

"She was."

"Cesari, you don't even see how badly you're being framed."

"I need to think."

The Princess Grill was on the same deck and not too far from the Commodore's Lounge. We arrived five minutes later and were seated next to a table of four much older women. One of them was a friend of Betsy's and recognized me. She began whispering to the others who started glancing furtively in my direction. I pretended not to notice.

The waiter handed us menus and I continued our conversation. What he said about Bjorn was weighing heavily on me. At the risk of validating Vito's powers of deduction I said, "Look, what you said makes sense, and I admit I hadn't considered it."

He gave me a mocking grin. "That had to hurt, didn't it?"

"You'll never know how much."

We both ordered sixteen ounce strip steaks, medium rare, creamed spinach, fries, and a bottle of Chianti. The old ladies at the next table kept looking my way on and off. I didn't blame them. I was almost a celebrity now. I couldn't even begin to imagine the story-telling going on; the slick New York doctor romancing an old woman for her money. The nurses I worked with back home would get a kick out of that.

The wine came first with some fresh baked rolls and butter. I took a sip and said, "How do you propose I investigate the captain? He's the one guy on board no one can touch."

"Why not?"

"Are you trying to be funny? The captain of a ship at sea is essentially a king. No one challenges him. He has ultimate authority over everyone on board."

"Fine, but he has a room where he keeps things like everyone else, doesn't he? Let's start by searching his cabin."

I raised my eyebrows. That was stupid even for him. "Search his room? You must be nuts. You'll wind up spending the rest of the cruise in the brig on the lower deck. Besides, anything important he probably keeps in his safe so even if we were able to search his room we would never be able to get into that."

"What's wrong with you, Cesari? What's with all the doom and gloom? The only other real suspect besides yourself and you're afraid to search his room. We should at least give it a try. There might be other clues we may find there."

The steaks came and we started eating. I hadn't eaten since breakfast and was ravenous. He took a few bites, scrunched his face and said, "This creamed spinach sucks. I'm sending it back."

"It's not that bad. Don't get all worked up. It just needs some seasoning." I signaled the waiter and asked if he could bring some fresh nutmeg to the table with a microplane spice grater and he agreed. I said, "See. No need for a scene."

"So what's it going to be, Cesari? It's time to man up. That is, if you really care about the old broad."

That hurt. I did care and wanted very much to bring whoever it was to justice. It was just very hard to believe it might be Bjorn. Still, Vito had a point. If he was guilty then he needed to have his ass kicked. Alternatively, the best way to clear him was to prove he had nothing to do with it. "Okay, I'm in."

He smiled, proud of himself. Nothing like talking a friend into crimes on the high seas in international waters under the jurisdiction of foreign nationals. I suddenly had this image of myself walking the plank over a pack of hammerhead sharks.

The old ladies next door finished their meal and were debating dessert options. One of them nodded in my direction and asked the waiter, "I'd like whatever he's having."

The waiter glanced at me and then back at her saying, "But, madam, he is having steak, not dessert."

She looked at my plate. "That can't be right. I smell something sweet coming from that direction. It smells like… cinnamon…that's it. Is he having an apple crisp or something like that?"

The waiter assured her that I was not eating an apple crisp and she ordered something else.

Vito saw I was distracted and snapped his fingers at me. "Earth to Cesari."

"I'm here."

"So let's get started."

"Tonight?"

"No time like the present."

"Fine, but I have a better idea than breaking and entering the room of someone who could potentially have me executed without a trial."

He looked surprised. "I'm listening."

"I'm just going to talk with him."

"Who? The captain? Now why didn't I think of that? Let's just go up to him and ask him if he murdered the old guy, stole the necklace, and then tried to murder the wife to cover his tracks? When confronted like that he'll probably slap the handcuffs on his own wrists. You're a genius, Cesari. Did you know that?"

"Shut up and eat. I'm thinking."

The women next door stood to leave. The first three looked down their noses at me as they walked by. They were clearly disgusted by my very existence and I hoped they weren't picked for my jury pool when the time came.

The one who smelled cinnamon moved a little more slowly, smiled politely, and dropped something right next to my foot. I bent to retrieve it for her, but she hurriedly left to catch up to her friends before I could reach it.

It was her room key.

Chapter 36

Vito went to the casino and I searched for Bjorn. The ship's information center told me he was at a reception for the first class passengers in the Churchill Room on deck 12 overlooking the bow. The Churchill Room was a cigar lounge and bar, which meant lots of wood, whiskey and dark leather. Oil paintings of fox hunts, the queen, and past glories adorned the walls as old money cruised the room sipping their drinks politely discussing all that was wrong with the modern world. Roger and Betsy would have been at home here.

Bjorn, in his dress whites, was surrounded by men in tuxedoes and women in long gowns. I was a little under-dressed for the occasion, but clouds of cigar smoke and alcohol distracted anyone from passing comment. I took up position behind several passengers eagerly waiting their turn to speak to Bjorn. He noticed me lingering in the background, excused himself, and came over. Greeting me warmly, we shook hands.

"Doctor, so nice of you to come."

"Well, I wasn't actually invited, and I apologize for my attire."

"Nonsense, you are welcome anywhere on this ship."

"Do you mean that?"

"Of course, I do."

"I'm glad to hear that. May I have a word with you in private, Bjorn?"

He looked curious. "Certainly. Is it about Betsy?"

"It is."

He nodded and put his arm around my shoulder. "Let's take a walk."

As we left the Churchill Room, he let one of his officers know he would return shortly. We walked outside and leaned against the metal railing. A full moon lit up the sky. He turned around and leaned back against the railing. Reaching into his jacket, he came out with a Cuban cigar, bit off one end, and fired it up with a torch lighter.

"I'm sorry that I don't have another cigar to offer you, doctor."

"Thank you and that's okay. I should have thought to grab one while I was in the lounge. Maybe we'll sit down with a brandy some other time."

"Definitely."

I said, "Any word on how she is doing?"

"Nothing since this morning."

I nodded. "She looked well when I last saw her."

"As a doctor, you have a different perspective on what "well" looks like. As a non-medical person, she looked awful to me. Spirited as always but awful nonetheless."

"I can understand that. Back in the states when I would discuss informed consent with patients prior to a procedure I would explain all the things that could potentially go wrong. I'd watch as people nodded their heads and without hesitation would sign even though they had no idea what I was talking about. I would ask them if they understood and they would say, *Sure, I could get very sick*. And then I would say yes, but your concept of very sick is different from what my concept of very sick is."

He puffed on his cigar. "I agree. In your practice, you probably see things every day that most of us never see in a lifetime."

"Exactly. You know, Betsy didn't want me to stay with her because she wanted me to continue searching for her necklace. She has every confidence in you but thought that maybe I could see things in a different light than you or your security team."

"I know. She told me, and she directed me to give you the widest latitude possible so long as it did not disrupt or jeopardize the voyage."

I raised my eyebrows at that. "I didn't know. I hope you didn't take that personally."

"Well, maybe a little, but she is the majority owner of the ship. So whatever you need…"

"Could you tell me about the day you searched the ship looking for the murder weapon and her necklace?"

"What would you like to know?"

"Was it a room to room search and how thorough?"

"Every room was searched from top to bottom, including the safes."

"The crew as well?"

"Everyone's room was searched including all of the crew."

I hesitated thinking of how to say it out loud and finally said softly, studying his face carefully. "Everyone's room? Even the captain's?"

He hesitated slightly and turned to me, his face showed no emotion. "No, not the captain's."

I nodded. "Bjorn, did you know that Betsy kept a faux necklace, an exact replica, that she left lying around to distract would be jewel thieves?"

Slowly, the way people do when they suddenly realize how important their words might be, he said, "Yes, I did. We talked about it often how to best protect her necklace and decided together years ago that sometimes the best way to hide something is in plain sight."

"The most important tool every magician must master to be successful is the art of misdirection."

"Exactly," he said, blowing a puff of smoke into the night air.

"It was actually a great idea, although the fact that the thief left the fake one behind sort of limits the investigation to those who might have known."

He let that float around for a couple of seconds before responding, "And since I knew the necklace was fake and had access, that places me on a very short list of suspects?"

"You just said your room was the only one that wasn't searched."

Without missing a beat, he said, "Doctor, I could have you slapped in irons and tossed into the brig below and not a soul alive would disapprove. Everyone on this boat already thinks you're guilty. It wouldn't be too hard to convince the Admiralty Board in London the same."

I swallowed hard. "I know that, but I have to do what's right for Betsy."

He sized me up as he thought about that. Standing to full height, he reached into his pocket and came out with the key to his room. Handing it to me, he said, "The combination to the safe is 1-7-5-8. Don't break anything. I'll be at the reception for the rest of the night. Leave the key on the dresser by the door. I have the spare key on me."

He walked away without saying another word, and I hoped I didn't just destroy our relationship. I knew he was innocent, but I went to search his room anyway just in case he was the greatest poker player on earth.

An hour later, I came up empty. His safe had nothing in it but his passport. I left the key where he had told me to, and with my tail between my legs went to find Vito in the casino.

He was sitting at a slot machine smoking a Camel, sipping bourbon and dropping quarters in like a drunken sailor. "So how'd it go?" he asked.

I was shaken and sat next to him. "Just great. He invited me to his house for Christmas. Wants to know what size I am in sweaters."

He snorted, "Did Uncle Bjorn spank you?"

"I may have burned a few bridges."

"He wasn't cooperative, I gather?"

"On the contrary, he was very obliging, and let me search his room completely, without any restriction or supervision. He even gave me access to his safe."

"Really?"

"Yeah, he's clean."

"So what are you whining about?"

"Because now he hates me."

He rolled his eyes. "Who cares? At least now you can scratch him off the list."

"That's the problem. Besides, me he was the only one on the list. Do you have any idea how uncomfortable it was to tell a guy like that he's a suspect?"

Vito turned to me, sipped his drink and said, "I don't give a rat's ass. I get accused of much worse every day."

"Yeah, but you're usually guilty."

He grinned. "It still hurts, Cesari. I have feelings too."

I looked at my watch. It was almost midnight. "You going to stay here all night?" I asked.

"No, I'm working on one of the cocktail waitresses. She gets off in an hour. She walks by every ten minutes so I can stare at her butt."

"Are you sure that's why she walks by, or is it possible she's just doing her job?"

He dropped another quarter in the machine and was rewarded with a two dollar credit which made him happy. "Please, Cesari, spare me the politically correct bull. I know when a chick is flirting with me."

"I just don't want you to get into trouble."

He snorted. "Thanks for the advice but I think I'll take my chances. So are you going to play, get a drink, or keep crying about you and Bjorn not being pals anymore?"

I spotted Brad across the room heading toward the twenty-five dollar black jack tables. I said, "There's Brad. I think I'll see what he's up to."

Vito turned to look. "Be smart and leave him alone unless he bothers you again."

"His breathing is bothering me right now."

"You heard my advice, right? Leave him alone."

"Never. I'll see you later."

He grabbed my arm. "As long as you're hell bent on starting trouble you might as well see this. It's hot off the presses." He reached into his jacket and pulled out a couple of pieces of folded paper and handed them to me. "While you were with the captain, my guy in New York faxed me this. You might find it interesting."

I took the pages and unfolded them. Nodding as I read, I said, "Thanks. This is great. He's an even bigger jerk than I thought. Why were you holding out on me?"

"I wasn't holding out on you. I didn't think I'd see you until morning. It never occurred to me that you were going to have it out with Brad in the middle of the casino tonight. Believe it or not Cesari, I don't spend every waking moment worrying about how I can better serve you."

"Well maybe you should."

He smiled, "Yeah, well, tell him I said hello."

Brad's back was to me as I walked up to the black jack table and sat beside him. I ordered a Manhattan and a hundred bucks in chips. I noticed a small bandage on his forehead over his right eye.

I said, "Hi Brad."

He looked at me suspiciously. "Doctor."

"What happened to your head?"

"I slipped on a wet bathroom floor in Corfu."

"Ouch. I'm sorry."

"Not as much as they will be when my lawyers sink their teeth into them."

"We haven't talked in a while, Brad. I'm sorry I missed my appointment with you the other night. The weather was atrocious, and I don't like getting wet."

He sneered, "You think you're a funny guy, don't you?"

The dealer tossed cards our way. Brad was showing a deuce and tapped for another. I held with a king and a six. "I'm not sure what you mean?"

"I don't know how you did it, and maybe you won round one, but I know you've got that necklace and I'm going to get it. Only now I have a secondary mission, and that is too prove to everyone what a skunk you really are."

I smiled. "That's too bad because I was hoping we could be friends. In fact, I was thinking of visiting that hospital of yours. What's it called again? Oh yeah, Hoosick General Hospital."

"What about it?" he asked warily.

"It's located in the town of Hoosick Falls, isn't it? That's in upstate New York, not too far from Albany. I think I know the area. Well, I've been doing some research on Hoosick General. I wonder if the proud citizens of that town know about the economic disaster that's looming on the horizon for them in the not too distant future."

"What's that supposed to mean?"

"Well, from what I've been reading, Hoosick General is on the verge of declaring bankruptcy and that a couple of thousand people may soon be out of work just in time for the holidays. For a small town, the economic impact will be devastating. It's interesting though because according to the financial records, there should have been plenty of cash on reserve for a rainy day, but I'm guessing that somebody's been sticking his hand in the cookie jar. My guys haven't nailed it down yet, but I suspect the accounting there is going to show some significant irregularities." I took a moment to smile at him. "I wonder how the board's going to react when they find out?"

Not so easily chastised, he grinned, "Okay, so you've done some homework and caught wind of some rumors. Congratulations. But trust me, doctor. When I say jump, the board says how high. Each one of them has been hand-picked by myself and has had their palms greased nicely from that same cookie jar. So do your best. You can't hurt me."

"Maybe you're right, but I wonder how high your wife would jump if you ever told her to? I mean, you did such a great job at handpicking everyone on the board that you even made her the chairwoman. Smart move loading the dice like that. You can never be fired as long she's the boss. I got to hand it to you. On the other hand, she's the only one who *can* fire you, isn't she? I guess you wouldn't want to piss her off?"

He hesitated and blinked. That one caught him off-guard, and not sure where I was heading with it, said, "Joycie's a good egg. She does what she's told."

I stood and tossed a chip at the dealer. "Joyce's a sweetheart, Brad. I have no doubt about that, but I was talking about your real wife, Gloria. Remember her, the woman who's visiting her sick mother in L.A., the woman whose name is on the title of your house, your car, and all your bank accounts, even the phony ones that you've been siphoning off hospital money into."

I watched the color drain from his face and added, "Checkmate, Brad."

God, I hated guys like him.

Chapter 37

The next morning, I tried calling the hospital in Corfu to see how Betsy was doing but the call dropped. After three more similarly unsuccessful attempts, I gave up, planning to try again later. Phone reception in Europe was almost always spotty and on a ship at sea downright pathetic. Frustrated, I went down to the sick bay to see if Aimée needed any help. The infirmary was quiet with only one or two patients in the waiting room perusing magazines. I said hello to the nurse and secretary and found her dictating a patient's chart in her office. She looked up and smiled, "Good morning, Jean."

"Good morning Aimée. How are you today?"

"I am wonderful. I haven't seen you in a while. I was wondering what happened. I could have used your help yesterday. The storm kept us very busy."

"I'm sorry I wasn't available. I was a little tied up. My cousin insisted on seeing Corfu and I couldn't let him run around the island unattended. He exhausted me so much that when I returned yesterday, I slept all day. I promise you that I wasn't hiding from you."

That brought an even bigger smile to her face. She stood and came around from her desk. "You should get a medal for the way you take care of him, but have no worry, I did not think you were hiding from me. In fact, I do not think I ever met a man that did."

I liked her self-confidence. She wrapped her arms around me and we kissed. "Do you need any help?" I asked.

"No, so far today is very light, but you never know what will happen. All it takes is one box of tainted lettuce and half the passengers will be in here with food poisoning. I could use the rest. The storm really taxed our resources."

"I'll bet. Well, let's hope no one eats salad for the rest of the voyage. There's enough going on around here as it is. Well, I won't keep you from your work. I just dropped in to say hi and to see if you needed anything."

"Thank you so much, Jean. Maybe we can meet later tonight?"

"That would be very nice. I've been very busy lately, but I'll do my best."

"I understand. Your cousin is a handful. Well, if not tonight, then perhaps we can visit Santorini tomorrow. It is the most beautiful island in the Mediterranean."

"Is it really?"

"Without question."

"Well then, I would like that very much. Hopefully, my cousin will settle down. I brought a DVD player and several Disney movies for him to watch. *The Little Mermaid* is his favorite."

"How adorable..."

"Yes, and I always leave a bowl of sedative-laced gummy bears nearby for him in case he is frightened by the scenes with the sea witch."

She looked at me sympathetically and touched my face lightly with one hand. "You think of everything."

"If I don't, who will?"

"What a cross you bear."

"Yes, I know. It has been difficult, but I don't wish to seem a martyr. It's just that if I can't be with you, I want you to know the reason why."

"I will understand perfectly." She smiled and hugged me. "I will not feel rejected."

"Thank you."

Leaving her, I felt really bad as I went to find Vito. I wanted to tell her the truth, the whole truth and nothing but the truth, but I was in too deep at this point. I could just stay away from her. Let her think that I had lost interest or was too distracted by my poor sick cousin to continue to pursue romantic interests. Just allow our relationship to die on the vine as it were. Would she buy that? She was a very polite and respectful person so she might. On the other hand, she was well aware of how attractive she was and the effect she had on me. Once you put your tongue in places you shouldn't have, it was hard to turn around and pretend you didn't want to do it again, and again, and again.

Vito was sipping an espresso at a coffee bar when I walked in and took a seat. There was a half-eaten chocolate croissant on a plate in front of him. I picked it up and took a large bite.

With crumbs falling out of my mouth I said, "You don't mind?"

He looked at me and shook his head. "Why would I mind?"

I chuckled. "How'd it go with the cocktail waitress?"

He snorted. "Great. We were up all night. We did it six or seven times. I can't remember exactly. I lost count because she was moaning so much."

Laughing I said, "Didn't go too well, huh?"

"Unbelievable, the girl flirts with me half the night, lets me buy her a drink after she gets off from work, and then she tells me she has a boyfriend who's a steward on this same ship and that she doesn't feel comfortable cheating on him but that she hopes we can still be friends." He slammed his empty espresso cup into the saucer. “I don’t need any more friends, Cesari. I need…”

I raised my hand. “I know what you need. You don’t have to spell it out. Now take it easy. You’re a big boy. You have to learn to deal with adversity.”

He made an exasperated sound. “Look who’s talking. Some girl hurts your feelings and you get on a jet and fly half-way around the world to get away from her.”

He pushed the wrong button this time. “You son-of-a-bitch. How dare you bring that up. Pam didn’t just hurt my feelings. I walked in on her servicing two guys.”

“Cry me a river, Cesari. You’re still a big baby for running like you did.”

I picked up the remains of the croissant and chucked it at him. He ducked, and it went past him onto the floor. I said, “Shut up about Pam.”

We stared at each other for a long moment and then started laughing. He said, “Big baby.”

“Schmuck.”

Changing the subject, he said, “So how’d it go with Brad?”

“He was duly impressed. In fact, if he was any more impressed he might have wet himself.”

“Good. Maybe we can scratch him off the list of people you need to worry about.”

“Either that or he just climbed to the very top of the list of people who would like to see me dead.”

“He’ll have to arm wrestle me for that spot.”

“C’mon, let’s go. We have work to do.”

“Where are we going?”

“Betsy’s room. I want to go over the crime scene again. I need to understand what happened better.”

“What’s there to understand? Some guy robs a necklace worth millions and then shoots the husband who’s trying to defend his wife. It happens all the time just like that. Maybe not with such high stakes but nonetheless…"

We stood to leave. I said, "All the time? Just like that? Since when did you become so well versed on international crime statistics? We're on a cruise ship, Vito. Crime rates are pretty low in general and violent murder almost unheard of. I don't know it for a fact, but I would bet that a crime like this hasn't happened in decades if at all."

"Fine, if you say so, but I think you're giving these Europeans too much credit. I'm sure they knock each other off as much as we do."

We found Betsy's room and let ourselves in uneventfully. Vito sat in a chair and, standing in the middle of the room, I appraised my surroundings as if looking for the first time. I closed my eyes and pretended to be the killer. Somehow I was in possession of her room key and could access the apartment safely. I knew there was a set of phony diamonds lying around as bait. I also knew that Roger and Betsy were at a party and wouldn't return until late. I enter the room and look around. No point in tearing the place apart because I knew the jewels were coming, so I would just set up shop and wait. I have my mask with me to disguise my appearance and a gun in my pocket.

Wouldn't I look around just in case there were other valuables to pluck? Of course I would. Go big or go home. Wasn't that the saying? Yet nothing else was disturbed. Betsy had said that everything was perfectly in its place and I knew that for a fact because I was there right after the crime occurred. What about the safe? He came all this way, committed a murder, and didn't even try to access the safe? Did that make sense?

I walked into her closet and looked at the wall safe. It was closed and locked. I thought about that again. I'm the killer. I'm in the bathroom waiting for my victims. They're rich beyond all my dreams and the prize jewel is around her neck. They come home. Two old people, defenseless against me and my weapon. Scared, confused, confronted by evil, they would have done anything to stave off the violence that was sure to come.

And yet, for some reason, I don't order them to open the safe. I demand the necklace. Betsy refuses, I snatch it and the old man tries to fight me off. A shot goes off and he's gone. I slap her and she falls hitting her head. I run, now scared that things have gone awry. I guess it could have happened that way. Maybe Vito was right. Botched robberies leading to unexpected consequences did happen all the time.

"Hey, Cesari, I'm getting bored." The sound of Vito's raspy voice startled me.

"Shh, give me a minute."

"Do you mind if I smoke?"

"Will you shut up."

He lit a cigarette as I walked into the bathroom, still in the killer's mindset. I have arrived early, entered the room unseen and decided it would be best to wait there for my prey. I'm nervous, probably perspiring. I try to stay calm. More than likely I'm wearing gloves. I observe the phony necklace sitting there on the counter. I get a chuckle out of the failed ruse. That helps settle down my nerves. I turn the lights off. It won't be long. They're old. How late can they stay out?

Suddenly, I hear someone access the door. It's them. They come into their apartment, tired and happy, and turn the lights on. I listen to their chatter. I wait until I hear the door close firmly. One, two, three. I burst out from my hiding place. They gasp in surprise and shock. I act quickly to take advantage of their paralysis.

I flung the bathroom door open and charged into the living room, hand extended as if I were holding a gun. Vito jumped in surprise. Still deep in thought and simulation I ignored him. He didn't say anything and caught on to what I was doing.

I waved the imaginary couple into the middle of the room, admonishing them to remain silent. Still in shock, they do as they are told. They both face me now and the action starts for real. I act quickly and grab the necklace. Roger engages me in Betsy's defense. We struggle, the gun goes off. He is now lying face up dead, and Betsy is unconscious. I recalled the wound I observed in Rogers chest the morning I came to the room. It appeared to be a large caliber weapon, a .45, the kind the Croatian police used, and the kind Vito purchased in Dubrovnik before coming on board the ship. He said you could find them on every street corner; a common weapon almost anyone could have purchased.

I closed my eyes again and zoned into another dimension. Now I was on the ceiling looking down at the players, running through various combinations of events. None of them ended well, but something bothered me, and it bothered me real bad. Then something played out in my mind that startled me. I didn't like what I saw at all.

I snapped out of it. "Vito, I have to go find the head of security."

"What's going on?"

"I'm not sure yet, but I need to see what's inside Betsy's safe."

"You think they're going to open it for you?"

"Yes, I do."

"Fine."

We walked down to the security office on deck 1 and were greeted by a pleasant woman in uniform who asked us to take a seat while she called the boss. A few minutes later, a large, formal looking man of about fifty, greeted us and we introduced ourselves. After I explained who I was and what I needed, he politely asked me to wait while he phoned the captain for instructions. Apparently, word hadn't reached him about my special investigatory status.

When he returned, he was accompanied by another officer. He said, "Gentlemen, the captain informs me that I am to cooperate with you fully in your request. This is Ensign Taylor. He will accompany us and record the proceedings. It is the ship's policy to never open a passenger's safe unless in an emergency or at their specific request should they forget their passcode. Once the decision has been made to do so, it is always performed with a witness. We have the ability to reprogram the electronic lock of Lady Beth's safe and when we do so the action itself will be registered in the ship's security office."

Back in Betsy's room, they approached her safe very formally. Ensign Taylor used a small video recorder to document the proceedings. The security chief, using a key and a series of numbers much longer than a typical passcode, reprogrammed the safe. The tension was pretty high in anticipation at this point which made our disappointment that much greater when the door swung open and we found nothing inside. I let out a deep breath and thanked the men for their time.

Outside Vito said, "Now what, Cesari?"

I was puzzled. "Let's go to the morgue."

"Oh c'mon. Really? The morgue?"

"You heard me."

Chapter 38

In the morgue, we went through the same drill with the attendant, and after calling the captain, he showed us into the small room with Roger's body and left us alone to examine him.

Vito shook his head. "What do you hope to accomplish here, Cesari."

"That's for me to know and you to find out."

I reached down, pulled the drawer out to its fullest extent, and unzipped Roger's body bag. Vito scrunched his nose at the sight. The room was icy cold and Roger's corpse was still in very good condition but an eerie, whitish gray nonetheless. I examined the chest wound. It was quite large and irregular and I had assumed the killer used a large caliber handgun like a .45. It didn't occur to me at the time that this might have been an exit wound.

I said, "Vito, help me lift him. I want to see something."

"You have got to be kidding me? I'm not touching that thing."

"Don't bail on me now, all right?"

"Fine, but there have to be gloves somewhere down here."

I looked around. "Over there by the door. There's a box. Get me a pair while you're at it."

We gloved up and together we lifted him to a sitting position. I shook my head at how stupid I had been. There was a small caliber entry wound in his back. He hadn't been shot fighting with Betsy's attacker and he hadn't been shot by a .45. The hole was probably made by a .32 or .38 using hollow points which if they didn't hit bone would have passed through tearing a hole twice as big on the way out. I thought about that. This didn't match up with what Betsy told us had happened.

"Are you happy now?" he asked.

"No, I'm extremely unhappy and twice as confused. Lay him back down and we'll zip him up."

We closed the drawer, thanked the sailor for his cooperation and left the morgue. I was missing something. That was for sure. Something big. I could feel it. I said, "I have to talk to Bjorn again. Why don't you grab a bite to eat and we'll regroup for dinner."

He looked at his watch. "It's a quarter after twelve. Six o'clock cocktails in the Commodore's Lounge?"

"Same place? Again?"

"Sure. Why not? I liked it there."

"Fine."

Taking an educated guess as to where he might be, I went to the bridge and asked to speak to the captain. A minute later, Bjorn appeared, stiff and formal and didn't offer me his hand. His feelings had been hurt and he scowled at me.

I said, "Captain, I would like to clear the air between us."

"Go on, doctor."

"I want to apologize for last night's invasion of your personal quarters and want you to know that it never once even entered my mind that you were in any way involved in this tragedy."

"You mean you felt that way after you rummaged through my personal effects?"

"No, I felt that way before, but I am a very analytical person and I needed to follow the logical progression of my thoughts. For instance, if you came to me complaining of abdominal pain, I would ask you what you ate for dinner the preceding night. You might say, doctor, you sat next to me all evening, you must know the answer to that question. The answer is yes, but I would still like you to tell me anyway just to make sure I didn't miss anything."

He nodded seeming to accept that and I added. "For your sake as well, it was good for me to search your room. The inquiry board will certainly want to know that their captain is above reproach and now I am an independent witness to verify that you were treated in the same regard as everyone else on board for whatever that's worth."

"I am undoubtedly going to be dragged over the coals no matter what the outcome. That's just the way it is, but I suppose you are right. I should thank you."

His appearance softened, and I saw the old Bjorn peeking out from behind the frowny face. I said, "That's not necessary, but I would like to talk to you some more. If you have the time."

"Why don't you join me for tea, doctor?"

"And crumpets if you have them?"

He smiled. "I think we'll find something to your satisfaction."

We sat in thick leather chairs in his office inside the bridge. He ordered tea and finger food. I was glad he was back on my side. He asked, "So what did you find out from this morning's inquiries? My crew tells me you and your friend have been very busy."

"That is true. Sometimes, when I'm confronted with a difficult diagnostic dilemma, I find it helpful to take a step back and think it through again."

"Take a fresh look?"

"Exactly, although that can be difficult because as human beings we suffer from prejudices and sentiment. For instance, take a man who has been happily married for many years and comes home early from work one day. He finds his best friend naked in his living room and his wife nowhere in sight. His first reaction isn't that his wife is cheating on him. No, not at all. His mind won't allow him to jump to that conclusion at least not at first. He will go through a litany of all the possible reasons why he is seeing what he is seeing other than what would be obvious to everyone else in a heartbeat. As a last resort, with no choice but to accept reality for what it is, he will slowly come to the correct conclusion."

"Why is that?"

"It's called denial, and we are all guilty of it from time to time. It's our subconscious way of protecting ourselves from hurtful truths."

He nodded thinking it over. "And how does that apply to this situation?"

We paused for a moment as tea was served and a plate of sandwiches and cakes was placed on a table in front of us. We thanked the server and continued.

I said, "I'm not one hundred percent sure yet, but I would like to ask a few pointed questions if you're okay with that."

He smiled. "Doctor, you already accused me once and searched my room. I doubt that you could offend me more than that."

I chuckled. "Once again, I'm sorry about that, but don't underestimate my ability to offend you or anyone else for that matter."

"Go on with your questions."

"As your head of security probably told you, I found nothing in Betsy's safe."

"Yes, he called me as soon he left the room. What exactly were you thinking you would find?"

"Anything but what we did. If that makes any sense?"

He thought that over, rubbing his chin and crossing his legs. "You think it's strange there was nothing in the safe?"

"It seems very odd, don't you think? One of the wealthiest women on two continents, wears a twenty million dollar necklace every night, and there's nothing in her safe? I mean absolutely nothing, not even any personal documents such as her passport."

"I agree, it seems a tad peculiar, but she must have cleared the safe out at some point before she took ill. That seems like a reasonable explanation."

I studied him carefully. "Possibly, but she was staying with me and she didn't put anything in my safe. Furthermore, I packed all her belongings and trust me, there was nothing safe-worthy among the things I brought back to my room for her."

"What are you suggesting?"

"Like I said, I'm not sure, but there's something here that doesn't seem to fit. The other thing I'd like to talk about is Roger. I went to the morgue this morning as you are aware."

"They called me as well, yes. And why did you need to see Roger?"

"Well, the morning of the murder when I came to Betsy's room, I only casually glanced at the bullet wound as I walked by his body. I took things at face value and it occurred to me what a mistake that might have been."

"Go on. What did you find?"

"That morning he was lying face up with a hole in his chest which I assumed was the result of a large caliber weapon discharged at close range during his struggle to protect Betsy. It turns out, that he was actually shot in the back with a much smaller caliber weapon, and what I saw in front was actually the exit wound. The killer probably used hollow point bullets which caused the much larger hole as it exited his chest. Were you aware of this?"

Casually sipping his tea, he replied, "Yes, of course. Why does it matter?"

I was surprised by that. "Because it changes the narrative somewhat. Betsy said Roger struggled with the killer and the gun went off. That scenario almost demands the entry wound be in the front not the back."

He thought about that for a few seconds. "I'm not sure I agree with you. Perhaps during the struggle, the assailant spun Roger around, maybe even grabbing him around the neck from behind before firing. Betsy was hysterical that night, and her recollection of events would undoubtedly be muddled by the emotional stress she was under. After all, when your husband is murdered in front of your eyes, does it really matter from which angle the bullet was fired? Furthermore, I don't recall pressing Betsy on the details beyond what she told me. Maybe that was an error on my part, but I just didn't see what difference it would make."

That made sense…a little anyway. I didn't like it, but it did make sense. I put some strawberry jam on a crumpet and took a bite. "This is delicious."

"Thank you. Our chefs are world class. Is there anything else, doctor?"

"As a matter fact there is. Despite my friendship with Betsy, I realize that I am just an outsider looking in. Roger's relationship with Betsy was rather strained. You alluded to this in a previous conversation, but I was hoping you wouldn't mind elaborating on it a bit more if you could."

He hesitated, choosing his words carefully. Finally, he nodded somberly and said, "It was complicated that's for sure. They married young I know that. He may have been eighteen and I think she was only seventeen. I don't know the details but I get the feeling they were never truly in love the way people ought to be. He looked much older than her now, but he wasn't. Years of alcohol excess, cigarettes, and debauchery took their toll on his appearance."

"Was it common for Betsy to have friends like... me?"

"No, not common, but once in a great while she met someone she took a fancy to. She told me she was drawn to you because you reminded her of someone she knew long ago. Someone who made her happy."

I remembered her telling me that when we were sitting on the promenade. I said, "Yes, she told me that too, but she didn't say who. I got the feeling it might have been a childhood sweetheart."

"Whoever it was must have been very special because when she told me she became teary."

That was interesting. "Did Roger have Alzheimer's? You mentioned once that his health was declining. Your exact words were 'he wasn't always on the same page as everyone else in the room.' What did you mean by that?"

"You have a good memory, doctor. Not much gets by you. Frankly, I'm impressed."

"Years of interrogating less-than-forthright patients about their drinking habits have trained me to pay attention to details; a word here, a word there. Sometimes, it's the things that aren't said that scream to me the loudest. Besides, I noticed a few oddities about Roger myself. My first night on the ship he was conducting music to himself at dinner. He looked like Beethoven only twice as fervent."

Nodding and letting out a deep breath, he said, "One of Roger's passions was the symphony. He was an accomplished classical pianist and he composed several concertos. The Boston

Philharmonic actually allowed him to conduct them for several charity events one summer."

I felt like this was leading somewhere and let him speak without interruption.

He continued, "Betsy and I talked about Roger's mental condition a lot. For a couple of years now, he'd been slipping. Not in the typical way you would think however. He had the usual forgetfulness that accompanies age, yes, but there was something else…something different. Most of the time he was perfectly lucid, but then at others he could be off the charts, if you know what I mean. He lost all interest in Betsy as a woman, and as you have seen for yourself, she is still quite a striking specimen." He drew in a deep breath looking pensive. "May I ask why are you asking all these questions about them?"

"I'm just trying to understand the situation. If Roger was mentally unstable, then it may have played a role in what happened that night. Did he go 'off the charts' frequently?"

"No, not frequently. On any given day, the odds are he would have been totally normal. On some days, however, he could be completely irrational. Once I was having lunch with him and he launched into a tirade about some argument he had over politics with one of his business partners back in Boston. With extreme detail, he regaled me with all of the colorful terms he called the man and how he was so angry he even had the man's Cadillac towed from its parking spot. I asked when this happened, and he looked at me like I was crazy. 'I just told you,' he said, 'it was last week on the day Reagan was sworn in. How could you forget? It was snowing like crazy. You should have your memory checked.'" Bjorn paused to take a breath before continuing. "I checked with Betsy afterward. It really did happen just like he said on the day he said it happened. Whether it was the effects of alcohol abuse or plain old fashioned senile dementia was impossible to tell. It was like he would slip into a time zone tucked away in his memory banks where he really couldn't tell where he was."

"Interesting."

"It gets better. So I'm sitting there in the Commodore's Lounge listening to this story about what happened in 1981, and suddenly he says, 'Gary, would you and your wife like to join Betsy and me on Martha's Vineyard this weekend?'"

I was enthralled by this. "Gary?"

"Gary Templeton was his third and most junior partner. He passed away ten years ago from a heart attack. Never mind the fact that we were just off the coast of Libya."

"So he actually thought you were this person?"

"One hundred percent. I tried to explain to him who I really was, and he started laughing. He thought I was playing some sort of game with him, so I let it go. A few minutes later he was back to normal like nothing had happened."

"Wow…So he had these brief periods where he would become completely immersed in some sort of flashback experience."

"Exactly."

"And when I saw him conducting music that night…"

"He probably believed he was with the Boston Philharmonic that summer twenty years ago."

"Did he see a physician for this?"

"Only the finest neurologists and psychiatrists in Boston. The kind that expect fifteen hundred dollars in cash to be paid up front at the time of service."

"Were they helpful?"

He smirked wryly. "I don't mean to be cynical, but if throwing your hands up in the air and saying you have no idea what's wrong is helpful, then they were very helpful."

I chuckled, "Is it safe to assume they did the usual things like MRI's, CAT scans…?"

"Gaggles of them and therapy and medications. They had no effect. It was eventually concluded that since he wasn't hurting anyone, and it didn't occur frequently enough to be a problem, to just leave him be. Keep an eye on him they said."

"I guess that makes sense." I hesitated and then asked, "Did Roger have a temper?"

"He used to. Not so much lately although he could be mean and even a little nasty to Betsy at times. I just assumed that was part and parcel of his mental condition. It didn't bother her. She was past that. No, it was the years of neglect and isolation that hurt Betsy the most. I think she just resigned herself to her fate which is why when she meets someone like you, who cheers her up, however temporarily, I try not to pass judgement. For the most part she is a very sad person."

"And her daughter?"

"You'd have to ask Betsy about her. As I mentioned to you previously, I never met her and Betsy rarely spoke about her. Well, doctor, I really do have to get back to the business of this ship."

We stood. "One last question if you don't mind, Bjorn?"

"Certainly."

"Are firearms allowed on board? I mean, with special permission like say for instance, law enforcement?" I was thinking about Antonela and her partner, Niko.

"The short answer is yes, with proper authorization, that would be possible as long as the weapons were kept secured at all times and registered with security. We strongly discourage that of course, but in these trying times we have learned to be flexible. Under no circumstances, however, is that permitted for ordinary passengers, and everyone who boards the ship must pass through metal detectors with their luggage."

"What about crew members? I know I saw security with sidearms outside Betsy's room the day of the murder."

"The ship has a small weapons cache in the lower deck under lock and key for emergency situations. You know, pirates, terrorists, and the like. Unfortunately, we have to brace ourselves for unpleasant events although I pray constantly it never happens."

"I guess it wouldn't be very easy to get one of those weapons?"

"Impossible. They are under lock and key, 24-hour surveillance, and guarded by two armed security officers at all times."

"Well, Captain, this little chat was very helpful."

"Good day, doctor."

I thanked him for the tea and crumpets and left. I had learned a lot but nothing that really pointed in the direction of who might have killed Roger. His mental condition fascinated me and I wasn't sure if I'd ever heard of anything like that. My psychiatric training had consisted of only a six week rotation at the Erie County Medical Center inpatient facility in Buffalo during medical school. That hardly qualified me as an expert in psychiatry. However, it was my considered opinion that most mental disorders went undiagnosed anyway, and that most psychiatrists needed therapy themselves.

Would Roger's mental condition have played a role that night? Good question. I tried to imagine him wrestling with a presumably much younger and healthier intruder. With a mighty heave, the assailant spins Roger around, gets him in a headlock, shoves the gun into his back, and fires. Roger staggers and falls forward…but he was found face up. So Roger staggers, turns around, and falls backward. Possibly, or Roger staggers, falls forward, and the killer turns him around to see if he is dead. Maybe.

I shrugged it off and went to my room to lie down for a couple of minutes. That was a hell of a morning and I was exhausted. I went in, flopped onto the bed, and stared at the ceiling fan twirling around slowly. Poor Betsy. She was a tormented soul; an unhappy marriage, an estranged daughter, and now adrift at sea.

I was just starting to doze off when there was a knock on the door. It was Vito. He was wearing a bathing suit, dark sunglasses, and sandals. He held a terry cloth robe over his arm and was sipping a piña colada through a straw. I said, "I thought we were going to meet for cocktails at six?"

He gave me a big smile. "It's five o'clock somewhere. Put your suit on."

I took a deep breath and let it out. "Give me a minute."

Down at the pool, we positioned our recliners to face the sun, oiled up, and lay back. Vito said, "Who's got it better than us, Cesari?"

He was a simple man with simple needs. I said, "No one, Vito. No one."

A waitress brought me a Mai Tai and we toasted each other's good health. I told him about my conversation with the captain and he said, "Seems like a pretty straight up guy, this Bjorn. Doesn't he?"

"Yes, he does. Not much there that doesn't meet the eye. Still, I get the feeling he knows something he'd rather not talk about. Maybe I'm just being paranoid."

"Relax, Cesari and soak up the rays. The poor guy's got a lot on his plate. Think about it from his point of view. Besides, look at what he told you about Roger. That was a mouthful."

"You're right about that. I feel for him. This is going to get ugly real fast when the ship returns to London. There's going to be a nasty inquiry. There always is in these situations. They will undoubtedly drag his name through the mud. It's sad, but that's always the way it is with bureaucracies. The pencil pushers get off by destroying whoever they can."

"Yup, little people always try to make themselves feel important by destroying others they think are really important. It's almost as if they think they're going to absorb their powers or something."

A shadow came over my face and I looked up. "Hi Joyce."

Grinning ear to ear she said, "Hey there, Tarzan. Can I sit with you and your friend?"

"Sure, pull up a chair."

When she settled in, I introduced her to Vito. "Joyce, this is my friend, Vito. Vito, this is Joyce."

She said, "Hi Vito."

Vito said, "Hi Joyce."

"Boy, look at you two guys. You got the best bods here."

I said, "Not counting yours, I presume."

"Aww, you're sweet."

"How's Brad?"

"Oh my God. What did you do to him last night? He was in a mood this morning. All he did was pace back and forth in the room for hours muttering Cesari, Cesari, effin' Cesari. Then he was on the phone for an hour talking to a friend of his back in the states and all I heard was Cesari, Cesari, effin' Cesari. And honey, you have no idea how much he hates making calls from the ship because they're so expensive. My God, I've never seen him like this. He was just starting to get over the email thing but now…forget it."

"Well, important guys like Brad sometimes let the stress get to them. It's a shame really. I think the bigger picture is that our society as a whole seems to be losing its coping skills. I don't know how much he listens to you Joyce, but you may want to suggest counseling."

She started laughing as she rubbed sun tan lotion on her chest. Vito unabashedly ogled her as she wiggled and jiggled her cannons. She said, "That'll be the day. Brad in counseling? Now that's a good one. He'll cool off. He always does and then he'll move on to the next crisis."

She struggled to reach her back with the lotion and Vito offered to help her. "Do you need a hand there, Joyce?" he asked as pleasantly as I've ever heard him.

"Thanks, but no thanks, honey. Dr. Cesari can handle it. Besides being a lot closer, he owes me. Don't you, honey?"

She had turned her back to me and Vito glared from beneath his shades. I suppressed a smile and began massaging the lotion into her skin. I said, "I sure do, Joyce."

"That's a good boy. Make sure you get real low down and don't miss any spots."

After a minute or two, she said, "Okay, that's enough. How about I lay down and you do the backs of my legs?"

She sprawled face down and I knelt beside her chair, spreading lotion up and down. She was wearing her thong bikini which presented a problem deciding where the top of her legs ended, and the rest began. Vito was salivating at my predicament. I picked a point and didn't go beyond with the lotion prompting her to say, "Higher. Do the whole leg or I'll burn."

I glanced at Vito and he mouthed *I hate you* at me. I said, "How am I doing Joyce?"

"Getting better. All you needed was a little guidance."

"That's all most men need, Joyce."

"Ain't that the gospel truth."

I finished, and she turned around. "Thanks, you're a prince. So, do you have plans for this evening? Brad's going on a bender for sure. I'm not even going to pretend I wanna be around him."

"You know Joyce. You're a pretty nice person. Don't you think you could do better than Brad?"

She sat up suddenly all excited, her breasts dangling about a foot from my face. “Are you offering me an upgrade, Dr. Cesari?”

Vito stood up disgusted. “I can’t take any more of this. I’m going for a swim.”

Joyce was put out, and as he walked out of hearing range, said, “What’s his problem? He’s got sort of a nasty disposition. Does he know that?”

“Never mind him, Joyce. He fell out of the wrong side of the bed this morning. You know what I mean? He’ll be fine as soon he meets the right girl.”

“Well, he ain’t gonna meet anyone with that attitude. Anyway, back to what I was saying. Were you making me an offer I wouldn’t dream of refusing?”

“Actually, I was just offering you advice because I think you’re nice and I think Brad is an obnoxious buffoon. You’re selling yourself short with him.”

“Don’t I know it. He’ll never leave his wife. I know that, but he can be fun sometimes. You can be fun too, and don’t think I’ve forgotten about our little deal. You owe me one more time in a bed, remember?”

“I remember.”

“A deal’s a deal.”

I nodded, “A deal’s a deal.”

“How about tonight?”

I thought about that and resigned myself to my fate. Tonight was as good as any other and I did owe her. I didn’t have any specific plans. Betsy was out of the picture and Aimée would think I was tied up with my addled cousin. That left only the balcony climbing, irrepressible Katarina who I would order to stand down.

“Tonight will work just fine Joyce.”

She clapped her hands. “Oh goodie. What time and where?”

"My room, say elevenish. I'll give you my room key just in case I'm late. I wouldn't want you hanging around in the hallway for Brad to find. Just let yourself in and make yourself at home. That sound good to you?"

"Are you kidding? I'll probably spend the rest of the afternoon picking out baby names."

She was funny.

Chapter 39

At 6:30 p.m. there was a knock on my door as I was getting ready to meet Vito for cocktails. We'd had enough red meat for a lifetime and agreed it was time for some red sauce. The ship boasted a small and casual Italian bistro called Carmine's on deck 3 not far from the casino. Supposedly, it served classic Italian fare on checkered red and white table cloths with an accordion player singing Italian love songs.

I finished splashing on after-shave and greeted my visitor. With some mild surprise I said, "Hi Captain."

"Good evening, doctor. May I come in?"

"Certainly. Have a seat. Can I get you something to drink?"

"No, thank you."

He took his hat off and sat at my table, crossing his legs. After letting out a deep breath, he said, "Doctor, I'll get right to it. My nerves are frazzled. I don't like this situation at all. I don't like having a killer running around and I don't like the idea that Lady Beth is all alone in a hospital in a foreign country. Yes, as you can imagine I am, in addition, deeply disturbed at the prospect of having to face an inquiry with all these loose ends; however, the reason I came by is to let you know you were one hundred percent right about Sven. They caught him this afternoon in Oslo and notified me immediately. He was indeed married and trying to win his runaway wife back as you said, and just for the record, he did not have Lady Beth's necklace on him."

I sat opposite him. "What will happen to him?"

"Nothing good, and he may even face prison time. He's a good man, but he made an extraordinarily poor decision. I hope they don't go too hard on him. Kept babbling about a man's got to do what a man's got to do. God knows where he heard that one."

"His heart was in the right place. I hope the court takes that into account."

He nodded and I looked at my watch. There was a long pause while I waited for him to speak. He seemed very uncomfortable and shifted in his chair several times. Finally, he said, "Doctor, I wasn't entirely forthright with you about something."

I was curious. "About which part?"

"About Betsy's daughter. You asked me about her twice and twice I told you I didn't know anything. I don't like to lie. It makes me very uncomfortable. I know a little...no...a lot more about her. It's just that it's such a deeply personal and intensely painful situation for Betsy, I was reluctant to tell you. In addition, I didn't see how it had any bearing on the matter at hand, but upon reflection I may be wrong about that."

I waited patiently as he collected his thoughts. He continued, "I started thinking about the media frenzy that is going to hound the poor woman when she returns to London. Sooner or later someone is going to track her daughter down and then it will be a free for all."

I was intrigued now for sure. "I'm listening."

"Her name is Veronica and we've never met, that part was true, but Betsy told me the whole story. Veronica is a troubled woman. As a teenager she became involved with drugs and alcohol. It was bad...really bad, and it got worse. When she was nineteen, she developed schizophrenia and was in and out of psychiatric and rehabilitation centers. Whether it was related to the drugs or not is unclear. You can only imagine the effect this had on Betsy and Roger."

I didn't say anything as he paused to take a breath before continuing, "To make a long story short, she intermittently experienced psychotic breaks; hearing voices, seeing things, the whole bit. Many years ago, during one of these periods she accused Betsy of hiding the fact that she was adopted which of course is poppycock and…"

"And?"

"And she accused Roger of murdering her real father."

I raised my eyebrows at that. "Oh my. So what happened?"

"Her delusion was so strong in her mind that she even went so far as to say she had proof. She claimed to have found a diary in which Roger admitted his guilt, but no diary was ever found. She persisted, even to the point of standing around the house screaming murderer at him over and over, all day and all night. At first they tried to ignore her, but she threatened him with physical violence if he didn't confess. Eventually, the Harringtons were forced to have her committed and to this day she still believes Roger murdered her father. She's in Rome residing in a psychiatric hospital not too far from the Spanish Steps. She has refused to see Betsy and Roger ever since. My understanding of the situation is that even now, almost two decades later, she is still completely wrapped up in her nightmare."

He was upset and when he finished I said consolingly, "Thank you for trusting me with this, Bjorn."

"I wanted you to know the full extent of the living hell Betsy's life has been. I can't bear the thought of her being raked over the coals. I know you care about her too. The press is going to latch onto this and destroy her and Roger's reputation."

I nodded and thought about Brad's attempt to use the press to hurt Betsy. I suddenly felt even angrier than I was at him. "I'll guard this information with my life, Bjorn, and I will do my best to protect Betsy."

He stood, placed his hat on, and extended his hand. I shook it and he turned to leave. As he did, I said, "Bjorn."

"Yes?"

"I realize that win, lose or draw, the ship and you are going to come out of it with a blackeye."

"I am profoundly aware of that."

"It could get worse."

"How so?"

"There's always the possibility that the murderer is one of your crew."

"I have already considered that."

"Bjorn, I grew up with a very strict sense of right and wrong. Life was simpler then, I know, but my mother used to tell me all the time that no one is above the law."

He nodded. "She was a wise woman, doctor, and no one is above the law on my boat…no one."

I believed him. He left and I put the final touches on my ensemble. I looked at my watch and decided to call Betsy before it got too late. I got lucky this time and the operator picked up on the third ring.

"Hello, I'd like to speak with Mrs. Harrington."

"Hold, please."

I listened to elevator music for a minute and eventually a woman with a Greek accent said, "Hello, may I ask who this is?"

"My name is John Cesari, Dr. Cesari, and I'm a friend of Mrs. Harrington's. I'd like to speak to her. She's on the surgical floor."

"I am so sorry Mr. Cesari but that is no possible."

I was confused. "That's Dr. Cesari and why not?"

"Mrs. Harrington she has left specific instructions that she does no wish to receive any calls."

"Seriously?"

"I'm afraid that is so."

"Would you at least tell her who it is? I think she will want to speak to me."

"She gave the staff a list of names of people she specifically does no wish to speak to and your name is on top. I am look at list right now."

I was indignant. "That, is impossible. I assure you."

"Is your name spelled C-E-S-A-R-I?"

"May I speak to the nurse in charge?" I was getting angry.

"That would be me."

My heart sank. This didn't make any sense. "Fine, could you at least tell her I called?"

"I will, Mr. Cesari. Have good day."

What the hell was that all about? I stormed off to find Vito loitering at the entrance to Carmine's, admiring himself in a wall mirror. As we were seated and waiting for our martinis, I told him about Betsy's daughter and my phone call to the hospital. A few minutes later, a basket of bread and olive oil was placed in front of us along with our cocktails. I still had steam coming out of my ears and practically inhaled my gin.

He said, "Hey, pace yourself, all right?"

"I'm fine. Just a little frustrated."

"I can see that. Well, anyway, the good news is that you and Bjorn are pals again."

"Yes, I think so. That was a painful story for him to tell and for me to listen to."

"Incredible."

I was very depressed. "I can't believe how much suffering some people go through."

"No one is born with a certificate guaranteeing health, wealth, and happiness, Cesari."

"I know."

"So why doesn't she want to talk to you?"

"I have no idea."

He dipped a piece of bread in the olive oil and shoved it into his mouth thinking about it. "Maybe, she's walling herself off emotionally? You know what I mean? People do that when they're under stress. Maybe she's afraid that if she lets you keep calling her, she's going to feel even worse than she already does."

He made a good point and I wondered how a guy as primitive as he was could possibly come up with as complicated a train of thought as the one he just offered. For a moment, it crossed my mind that he was wired, and somebody was feeding him intelligent answers.

I said, "It's possible."

"You know, the captain's a good guy. I feel kind of sorry for him. Sounds like he's going to have a helluva moral dilemma when he gets back to port. The inquiry board is going to crawl up and down his ass about the Harringtons and if he don't fess up all he knows they'll fry him good."

I nodded. "He's like family to the Harringtons. He'll do everything he can to protect Betsy from scandal. I think he would even perjure himself for her. In fact, I think he was actually telling me that's what he was going to do. Not in so many words, mind you, but nonetheless, I think he wanted me to know what really went down when the shit hits the fan and they slap the cuffs on him."

"I can respect that. You think he has any idea who snuffed the old guy?"

"No, but I think he doesn't care at this point. As far as he's concerned, the only thing that matters is to protect Betsy from further pain and anguish."

"It had to be one of the crew. Who else would have a weapon on board?"

"Oh, I don't know; a couple of Croatian gangsters, a mobster from the Bronx…"

He chuckled, "Okay, I get it."

We both ordered lasagna and Brunello di Montalcino. After a few mouthfuls, Vito said, "This is pretty good."

It was and I agreed. "I'd enjoy it more if you would eat with your mouth closed."

"Fine, so where does all this leave you?"

"Confused mostly. No real suspects. The only motive is the necklace and that is a very big motive. Almost anyone could have been tempted by such a big prize. The part that really bothers me is the killer coming back to finish off Betsy. She must have seen or heard something that he was afraid of, yet she didn't remember anything special."

We finished our meal with tiramisu and left the restaurant thoroughly sated. It was 9:30 p.m. and we headed to the casino, Vito looking for agreeable women, and me, looking for Katarina. He seemed to find what he needed at the roulette table and I spotted Katarina sitting with her fiancée. Approaching with a big smile, I said hi to the both of them. Edvard didn't seem to remember me and as I leaned close to shake his hand, he said something in Croatian. I looked to Katarina for a translation.

She said, "He would like vodka martini, dry with two olives."

I chuckled and said, "Tell him I said right away."

Smiling she replied, "I tell." She leaned over and whispered in the old guy's ear and he nodded thank you.

I signaled a cocktail waitress and placed his order. I said to Katarina, “So the wedding is still on?”

She looked surprised. “Of course is still on. He is worth three hundred million American dollar. I am going to be rich widow.” She stroked the old man’s remaining wisps of white hair.

“Well, that’s good I guess.”

“Don’t be jealous. I still like you but must put Edvard to bed first. In one hour, I come to room.”

“I put my hand up. “No, not tonight. I’m expecting company. Grown up company. So please…”

She shook her head. “When are you going to learn? I am only woman for you.”

Chuckling, I said, “Just don’t bother me tonight. All right?”

“Fine.”

“Thanks.”

The old man whispered something to her and she said, “You must go now. Edvard don’t like I flirt with the help.”

Edvard smiled at me politely, and then shooed me away with his hand.

Chapter 40

I brushed my teeth and spruced up in the bathroom. It was almost eleven and I was sure Joyce would be prompt. I had made up my mind to show her a good time and not just go through the motions. She'd been very helpful to me, and overall, I honestly did like her, botox notwithstanding. She was as they say…amusing in her own way.

Looking down one more time at my lady-charmer, I was sure that she would be pleased, and donned my royal blue bathrobe. I had a bottle of champagne sitting in an ice bucket and a basket of fresh fruit for us to nibble on in case we needed extra energy. I really knew how to say thank you to a girl.

By the time I heard the knock on the door, I had pretty much worked myself up into a fever. I looked at my watch. Eleven on the dot. Without hesitation I opened the door wide and saw nothing…at first. Then I looked down into the wrong end of a can of mace. Antonela sprayed a long burst directly into my face. I groaned, clutched my eyes in pain and staggered backward into the room. I heard the door slam shut as I tripped and fell back onto the bed. Blinded and confused, I felt a jolt of electricity as she triggered a taser into my chest. I twitched and convulsed, stunned and barely conscious.

Several minutes passed. I felt her working on me, but was too weak to defend myself. My head eventually cleared, and I found that I was tied to the bed naked. I looked around, my eyes still watery and my vision a little slow to come into focus. My wrists were bound tightly to the bed posts with my own neckties. I tugged on them unsuccessfully to see if I could pull free. A sinister laugh caught my attention and I discovered her at the foot of the bed eating grapes and sipping champagne. I wondered where Joyce was. She said, "Are you ready?"

Shit!

"Antonela, c'mon. Aren't you getting carried away?" Realizing my error, I quickly added, "I'm sorry. I meant my Shwimbo."

In response she put down the champagne flute, reached into a bag she brought with her, and came out with a long, serrated bread knife. My eyes went wide, and I remembered what she had said about cutting me up into little pieces. She said, "Is no matter now."

"Antonela, no. Don't do this. Please."

She smiled and touched my foot with the tip of the cold blade. I flinched, and she said, "Antonela yes, but first, we play."

I breathed a sigh of relief. Anything to buy time. She stood and put the knife down on the night table where I could see it, and then slowly undressed in front of me. Down to her panties, she cocked her head and smiled. "You like Antonela?"

"I love Antonela."

She chuckled. "You remember. Is good. This go easier than last time, but maybe we try new trick?"

"I'll do whatever Antonela wants."

"Yes, you will. No scream like girl this time, all right?"

"I'll try."

"Okay, you stay here. I need one more thing."

She walked over to my closet and I realized that I had broken out into a cold sweat. I jiggled my wrists again but knew there was no way I could break free. She was a professional and knew how to tie a knot well. She rummaged around for a minute, found what she was looking for and came back holding one of my belts. "You change where you keep belts, but I find."

Suddenly, I was curious. How did she know where I kept my belts? She stood by the side of the bed and snapped the belt loudly. She had a devilish grin on her face as she pulled her panties down and climbed on top of me.

Suddenly it came to me. "It was you, wasn't it? You strangled Betsy."

She shrugged. "I lose temper. No mean hurt old lady."

"You bitch. How could you?"

She slapped me hard once and then again. My face stung from her blows. Her eyes glazed with excitement, she looped the belt around my neck and slipped one end through the buckle. Tugging it taut, to remove any slack, she sat back and began grinding herself slowly into me as she held onto the belt as if it were the reins on a horse. I tried to stay calm but felt my pulse quicken. I couldn't help myself. I was starting to breathe quickly, and I deliberately tried to slow it down. She closed her eyes and quietly moaned as I watched her rhythmic movement. Her breasts were tiny, like the rest of her, and her nipples were erect. Moving faster, back and forth, she was losing control and despite my best efforts, so was I. Abruptly, she stopped and gave me a mischievous glance.

She reached down between her legs and positioned me. The look on her face told me that whatever was coming wasn't too far away. Leaning down, she kissed me and adjusted the buckle off to one side of my neck. Without warning and with both hands, she pulled back on the belt with all her might, choking me. I bucked involuntarily in response. She rode me hard as I thrust violently, trying futilely to break free. My lungs screamed for oxygen and my head felt like it was going to explode as she slowly crushed my larynx. Her face was wild with excitement and as my efforts weakened she pulled on the belt with even greater force. It wouldn't be long before I passed out. I gave it everything I had but to no avail and felt my strength waning as she climaxed in a loud, sadistic, almost primal grunt.

The room was just starting to go dark when her grip loosened, and I sucked in a deep breath coughing spasmodically. Gasping and wheezing, it was a few seconds before I realized she had fallen off me onto the floor. I saw Joyce standing at the foot of the bed holding the bottle of champagne by its neck.

"Are you all right?" she asked.

My chest heaving and carotids pounding, I nodded and said hoarsely, "Quick untie me before she wakes up. She's extremely dangerous."

"I can see that."

A moment later the tables had turned. I carried Antonela into the bathroom, her hands tied behind her back, and put her in the bathtub.

I came out and put my arms around Joyce. "Thank you."

"Thank goodness I let myself in. For a minute, I was starting to get jealous until I saw your face turning blue and your eyes bulging out of their sockets. So who's the crazy girl?"

"It's a long story, Joyce."

I went over to the sink, poured myself a glass of water and rubbed my throat as I thought about Betsy. Antonela had come here to exact her revenge on me and took it out on the first person she saw. Well, that answered a lot of questions and suddenly the pieces started to fall into place.

Joyce came up from behind and slid her arms around me, resting her head against my back. I turned around and kissed her. She said, "I guess it ain't going to happen tonight?"

I shook my head. "Not tonight."

"Do I get a raincheck? After all, I did just save your life."

Smiling I said, "Definitely."

She chuckled and I asked, "What's so funny?"

"I can't remember the last time I was standing this close to a hot, naked guy and had to settle for a raincheck."

I smiled. "I like you, Joyce."

That made her happy. "I like you too. I wish I had met you twenty years ago."

"I would have been in high school."

"Even better. Easier to train."

"Trust me, I'm no bargain."

"So what are you going to do with the troll? She's bad news."

"The less you know, the better."

"I guess you're not going to call security."

"That's a good guess."

She smiled and said, "Man, I knew you were my kind of guy. Well, it's getting late, I might as well go back to the casino and see what Brad's up to."

"Say hi for me, and Joyce...?"

"Yeah?"

"You were never here."

She smiled. "Never where?"

She left and I propped a chair up against the bathroom door just in case Antonela woke up and managed to undo her restraints. She was out cold, and I doubted she'd be much trouble, but it couldn't hurt to be safe. She'd caused me too much aggravation already. I dressed quickly and went to find Vito. He was in the casino nursing a pair of deuces and an unfiltered Camel.

"Vito, I got trouble. Cash your chips in."

"What kind of trouble? I'm busy." he growled.

"I leaned close to his ear and whispered, "I have a naked Croatian cop tied up in my bathroom kind of trouble. Now cash in."

He shook his huge head and grinned. "The midget?" I nodded and he added, "This, I got to see."

Tossing his cards in, he pocketed his chips and we walked outside. He took a last puff from his cigarette and tossed it over the side of the railing. I looked at him with disgust. "Really? You're littering in the middle of the Mediterranean?"

"Actually, it's not the Mediterranean. We are now in the Ionian Sea. You should read more."

"What difference does it make? You're still littering."

"You going to tell me what happened or not?"

As we walked, I quickly filled him in. He stopped and pulled me by the arm under a light. "Look up."

I did, and he examined my bruised neck. He whistled, "Damn, she's hardcore."

"You're telling me?"

"Well, at least you would have died with a smile on your face. Not every guy has that much luck."

"Thanks, but believe me I wasn't smiling. Being strangled is an awful way to die. I can't believe she did that to poor Betsy."

He nodded, "You're right. You know, it's a miracle you're alive, Cesari. Both neck ties just happened to tear apart at the same time? That's amazing. It almost seems impossible. I mean, I know you like to work out and everything, but no one is that strong. I bet you have cheap ties. That would make sense. That would never happen with mine. Okay so what's her status?"

I didn't want to go into a long explanation about Joyce. It was always best to keep him on a need to know basis anyway.

"She was unconscious when I left her but okay. Maybe a little uncomfortable."

As we walked, we passed a series of circular life preservers hanging on the railing next to the life boats. He stopped and stared at them They were orange and white and had ropes attached to them. He looked up at the sky and I asked, "What are you thinking?"

"It's a beautiful night. At least seventy degrees maybe more."

"What's your point?"

"I think I have a solution to your problem. Let's grab a couple of life preservers and go back to your room."

We looked both ways, grabbed two life preservers and hustled back to my cabin. Antonela was still unconscious but otherwise looked comfortable. Joyce had given her a pretty good whack with the champagne bottle and she had a lump on the back of her head. I turned the shower on, and the cold water woke her with a start. She shook her head and yelled out loud from the shock.

Turning off the shower, I lifted her to a standing position as she tried to orient herself. She was very confused and having trouble understanding what was going on. I spun her around and untied her wrists.

"What you do?" she asked groggily.

I handed her a towel. "Never mind asking questions. Just shut up and put your clothes on. They're on the floor next to the tub. I'll wait for you in the living room."

Vito was lying on my bed with his legs crossed examining the bread knife Antonela had brought. I sat on a chair next to the door, so she couldn't make a run for it. A minute or two later she came out looking sheepish and was surprised when she saw Vito.

"Who is friend?"

"His name is Vito and he doesn't like it when people try to kill me. Now sit on the floor, and I'm going to give you a couple of choices."

Defeated, she let out a deep breath and sat cross-legged, leaning back against the bathroom door. I said, "You know Antonela, what you've done to me twice now I could possibly get over. I understand that sometimes I do things that make people angry…even angry enough to want to hurt me, but I cannot forgive what you did to Mrs. Harrington. You crossed a line and no amount of begging is going to uncross it. Understood?"

She nodded. "Is understood. Now what? You kill Antonela?"

"Honestly, I really think that's what you deserve, but I'm hopelessly romantic when it comes to women so I'm going to let you decide your own fate."

She looked confused. "What mean?"

"We are in the middle of the Mediterranean…"

Vito interrupted me. "The Ionian Sea."

I shot him a dirty look. "We are in the middle of the Ionian Sea very near the island of Santorini. It's a very busy vacation spot and thousands of tourists and locals take their boats out every day to fish, sail, and play. The water at this time of year is quite warm. If someone were to fall overboard, they would only have to stay afloat for a couple of hours until daybreak and I'm sure they would be rescued right away."

She looked concerned. "You throw Antonela overboard? What is other choices?"

I shook my head. "You misunderstood."

"You say Antonela decide."

"What I meant is I can either throw you overboard with a life preserver or without a life preserver. That's what you get to decide."

Her eyes went wide, and I continued, "Now, now, don't look so upset. Remember, wet is better than dead. As far as I'm concerned, you're getting off easy. And I don't ever want to see you again. Okay, the clock is ticking. Which is it going to be?"

She let out a deep breath. "I take life preserver option."

"Okay, then, let's go onto the balcony. C'mon Vito."

The warm night air felt good. We helped her wiggle into the two life preservers. She was tiny, and they fit easily over her torso. Then we picked her up and got close to the railing. If you didn't know what was about to happen, you might think we were playing in someone's backyard pool. I had one arm under her shoulder and one under her leg. Vito had the other side. She clutched the life preservers with all her might.

I looked at her and asked, "Ready for a Shwim…bo?"

She looked back over the side of the ship, rolled her eyes, and nodded. We swung her back and forth building up momentum, and on the count of three, we tossed her over the side. As she became airborne she shouted, "Hole in butt!"

She was small and light and we were big and strong. She went pretty far with good trajectory and we watched as she cleared the side of the ship easily on the way down, making a small splash.

Watching her bob up and down for a minute, I said, "Well, that felt pretty good."

"You think there are any sharks?"

"Hadn't given it much thought."

Chapter 41

The next morning Vito and I ate eggs benedict, bangers, and black coffee with a view of Santorini. I said, "Man, look how beautiful this place is. We're in paradise, Vito."

"You're right about that. It's gorgeous. A guy could get used to the cruising life."

I nodded, thinking about all the terrible things that happened so far. "Maybe."

"So do you think we'll see Antonela again?"

"I'd like to think not, but if she's anything like all the other women I've ever known, then I doubt she'll do anything I told her to do."

He chuckled, "Ain't that the truth, brother."

"I know it sounds ridiculous, but last night has actually helped shed some light on Roger's death."

"How so?"

I sipped my steaming French roast and said, "Well, before last night, I had assumed that the same person who had murdered Roger had come after Betsy too. It's obvious now that Betsy's assault was unrelated to Roger's death."

"And how does that help?"

"For one thing it means that whoever stole the diamonds and killed Roger is probably sitting around pretty smug at having gotten away with the crime."

He nodded. "And overconfidence killed the cat."

I didn't have the heart to correct him. "Exactly, and the other thing it means is that I need to consider other possible motives for the crime."

"What does that mean?"

"It means that all that glitters is not gold."

"Would you please speak English."

"You know, Vito, you said something the other night that made me wonder if you're some sort of idiot-savant."

"What's that?"

"Genius, my friend. You just may be a genius disguised as a…well…let's just say…not genius."

"Shut up. What did I say?"

"You said, 'when you eliminate the impossible, whatever's left, no matter how improbable, must be the truth.'"

"I didn't say that. Sherlock Holmes said it."

I laughed. "Stunningly handsome and humble too. You're going to make some woman very happy one day."

He liked that and grinned.

As we finished breakfast, Bjorn entered the dining room, spotted us and came over. He wore a very solemn expression and his eyes looked red as if he'd been crying.

"Good morning, gentlemen."

We both stood to greet him and he waved us back into our seats, joining us. I said, "Good morning, Bjorn. Is everything okay?"

He looked at Vito who took the signal and said, "Please excuse me, I need to use the men's room."

He left us alone and Bjorn turned to me, a solitary tear running down his face. "Lady Beth is dead. The doctor called me this morning."

I was shocked. She looked great when I last saw her. "What happened?"

My mind ran through the litany of post-operative complications; pneumonia, pulmonary embolus, arrhythmias. He said, "She committed suicide."

My jaw dropped and I sat back in my chair speechless. I was having trouble wrapping my head around it. Eventually I stammered, "I don't understand. Why would she do that? How could she do that?"

"Apparently, the ulcer they removed proved to be cancerous. They did some further testing and scans which showed that it had already spread throughout her body. She decided that she didn't want to drag things out. The doctor said she didn't suffer."

"How did it happen?"

"She complained of progressively severe pain and requested they increase her medications. Given her recent surgery and terminal diagnosis that seemed reasonable so they doubled the amount of morphine in her IV bag. She could control how much she received with a button which would deliver a measured dose. When she was alone, she removed the IV tubing from the control pump and turned it wide open. The entire bag ran into her veins in minutes. They discovered her shortly after midnight. It took the staff several hours to sort out the confusion. She left a detailed note apologizing to everyone for what she did so no one would get in trouble."

He became all choked up and I reached across the table and touched his hand consolingly. "Bjorn, I'm sorry."

"Thank you. I know you cared about her. She wrote us both letters which, in view of the circumstances, the physicians there are graciously having express couriered to us by a small private plane that shuttles from Corfu to Santorini. They will arrive this afternoon and be brought directly here."

He was devastated, that was plain to see, and I wondered how he was going to be able to carry on the task of managing the ship. He stood to leave as Vito returned to the table. We shook hands stiffly, he nodded to Vito and walked away.

After I told him the news, Vito stared down at his coffee cup and said, "Damn."

I nodded in silence. What more was there to say?

He broke the silence a moment later as I sat dolefully. "I'm sorry, Cesari. I know you really liked her."

"Thanks, I really did. Man, this sucks."

"That would explain why she didn't want to talk to you."

"How so?"

"She had feelings for you. She probably made up her mind what she was going to do and was afraid that if she talked to you, her resolve might weaken."

I looked at him and said, "I think you're right. In fact, I think she knew when I was there. That's why she didn't want me to stay with her. I could feel something was wrong. I offered to speak with her doctors and she ordered me not to go near them. She must have known then. Damn."

We sat there in silence for a few moments. Eventually, he said, "Why don't we get off the ship for a couple of hours and walk around. There's not a whole lot to do at this point, and you could use some fresh air."

My head was still spinning and I felt like garbage. I felt so sorry for her. All alone on a Greek island to find out you had a disease that would allow you to live maybe six more miserable months under the best of circumstances had to be depressing news. Younger, stronger with family and support, she might have chosen to fight it, but without Roger and her daughter, she despaired. I couldn't really blame her. Metastatic stomach cancer was a brutally aggressive disease and the European healthcare system was far more fatalistic in their attitudes and approach to end of life care. Who knows how it was presented to her? It didn't matter now.

I let out a deep breath and replied, "Yeah, that sounds like a good idea."

It was a forty-five minute cab ride from the port to the small town of Oia. Vito reassured me that his guidebook said this was the place to see. He was right. It was breathtaking with marble sidewalks and white buildings with blue domes, shutters, and doors. Most of the town was carved into the side of a steep cliff which led down to the shoreline. The bustling commercial center was on the plateau at the top and stretched east-west for about a mile. It was quite a walk to the bottom and after trudging all the way down in the blazing late-morning sun I was wondering how we were going to make it back up again to where all the restaurants were.

Foolishly, we hadn't brought any water with us and were now paying the price as we leaned against a large rock watching the pristine blue water gently lap up against the beach.

He looked up and said, "I'm not sure if this was the best idea I ever had."

"Possibly not even the second best idea. I'm drenched with sweat and already dehydrated."

"You? I'm wearing a suit."

I laughed. "Would you at least loosen your tie?"

He took off his jacket, rolled up his sleeves, and undid his tie. "Well, we might as well get started."

The cobblestone steps were winding, wide, and steep and I had counted three hundred on the way down. Going up, we felt our thighs ache and we sucked wind. The sun was merciless and seemed twice as hot going up. By the time we were half way, he sat down on the stone wall, perspiring. "I need to rest Cesari."

"All right, this is as good a spot as any."

"How do people live here?"

"They must be in great shape; lots of yogurt and honey, very little salami."

He chuckled. As we recovered, we heard a clopping sound coming from below. We looked back and coming from around a bend, we saw an old guy with unkempt hair and mustache leading a column of brightly adorned donkeys. One of them carried a saddle bag bursting with water bottles. Every now and then one of the donkeys would fall out of formation and he would call out to it and patiently wait for it to resume its position. Nearing, he called to the caravan to halt, and greeted us in broken English.

"Good morning."

We said hello.

"You tired, want ride to top?" We looked at each other and then at the donkeys.

We were exhausted and hot. I glanced at the top of the cliff. "How much?"

He smiled. "Only seventy euros…each."

Vito snorted. "Oh brother. What a scam."

I chuckled. We were healthy. A few more minutes of rest and we'd be fine again. What we really needed was water. I was starting to feel light-headed. I said, "No thanks, but how much for a bottle of water?"

He smiled politely and said, "Seventy euros…each, but free with you ride donkey."

Vito chortled. "So much for socialism."

Twenty minutes later we dismounted at the top and paid the man. I said, "That was the most expensive taxi ride I've ever taken."

"A hundred and forty euros for fleas and a hot bottle of water."

Laughing, I said, "It's better than a heart attack. C'mon, it's almost one. I'm not hungry but I wouldn't mind getting out of the heat and having a cocktail."

We found a shaded rooftop bar that overlooked the water and ordered a bottle of Assyrtiko, a light and flavorful white wine made from grapes grown right here on Santorini. I was pleasantly surprised to see Joyce sitting by herself staring out at the sea. She hadn't seen me and as Vito waited for our order I walked over to say hello.

She was wearing short shorts, a wide brimmed sun hat, and designer sunglasses. She looked up, surprised to see me and then turned away quickly to look at the water, but not before I noticed the bruise mark on her cheek. "Hello, Dr. Cesari. How nice to see you again."

Looking at the back of her hat I said, "Nice to see you too, Joyce." She was sipping sangria. "Thank you again for your help last night. Can I pay for your drink?"

"Oh, that's not necessary."

"I know but it would make me happy."

"In that case, feel free to be as happy as you want."

"Where's Brad?"

"Somewhere on the island. I don't really know where. We're not really on speaking terms at the moment. He…"

She hesitated and I could tell something big had happened. I sat down next to her and waited patiently. She finished, "He threw me out."

Surprised I said, "He threw you out?"

"Lock, stock, and barrel."

"Is that what happened to your face?"

She turned around and looked at me. "No, I fell."

"I see."

She let out a deep breath. "We had a big fight last night. He was totally drunk and saying awful things about you. He said a friend of his back in New York looked you up and that you're a gangster or something. Whatever dirt he had on you he was going to the captain with it. I defended you and said you weren't such a bad guy. Oh my God. You would think that I had cursed out his mother or something. He made me sleep on the couch and this morning with his hangover he was even meaner. He started going on about you again. When I wouldn't back down about you, I thought he was going to have a stroke. He told me to leave and don't come back and that's exactly what I'm doing. Who needs him?"

"Is that when you fell?"

She didn't say anything, so I asked, "Where are you going?"

"I have a four o'clock flight on a puddle jumper to Athens. I'll stay overnight and catch the first flight I can back to New York."

I scanned the bar. "Where's your luggage?"

"In his room. He grabbed my arm and dragged me to the door. He said you want Cesari then you can have him and locked me out. I was lucky he let me take my bag and passport. All I said was why can't you cut the guy some slack. You've been leaning on him ever since the first night."

"Joyce, I'm sorry."

"Don't be. I'm sort of glad it's over. He's too high maintenance. I didn't leave anything behind that can't be replaced and I've got my credit cards so I'll be all right."

"Can he do that? Just toss you out? I mean you paid for your ticket. You have a right to stay."

"Actually, he paid for my ticket or to be more specific, his hospital paid for it. He's very clever with stuff like that. They pay for everything…even these guys." She wiggled her chest at me. "But I don't care. I don't want to stay where I'm not wanted. I'll be fine."

I shook my head. "Well, I can't believe it. I feel terrible you guys had a fight over me."

"What does it matter whether it was about you or somebody else? It was bound to happen over something. He drinks too much and I told him so."

"Hey, Cesari, the wine's here." Vito called out gruffly.

I called back, "I'll be there in a minute."

Joyce looked back over her shoulder at him. "He really is uncivilized, isn't he?"

"He's got some issues but his heart's in the right place." I snapped my fingers. "Hey, I have an idea. Would you like to finish the cruise without Brad?"

"What do you mean?"

"I mean that me and Vito both have very nice rooms."

Smiling, she said, "I don't mind sharing a room with you but him…never."

"I didn't mean sharing a room. We'll give you one of our rooms and we'll move in with each other."

She looked astonished. "You're so sweet but you don't have to do that for me."

"But I want to. You saved my life. It's the least I can do."

"Don't you think you ought to check with mouthzilla over there first?"

I smiled. "Don't worry about mouthzilla."

She laughed. "All right, I'd love to finish the cruise. Maybe now I can do it like a grown-up."

"Great, it's settled. I'll talk to Brad about giving you your clothes back."

"I'd stay away from him if I were you."

"You're probably right, but it's not fair that he won't give you your stuff. I'll try to reason with him."

"And if he says no? What are you going to do? Call security?"

I smirked. "Guess again."

"Jesus, you're too funny."

"Well, I think Brad and I need to find some closure."

"I hope you closure him good."

"That's a definite possibility. Would you like to join us at our table?"

"I'd love to, but your friend better not get nasty. I'm not going to take it anymore. I'm feeling very empowered right now."

"Feel free to let him have it."

Chapter 42

Later, Vito was unpacking his suitcase in my room grumbling under his breath. "I can't believe this is happening. I paid top dollar for that stateroom and you give it to a bleach blonde who insults me every chance she gets. This is total bullshit, Cesari, and you know it, and another thing, I get the bed and you get the couch or lounge chair on the balcony or whatever because I don't care."

"Take a deep breath, will you? You did the right thing."

"Oh, spare me about doing the right thing, will you? I'm getting tired of being pushed around."

"C'mon, how could we let her get thrown out of her own stateroom?"

"Oh, that's great. She can't get thrown out but I can? It's not my job to save every broad you feel sorry for, Cesari. She don't even like me for crying out loud and I have to give her my room? Total B.S."

"Is that what this is all about? She hurt your big baby feelings?"

"Well she did."

"I'll tell her to apologize before you start crying."

"I can fight my own battles."

"You should try listening more to women instead of telling them how great you think you are. It's more attractive. From now on, do what I do; listen, don't talk, just listen. I try to understand women and let them be themselves. I let them know that John Cesari is a safe space where they're going to find validation and support. Here's a tip. The next time you're talking to a woman keep repeating to yourself, 'she's a human being just like me, she's a human being just like me.'"

"Will you shut up?"

"Look, I'll sleep on the couch but I don't understand why we can't share a king bed. For God's sake, we're in Europe. Heterosexual men share beds all the time here. We could even sleep head to toe if it'd make you feel more comfortable."

"Stop. It ain't going to happen, and whether or not you're heterosexual is still an open question, and I ain't doing that head to toe stuff with you or anybody else from Broke Back Mountain"

"You should consider it. It's a very sophisticated thing to do. It would give you something to talk about at cocktail parties."

"Stop it."

"Fine, do you have the photos you took of Brad and Joyce?"

He rummaged briefly through his stuff and tossed me an envelope. I looked through the amorous pictures and shoved them into my sport coat pocket.

He finished putting his clothes away and stretched out on the sofa. "This is very comfortable. A little on the short side, but if you curl up, you'll be fine."

I looked at my watch. It was 8:00 p.m., Joyce was tucked away in Vito's room, and the ship was about to set sail. I needed one more thing before I went to visit Brad.

I said, "Why don't you relax here for a while, I have a few things to do. Maybe we can catch a bite when I come back? My treat."

He flipped me the bird.

I grabbed a towel from the bathroom and went down to the lower deck in search of the engine room. Once again I was appalled at the lack of security. There were signs here and there that said *Crew Only* but that was it. Doors weren't locked and there was no one to challenge me. I passed one crew member in the hallway who nodded amiably and kept moving. I guessed that passengers rarely wandered around in the bowels of the ship and this just wasn't a concern. But what if someone did and was injured? Then again, this was Europe, if you got hurt doing something you shouldn't have no one gave a crap. There was something to be said for personal accountability.

The loud clanging of metal and hissing of pistons caught my attention as I approached my destination. The entrance to the main engine room was marked *No Admittance* but swinging doors allowed easy ingress into a hot and markedly humid room the size of a warehouse with tall ceilings, institutional overhead lighting, and massive machinery. Less than a minute in and I was already regretting wearing my sport coat.

Everything was painted battleship gray, and I tried to keep a low profile, ducking discreetly behind huge metal pipes and machines as I darted secretively through the room trying desperately to stay out of sight. Thankfully, there were only a handful of crew doing routine maintenance work. I had the feeling they wouldn't particularly care if they saw me, but I had no desire to tempt fate.

Twenty minutes later I was drenched with perspiration when I finally spotted what I was looking for…sort of. I had been hunting for a crowbar but that was more of a construction worker's tool; instead, I found a large metal wrench, fully two feet long and made of heavy duty steel. It was old and dirty and...perfect. I looked around in all directions, picked it up, wrapped it in the towel and danced my way back to the exit. It was heavy and weighed at least six or seven pounds and I couldn't wait to test it. I had always been fond of blunt objects.

Once I left the lower levels, I breathed a sigh of relief as the temperature cooled and my anxiety became a memory. On the elevator to Brad's room, I took the massive wrench out and used the towel to wipe sweat from my face. I threw the towel over my shoulder and stood there thinking about what I had to do. The elevator came to a stop, and preoccupied, I started to get off before realizing I wasn't on the right floor. A couple got on and stared at me. I appreciated their consternation. I was a mess; sweaty, a bath towel over my shoulder and holding a huge, dirty, dangerous-looking piece of metal.

I smiled affably, shrugged, and said, "I have a leaky pipe in my room. Apparently it wasn't covered in my package. What're you going to do?"

In response, they hugged each other tightly and nodded. They got off in a hurry at the next stop, and it was close to 9:00 p.m. when I arrived at Brad's room. Rapping on his door with the wrench, I hoped he was home, but if he wasn't I'd return. I had the rest of my life to take care of him if it was necessary. I was very committed. CEO's brought out the worst in me. I probably needed some sort of counseling for that.

He didn't answer so I knocked even harder with the wrench. Eventually, I was rewarded with a distant 'hold on I'm coming'. I blocked the peep hole with my index finger. In a split second I went through the situation in my mind as I waited. He had me by almost half a foot and at least fifty pounds, but he was soft and I was hard. After observing him for a week, I guessed he'd been drinking today just as every day. He might have company.

A chance I would have to take. I should be afraid but I was never that smart.

Scenario number one; he opens the door and I greet him with a smile. "Hi Brad, can we talk about Joyce?"

"Sure, doctor. Please come in and have a seat. I'll get you a drink. Do you like top shelf bourbon?"

I shook my head. Not a chance. Start over. Scenario number two; "Hi Brad, can we talk about Joyce?"

"Sure, but first get on your hands and knees and bark like a dog."

Closer to reality. One more try. Scenario number three; "Hi Brad, Joyce is staying with me. Did you know she was a nymphomaniac and really likes being on top?"

He doesn't answer because he turns beet red and drops from a stroke.

I smiled. I really liked that one. I heard footsteps approaching the door and then the sounds of him muttering when he couldn't see through the peephole. I braced myself as he unlocked the door and pulled it open His face registered surprise at seeing me He had just come out of the shower and was barefoot, wearing his bathrobe.

Perfect.

I knelt down quickly and without warning swung the wrench like a hammer, bringing it down hard on the top of the foot nearest me. Bones cracked and he howled in pain. I lunged into him like a linebacker and he fell backward into the room, landing on the coffee table which collapsed under his weight. I closed and locked the door behind me while he lay there confused clutching his injured foot.

He was in agony and it took a while for him to collect himself, and while he did, I poured myself Wild Turkey from an open bottle on a nearby credenza. I took a sip and handed him the bottle as I sat down on the sofa in front of him.

"You suck, Cesari," he hissed, but he grabbed the bottle and took a long swallow. "I can't believe how much you suck."

I said, "What, no more doctor? C'mon, where's your respect?"

Lying on the remains of the broken coffee table, he took a deep breath, grimaced with pain, and said, "What exactly were you hoping to accomplish with this felony?"

I said, "Cover yourself up will you? I hope you don't think that's an attractive sight." I hadn't seen many CEO's private parts but I was convinced there was an inverse relationship between the power a man had over other human beings and the size of his you know what.

He pulled his robe closed and I continued, "I don't think they call it a felony in Great Britain but whatever. Look, this little social call I'm making is for two reasons. One, ever since the cruise began I've been trying to convince you to stay out of my face but every time I turn around you're right there. It's frustrating for me, but do you know what the real problem here is?"

Disgusted he asked, practically spitting the word out, "What?"

"You were mean to a friend of mine."

Suddenly he looked puzzled. "Who?"

"Joyce."

Despite his pain, he chuckled, "Joyce? You can't be serious? She's a stripper. I met her in a club doing lap dances. How could she be a friend of yours? What is it with you two anyway? She spent the whole night defending you."

"That's just it. I'm a very good judge of people and there's something about her I like, and you weren't very nice to her. She told me how you threw her out."

"Ain't that sweet. You got a hard on for a retired sex-worker. I feel like I'm in the middle of a romance novel. What else did she tell you?"

"That you found out something about me you shouldn't have and were going to try to hurt me by going to the captain with it."

"That's right. He's got a right to know. You got a rap sheet back in New York as long as my arm and even have a felony conviction. You got more mob connections than any doctor I ever heard of. That is, if you really are a doctor."

I tapped the heavy part of the wrench on his good leg. "I'm a doctor all right which is why I can tell you with a great deal of confidence how much it's going to hurt if I have to hit you again with this wrench." I took a breath and continued, "So you think that you know all about me and my friends?"

"I know you're dirty and not what you seem to be."

"All the more reason for you not to piss me off."

He was quiet as he digested that part."

"This is the deal, Brad. You're not going to tell anyone anything because I'm done playing."

I tossed him the envelope with the pictures of him grabbing Joyce's ass the night of the ball. He looked at them and took a deep breath in frustration. I said, "I particularly like the one where you push her against the wall and put your hand up her dress. You leave me alone and I won't send those pictures to your wife accompanied by a note explaining what a great vacation you had without her. If memory serves me correctly, she's chairwoman of the board at your hospital."

He shook his head in defeat and hissed. "Fine."

"Joyce will be coming by in the morning to gather her belongings. You'd better be nice. Understand?"

"Fine."

"That's all. Drink a lot of whiskey tonight and put ice on your foot. That will help with the pain and swelling. We dock in Athens tomorrow. You can see a doctor then."

I stood to leave, and he said, "That's it? That's all you wanted to say? You didn't have to break my foot."

"That was for slapping Joyce around, and if you touch her again I'm going to come back and break a lot more than your foot. Understand?"

"Fine."

"Now I'm going to throw this wrench overboard. Unless you want to go over the side with it, you'll forget you ever saw me tonight or ever."

"What am I supposed to tell people about what happened here?"

I thought it over for a second. "Tell them you were sea sick."

"Sea sick?" He was incredulous. "Who breaks their foot from being sea sick? Besides, we're barely moving."

"Brad, I don't care what you tell people. Just don't make me have to come back here to see you again."

"Fine."

Chapter 43

By the time I got back to my cabin it was well after 10:00 p.m. and Vito was sipping a glass of Barolo on the balcony. I picked up the bottle and looked at the label. It was twelve years old and I wondered if he charged it to my room. Most of it was already gone. He had ordered room service and his tray was to one side. I scavenged for scraps and found a half-eaten parker roll. As I buttered it up, he laughed. "I had a pet dog like you once."

He was in a decidedly better mood than when I left. "Your dog used to butter its bread?"

"I meant he was always checking out my plate for leftovers, wise guy, and don't kid yourself, my dog was pretty smart. So how'd it go with the big man?"

"Pretty good. I talked to him very reasonably and I think he saw my point of view. I felt bad for him though. He wasn't feeling very well. I think he may be sea sick."

"Sea sick? But we're barely moving. Well, I'm glad he's coming around. By the way, right after you left, the captain came. He left an envelope for you. It's on the desk in the living room. He said he was tied up with the ship's departure or he would have dropped it off sooner. He said you would know what it's about."

I went back into the living room and found an envelope with my name written on it. I opened it and sat on the edge of the bed. It was the letter from Betsy that Bjorn had told me about this morning. Between the excursion to Santorini and Brad, I had almost forgotten about it.

As I read it, Vito came in the room and asked, "So what is it?"

"It's a letter from Betsy explaining what happened and saying goodbye."

He nodded and sat down. "Letter? It looks like a book."

The letter was long and took up nearly three full pages but explained a lot. I let out a deep sigh as I read. I almost didn't want to finish, but I knew I had to. I took my time soaking in revelation after painful revelation, re-reading certain sections once, twice, and sometimes three times to make sure I fully absorbed the meaning. This was a woman's life laid bare, all the warts and blemishes exposed. Her soul was on display for me and I didn't want to misunderstand or misinterpret even one word. She had placed her trust in me and I would not let her down.

Vito noticed the concerned look on my face as I finally put the letter down and stared at the floor too stunned to speak. "Are you okay?" he asked.

Ignoring him my mind raced with disbelief. I'd had my suspicions but I didn't want to believe it. I had hoped that something would give and I would find another explanation.

"Cesari?"

"I'm okay. Give me a second to think." I walked over to my room safe in the back of the closet and secured the letter there. When I returned, I said, "C'mon we have work to do."

"You going to tell me what's going on?"

"You'll find out the same as I will. Betsy said in her letter that all the answers are in her room."

"But we've been there."

"Have we?"

We went to her suite and let ourselves in. For the first time I noticed the large full-length wall mirror framed in black walnut next to her armoire. It always amazed me how sometimes you can look at a thing and never really see it. Life was like that too. In her letter, Betsy challenged me to see things…to see her… on a deeper, more complex level. 'Beginning with the mirror, she said. Look, think outside the box, and most of all, assume nothing.'

Standing in front of it, I studied my image half expecting something magical to suddenly happen. Vito said, "I'm waiting?"

I searched the edges and then grasped one side of the wood frame and pulled. The mirror swung away from the wall revealing a second wall safe. I let out a deep breath. I was starting to become apprehensive that my worst fears were about to be confirmed. Part of me didn't want to know the truth, but the other part was compelled to know. Now it made sense why we found nothing in the other safe. That one was a decoy just like the fake diamond necklace.

Vito whistled, "The old broad had it all going on, didn't she? How smart is this?"

"She was smart, all right."

Without telling me what their significance was she left me a four digit number which she had hinted would be important. Realizing now this was the code to the second safe, I punched the numbers in and held my breath as the door opened, and then I saw it. There was no escaping the truth now and I took a deep breath.

"Cesari, what's there?"

I reached in and took out a black Smith and Wesson .38. Releasing the cylinder, I emptied the bullets into my palm. They were hollow points and one round was missing. The round that had killed Roger. I handed it to Vito and his eyes went wide seeing it.

He said wryly, "I thought there were no guns allowed on the ship?"

"Being the VIP's they were, Betsy and Roger didn't board the way the rest of the passengers did. They didn't have to pass through metal detectors or security checkpoints."

"Do you think Bjorn knew they had a weapon?"

I shook my head. "I don't know, but I doubt it, and I doubt they would have told him. It's one of those subjects that probably never came up, so no one brought it up. It would have been hard to argue against a little personal protection anyway. After all, they did practically live on the ship."

Understanding its significance, he said, "Cesari, I'm sorry."

Nodding glumly I barely uttered, "You and me."

"What else is in there?"

Peering back into the safe, I found Roger and Betsy's passports, stacks of cash in rubber bands, paperwork including health records, contact information in case something happened to them, a Rolex watch, and a rectangular black leather case.

I opened the leather case in front of Vito and found Betsy's jewel studded necklace. Vito whistled, "Not much to say, is there?"

"No, there isn't, she killed Roger and pretended it was a robbery."

"Why?"

I slumped into an armchair. I was so depressed. "Sit down, Vito."

He sat opposite me on the sofa. I said, "Betsy's letter was a bit more than a goodbye letter." I paused, inhaling deeply. "It was sort of a confession...and a request."

"Sort of a confession? Is that like sort of pregnant?"

"She didn't actually say she shot him, but my guess is that it was either too difficult for her to put in writing, or she was concerned that if the letter never reached me and went public it would destroy her daughter. So rather than spell it out, she explained the circumstances of what happened that night and then led me to the safe, assuming I would be smart enough to piece it together. Additionally, she wanted to put me in her shoes before I found out the truth. She didn't want me to judge her before I had a chance to let her words sink in. In other words, now that I know the truth, I can't help but wonder if I or anyone else would have done exactly the same thing."

"You said there was a request?"

"Yes, a request. She'd like me to bring the necklace to her daughter in Rome and deliver a message to her."

"The crazy girl?"

"Well, it seems she may not be quite as crazy as everyone believed. She's had drug problems and schizophrenia sure, but the reason she's hospitalized all these years had nothing to do with that."

I paused organizing my thoughts and recollecting the letter from Betsy I had just read. "The story begins a lifetime ago when Betsy was still in high school. She met an upper classman named Flynn. He had it all, looks, smarts, a sense of humor. They fell head over heels in love and planned to marry as soon as they graduated. It was her junior year when it happened, a terrible tragedy by any standards. Flynn disappeared during spring break in Florida. His body was never discovered so it was never clear what happened. Roger and Flynn were good friends. Roger told everyone they'd been drinking late at night on the beach and Flynn insisted on going for a swim against his advice. He never returned. Betsy was in Boston when she received the news and of course was devastated, almost suicidal."

Vito let out a deep breath, "Jesus Christ."

Nodding, I continued, "It gets worse. Betsy had just found out she was pregnant with Flynn's baby. The plan was that when he returned from spring break, they were going to elope and to hell with what people thought. Try to picture this Vito: a seventeen year old girl, upper crust family, a different era, no one to talk to, no choices, distraught…isolated, pregnant, her boyfriend is missing and presumed dead."

"What happened?"

"Roger happened. He and Betsy were friends also and had even dated briefly before Flynn came into the picture. When he returned from break he became her shoulder to cry on in her time of need. She confided in him about the pregnancy and he offered to marry her to protect her reputation. The other options were too terrifying for her."

"I still don't understand."

"You will. Just hold on. That spring break so many years ago, two boys on the cusp of manhood took a walk in the woods, drinking beer and talking about girls. The only problem was that one had the girl and the other didn't. One was on top of the world and the other consumed with jealousy."

Vito's face took on a distressed look, "Don't say it, Cesari. Don't say it."

"Flynn told Roger that Betsy was pregnant with his child and that they were going to run away as soon as he returned. Roger lost it and smashed his head in with rock. He buried the body deep in the woods in a shallow grave and the next day told everyone the made-up story about a midnight swim. The search went on for quite a while before the authorities finally gave up and assumed he was inside some shark's belly.

Over the coming weeks, Roger was racked with guilt and his initial inclination was to confess so he wrote it all down in his journal, planning on turning himself in. He wanted to explain to Betsy first and tell her how sorry he was and how much he loved her, but when he saw her, he couldn't go through with it. He let it drop and played dumb all these years. Why he held onto the diary is anyone's guess. Maybe he even forgot about it. Now spin the clock ahead. Their daughter, Veronica, desperate to find money for drugs goes ransacking their room for things of value to trade or sell and comes across the diary hidden deep in his closet in a box buried under high school memorabilia. Surprised by the finding, she read it and you know the rest."

"And he confessed to Betsy after all these years?"

"No, at least not intentionally. The last few years, he's been experiencing flashbacks where he relives past experiences. When this happens, he can't differentiate reality from memories. He actually thinks he is in the moment."

"What are you saying?"

"The night he and Betsy returned to their room, he flashbacked to that day when he and Flynn were alone in the woods on spring break. He relived it all in gory detail including the fact that it was her pregnancy which tipped him over. While he talked to himself, she calmly went over to the safe and got the gun. At least that's my best guess as to how it went down."

We were silent for a long moment contemplating this series of events. I tried to imagine Betsy's state of mind at having found out that the love of her life was brutally murdered, and that the man who did it had been sharing her bed for fifty years, and her daughter…so cruelly mistreated. I could see how anybody could have snapped under those circumstances.

I glanced over at Vito. "Are you crying?"

He wiped his eyes, "Hell no. My allergies are bothering me."

I snorted. "You keep it up and girls might start liking you."

"Shut up. What now?"

I thought about that. "Now begins the cover up."

"Seriously, you're not going to tell anyone?"

"Don't be ridiculous. The woman has suffered enough, and what would be the point? She's dead."

"And…?"

"First, we dump the gun into the Mediterra…Ionian Sea."

He grinned. "For a guy who don't like to litter, you sure throw a lot of things overboard."

Despite my mood, I chuckled. "C'mon, let's put everything away and lock up."

"What about the necklace?"

"I'm taking it. Betsy asked me to bring the necklace to her daughter and that's what I'm going to do."

"Are you at least going to tell Bjorn the truth?"

"No, if Betsy had wanted him to know what happened then she would have told him so herself. He obviously knew nothing about the second safe or else we wouldn't be sitting here holding the murder weapon and a twenty million dollar heirloom necklace that doesn't belong to us. Personally, I think she wants to protect him from the truth. It'll be easier for him."

"I can see that. The less he knows, the less he has to lie."

"That's part of it. The other part is that he was so close to them, the truth would be extraordinarily painful."

"Kind of like finding out there's no Santa Claus?"

"There you go."

As we walked back to the room to secure the necklace in my safe, he asked, "So how much did you know or suspect?"

"Well these things don't hit you like a bolt of lightning, Vito. They kind of creep up on you over time. At first, I took events at face value like everyone else, but my suspicions began when Betsy and I went to see Roger in the morgue. Her reaction there was odd to say the least. She was angry, not grief-stricken. I mean, really angry. I wrote it off at the time. Death sometimes brings out strange emotions in people, but it struck me as unusual nonetheless. Then there were the peculiar circumstances of the murder scene itself. Very few people could have known about the phony diamonds and had a key to her room. That alone should have made me number one, two, and three on the suspect list by any standards, yet she emphatically told me she didn't believe I could have done it. But it was something she said that bothered me. She said I *know* you didn't do it, and the way she said it was more like a cold hard fact. Then she told the captain to stand down as well."

I paused to look at him. "Think about that. Just like that? Her precious diamonds are gone and her husband is dead, and the most likely suspect is given a pass. No one even asked me for an alibi. I mean, I'm not that great a lay, am I?"

"Knowing how selfish you are, Cesari, I'd have to say probably not."

I smiled, "At the time, I was too relieved at not being a suspect to argue the point. Plus, I was preoccupied with Brad and Katarina and everything else that was going on. It wasn't until I realized Roger had been shot in the back that I started to wonder if all was not what it seemed."

We entered my room and I put the necklace in the wall safe and took out Betsy's letter. I continued to talk as he sat down and lit a smoke. Totally against the rules, but he didn't care. I said, "Still, I couldn't reconcile events because of the attack on Betsy in my room. Then she became sick and things started to spiral out of control. However, once I realized that Antonela was the one who tried to strangle Betsy and not Roger's killer things started to make sense. The only thing missing was the motive, but now we have that."

As he mulled that over, I grabbed his cigarette lighter and burned Betsy's letter in a metal trash can and placed it out on the balcony.

"Revenge?" he asked as I returned to the room.

"No...and not even anger."

"Then what?"

"Are you listening to me at all? Love, Vito, love. That's why she did it. Flynn was Betsy's first, true and only real love. The kind of love that makes your heart skip a beat when you're near the person and your toes curl when you kiss. That kind of love can never be replaced or substituted, and you never stop being in love with that person. You can move on from it, maybe even love again, but it's never the same. You can never really forget it or put it behind you. It's always there lurking around every corner, and in Betsy's case it was even more difficult because of the pregnancy. She clung to Roger because of the baby but she never loved Roger. Veronica was Flynn's daughter. Don't you think that every day of her life Betsy thought of Flynn whenever she looked at Veronica?

"Try to imagine how painful it had to be when Veronica started talking about her real father being murdered. That must have been a nightmare for Betsy even though she didn't know the truth at that point. Try to imagine this scene, Vito. Roger's standing there babbling to himself about how he picked up a rock and bashed in the skull of the love of her life and then covered it up. Betsy's listening, in shock, crying. It dawns on her suddenly that her whole life had been a sham; that all the pain and anguish she had endured had been caused by this one man. Then the realization must have come that she institutionalized Veronica unfairly. How cruel a thing to do to mask a heinous crime? Roger took advantage of the fact that Veronica was mentally ill. But the biggest injustice of all was that Betsy had been kept from her soulmate all these years by a singularly barbaric act of treachery." I took a deep breath and let it out. "Now somebody has to tell her daughter what happened and it looks like I've been elected."

I looked over at him and said, "Are you crying?"

"Shut up."

Chapter 44

The ship's small chapel was filled to capacity with standing room only. The groom leaned against his walker at the altar, and the chaplain, Allison, stood in dress whites next to him waiting eagerly. This was a big day for her and she was excited to preside over a wedding ceremony, even one as unusual as this. Pleasant, Bach-inspired organ music played overhead. Vito and I wore our tuxedoes for the occasion. It wasn't every day you got to see a twenty-five-year-old volleyball star marry an eighty-eight-year-old millionaire. I was pretty excited too.

We had docked in Rome and were waiting to disembark. This was the last stop for most of the passengers and was our final hurrah, so to speak. I had said goodbye to Aimée the night before in grand fashion. Two bottles of champagne over roast duck with Cesari jubilee for dessert. I doubted she'd forget that night any time soon. She was planning a trip to New York next year and promised to look me up. I was keeping my fingers crossed on that one.

I left my chair and went down to the vestibule to see what was going on. Katarina was just arriving and saw me. Berislav frowned but politely gave us some space. She wore a traditional long, white, sequined gown which trailed in the back and held a bouquet of long-stemmed red roses. She was stunning. I lifted her veil and looked at her face; just the right amount of make-up, eye shadow, rouge and lipstick. Even her freckles were adorable. Her eyes twinkled.

"You're a beautiful bride, Katarina."

She smiled and threw her arms around me. "Most beautiful bride ever. Now kiss."

I kissed her gently on the lips not wanting to smudge anything. I said, "I wish you all the luck in the world. I really do."

"Luck has nothing to do with. I work very hard for this day."

She was too much. Nodding, I chuckled and said, "I agree. No woman ever worked harder."

She liked that. "You stay in Rome for few days?"

"No, just for one night, and then I'm flying back to the states."

She pouted. "Is no fair. Honeymoon won't be same without you."

I smiled, "You have a husband now. You can't just come crawling in through my bedroom window anymore."

"Oh yeah, how could forget? No matter, I rich widow soon. I come America to find you."

That could have been interpreted as a threat but I took it as more of a suggestion. "I'll be waiting."

As Mendelsohn's wedding march began, Berislav approached. He was nervous and sweating like an expectant father. He acknowledged me curtly and said, "Is time, Katarina. Husband wait."

She replaced her veil, put her arm through mine, and said, "Walk me down aisle."

Berislav's jaw dropped and he started to object. She said sharply, "You want I change mind, stepfather?"

He threw his hands up in the air and took a step back. I was too stunned to respond and let myself be pulled down the aisle. Vito's eyes went wide when he saw us and I knew he was worried about the same thing I was. She was just wild enough that when we arrived at the altar she might throw caution to the wind and announce to everyone that there had been a change of plans and she was marrying me instead.

It didn't happen. When we reached the altar, Allison smiled and Edvard, looking tired, yawned. It could have been time for his nap. Katarina turned to me and waited. I wasn't sure what I was supposed to do so she whispered, "Lift veil and kiss like before."

I gently lifted her veil and leaned in to kiss her on the cheek, but she was having none of that. With one hand holding the bouquet, she put the other around my neck, and planted a big wet one on my lips. It went on a little too long and I heard an older woman in the front row cluck her disapproval. Allison cleared her throat and finally, Katarina set me free. With one last big smile, she turned to Allison and stepped toward Edvard.

After the ceremony we begged out of the reception, bid Katarina good luck and goodbye and went directly to check into our hotel by the Spanish Steps, aptly named the Hotel Piazza di Spagna. It was a small, family run boutique hotel with modest but comfortable rooms. We booked a double with two twin beds and settled down, waiting for our appointment at the Sisters of Charity Home for Troubled Women several blocks away. It was the Italian version of a psychiatric hospital. Instead of medicating people into a coma, they prayed and ate a lot of pasta.

Still wearing his tux, Vito laid down, legs crossed at the ankles with his hands behind his head. We had an hour to kill. I sat on the edge of my bed studying the necklace, twirling it around so the yellow, red, green, and blue baubles sparkled in the light. The brilliance of the large pendant diamond took my breath away.

He said, "How do you think she's going to handle all this?"

He was talking about, Veronica, Betsy's daughter. I let out a deep breath. "Lots of tears I expect."

"You're probably right. It's a shame."

"I know. All I can do is be honest and supportive. Betsy knew that she'd never be able to make up for all the years of injustice, but figured the healing if there were to be any, should at least begin with an apology."

"Why does life have to suck so much, Cesari?"

"I don't know. I wish it didn't have to, but I don't have any say in it."

"What's going to happen to her? I mean, she just inherited a fortune in addition to the necklace. Can she handle it all?"

"No, of course not. She's not well enough, but Betsy said in her letter that she contacted her attorneys and they will make arrangements so that she can be taken care of properly at home. She'll never have to want for anything. That's something."

"And the necklace? You just going to hand it to her?"

"The necklace belongs to her. If she wants to keep it here, then I'll give it to her. It's her decision, but I'll suggest she let me set up a safe-deposit box for her. We can do that here in Rome or if she wants, I can bring it back to Boston and leave it with the executor of Betsy's estate."

He nodded. "That seems reasonable, and then what? You'll probably need another vacation to get over this one."

I sighed. "Yeah well, the fun's not quite over yet for us."

He frowned. "What's that supposed to mean?"

"It means, we're going to Ft. Lauderdale when we get back, to look for Flynn."

Rolling his eyes he said, “Are you crazy? It’s been fifty years since he was murdered. There’s probably a parking lot or a mall over his remains.”

“You’re right. The odds are against it, but we’re going to give it the old college try anyway. Betsy wrote in her letter, that Roger and Flynn were staying at a rental home not too far from the beach that summer, and that there was a state park nearby where guys used to hike, drink beer, and go for walks with girls. As far as she knows, the park was federally protected land and is still there. Roger practically told her the exact location of the murder when he was in his trance.”

“Wouldn’t anyone have thought of this back then?”

“Why would they? Roger had convinced everyone Flynn drowned or was eaten by a shark. I’ll order us metal detectors. Betsy said that she had given him a ring that he wore around his neck on a gold chain. We might get lucky.”

“And just why are we doing this?”

“Betsy made arrangements to be buried in a separate grave far away from Roger. She asked the executor of her will to arrange for an adjoining plot. We’re going to bring Flynn home to be with the woman he loved so she can find peace, and maybe for the first time in a long time…happiness.”

He thought about that for a moment. “So we’re doing this for…love?” he asked quietly in a hushed voice.

I looked at him, nodded, and handed him a tissue from a box on the night table. I said, “Here.”

He grabbed the tissue, blew his nose, and sniffled.

“Thank you.”

The End

Jailhouse Doc

About the Author

John Avanzato grew up in the Bronx. After receiving a bachelor's degree in biology from Fordham University, he went on to earn his medical degree at the State University of New York at Buffalo, School of Medicine. He is currently a board-certified gastroenterologist practicing in upstate, New York, where he lives with his wife of thirty years. Dr. Avanzato co-teaches a course on pulp fiction at Hobart and William Smith Colleges in Geneva, New York.

Inspired by authors like Tom Clancy, John Grisham, and Lee Child, John writes about strong but flawed heroes.

His first six novels, Hostile Hospital, Prescription for Disaster, Temperature Rising, Claimed Denied, The Gas Man Cometh and Jailhouse Doc have been received well.

Author's Note

Dear Reader,

I hope you enjoyed reading Sea Sick as much as I enjoyed writing it. Please do me a favor and write a review on amazon.com. The reviews are important, and your support is greatly appreciated.

Thank you,

John Avanzato

Hostile Hospital

When former mob thug turned doctor, John Cesari, takes a job as a gastroenterologist at a small hospital in upstate New York, he assumes he's outrun his past and started life anew. But trouble has a way of finding the scrappy Bronx native.

Things go awry one night at a bar when he punches out an obnoxious drunk who won't leave his date alone. Unbeknownst to Dr. Cesari, that drunk is his date's stalker ex-boyfriend—and a crooked cop.

Over the course of several action-packed days, Cesari uncovers the dirty little secrets of a small town hospital. As the bodies pile up, he is forced to confront his own bloody past.

Hostile Hospital is a fast-paced journey that is not only entertaining but maintains an interesting view on the philosophy of healthcare. If you aren't too scared after reading, get the sequel, Prescription for Disaster.

Prescription for Disaster

Dr. John Cesari is a gastroenterologist employed at Saint Matt's Hospital in Manhattan. He tries to escape his unsavory past on the Bronx streets by settling into a Greenwich Village apartment with his girlfriend, Kelly. After his adventures in

Hostile Hospital, Cesari wants to stay under the radar of his many enemies.

Through no fault of his own, Cesari winds up in the wrong place at the wrong time. A chance encounter with a mugger turns on its head when Cesari watches his assailant get murdered right before his eyes.

After being framed for the crime, he attempts to unravel the mystery, propelling himself deeply into the world of international diamond smuggling. He is surrounded by bad guys at every turn and behind it all are Russian and Italian mobsters determined to ensure Cesari has an untimely and unpleasant demise.

His prescription is to beat them at their own game, but before he can do that he must deal with a corrupt boss and an environment filled with temptation and danger from all sides. Everywhere Cesari goes, someone is watching. The dramatic climax will leave you breathless and wanting more.

Temperature Rising

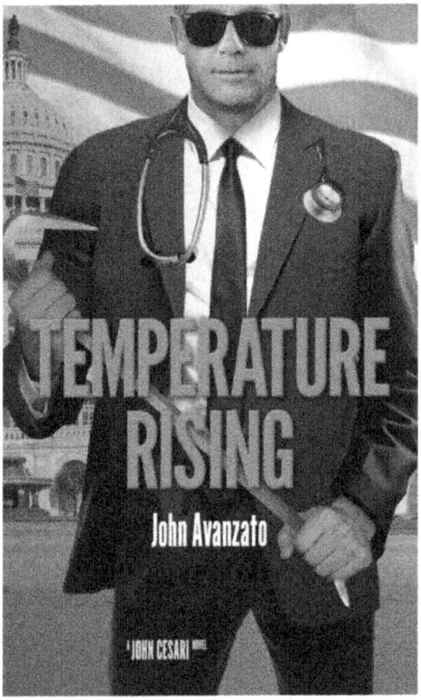

John Cesari is a gangster turned doctor living in Manhattan saving lives one colonoscopy at a time. While on a well-deserved vacation, he stumbles upon a murder scene and becomes embroiled in political intrigue involving the world's oldest profession.

His hot pursuit of the truth leads him to the highest levels of government, where individuals operate above the law. As always, girl trouble hounds him along the way making his already edgy life that much more complex.

The bad guys are ruthless, powerful and nasty but they are no match for this tough, street-smart doctor from the Bronx who is as comfortable with a crowbar as he is with a stethoscope. Get ready for a wild ride in Temperature Rising. The exciting and unexpected conclusion will leave you on the edge of your seat.

Claim Denied

In Manhattan, a cancer ridden patient commits suicide rather than become a financial burden to his family. Accusations of malfeasance are leveled against his caregivers. Rogue gastroenterologist, part-time mobster, John Cesari, is tasked to look into the matter on behalf of St. Matt's hospital.

The chaos and inequities of a healthcare system run amok, driven by corporate greed and endless bureaucratic red tape, become all too apparent to him as his inquiry into this tragedy proceeds. On his way to interview the wife of the dead man, Cesari is the victim of seemingly random gun violence and finds himself on life support.

Recovering from his wounds, he finds that both he and his world are a very different place. His journey back to normalcy rouses in him a burning desire for justice, placing him in constant danger as evil forces conspire to keep him in the dark.

The Gas Man Cometh

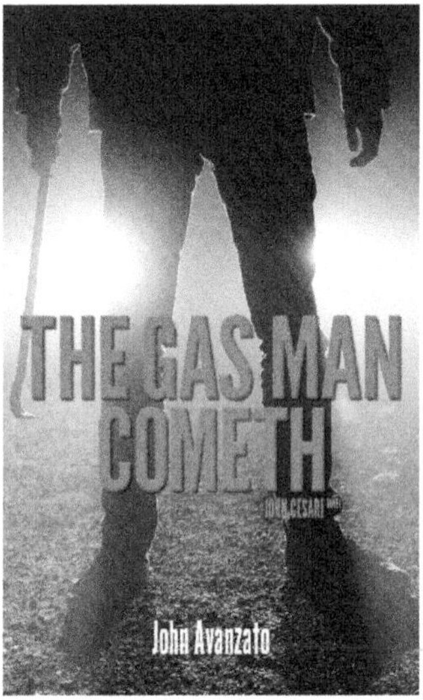

A deranged anesthesiologist with unnatural desires lures innocent women to his brownstone in a swank section of Manhattan. All was going well until John Cesari M.D. came along becoming a thorn in his side.

Known as The Gas Man, his hatred of Cesari reaches the boiling point. He plots to take him down once and for all turning an ordinary medical conference into a Las Vegas bloodbath.

Hungover and disoriented, Cesari awakens next to a mobster's dead girlfriend in a high-end brothel. Wanted dead or alive by more than a few people, Cesari is on the run with gangsters and the police hot on his trail.

There is never a dull moment in this new thriller as Cesari blazes a trail from Sin City to lower Manhattan desperately trying to stay one step ahead of The Gas Man.

Jailhouse Doc

Dr. John Cesari, former mobster turned gastroenterologist, finds himself on the wrong end of the law. A felony conviction lands him in Riker's Island, one of the country's most dangerous correctional facilities, doing community service.

Fighting to survive, he becomes trapped in the web of a vicious criminal gang dealing in drugs and human flesh.

A seemingly unrelated and mysterious death of a college student in Greenwich Village thrusts Cesari into the middle of the action, and forced to take sides, his options are to either cooperate or die. Which will it be?

KCM Publishing
a division of KCM Digital Media, LLC

Made in United States
North Haven, CT
23 December 2022

30054132R00235